ENCHAINED HEART

Jamie slammed the back bedroom door with his foot then slowly put the girl down. She was all soft curves and warm, fresh scent. The most feminine thing he'd ever touched.

She said his name but he covered her mouth with his before any more words came out. He didn't want words, he wanted her sweet taste, the soft caress of her lips. Her mouth opened to him with a languorous slowness, with a breathy sigh from her trembling lips.

His fingers stayed splayed around her ribcage while his thumbs languidly stroked along the sides.

She pulled away from his kiss, flinging her head back.

"Oh, Jamie Scott," she murmured, voice husky and hungry and on the edge of laughter, "you're all thumbs."

He pressed his thigh against hers. "Not quite."

ALSO BY SUSAN SIZEMORE

Wings of the Storm

Available from HarperPaperbacks

My First Duchess

Susan Sizemore

HarperPaperbacks
A Division of HarperCollinsPublishers

This is a work of fiction. The characters, incidents, and dialogues are products of the author's imagination and are not to be construed as real. Any resemblance to actual events or persons, living or dead, is entirely coincidental.

HarperPaperbacks *A Division of* HarperCollins*Publishers*
10 East 53rd Street, New York, N.Y. 10022

Cover illustration by John Ennis

First printing: December 1993

Printed in the United States of America

HarperPaperbacks, HarperMonogram, and colophon are trademarks of HarperCollins*Publishers*

10 9 8 7 6 5 4 3 2 1

For James Murray Sizemore for the name,
Dr. Iain Ross Mactaggart for the voice, and
Scott Rockenfield on drums

1

Spring, 1749

"Leave, Your Grace? Why?"

"I want to go home to Lacey House," Margaret answered her maid's shocked question. "And I want to go now. I'm sorry about the bother, but—"

"But, Your Grace," Maude countered, "the packing, your levee . . ." The woman's plain face was pink with indignation. "You can't just leave," she insisted. "There's too much to do!"

Margaret, duchess of Pyneham, stood very still while her dresser's agile fingers buttoned, tied, and laced her into a blue velvet traveling dress. A housemaid bustled around the bedchamber, hastily filling a traveling bag with the few essentials Margaret had ordered for the trip. Footmen had carried in trunks and waited outside the door for further orders. Despite Maude's protests, the arrangements for the duchess's journey from her London townhouse to her county seat were well under way.

Maude, who was supposed to be supervising all the activity, continued to stand in front of her mistress, looking worried. Margaret didn't blame her maid for this uncharacteristic behavior. After all, it was Margaret's behavior that was uncharacteristic, and Maude was merely reacting to it. She'd spent the whole forenoon being upbraided by the king because she refused to marry his cousin. In German. In front of the whole Court.

Margaret had come back from Court in tears, pushed through the downstairs hall crowded with petitioners, and marched into her private chamber with the loud announcement that she was going home. She'd then started giving orders like the martinet she tried so hard not to be.

She risked disturbing the fit of her sleeve to reach out and touch Maude on the shoulder. Maude deserved more than terse orders and harsh looks from her mistress.

"I just want to go home," she explained. "I don't want to hold a levee today. I don't want to see anyone. And those people in the hall don't really want to see me. I've already told Edwards to bring the coach around." She gave the older woman a coaxing smile. "You can follow with the luggage and everyone else at your leisure."

"But . . . you can't go alone."

"Of course I can. I want to be alone."

Her dresser approached with the jewelry box, but Margaret waved her away. She was in too much of a hurry to worry about wearing the correct jewelry with every outfit. She was still dressed half in Court finery. But who was to see her to comment on her wearing the heirloom topaz and gold earbobs and necklace and several rings with a simple blue traveling dress?

Maude decided to give in. She had no choice, as Margaret was already heading for the door.

"Go alone? Follow later? Yes, Your Grace."

"The blasted scarf itches," James Scott McKay complained to his horse. The roan stallion tossed its head, pawed the ground, then subsided under his master's gentling hands. "Aye, and you're restive, I know," Jamie soothed. "It'll be soon now. Soon. I hope."

Jamie adjusted the scarf over the lower half of his face, then looked up and down the empty road once more. It was a cool spring afternoon, the heath was green and empty, and a breeze stirred through the small copse of budding trees at his back. He'd been waiting near the edge of the road for the better part of two hours. He felt as if he might as well be alone in the world for all the traffic heading his way on the normally busy road.

He wanted to get the job over and done with and be on his way, but so far no wealthy pigeon was interested in passing by. The decision to take to the roads hadn't been easy for him, but now that it was made he was anxious to get his first robbery over with. He was beginning to think that perhaps he'd better head home and try his luck again on another day.

He yawned and removed his hat to scratch his head, uncovering his long brown hair. He'd debated with himself about wearing a wig, but had decided such formality of dress wasn't suitable for his new profession. A black crepe mask might have been better than the scarf, though. He wished he'd thought of the mask sooner.

He sighed, put his hat back on his head, and looked down the road in the direction of London.

He saw a puff of dust in the distance. Squinting, he could make out the form of a swiftly moving coach. He listened carefully and soon could hear the thunder of hoof-beats as the coach came barreling up the rutted road toward him. It wasn't long before he could identify the horses as a team of fine Cleveland bays, and could count only a footman and the driver on the high-perched driving seat. It was a fine coach, blue with silver trim. A rich man's coach, no doubt of that.

A pigeon. At last.

Jamie smiled beneath his scarf. He pulled the pistol from his belt and urged the roan forward. It looked like luck was with him at last.

The coach gave a lurch as it picked up speed.

What was Edwards doing? Margaret wondered as she woke from a doze. Why were they going so fast? A second later the sound of a pistol shot answered her question. The report came from nearby, close enough to the coach window that she caught a whiff of gunpowder and had to cover her mouth to keep from coughing.

She heard a Scots-accented voice call out, "Stand and deliver!"

There was an angry shout from her coachman in reply.

The Scotsman answered, cold as steel. "Do you want to die, laddie?"

There was a great deal of swearing from Edwards, but he responded to the threat, bringing the coach to a halt in the middle of the road.

Margaret didn't consider herself brave, but in the short silence following the coach's stopping, tension and curiosity grew rapidly within her. She was angry. Angry because her people were in danger. She wished she had a weapon and the ability to use it. Besides, the highwayman was bound to stick his nose into the coach any moment now and demand that she hand over her possessions as the price for her life.

No need to wait for the inevitable, she decided. She might as well meet the ruffian halfway. So, instead of cowering back on the satin-cushioned seat, she stuck her head out the coach window. She was just in time to see the footman toss the unused musket he'd been carrying to the ground, then hand over the moneybelt he'd been entrusted with for their travel expenses.

Margaret bristled angrily, and called out, "I suppose now I'll be sleeping in the coach tonight."

As she spoke the highwayman's attention turned from the men at the front of the coach to her. Their eyes met.

All Margaret could see of the man's face between the top of a large red scarf and the brim of a wide black hat were a pair of heavy straight brows and two enormous brown eyes. Lovely eyes, she thought, aware of the incongruity of her observation, considering the circumstances. She was supposed to be angry at him. After all, he was wearing the scarf to hide his face, and his long-fingered hand held a neatly poised pistol aimed at her coachman. She could see a second pistol stuck through a wide leather belt where his coat gaped open. His other hand held the reins of his horse with almost negligent skill. He hadn't stopped her coach on this remote stretch of road so the duchess of Pyneham could admire his eyes.

He was slender and respectably dressed in buff breeches and blue coat. He sat the fine horse with confident ease. After one swift glance at the rest of the man, Margaret met his eyes once more.

She waited for him to speak, but no words came from beneath the red scarf.

"Yes?" she inquired after the silence grew between them for several seconds.

The highwayman blinked. "What?"

Margaret wasn't sure what to make of his reaction. He seemed curiously hesitant about getting down to business. "The last time I was robbed," she confided, "it happened so quickly. Of course it was Ted Barton, and he was notoriously rude," she went on as the highwayman tilted his head curiously to one side. Strands of light brown hair brushed his shoulder as he moved. His hair was long and silky, unpowdered, and looked quite clean.

"And he was hanged as well," Edwards called down from the driver's seat.

Margaret leaned farther out the window and addressed the driver. "Yes, but it wasn't for being rude that they hanged him, it was for stealing."

"No more than he deserved," Edwards said.

"I don't know. I've always thought the death sentence was a bit harsh for anything short of murder. I suppose you'll be hanged someday," she added, feeling that perhaps she was being rude by leaving the highwayman out of the conversation.

Jamie wasn't quite sure what to say. She sounded as if she felt sorry for this Ted Barton, and for him. Her eyes reminded him of smoke, soft and warm and gray. He urged his horse closer to the coach. His first look at the woman leaning out the window had momentarily knocked all thought of what he was about out of his head. At the sight of her honey-blonde hair and heart-shaped face he'd almost doffed his hat like the gentleman he'd been raised to be. A flare of outrage kindled in him at her matter-of-fact words.

"You've been robbed before?"

"Three times," she answered. "No, twice. The time when I was eight doesn't count since Father shot the horse out from under the robber before he could stop the coach. I remember how Father laughed when the horse went down. The second time was Ted, and you make three. And I suppose being stopped by you is all my fault." She sighed. "I can't seem to do anything right today. I should have known better than to travel alone."

"My lady," Jamie protested. Her smoke-gray eyes brimmed briefly with tears, which she quickly blinked away. Jamie had to fight the impulse to step down and brush the tears away. "Now, lass—"

"Your Grace," the driver interjected.

Jamie aimed his pistol at the man. "What?"

"Your Grace," the man repeated. "If you're going to rob the duchess of Pyneham you can show a bit of respect."

Jamie was glad the itchy red wool scarf covered the look of consternation on his face. "Pyneham? I've heard of your grandmother."

"My great-grandmother," Margaret corrected swiftly. "Everyone's heard of the first duchess. Orange girl to actress to great lady all because of her liaison with a king."

"That wasn't what I—"

"Not that I'm ashamed of the connection," Margaret went on. The thought of her scandalous ancestress brought a smile to her lips. "She'd have sent you packing, Scotsman. She could have faced down the king himself." Margaret felt the tears starting to threaten again. "Not like me," she added. "And now I suppose you want my jewels?"

Jamie tried very hard to hold his curiosity, and sympathy, in check. He did have a robbery to get on with. He held the pistol suggestively in one hand. He removed his wide-brimmed hat with the other and held it toward the beautiful young duchess. "If you wouldn't mind."

"I do, actually."

"Think of them as charitable contributions," Jamie consoled her.

He looked around quickly, making sure the men on the box knew he hadn't forgotten them. They were sensibly staying put, the coachman holding the reins of his team loosely in his hand. The road stretched out across the heath with no other traffic in sight. The occasional lowing of a cow from a herd grazing in the distance was the only sound to be heard. He returned his attention to the duchess.

"That's a lovely diamond ring. I'll be having it first, if you please."

"For your favorite charity?" She dropped the ring into the bowl of the hat.

"A widows and orphans fund," he replied. "The other ring as well. Is it a ruby?"

"Yes. It's not that I'm opposed to charity," she told him. "But it's your direct method of soliciting funds I'm not so sure about."

"You'd be direct too if you had four sisters to find dowries for."

She threw back her head and laughed. Her mouth was generous and her throat was quite lovely, long and slender. He wondered what it would be like to take her face between his hands, to rest his palms on the warm pulse points at the base of her throat, to taste her laughing mouth.

"Four sisters," she scoffed, bringing him out of his reverie. The gray eyes were cloudy with annoyance when she added, "Oh, that's a fine tale. I suppose you turned highwayman to care for them."

"Aye, lass, that I did."

"Of course."

"The necklace."

"Must you? It belonged to my great-grandmother."

"The doxy. Aye. I'm sure she won't miss it."

"No, but I will. If you must," Margaret complained. She slowly undid the clasp.

Her traveling dress was as low cut as any fashionable costume, showing her long, slender throat and well-shaped breasts to fine advantage. Jamie watched with delighted interest as the glittering yellow jewels slid sensuously across the creamy swell of the duchess's half-exposed bosom. He was waiting for them to dip down into the shadowy cleft between her breasts where his fingers were itching to go. Instead, she plucked them off her bosom and deposited them in the hat.

She would miss the necklace very much. And she certainly didn't like the covetous way the Scotsman stared at the necklace until he had it in his possession. She didn't blame him for wanting it, not that he'd keep it for long, she knew.

An idea occurred to her as she added it to the growing pile in the hat. "Tell me who your pawnbroker is, Scotsman."

"Jamie." He didn't know why he didn't like her calling him Scotsman. Perhaps it was the hint of contempt he thought he heard in the word. "My name's James Scott M—"

He choked back the word just in time. Lord, what was he doing? He'd almost told her his name. What sort of fool was he? It was bad enough he'd had to take to the roads to earn his keep. If he wanted to stay alive he'd better not make any more foolish, sentimental mistakes. Or his first robbery would be his last.

"Very well, Jamie Scott," Margaret said, oddly pleased that he'd introduced himself.

He nodded emphatically, and the scarf slid down his face a bit, revealing a pair of high cheekbones and part of a straight, aquiline nose. She hoped his disguise would come off completely so she could get a good look at him. She needed a description to report to the magistrates, of course. She wondered if he was handsome. She had the impression of a long face, with a fair complexion; a face dominated by those extraordinarily large, brandy-brown eyes. Eyes which were presently looking at her with an expression of deep puzzlement.

"Pawnbroker?" Jamie asked the honey-haired duchess. "What pawnbroker? You mean, where will I be disposing of your jewels?"

She nodded, and he was struck by the realization that he hadn't thought any further than the actual highway robbery part of his new trade. Of course he was going to have to exchange her jewels for cash, but where? Cripham? No, Cripham dealt with the Quality. He needed someone who wouldn't ask any questions. He reached under the scarf to scratch his jaw thoughtfully while the duchess watched him curiously.

"Might I make a suggestion?" Margaret asked after Jamie Scott stared at her in bemused silence for a while.

"By all means," Jamie replied. "Do you have a pawn-broker in mind, Your Grace?"

"I'm told John Hewitt of Copper Street is quite reputable, for a receiver of stolen goods. Or so a neighbor of mine who was robbed last Christmas told me. My neighbor went to Hewitt's shop and retrieved all his property." She tried a cajoling smile. "If you take my jewels to Hewitt I'll be able to buy them back." She couldn't help but add bitterly, "Everyone makes a profit on the exchange but me."

Her self-possession amazed him. Here he was robbing her at gunpoint, and she was teaching him his business. Of course, if she could spend her morning dealing with the king, why shouldn't she be able to cope with a ruffian on her way home? All that was needed to stand up to either was raw courage. He suspected she had more than her share of that. She was quite a woman, was the lovely young duchess of Pyneham. So lovely that he kept trying to forget why they were holding a conversation in the middle of Hounslow Heath.

"Hewitt," he said, getting back to business. "Very well, lass. You'll find your baubles at Hewitt's in Copper Street."

"Thank you. And it isn't 'lass.'"

"Beg, pardon, Your Grace."

She made an impatient gesture, then drummed her fingers on the edge of the coach window. "Never mind the title, Jamie Scott," she told him sternly. "My name is Margaret."

There were gasps from the men at the front of the coach. Jamie chuckled at their shocked reaction.

"Your Grace!" the coachman protested. "What would the dowager say if she heard—"

The duchess ignored her driver's indignation. "There are a lot of other names to go with it, of course," she went on. "And a few more titles strung on behind, but it boils down to Margaret."

Margaret didn't know why she was rattling on like this. As if the man cared about her name. Or anything else but the fortune in jewels he was stripping from her. She should be berating him for the insolent cur he was. Or facing him in chilly silence. She should let him get on with it, so they could go their separate ways never to meet again.

But there was something that inspired her to confide in him. Maybe it was the intelligent humor in his eyes, or the soft burr of his Scots-accented voice. Probably, she forced herself to admit, it was the anonymity of his masked face that was making her chatter at him like a complete ninny. Here was someone who didn't depend on her for anything, who wanted nothing more from her than the obvious.

Jamie was both shocked and pleased by her informal introduction. "Margaret?"

She smiled encouragingly. "Yes. Maggie to my—well, no one but my sister and grandmother call me Maggie. Not that I've heard from my sister in ages. Is it the state of the roads, do you think?" she went on anxiously. "Or the frequency of mail coach robberies?"

"What?" She looked deeply troubled, the sadness he'd noticed when their eyes first met showed on her face again. Perhaps she was talking to him because she had no one else to confide in, he reasoned. Poor lass. "Road?" he questioned.

"I don't get letters and I worry because—" Margaret bit off the words, aware of just how much of her private anxiety she was giving away.

"You're worried because you don't get any mail?" the highwayman asked.

She nodded in reply.

"You're a duchess. You must get a hundred begging letters a week."

He was right, she did. From people who wanted favors from her. She'd learned early that to most people a duchess was the same as a fairy godmother in a French fairy tale.

"Ah, but it's not the begging letters you want," Jamie Scott added.

She'd been determined to press her lips together and remain silent after already saying too much. "No," she agreed. "Those aren't the sorts of letters I want."

He cocked his head to one side. The mask slipped further. She could see most of his face now. At least she could tell that he had a long, narrow face, and she could guess that his mouth was generously wide. She could see a hint of a smile. He pulled the scarf back up and went on.

"It's love letters you need, Margaret."

"No!" she answered quickly. "Love letters are the last things I want. Men aren't to be trusted, highwayman." She looked pointedly at the loot in his hat. "Are they?"

"No," he acknowledged, bowing slightly from the waist. "Perhaps some are more trustworthy than others."

"No, they're not."

Her firmness on the subject astonished him. "You do need love letters. Need," he went on before she could contradict him. "Even if they aren't what you want."

"I've had love letters."

"But not from the right man."

She laughed, but it was an angry sound. "There's no right man, Jamie Scott. Not for me."

He gave a confident chortle. "That's because you haven't yet had any from me."

What was he saying? I must be mad, he thought. I must be. Only a madman promises a sad little duchess love letters while he's holding a pistol on her.

"No, thank you," she replied. She lifted her pointed chin haughtily, an effect he thought she'd probably practiced in front of a mirror, and inquired coldly, "Are you through?"

"Almost."

He looked up and down the road again. Then took

another hard look at her, memorizing her features and checking for any treasure he might have missed.

"Could I have your earbobs, Your Grace? Margaret," he added, catching the glint in her eyes. "Eyes like fine blue steel."

He didn't realize he'd spoken aloud until she blushed and said, "That's not the most gallant compliment I've ever had."

Jamie covered his embarrassment with a bold laugh. "I'm not a very gallant sort," he reminded her. "I'm waiting for your earrings."

Margaret touched a finger to one of the gold-and-topaz earrings, hesitating to take it off. They were another gift from King Charles II to her scandalous great-grandmother. Never mind that they were heirlooms, they were her favorite pieces of jewelry. The design was quite charming, the square-cut topazes were a rich, warm sun-yellow in color suspended from a design of gold filigree work. She didn't want to give them up, even if she could ransom them back later.

"Please?"

Jamie wished she hadn't said the word. Or looked at him with such pleading when she said it. Maybe there was something of the gallant in him after all. He almost couldn't bear taking these last bits of finery from her. Almost. He sighed and fished the necklace and rings out of his hat. He put them in a deep coat-pocket, then placed his hat back on his head.

He sighed again, checked the road once more, and put away his pistol. Then he leaned toward the window and held out his hand, palm up.

"I'll have just one of the earrings," he told the staring woman.

She looked at his hand, then met his gaze. "What?"

"Just one, Margaret," he coaxed quietly, eyes holding hers. "To remember you by, lass."

"Oh."

Margaret didn't know what to think or say. He was robbing her. Of course he was robbing her, but why did it feel like he was a knight asking for a token? And why did she feel oddly pleased at the request? It really wasn't a request, was it?

"All right," she answered, her words independent of her thoughts. Her fingers moved almost as independently, unfastening the topaz earring and dropping it into his outstretched hand. She felt her lips lift in a smile, and his brown eyes smiled back. She felt lost, trapped in the silent if indecipherable communication flowing between them.

It was Jamie Scott who broke the spell, by suddenly wheeling his horse away from the coach. The roan stallion tossed its head, responding with surprising speed as Jamie called out, "Drive on!"

Within moments, Jamie Scott had disappeared into the woods lining the right side of the road. And Margaret was left to stare at where he'd been, aware of how empty and desolate this spot of countryside seemed without the highwayman's vibrant presence.

Edwards urged the horses forward with a sharp crack of the reins. She heard the footman call back a question, asking if she was all right? Should they stop to inform the magistrate in the next town?

She ignored the questions and sat back, crossing her bare-fingered hands in her lap. She was alone. And considerably poorer. And he was gone, having taken all he could.

How very like a man.

2

It took Jamie three days to get home. First there was the matter of disposing of his loot. The shady old man at the Copper Street address drove a hard bargain for the jewels. Jamie came away from the pawnbroker's shop with less than he had expected in coin, but the owner, suspicious at first, ended up believing that Jamie had the makings of a proper gentleman of the road. Jamie didn't know what it was he said or did to give the impression that he was a natural for the illegal trade, but he listened eagerly to the man's advice.

The pawnbroker's words led him to an inn on the outskirts of Hounslow Heath. It was a gathering spot for highwaymen and their doxies. The atmosphere was rough, but convivial. The description of his red scarf and roan stallion had preceded him via a broadsheet published by the magistrate who'd received the duchess's robbery report. The magistrate wasn't advertising to find the criminal, he was charging five pence apiece for the badly printed tale of how a lusty Scotsman got the better of one of the greatest ladies of the realm.

The tale was scurrilous and mostly false, but it bought Jamie easy entree into the thieves' den when both his horse and accent were recognized by the inn's patrons. There were a great many ribald toasts. He accepted the praise and bought plenty of rounds for the house. And he listened and learned from contact with men far more seasoned at the profession than himself. He ended up staying the better part of three days. Fortunately, he'd sent most of his ill-gotten gains home with a messenger before going to the inn.

When he finally got home, he entered his front door quietly, hoping not to be noticed. He strode into the small entrance hall with his mind on his family's troubles. There was no butler to answer the door. He was the lone male in the McKay establishment. For once Jamie was grateful. The fewer servants one had, the less questioning and gossip there'd be about any change in routine or circumstances in the coming weeks.

He didn't miss having servants, though his mother did, he knew. His sisters never complained that there was only one housemaid and a cook to serve the lot of them. Though the housemaid and cook complained loudly enough when they were late in getting paid.

Their townhouse was in a respectable, if no longer fashionable, neighborhood. Mother was dreadfully upset about that, as well. Bad investments, Jamie recalled bitterly as he started up the stairs to the first floor. Not just bad investments, but Father's gambling, his death, and then the Jacobite troubles had brought the family south to

London, to this townhouse Grannie McKay's English mother had left her. The vast estates were lost. This was the only property the once-proud McKay family now owned.

He'd been thinking of selling it to pay even more of Father's enormous debts, until Granny suggested an alternate means of support. Selling the townhouse would have fed them for a while, but where could they have gone? Debtors' prison? How could he hope to keep four innocent young sisters respectable once the family was turned out on the streets. Granny McKay was right, he told himself again. Better to feed off the rich English for a while, until he was able to find some alternate means of support.

He would rob again, he'd have to. Just until he'd earned enough to dower the girls, enough to see Mother and Granny well taken care of. Just until he had enough and no more. But he'd never be able to rob anyone like Margaret again. No more sweet, sad, talkative girls, he vowed.

He fervently hoped he'd never meet the duchess of Pyneham again. Not that it was likely, considering their different circumstances. Once it wouldn't have been so unthinkable. Once he had lands and station enough to match her own. But now . . .

Jamie, will you get your mind off the lass? He demanded angrily of himself.

In all the time since he'd sent her coach on its way he hadn't been able to get the duchess off his mind. It wasn't just her beauty, though Lord knew, those smoky eyes and heart-shaped face had haunted his dreams for three nights. He hadn't been able to drink the vision of her, golden-haired, fearless, out of his head. He could still see her voluptuous figure, clothed in stiff blue velvet, framed in the window of her coach. Like a portrait of everything he wanted but could never have.

His head still ached from too much spirits, so he tried not to shake it disapprovingly as he trudged up the threadbare carpet to the first floor. It didn't help his headache to find his sister Samantha waiting for him on the landing.

Beautiful, fair, eighteen-year-old, lively, loud Samantha.

"Where have you been?" she asked, at full volume, as usual. "We've been worried. We got the money."

She brushed a wisp of pale curls off her forehead as she went on in what passed for a whisper from her. "Were you gambling? You've got the same guilty look Father used to have. You look as if you've been whoring, actually, but Mummy would freeze if she heard me say it. Mummy's frantic. About the money you sent. I paid the grocer. Granny's keeping the rest. She said not to mind how you got it. Mummy's sure you've gone into trade. You haven't, have you?"

Samantha folded her arms across her bosom and gave him a stern look. He didn't get a chance to answer before she rattled on. "If you've gone into trade Mummy will freeze. She'd rather we'd all starve than have a McKay working like some common *merchant*. I don't mind. She'll get used to it sooner or later, and then she won't complain so much when I become a governess. I'm becoming a governess, Jamie. Don't tell Mummy."

"You are not," Jamie answered.

He'd heard this suggestion before. Not just from Samantha, but from Edwina, as well. They were the eldest of the girls. They thought they were the most practical. Or self-sacrificing. It was those bloody novels they read.

His tone carried grim finality, without a trace of the Lowland Scots lilt he'd adopted to play the role of Jamie Scott. Eton and Cambridge had long ago done away with his natural accent. The girls had had French and English governesses to serve the same purpose. He remembered those dried-up, out-of-place, hopeless women.

"No sister of mine is going to be a servant to other people's children," he declared.

"But—" Samantha began.

"We'll not discuss it," he commanded.

He squeezed past his sister's hooped skirts and walked down the hall. He heard the rustle of stiff cloth as she followed closely behind him. At the sitting room door he hesitated a moment to collect his thoughts. The sitting room was the women's domain. Today, knowing what he'd become, he felt like a wolf about to set himself among a peaceful group of sheep.

Samantha didn't leave him standing in guilty indecision for long. She gave a huffy sigh and took the opportunity to push past him. Opening the door, she strode in, head held at a haughty angle.

Jamie followed and savored the sight of his family in the moments before the inevitable chaos broke loose. Seventeen-year-old Edwina, of the dark, almond-shaped eyes and rich brown hair, was perched on the padded seat of the bay window, looking dreamily out. An abandoned pile of cloth and a sewing basket sat next to her. Mother, thin and nervous, hair white with powder, and Granny McKay, thin and willful, hair steel-gray from experience, were seated next to each other. They shared opposite ends of an enormous embroidery stand. Jamie was willing to wager they hadn't shared a word in hours. The younger girls, plump, thirteen-year-old Michelle and fifteen-year-old Alexandra, a thinner duplicate of Edwina, were seated on the floor. Both girls had their heads bent over books.

As everyone looked up at the sound of their entrance, Samantha announced needlessly, "Our lord and master's

home!" She gave him another haughty look and stalked off
to join Edwina by the window.

Edwina jumped up and ran to fling herself into his
arms. "Oh, Jamie! We've been so worried!"

Michelle and Alexandra abandoned their books. Jamie
pried himself away from Edwina and gave each of the girls
a quick hug before turning to face his elders.

Granny was seated as still as stone, head tilted speculatively to one side. He read the question in her sharp eyes
and nodded slowly. Her thin lips quirked in the faintest of
smiles, the question turning to a twinkle. He knew she'd
want to hear all about his highway adventures when they
could talk in private.

She folded her hands in her lap and said, "Welcome
home, lad."

His mother didn't so much look at him as through him,
expression frozen in a cold angry mask. She was behaving
just as Samantha had predicted.

"It's trade, isn't it? Dirtying his hands, besmirching our
proud name. All for the sake of money. How could he do
this to me?" she asked, not speaking precisely to anyone.
"I know it. Don't try to lie to me."

He didn't. Jamie wanted to say something comforting,
but he knew it wouldn't do any good to try just yet.

A tense silence followed while everyone waited uncom-
fortably. Soon a tear eased from Mother's eye and slowly
trickled down her cheek, bringing the predictable quick
thaw to the freeze. A great many tears followed immediately after the first. Mother bolted to her feet.

"Oh, Jamie! How could you?" she cried, and rushed
from the room.

Granny gazed placidly after her retreating daughter-in-
law. "Well, I'm glad that's over with." She sighed, and got

creakily to her feet. "I'll see you in my room after dinner, James. I'm going to take a rest now."

Jamie offered his arm to escort her to her room, but she waved him aside.

"I'm not feeble yet. Remember, after dinner."

"Yes, Granny."

After she was gone, Edwina tugged impatiently on his sleeve.

"Where were you?"

"Gambling," Samantha supplied before Jamie could answer. "And—cover your ears, girls—whoring."

The girls giggled and blushed. Samantha had picked up the sewing box and was poking through it. She picked up a large needle as Jamie stalked angrily toward her. He was very tall, but she pretended to be oblivious to his presence as he loomed above her. She certainly wasn't intimidated in any way.

"Mind your language," Jamie said sternly.

"Sit down, Jamie," she suggested affably. "You're tired."

Jamie's annoyance vanished. She was right. He was tired. And he'd been doing worse than gambling and whoring, though he'd been doing that as well. He took a seat beside his sister and stretched out his long legs.

"Ahh." He sighed contentedly. "It's good to be home."

"I'll fetch tea," Alexandra decided. "Come on Michelle."

The younger girls left. Edwina sat down on Jamie's other side. Jamie looked from one pretty girl to the other. He reveled in their company, as always, but something suddenly seemed wrong. Lovely company, but they were only his sisters. Sweet and entertaining, of course, but merely sisters. Both were attractive, but neither could compare with the woman he'd encountered on the road. Being with them was pleasant, but neither of them could stimulate his senses in the same way as the duchess. His duchess.

He missed her, he realized with a pang. He'd known her only a few minutes, but it was her company he was missing. It was damned foolish, and he knew it, but it was true, nonetheless.

He reached into his pocket and pulled out the topaz earring. He held it up to the light. The sun-fire facets glittered seductively. The girls gasped at the sight of the gorgeous jewel.

"It's a topaz!" Samantha declared.

"Gold like her hair," he whispered on a sigh.

"Where'd you get it?" Edwina demanded.

Quick as a snake, she snatched it from his hand. Edwina had very clever fingers. Granny McKay said she had the makings of a pickpocket. Jamie hoped she was joking.

"Can I have it?"

"No, you may not." The girls stared at him, waiting for an explanation. He should have kept the thing in his pocket. "Besides, I only have the one. It's . . . a token," he confessed. "From a lady. I promised her I'd keep it as a remembrance."

"You're in love!" Edwina deduced.

Jamie didn't bother answering such girlish nonsense.

"Well, this is a new wrinkle," Samantha declared. "You've never been in love before, Jamie McKay. I hope she's rich. She must be if she has baubles like that to give away. Is that how you're going to rescue our fortunes? Marry an heiress? You won't be happy, you know. Fortune hunters always come to a bad end in novels."

Edwina rushed into the lull while Samantha paused to draw breath. "Not if they're in love. It won't matter if she's rich if they're in love. Sammie reads the wrong sorts of books. She's trying to improve her mind. Who is she, Jamie?"

"Sammie doesn't have a mind," Jamie teased. He fingered one of her pale curls. "She's got dandelion fluff stuffed with words. And it won't do you any good to demand the lady's name."

"A secret love!" Edwina exclaimed. "How romantic!"

Samantha ignored the subject of romance and got back to the object at hand. The object in Edwina's hand, to be precise. "What are you going to do with the earring?" she wanted to know. "If it's a token you must wear it," she went on before he had a chance to answer her.

Jamie considered. He had promised the duchess he'd keep it. He always kept his promises. "Wear it on my vest?" he asked.

"It's an earbob," Edwina pointed out.

His light brown hair was loose around his shoulders this morning instead of properly tied at the back of his neck. Edwina flipped hair away from his face and held the small piece of jewelry up to his ear.

"It would look dashing if you wore it as it was intended," she advised.

"What?" Jamie snorted. "Wear an earbob?" He eyed his younger sister in pretended shock. "You'll have me in a bag wig and face patches, too, I suppose."

Her face lit up with pleasure. "Oh, yes, please! Jamie, you're ever so dull. Wear the earring." She appealed to Samantha. "It's all the fashion, isn't it, Sammie?"

Samantha nodded. She smiled and held up the large, sharp needle she'd been holding. "Very dashing she agreed."

"And it's a token from your lady. Do it, Sammie," Edwina urged. "You know how to pierce ears."

Jamie didn't like the girls' eager tones. He shook his

head. "Oh, no," he protested. "You're not piercing my ear. I'll not look like some . . . some . . . highwayman?"

He blinked and leaned his head back against the sun-warmed window pane. Highwayman. Highwaymen were dashing, weren't they? They had an aura of glamor to them, didn't they? Bravado. Style. Wasn't that one of the lessons he'd learned at the inn?

It was a cultivated glamor. Reputation was as important for a successful highwayman as a fast horse and a true aim with the pistols. He intended to be successful. He'd already adopted the alias of Jamie Scott. He had the beginnings of a reputation with his very first robbery. Why not add some glamor to the persona he was trying to cultivate? Why not let Jamie Scott wear the earring? Staid James McKay wouldn't hear of adopting any outlandish fashion. The more he did to divorce James McKay from Jamie Scott the better.

He sat up and addressed his eagerly waiting sisters.

"All right, prick away, Sammie. I'll wear the blasted earbob."

"You're going to wear your secret lady's token? I knew you were in love!" Edwina enthused.

"Mummy will freeze when she sees it," Samantha pointed out.

"I know," Jamie agreed. "I won't wear it at home."

He closed his eyes and sat very still, his rangy muscles bunched with tension. "Just do it, Sammie," he said between clenched teeth. "Before I lose my nerve."

3

"*Are you sure The Beggar's Opera is suitable,* Your Grace?" the vicar's wife questioned timidly.

Margaret smiled patiently at Mrs. Wendall and glanced briefly across the room at the dowager duchess. Grandmother was ignoring the whole conversation while she went through papers on Margaret's writing table near the terrace door. It was the middle of the afternoon, and Margaret and the vicar of Holborn Lacey's wife were seated in the morning room discussing plans for the midsummer fete.

Grandmother never discussed anything outside the family, but Margaret had a duty to be a leader in the life of the neighborhood. For the midsummer celebration Margaret had offered to finance the production of a play, in which she was also to take part. She'd always been fond of playacting, and saw the entertainment as a way of indulging this interest. Mrs. Wendall had been delighted at the idea, until Margaret mentioned which play she wished to perform.

There were times when Margaret wished she was of a more imperious, high-handed disposition. What was the good of being a duchess, she wondered petulantly, if she couldn't do whatever she wanted? Why had she thought that coming home would be any easier on her than living at Court? Instead of peace and quiet she'd just exchanged the boredom of Court life for the obligations of county life. She found herself becoming more and more restless as the days passed, wondering why she used to enjoy spending time at Lacey House.

She forced her mind back to the discussion.

"It's a wonderful play, Mrs. Wendall. I think you'll enjoy it."

"But, it's about criminals!" Mrs. Wendall whispered the words dramatically, as if revealing a dark secret. As if *The Beggar's Opera* hadn't been a popular production for many years.

"You fancy criminals. Don't you, m'dear?"

Margaret ignored her grandmother's teasing voice and the accusing rustle of paper. She looked, as if for help, to her great-grandmother's portrait instead. The Lely painting of the first Margaret Pyne, half-nude and smiling with sly pleasure, took up much of one wall. Beneath the picture was a glass case full of mementoes of that notorious lady's life. Margaret was fond of the portrait. Mostly because Great-Grandmother wasn't about to step out of the painting to make scathing comments.

"These are all about your Jamie Scott, I see," Grandmother went on, oblivious to Mrs. Wendall's presence. A worn and stained sheet was in the dowager's hand.

Margaret gave the vicar's wife a polite smile, then got up and stalked over to the writing table.

She plucked the broadsheet away. "This is mine."

"You collect every scrap of information about this ruffian as if they're love letters," the dowager said. "Lord, girl, Scott's a common criminal. Find yourself a husband and stop mooning over some fool robber."

Jamie Scott was no fool. Margaret didn't say it. She knew it would make her sound the fool to say it. She probably was a fool. She'd been told often enough in the last six weeks how lucky she'd been to escape from the encounter with only the loss of her jewels. And then she'd been able to retrieve them easily enough.

Meeting Jamie Scott had only made her loneliness and restlessness more evident to her. Memories of the man, of the incident, made her feel vulnerable. She wanted to know why she'd come away from the robbery feeling so different. So she'd asked after any news of him. Some had chosen to take her interest as a joke.

"People send them to me," Margaret said in her own defense, pointing at the papers. "And I don't want a husband."

She touched the topaz necklace at her throat. She couldn't help but remember Jamie Scott's eyes on her as she put the necklace in his hand. Hungry eyes. She couldn't get her mind off his eyes, his voice.

"I don't collect anything," she defended herself. "I'm just interested in him . . . his . . . activities."

The dowager looked at her in disgust. "I'll put him on my list," she said.

"What list?"

"List of suitors for you, Maggie," Grandmother answered with an emphatic nod. "I've been making one up for some time now. I'll add Jamie Scott to the bottom of the list."

Margaret frowned. "I'm not amused, Grandmother," she told the old woman. List of suitors, indeed!

"I'll offer him a few thousand pounds to take you off my hands, if you like. Over and above your dowry, of course."

Margaret ignored the scathing words. She returned to her guest. But Mrs. Wendall was already at the door, her china-blue eyes round as saucers.

"I must be going," she said hastily. She bobbed a curtsy. "Good-day, Your Grace."

"But the play—"

"Let the woman go," the dowager ordered. "I'm not done talking to you, Maggie."

Margaret heard the sound of the door opening and swiftly closing as she turned back to her grandmother. She closed her eyes for a moment, wondering what sort of gossip about her being infatuated with a highwayman the vicar's wife was about to spread throughout the neighborhood.

She approached her grandmother again. The dowager was smiling thinly, like a self-satisfied cat who'd broken into the creamery.

"Do you enjoy embarrassing me?" Margaret asked the old woman.

The dowager brushed a gnarled hand across Margaret's cheek. "I wouldn't hurt you for the world, child," she said gently. "I'm just trying to shock a bit of sense into you."

"Sense?" Margaret asked in complete puzzlement. "Sense about what?"

Sunlight slanted across the small table. It stirred up the heady scent of roses from the crystal vase full of blossoms on one corner of the inlaid desktop. Beside the roses was the ransacked pile of papers. Not all of them concerned Jamie Scott; most were invitations to various social functions. None were personal letters. She longed for a letter. Two letters, really, but neither Jamie Scott nor Frances had sent her any word.

"Sense about what?" she repeated.

The dowager picked up the assortment of papers constituting the adventures of a Scots highwayman. Most were printed in bad prose on cheap paper. "Burn these," she said earnestly. "Get on with your life."

Margaret folded her hands together. She didn't want an argument. She answered mildly. "I am living my life."

The dowager shook her head. "You're getting on with being the duchess of Pyneham. It's not the same thing. It's a man you need. Not a man like your father," she added hastily. "Or like your brother-in-law," she said before Margaret could.

"Is there any other kind?" Margaret asked.

She closed her eyes again, willing the bitterness and pain to stay inside. Damn you, Father! she cursed silently. Damn you for forcing Frances to marry that man. And damn me for being grateful it was she when it was me General Lake really wanted. She took a deep breath and opened her eyes once more. She looked at the portrait of the first duchess of Pyneham.

"I'll not marry," she said firmly. "Not now. Not ever. I don't have to." She pointed at the painting. "She saw to it that I don't have to." The first duchess had insisted the title be inherited by the eldest child, not the eldest male. Margaret was a duchess in her own right. She was as free as a woman could be, and she intended to stay that way.

"It would take an extraordinary male to get me to change my mind," she told her grandmother. She looked deep into the woman's eyes, gray eyes like her own, filled with concern, and added, "Find me a gentle man, a compassionate man, a sober, responsible man. Do you have any like that on your list? If such a creature exists, I'll reconsider."

The dowager shook her head sadly. She would have spoken but a knock on the door drew Margaret's attention. She was glad of the interruption, though she knew the people waiting to enter were only bringing her more work. There was no clock in the morning room, but she could tell the time by the angle of the sunbeams slanting across the blue and white carpet. It was nearly three o'clock, and she'd told Bartlett and Maude she'd see them at three o'clock. Her steward and maid were nothing if not prompt.

The dowager sighed and went out the terrace door, preferring a walk through the rose garden to the company of servants. Margaret resumed her seat on the brocade chair and called, "Come."

Adam Bartlett opened the door, then gallantly waved Maude in before him. Margaret noted the maid's plain features light with a shy smile at the gesture. She smiled at Bartlett herself as he entered.

Bartlett was a tall, sturdily built young man with a dark complexion and black hair. He had a strong, stubborn jaw and bright blue eyes. He was young for his position, no more than a year or two older than Margaret. Margaret had known him all her life, and he was the only man she trusted. He was the stablemaster's son. He'd left Lacey House when he was nineteen under unhappy circumstances, but at her father's death Margaret had sent for him and formally offered him his present position. He'd gravely accepted. They'd been grave and formal with each other most of the time since.

Margaret missed the closeness they'd had when they

were children, Maggie and Adam and Fanny. They were adults now, and everything had changed; the formality was necessary to remind them of it. She didn't ask Bartlett or Maude to sit, or offer them tea. They would have been shocked and disapproving. She was the one who found it hard to remember to keep them in their place.

She folded her hands in her lap and addressed her servants. "Why," she asked Bartlett, "did you strike and then dismiss the groom, Markham?" Before he could answer she spoke to Maude. "And why do you want to speak to me instead of the housekeeper about dismissing the new housemaid?"

"It's difficult to explain, Your Grace."

Bartlett looked and sounded nervous. If there was one thing she knew about stolid, dependable Adam Bartlett, it was that he was not a nervous man. Maude, usually so forthright, was looking at the floor instead of at her. It was a lovely, warm summer day, full of sunlight and the hum of bees from the garden. Suddenly the world seemed cold and silent, as though danger had entered the room with the two people she considered friends.

"What's wrong?" Margaret asked worriedly.

Bartlett met her eyes. "I struck Markham because my father found him tampering with a saddle. Your saddle, Your Grace." As Margaret stared at him in shock, he added. "I think you were meant to have an accident, Your Grace. And I didn't dismiss him. He ran off before I could finish questioning him."

Margaret shivered. "An accident? A fall? Making it look like an accident, you mean?" She heard Maude gasp. Bartlett nodded slowly. Who would want to hurt her? Why?

"I've checked up on the man," Bartlett answered without her having to voice the question. "Markham was a soldier, in General Lake's regiment."

Lake? Her brother-in-law? Margaret was cold with dread, but she wasn't surprised. She didn't doubt the unvoiced accusation against Lake for a moment. She saw the deep hatred of the man in Bartlett's eyes. The hatred and the pain. Her own feelings echoed the steward's.

"The bastard," she said, softly but with a great deal of emotion.

She turned her attention to the maid, but the unannounced entrance of the butler carrying a thick, folded piece of vellum as though it were a sacred object distracted Margaret from Maude's troubles.

"Yes, Dominick?" she asked the butler.

"For you, Your Grace." Dominick cleared his throat. The older man was slightly flushed with embarrassment. "You said to bring this to you immediately if it should ever arrive."

Her mind was still on General Lake, and she couldn't remember what her instructions about whatever this was had been. What was it? When had she told Dominick to . . . ? She looked at the folded paper. On the outside, in clear, bold handwriting, were the words "To Margaret, From Jamie Scott."

It had to be a joke. No. He'd remembered. She *knew* this had to be from him.

She dismissed the servants, forgetting their concerned looks and the conversation the instant the door closed behind them. She held the paper in her hand and noticed it was trembling. The light was better by the windows. She stood and walked a bit unsteadily into the sunlight. The vellum was sealed with dark red wax; some of it stuck under her nails as she pried it off.

She unfolded the large sheet of paper, holding the words

up before her eyes, scanning them with a hunger she hadn't known she'd felt. The room was silent, still, she was alone. But she could feel him, feel Jamie Scott's presence as though he'd just stepped through the garden door and come up behind her. She felt enfolded in his presence, surrounded. She could almost feel the heat of his body, the brush of his warm breath and soft brown hair on her cheek. His handwriting was as clear and sharp as crystal. She read.

Dear Margaret,

I promised you a love letter. I never forget a promise, though sometimes it's later than sooner that I fulfill them.

I'm sitting near a fire as I write. When I look into the smoke I think of your eyes. The smoke's not so expressive, not so tender. The fire's dying down and dawn is near. I'm drunk, or nearly so, or perhaps I wouldn't have recalled my promise. The brandy at the Red Bull is exceptional, Margaret. Exceptionally fine. Not near as fine or as burning on the tongue as a kiss from you would be, but it will have to do until I can claim the kiss for myself. And claim it some day, I will. Rob it from you, perhaps, as I did your jewels. Will stolen kisses taste like smuggled wine? Will there be a finer, sharper edge to the taking? Or will you give it freely, I wonder? I'll drink you a toast and think of the intoxication of drinking from your lips instead.

I'll drink to you and I'll write to you because I cannot get you off my mind. You're my first duchess, Margaret. Am I your first highwayman? No, you said there were others. I'd like to think I was the first to steal your heart. Could a duchess love a highwayman, I wonder? It's words of love I promised you. Read my words, lass, and dream that I'm touching you. For, truly, if I were to see you again, I'd steal more than a kiss. You'd be soft to the touch, once I freed you from all that wretched boning. Soft and pale and hot to the touch. There's a treasure of yours I crave more than gold and topaz. I'd bury my hands in your topaz hair and draw you to me. Draw you down on a soft white bed and take you. Take you into my arms, and myself into you. Would you have me, beautiful duchess?

Do you think of me ever, as I think of you?

Are these words of love enough for you? They're not enough for me. Good-bye, Duchess Margaret. Pray our paths never cross again. For if they do, I'll take you and make you my own.

The letter ended in a scrawled signature. Though she didn't know why, tears burned behind Margaret's eyes by the time she had reached the end of the page. She didn't know how long she'd been holding her breath, but now she let it out in an explosive sigh. She gasped for air as though she were drowning. Drowning in words. Possessive words. No suitor had ever written such words to her before. She didn't want to be possessed. Yet, Jamie Scott's words left her hot and trembling and aching for the promised kisses. She could almost feel his lips claiming hers, almost feel his hands touching her in places no one had ever touched before.

She pressed her forehead against the window, breathing in great gulps of air, trying to calm her senses. Trying to think. She was surrounded by the scent of roses, as heady and caressing as the images conjured by Jamie's words. If she was going to think, she had to get away from the roses. But she didn't want to think. The letter weighed heavily in her hand, the words calling her back to their embrace.

Margaret sighed, and read the letter again.

4

Fingers trembling just a little, Margaret lit a candle and touched the letter to the flame. The heavy vellum burned slowly, crisping around the edges before licking into the words on the page. The smell of smoke mingled with the aroma of the roses, but she didn't linger to inhale the scent. She didn't let herself grieve over destroying Jamie's words. She would not nurse secret hopes. She would not dream of lean, long-fingered hands playing across her skin. Or the caressing look in warm brown eyes. Or the touch of lips she'd never even seen. She would not!

She left the warm ashes heaped in her empty teacup and marched purposefully out of the morning room. Maggie Pyne could memorize love letters, but the duchess of Pyneham had far more important things to do. Besides, she lamely defended her actions to herself, the letter was evidence. He told me where he was. What if the constables should find his hideout? Do I want to see the man hanged even if it's what the law says he deserves?

"If they'd let me sit in Parliament . . ." she complained aloud.

She might have continued grumbling righteously to herself, but Maude was waiting just outside the door. The woman's worried expression caught Margaret's attention. She took Maude's hands in her own.

"Oh, dear. I didn't give you a chance to finish, did I?"

Maude looked uncomfortable with the familiarity. She gently detached herself from her mistress's grasp. Margaret clasped her hands at her waist instead, realizing how much the lack of another's touch bothered her. Her grandmother might give her the occasional hug or peck on the cheek, but no one, no one else at all, would ever presume to lay a finger on the duchess of Pyneham. Except to serve her, of course. She had people to bathe her and dress her and comb her hair, but no one just to hold her hand or stroke her cheek or— She firmly denied the images the memory of Jamie Scott's letter tried to conjure in her head.

"Tell me what's the matter," she bid instead.

Maude looked around, making sure there was no one else in sight. Margaret almost smiled at her furtiveness.

"It's Janet Cole, the new housemaid," Maude said at last. "I don't like her. Not one bit. And now that I heard General Lake's trying to kill you, I—"

"Let's not talk about Lake," Margaret cut her off. "What's wrong with Janet?"

Not that Margaret had any idea which housemaid Janet was. She didn't even know how many housemaids she employed. She did know her personal maid's dislike for another servant wasn't excuse enough to have the girl dismissed. She did know it wasn't like Maude to express her personal feelings about the other servants or to take advantage of their long-standing relationship. Margaret waited for her explanation.

Maude looked uncomfortable. She made a helpless gesture. "It's not anything the girl's done, Your Grace. It's the way she's always watching—lurking—slipping around like she wants to see everything but doesn't want to be noticed. She makes me . . . uncomfortable. I can't explain it."

Margaret didn't know how to respond, and she didn't have time to think of a response before Dominick appeared, striding quickly toward her down the hallway.

"Your Grace," the butler said as he reached her. "There's a delegation from Holborn Lacey asking to see you. They're waiting in the rotunda." He looked equally amused and uncomfortable. Dominick was not one of those blank-faced, unflappable butlers she'd heard bragged about, though he always tried hard to achieve the solemnity he thought his position required.

"Delegation?" she asked curiously. She dismissed Maude with a gesture. "We'll talk later. From the village?"

"Led by Mrs. Wendall, Your Grace."

"What could she want?"

Margaret set off toward the front of the house. She laughed a little as a thought struck her. Perhaps, after hearing about the dowager's list of suitors, the vicar's wife had gone out and rounded up some respectable yeomen as candidates for the duchess's hand.

Or more likely, it was about the play, she decided as she entered Lacey House's great, circular entry hall.

The rotunda, tiled in sea-green malachite and gray marble, stretched out before her. Huddled near the bottom of the sweeping grand staircase were a group of at least twenty familiar faces, Mrs. Wendall planted firmly in the foreground as their leader. Margaret noticed that the vicar's wife was attempting an expression of righteous sternness as she approached. The woman reverted to flustered indecision the moment she saw Margaret.

She curtsied and flapped her hands at her cohorts, who quickly followed her lead. By the time everyone was upright again Margaret had come to a halt in front of them.

"Yes?" she inquired sweetly.

While Mrs. Wendall was still clearing her throat someone in the crowd said, "It's about the play, Your Grace."

"It's indecent," a woman's voice trilled from the back of the group. "Even Eloise says so."

"We talked it over."

"We took a vote." This last statement was from Jordan the carter, who was known for reading political tracts.

Margaret folded her hands and addressed Mrs. Wendall. "The play? *The Beggar's Opera*? Indecent? I see. The people of Holborn Lacey think the production would be improper for the midsummer festivities?"

Mrs. Wendall nodded eagerly, obviously glad the duchess needed no further explanation. Margaret surveyed the group. She didn't show her disappointment. She didn't argue with them. It was their festival. She could always stage a private entertainment, she supposed, with the London circle that shared her interest in drawing-room theatrics. Never mind her longing to perform for a large audience. It was no more than a penchant she'd inherited from the first duchess, who'd managed to fit in a successful acting career while keeping King Charles company between the covers.

"You have another play in mind?"

"Yes, Your Grace," a chorus of voices answered.

"I see." Everyone looked at her with eager anticipation. Feet shuffled on the smooth tiles. There was an embarrassed cough. She didn't let them wait long before she made her decisions. "Very well," she agreed. "We'll perform your selection." She narrowed her eyes at Mrs. Wendall. "What play?"

"Well, I haven't actually read it, but it sounds ever so appropriate. It has fairies in it, so the children can have parts as well. I do think it's appropriate to include the children, don't you, Your Grace?"

"What play?" Margaret repeated, just about at the limit of her patience.

"*A Midsummer Night's Dream,*" Mrs. Wendall finally supplied. She gave Margaret a winning smile. "There's a role for a fairy queen. It's one of the main parts. You'd make a lovely fairy queen, Your Grace."

Margaret was not opposed to outright flattery. She let herself succumb to it to smooth over her disappointment. "I'd be happy to portray a fairy queen," she agreed. She ran her gaze around the now-smiling group. "We'll start rehearsals right away, shall we?"

"Right now?" Mrs. Wendall asked.

"Yes."

"But I don't have the book with me. I left Mr. Wendall's Shakespeare in his study."

"Shakespeare?" Margaret glanced at Dominick, who lingered unobtrusively behind her. "Do we have a volume of those plays in the book room?"

"I believe so, Your Grace."

"Good. Fetch it—" She pivoted around. "No, I'll fetch it. You take my guests up to the ballroom, then order refreshments. I'll bring the book and we can get started."

She didn't wait for Dominick to answer, but headed quickly across the rotunda. She entered the hallway, which led to the opposite side of the ground floor, and made her way quickly to the large room at the end of the corridor.

She passed the open door of the steward's office on her way. Bartlett was seated at his desk, a fierce frown of concentration on his face as he read a document. He glanced up briefly as she passed. She smiled but went on without disturbing him.

Her sense of purpose was replaced by dismay the moment she reached the book room. She rarely came here.

Leather-bound volumes, spines trimmed in gilt lettering, marched in thick rows from floor to ceiling on three walls. The shelves were interrupted only by four tall but narrow windows with cushioned window seats on the wall facing the front lawn and a wide fireplace opposite the windows. A polished oak table occupied the center of the room, and there were a group of chairs and heavy candle stands near the fireplace. This room had been her father's domain. He and his guests had come in there to get roaring drunk. It hadn't been safe for any servant girl to venture near the book room then. And their governess made sure neither she nor Frances went near the place, either. Except, Margaret recalled bitterly, for one very inauspicious occasion four years before.

Her errand forgotten for the moment, Margaret walked slowly around the perimeter of the room. The painful memory assailed her.

"Lake's my best friend," Father said, doing his best to stare them both down. "He's asked for the honor of my daughter's hand."

Frances looked at the parquet floor. Margaret wouldn't cower. She never cowered. Not when he shouted, nor when she saw him strike a servant. Nor when he struck her. She wouldn't let herself show fear. And she wouldn't obey him in this. She didn't have to and she wouldn't.

"I'm marrying Edward," she reminded him. Edward, whom she didn't love, but whom she'd known forever and

who was their nearest neighbor. Father couldn't object to Edward.

"Then it's Frances, who'll make the marriage. It's decided."

And Edward died at Culloden, she thought, pulling away from the too-vivid memory. And Frances married Lake, and it all started in this room when she said no to a marriage she didn't want.

"No wonder I haven't been in here in years," she murmured. She tried to keep her thoughts on the present. "I'm going to be a fairy queen," she reminded herself. "As soon as I can find the Shakespeare." She began searching the shelves.

She was holding the collected works of Shakespeare in her hands when she heard the ring of boot heels coming down the hall. The steward must have finished his work and come to check on her. The door opened, and she turned with a smile for Bartlett.

"They won't let their duchess be a strumpet," she announced.

The extraordinarily handsome gold-haired man framed in the doorway was not Bartlett. "Pity," General Sir Charles Lake drawled as he came toward her. "I've always thought you'd make a fine one."

Margaret felt herself blush, but bit back an angry retort. "What are you doing here?" she asked instead, looking up at the man who towered above her.

He gave her a slow, seductive smile. Attempts at seduction had always been his favorite way of irritating her. She ignored it. "Where's Frances?"

"Never mind Frances." He reached out for her.

She spun away, putting the table between them. She denied that she was afraid of him. She simply didn't want him touching her. She gave a silent, bitter laugh. To think she'd been craving someone's touch not so long before. She put the heavy book on the table.

His boots were covered in dust and his well-cut riding clothes were rumpled, but his disheveled appearance only enhanced his attractiveness. Lake was one of the handsomest men in Britain. He'd been trading on those looks for years. There weren't many women who could resist his lithe body and knowing smirk. He smirked at her now, and Margaret merely sighed. His looks had never impressed her. Not even when she'd been sixteen and he'd first tried to seduce her. He'd been a general at twenty-five, and though he was retired from the army and nearly forty, he hadn't let himself run to fat. He was too vain for that. His vanity never let him believe there was someone who didn't want him.

"But I do mind Frances," she said, forcing her voice to be sweet. "I would appreciate your bringing my sister for a visit from Rishford Abbey. Or allow me to visit her there. I thought I made that perfectly clear in the last letter I wrote you. All you need to do is let Frances visit while you enjoy yourself in London."

He pulled the letter out of his coat pocket and tossed it on the table. It landed beside the leather-bound volume.

His smirk turned to a snarl. "You were perfectly clear, Your Grace. That's why I'm here. What you 'suggested' was cutting off my allowance unless I separated from my beloved wife. I won't be bought off. I'll have what's rightfully mine. It's you and the Pyneham title, or nothing."

"Then it will be nothing," Margaret replied. She couldn't give herself to Lake. Not even for Frances's sake. Even if she could, she didn't think it would do her sister any good. Lake would still use Frances's safety as a hold over her. "It's a pity about your gambling debts," she added, using the only weapon she had. She just wished they were heavier. Pity the man won more than he lost, or her threat might have had more teeth. "I simply can't cover your expenses for this quarter," she went on. "Unless of course—"

"Don't threaten me," he told her coldly. "I'm better at it than you are." He moved swiftly around the table, looming over her. All hint of seductiveness was gone from his manner.

He was a big man, with a talent for intimidation. Margaret refused to acknowledge his threatening stance. "The groom ran away," she said. "I'm afraid there won't be any riding accidents in my future. Frances won't be inheriting the title for a while yet."

He didn't deny he'd sent the groom to kill her. Of course, she couldn't prove it, either.

"The title should be mine. Your father wanted it that way. I'll do what's necessary to get what's rightfully mine."

"My father's dead. I'm sick of my sister being a pawn."

"You're not the one who's sick," he told her with an evil smile. "It's Frances who is ill. Very ill. Mad, actually." The look he gave her was feral and predatory. His voice was soft and dangerous. "I must keep a strict, stern watch over her tender health. Especially since something could happen to you. Be careful of your health, little duchess. And of accidents."

Lake put his hands on her shoulders. She forced herself to stay still under the harsh touch. She'd only be acknowledging her revulsion. She didn't like showing a man with power over her that he affected her in any way.

His fingers dug into her shoulders. "Frances is mine," he told her. "I'll do whatever I want with your precious sister. And you'll pay me to take care of her. I say she's insane. Just a step away from being locked away in a madhouse."

Hard fingers pressed deeply into her shoulder blades. "I've heard of one place where the doctors recommend daily beatings and locking the patient away in darkness. It sounds like a fine treatment, don't you think?" His voice had a silky malevolence. "Shall I start such a treatment? She's frail, but I'll do what I have to help your dear sister and heir."

Margaret looked up at her brother-in-law in helpless, silent fury. She was more furious at herself than at Lake. Lake was a far more experienced gambler than she was. She should have known that her desperate bluff about cutting off his income wouldn't work. His nearness and the possessive weight of his hands was almost more than she could stand. A chill of revulsion swept through her, except at the heated points where his skin touched hers. She hardly felt the pain.

Margaret swallowed her pride and managed to say humbly enough, "I think your present care of Frances is quite enough."

"I'm glad you think so. And . . ."

"How much do you want?"

His thumbs stroked across the base of her throat. The smirk returned to his lips. "I'll start with an increase in my allowance. Then, perhaps I'll continue with a kiss."

"I think you should take your hands off the duchess."

Margaret's head turned at the welcome sound of the voice. Bartlett had come in quietly. A large footman was in the hallway behind him.

Lake's hands dropped from her shoulders. He laughed coldly. "It's the faithful hounds."

Bartlett ignored the other man. "Your guests are

becoming anxious, Your Grace," he told her. "Perhaps I can deal with the general while you rejoin them."

Margaret smiled gratefully at her friend. She picked up the book. "Thank you, Bartlett. The general has come on a matter of finance. See to it, please."

"Yes, Your Grace."

Bartlett bowed as she passed him. They exchanged the briefest of looks. Still, his disapproval was palpable. Of Lake. Of the necessity of dealing with his demands. Of himself for being helpless to defend the woman he loved— the woman who was Lake's wife and prisoner.

Oh, Frances, Margaret wished as she hurried off to try to forget herself in the role of a fairy queen, why can't we all be children again?

"Why don't you kill him before he kills you?" the dowager asked.

Before Margaret could answer, her grandmother turned away and marched restlessly from one side of the bedchamber to the other. The trio of maids in the room with them looked up in wide-eyed fright at the old woman's fierce words.

The pretty red-haired maid scurried off toward the dressing room like a terrified sheep. The other two just got out of the dowager's way. Behind Margaret, Maude *tsk*ed in annoyance at the girl's hasty departure. Margaret wished that her grandmother wasn't always so arrogantly oblivious of the servants' presence.

Margaret closed her eyes to enjoy more fully Maude's brushing her hair. She was exhausted, her emotions drained. The hour was late, and all she wanted was to sleep.

"Are you listening to me, Maggie?"

She opened her eyes and said, "I can't just order a man's death, Grandmother."

The dowager came back to the dressing table. "Why not? The man's threatened you. You've no friends at Court, but Lake does. And in the law courts. If you can't go to the law, take it into your own hands. Or—"

"Assassination? Don't be ridiculous." Sometimes the dowager was just a bit too high-handed. And sometimes it was hard to tell when she was joking. Margaret fervently hoped she was joking now. The idea of murdering Lake was ridiculous. This wasn't the Dark Ages. Very well, she conceded to herself, the idea of some sort of action against the man was tempting, but violence certainly wasn't the answer. Was it?

"What was that under butler thinking of," the dowager muttered. "Letting Lake in unattended just because the butler was busy. You can't trust your own staff, girl. The man could have had your honor or your life in the time it took for the steward to arrive." The old woman shook a finger at her. "You need to be looked after. Someone to keep you safe." She smiled, baring her few remaining teeth. "Hire someone to do it. Your Jamie Scott is a bold lad. Offer him enough coin and—"

"Grandmother!" Margaret jumped to her feet in outrage. "Jamie's no murderer!"

"Might as well be," the dowager answered, unperturbed by Margaret's outrage. "He's good with a pistol. Offer him a change of employment. Or can you see using any of the bumbling fools already in your employ as a bodyguard?"

Margaret sat back down suddenly. She looked at her grandmother speculatively. "Bodyguard?" Jamie Scott as a bodyguard. *Her* bodyguard? No, no, she thought hastily.

She didn't want him near her body. There was too much she'd be tempted to let him do with it. That wouldn't do at all. "He's a highwayman. A robber. A scoundrel."

"Just the sort you want," the dowager replied knowingly.

"What?" Margaret blinked. "Want for what?"

Instead of answering her question, her grandmother bid her good-night and left her to finish getting ready for bed. Margaret looked blankly at Maude. Her maid offered no explanations; she just finished braiding Margaret's hair in silence. Margaret sighed and climbed into bed as soon as Maude was through with her. The night was warm, so she ordered the bed curtains left open, the balcony doors left ajar, the candles extinguished, and the group of servants off to their own rest.

Once she was alone in the dark room, she rubbed her aching temples. She wanted to sleep, not think about what a long, trying day it had been. It hadn't been completely terrible, she told herself. The villagers enjoyed the reading of the play. Jamie Scott's letter had come.

The memory brought a smile to her lips, though her body moved restlessly, stirred by the memory of the highwayman's bold words. She closed her eyes and turned on her side, silently reciting Jamie's words to herself, mixing them up with one of the speeches from the play, as sleep made her mind first fuzzy, then claimed her altogether.

She dreamed she was touching the letter to the candle flame, then dreamed it again. When her hand started to repeat the gesture a third time she drew the paper back. "I have to," she explained. "I have to. If I keep you I'll keep wanting you, and I can't want anymore. I can't trust anyone. I can't let you matter. It's hopeless to let you matter. It breaks my heart not to let you matter. I can't run off and be your doxy and play the strumpet no matter how much I want to. I'm a duchess, you see. Your first duchess."

The flame beckoned. Her hand moved inexorably forward. The paper caught, flared. The edges curled and smoked. The smoke mingled with the scent of roses borne in on the night air from the garden below her balcony.

Margaret sat up in bed, wide awake. She smelled smoke. Her eyes burned, and she coughed on acrid fumes. Fire. Something nearby was on fire. A flicker of light caught the corner of her eye. The flame was coming from the end of the bed!

She rolled over and out of the soft embrace of the feather mattress, calling out for the maid sleeping in the antechamber as she reached for the flower vase on the bedside table. She dumped the contents, flowers and all, onto the burning blanket. Even as the water sizzled out part of the fire, a tongue of flame reached from the blanket toward the bed curtain. She called again, but didn't wait for an answer. She bunched the blanket up, pulled it off the bed, and ran onto the balcony. She threw it over the side before the flames could touch her. She looked down, watching the track of fire as it slowly descended to the terrace two floors below. Safe, shaking from reaction, she leaned against the marble rail, her mind racing. She heard the door open behind her, Maude's voice calling out a question. She ignored the sounds.

Someone had set the fire. Someone had come into the room as she slept and set her bed on fire. Her own bed! She wasn't safe in her own bed. Lake really was trying to kill her.

Bodyguard, her grandmother had said. She needed someone to protect her.

She closed her eyes. The memory of warm, brown eyes

and a pistol held in a steady hand appeared before her, bringing an odd comfort.

"Jamie Scott," she said. "Bodyguard. The Red Bull Inn."

5

"*You're not really* going in there are you, Your Grace?" Huseby moved as subtly as a man his size could, trying to keep her from the door.

Margaret had to look a long way up to glare menacingly at the oversized young footman. "Yes, Huseby," she told him, "I'm going in there. That's what I came here for."

"I understand the playacting and all, Your Grace, but it's not right for you to be in such a place. It's full of wicked men and shameless women."

Margaret had hennaed her hair for the occasion and put on a coating of face paint and a couple of small, round beauty patches. The henna had come from the possessions left by Janet Cole, the maid who'd fled Lacey House after Margaret's bed was set on fire.

The gown Margaret was wearing had once belonged to Eloise Huseby, Holborn Lacey's only professional jezebel, elder sister to young Alfred Huseby here. Eloise was as small as her brother was large. The bodice of the faded red wool dress was tight and ill-fitting. It left a great deal more of Margaret exposed to the open air than even her most fashionable Court gowns. The hem was mud-splattered, as were her bare feet.

She'd left her coach at another inn down the road and walked to the Red Bull, the formidable-looking figure of Huseby trailing behind her. The lad was being altogether too protective. She wasn't sure whether she was pleased or annoyed at his earnest solicitousness. She did know she wasn't going to let him keep her out of the Red Bull. After making her plans in secret for the last week and sneaking out of her own estate in the middle of the night and the long, tiring trip to the stinking outskirts of London, she wasn't going to be stopped now. She'd come to the Red Bull to acquire a proper bodyguard, someone as dangerous and daring and calculating as all the two-pence broadsheets claimed Jamie was. She wasn't leaving until she had Jamie Scott by her side—in her employ, she corrected the thought quickly.

She was going to save him. It hadn't been her original intention in coming here. Or maybe it had been and she just hadn't wanted to admit it. She wasn't the only one who needed help. Jamie Scott needed to be saved from the destructive course he'd set out upon before it was too late.

They'd passed a gibbet at a crossroads not far from the Red Bull. She couldn't get the image of the rotting body hanging there in chains, the chains rattling gently in the wind, out of her mind. The body was of a highwayman, denied proper burial, his gruesome remains left as an example of the penalty awaiting lawbreakers. She knew she couldn't let the man who'd written her such beautiful, heart-stirring words end up as just another roadside corpse. She'd offer him honest employment, a new beginning. It was all she could offer.

She tried to edge past Huseby again. He blocked her way again. Margaret sighed. It was very difficult to act on her good intentions when she couldn't even get past the inn door.

"You wouldn't stop Eloise from going in there," she pointed out.

"But it's her business, Your Grace. She's a fallen woman," he added, not without a trace of pride in his sister's industriousness. "She'd make a fine night's work of every whoremaster in the taproom."

"Indeed," Margaret agreed, not quite sure what she was agreeing to. She told herself she really wasn't all that innocent, but surely no woman would willingly submit to so many men for so little coin in such a short space of time. Not that this was the time for speculating on the behavior of loose women. It was a role she'd taken on for a few hours, until she could speak to Jamie Scott alone. Then she could get out of this filthy rag and order it burned, bugs and all. At the moment it was time to play the imperious duchess to get this lummox out of her way.

"Stand aside," she ordered. "I want to get this over with as quickly as possible. Mind your place or I'll have you beaten."

He didn't budge. He smiled knowingly instead.

"Why is it," she asked, hands on hips, "that no one believes me when I threaten them?"

"You're too good to us, Your Grace."

"So it would appear. I suppose you expect me to wait here while you fetch Scott out? No," she continued firmly. "You don't even know what he looks like." Not that she did, either. But at least she'd met him. She was certain she'd be able to recognize his eyes, his hands, his voice. "Move," she ordered.

"Please, Your Grace," Huseby entreated as she began to step around him. He plucked tentatively at the soiled sleeve of the red dress.

Margaret whirled on him. "Not, 'Your Grace'! Maggie," she reminded him, easily falling into the Cheapside accent she'd picked up with milk and caresses from her wet nurse. "I'm Maggie Pyne."

The sound of an approaching rider drew her attention. She looked across the innyard as a roan stallion was reined to a halt a few feet from where she and Huseby stood. The rider was young, straight, and slender, in a dark hat and coat. His long face was set in lines of cold anger. She stared at him openly, trying to discern if there was anything familiar about him.

He paid her no mind, except for a fleeting glance aimed mostly at her overexposed bosom. He was too wrapped up in his own black mood to notice her interest in him. She studied his swift movements as he dismounted and moved, sleek and dangerous, across the innyard.

Was that he? she wondered. Was that Jamie Scott? The build was the same. He sat his horse the same. The horse itself looked familiar. The young man's eyes were large and brown. Jamie's color, but the expression in them was very different. This man's eyes were cold and hard and dangerous. Not Jamie. Not like Jamie at all, she decided. She made herself look away as the black-clad stranger moved to the door. She concentrated on getting past her protective footman once again.

* * *

There was a pair of newcomers standing in the courtyard of the Red Bull when Jamie came riding in. He paid them very little mind, noting only that the man was a hulking bumpkin in muddy homespun and the doxy had badly dyed red hair and too much bosom for the worn scarlet dress she wore. Normally he'd have taken at least a few more moments to appreciate the ripe charms of the lass, but at the moment he was angry and in a hurry.

It was Taggert he was after. Once he was finished with the cheating bastard he might have attention to spare for a lively looking piece of goods like the redhead. She'd probably be finished with the customer from the country by the time he finished his business with that cheating cove, Taggert. Mayhap he and the redhead could comfort each other after the exertions of dealing with more distasteful customers.

He slid off his tired horse and handed the reins to the waiting ostler. He flipped the boy a shilling, checked the pistols at his belt and the knife up his sleeve, then strode purposefully into the inn. He felt the girl's eyes on his back but ignored the urge to look her way. Later, he promised himself. Later.

Only a fool would sit with his back to the door in a place like the Red Bull. Taggert was a fool. His back was not only turned but he was half out of his chair, his ugly face planted firmly between the breasts of Lucy, the Red Bull's most willing barmaid. The rest of the customers scattered at the tables were minding their own business.

Only one pair of eyes looked up at Jamie's entrance. Lucy, seemingly oblivious to Taggert's attentions, beamed a shining, if a bit gap-toothed, smile of welcome at Jamie. When she would have called out a greeting, Jamie put a cautioning finger to his lips and cat-footed forward. The girl giggled and ran her fingers through Taggert's sparse supply of hair.

Behind him, he heard the door open again and glanced around briefly enough to see the country lummox hesitating in the doorway. The red-haired girl was behind him. It looked as if she was trying to squeeze past the big fellow. He heard an "oomph," followed by a satisfied sigh as the girl pushed her way inside. This was no time to let himself be distracted. He dismissed the odd pair and went back to approaching his quarry.

Taggert was still busily engaged with Lucy's breasts when Jamie bent over him and murmured icily, "A word in your ear, perhaps?"

Taggert was off his chair like a shot, tumbling Lucy to the floor. He snatched up his ale mug and sent it flying at Jamie's head. Anticipating the move, Jamie had already danced away. He had his knife out. Even though he was furious enough to want Taggert dead, showing a pistol in the Red Bull was an invitation for every man in the room to draw his own weapons. Steel would do.

Taggert snarled, but didn't move. He'd seen the knife. Though the light in the taproom was dim and smoky, the glint of steel was bright enough to draw the attention of the rest of the wary patrons. The silence was sudden, heavy, and expectant. Lucy's scrambling to get to her feet and out of the way was the only motion in the otherwise frozen atmosphere.

Taggert's snarl turned slowly into a false smile as he raised his gaze to meet Jamie's.

"You startled me, lad," he said, false cheerfulness doing nothing to disguise suppressed anger and fear. "Didn't think I'd see you this side of Tyburn. Not with the way the constables were on your heels when we parted company."

"And just why were the constables waiting at that particular spot?" Jamie wondered.

His voice was low, but the dangerous tone carried to every waiting ear. He'd learned to never let any man take advantage of him, and it was fear of the most dangerous predators that kept the beasts in the Red Bull friends and allies. Nobody here was a sheep, but Jamie was definitely one of the wolves.

He continued before Taggert could reply. "Master Taggert, it seems," he announced, "has ambitions of replacing Jonathan Wild as the Thief-Taker General of England."

Mutters and the glitter of hostile eyes greeted this statement. Rats, Jamie thought, hating his compatriots. They reminded him of rats. And he himself was among the worst of them.

He kept most of his hatred aimed at the man who'd betrayed him to the constables. He'd barely made his escape. Worst of all, his face had been seen. He was going to have to lay low for a while, which he could ill afford to do.

Taggert spread his hands before him and looked pleadingly at the crowd. "I don't know what he's talking about."

Jamie laughed coldly. "The laddie thought the price on my head was worth the risk of setting an ambush for me. We arranged to meet at Hargate Cross. He was there, and so were a trio of thief takers. Well, the constables didn't arrest me. It's taken me three days to get safely back here. You shouldn't have been fool enough to come here until you heard I was hanged."

Jamie heard the scrapes of chairs being pushed back across the sagging boards of the floor. Men preparing to defend or attack Taggert. The patrons of the Red Bull were judge and jury of their own. He felt more than saw the circle of bodies drawing in around where he and Taggert stood.

The place was barely lit; two grimy windows and a lantern hung over the bar providing what little illumination there was. If this was what it was like in the middle of the day, Margaret thought as she made her way around the tables, they must stumble around like blind men after sunset. Probably just as well for the innkeeper's sake, she decided as she got a whiff of the greasy, sour smell from the kitchen. She ignored Huseby's hand plucking at her sleeve, urging her to a place by the wall. The patrons, hard-faced men and a few blowsy women, ignored her as she moved among them. They were all intent on the confrontation in the center of the room.

Margaret's attention was riveted there as well, on the slender, dangerous man holding the knife. There was something too familiar about him, though what she saw was more impressions than actual detail. She could make out that his brows, heavy and straight, were lowered over narrowed eyes, his long jaw was angrily clenched, and with the arrogance of a lord, he was looking down his long nose at the object of his fury. His fury seemed justified as he explained that the bald man had betrayed him for the sake of a reward. Explained in the Scots-burred voice she'd heard so often in her romantic musings.

Well, there was nothing romantic in this situation. The room was crackling with danger. Margaret could feel it vibrating around her, but she was too intently aware of the man with the knife to take much notice of anything else. Was it really he? This man was as sharp and deadly as the blade in his hand. It sent a shiver through her, hot and cold. She told herself it was fear, but it felt more like hunger.

"I want to see you swing," the bald man declared, giving up all pretense of innocence. "I hate you, you bastard whoreson. Hated you ever since you bedded my woman."

The Scotsman looked puzzled. "Bedded your woman?" He gestured with his free hand. "Which one's yours? God's death, man, they're all for hire."

The girl who'd been knocked to the floor laughed louder than the rest. "You did it for me, Taggert?" she questioned, edging toward the men.

The bald man turned a look of adoration on the girl. "You know I love you, but all you can talk about is 'sweet Jamie.'"

"Sweeter than honey," the girl declared. "At least he bathes, which you've never been known to do."

There was a low rumble of laughter from the crowd. Margaret took a step closer to the quarreling men. The Scotsman tossed hair off his shoulder, and she caught the yellow gleam of the jewel he wore in his ear.

She gasped and said loudly, "You are Jamie Scott!"

Jamie didn't know why he let the girl distract him, but he turned his head toward her. He got a glimpse of a shocked face staring out of the room's shadows, and then Taggert was on top of him. The knife went flying out of his hand, and he had to defend himself with his fists against one of the nastiest street fighters in the London underworld.

There was a collective roar of outrage from the patrons of the Red Bull, and they all seemed to be on their feet, flailing in deadly fury. Furniture began flying, along with fists. Bodies crashed over tables, crockery crashed against walls and skulls. A flying bottle hit the lantern, which began to swing wildly, making the already uncertain light even more flickering and eerie. Margaret dropped to the floor, searching for the lost knife, following a half-formed notion that Jamie might need it.

She heard a bellow and looked up to see Huseby breasting through the sea of thrashing bodies, trying to make his way to her. Another bottle sailed through the smoky air. Huseby's head got in its way. The big footman went down like a stone.

Margaret lost track of Jamie Scott in the melee as she crawled in a winding path under the tables to reach Huseby. When she got to him it didn't take long to discover that the hit on the head had done little damage. There was a growing lump, and he was out for a while, but she didn't think he was badly hurt. She dragged a table away from a wall, and positioned it protectively over the footman's fallen form. Then she inched back to the center of the fray. She stayed low, dodging the jostling, swearing combatants when she had to.

She found Jamie Scott standing over the body of the bald man, shaking his own right hand as though it hurt. Margaret didn't know what condition Jamie had left his attacker in, but she could tell that the highwayman's knuckles were bruised and swollen. He was alone in a sea of calm while the fight continued around him.

Margaret got up cautiously off her knees and approached him. He looked at her, but before she could say anything, the other girl, Lucy, sidled over to Jamie. She kissed him on his throat. Margaret looked at the knife she'd retrieved.

"You're just the kind of man I want, Jamie love," Lucy declared.

The girl's hand landed possessively on Jamie Scott's

upper thigh, a bit too close to the bulge in his breeches for Margaret's taste.

"Is he now?" Margaret heard herself say, low and menacing.

Jamie paid no mind to Lucy's pawing him. His gaze dropped instead to the knife in the redhead's hand. It was a small hand, grimy but delicately made. He'd found her words amusing, especially since he felt Lucy, pressed so very close to his side, go tense when the other doxy spoke. He'd never had his favors fought over before and wondered if perhaps the girls had made a mistake. They must think he was some dashing, handsome highwayman.

Much of the fighting had died down by now. Grudging peace was returning to the room. The barmaids and the tavern keeper were already beginning to set the place to rights. The bar patrons were hauling unconscious bodies outside, as much in order to rifle their pockets in decent light as to attend to their wounds.

"Your lover's bleeding," he told Lucy, pushing her hand away. "You'd best tend him if you don't want him dead." Not that he thought Taggert was fatally injured. He'd only broken a few of the man's bones. More's the pity.

"It's you I'm worried about," Lucy said persisting.

The other girl came closer. Jamie kept his attention on the knife. There was something dangerous about the girl.

"Would you like this back?" she inquired. "Could we talk? In private?"

Jamie's gaze slowly drifted upward, past a slender waist he could easily span with his big hands, and came to rest on the girl's almost completely exposed breasts. Her bodice, already ill-fitting, had gotten disarranged. The top edges of a pair of rose-pink nipples greeted his sight. He found himself smiling at them and licking his lips.

He wanted to get the girl in private all right, but not to talk. The excitement from the fight was still coursing through him. The redhead's body was lush and inviting. She was fresh and different from the Red Bull's usual complement of whores. There was something almost familiar about her, but also a hint of mystery that stirred his blood.

"I know what I'd like," he said, firmly pushing Lucy aside to get closer to the redhead. He was the victor. This new girl would more than do as spoils.

" 'Old on, Jamie, love," Lucy demanded, grabbing his shoulder. "What about me?"

Margaret put herself between the highwayman and the barmaid. "Go away," she commanded. She brandished the knife. "Mr. Scott and I are going to—"

She didn't get a chance to finish what she was about to say. Hands came around her waist, turning her. The knife was plucked out of her grasp. Lips brushed her cheek as she was lifted off her feet. She heard a deep, throaty laugh in her ear. The next thing she knew she was dangling over Jamie Scott's shoulder and being carried out of the taproom.

6

Jamie slammed the back bedroom door with his foot, then put the girl down, slowly, sliding her body down his until her bare toes just touched the floor. She was all soft curves and warm, fresh scent. The most feminine thing he'd ever touched.

A loose strand of her hair flowed gently across his cheek, heavy and smooth, beautiful to the touch despite its ridiculous false color. His lips brushed her ear as it passed him, drawing a surprised sound from the girl. She gasped, and almost jumped away. He kept his hands on her waist, pinning her between himself and the rough wood of the door. Weak rays of sun slanted across his back from the thick diamond panes in the room's only window, framing the two of them in a puddle of watery light.

She said his name, but he covered her mouth with his

before any more words came out. He didn't want words, he wanted her sweet taste, the soft caress of her lips. Her mouth opened to him with langorous slowness. He reined in his own urgency, and made the intrusion of his tongue into the heady warmth of her mouth a gentle thing, teasing a sensual response from her, feeding rather than forcing quick passion.

When her mouth was at last clinging hotly to his, her hands came up to his shoulders, palms sliding up the worn wool of his coat, making Jamie wish she'd touched bare skin instead of cloth. Then her fingers found his hair, twisted and tangled in it, pulling him closer. He didn't need her urging.

His fingers stayed splayed across her ribcage, while his thumbs languidly stroked the undersides of her breasts, traced up around the sides, circled but didn't settle on the hard nipples peaking over the top of her dress.

She pulled away from his kiss, flinging her head back against the door, lost to the sensation. He let his gaze as well as his fingers stroke her breasts. The round, pale globes were as beautiful to look at as they were to touch, and they felt like yielding, warm satin beneath the pressure of his fingers.

"Sweet Jesus, Jamie Scott," she murmured, voice husky and hungry and on the edge of laughter, "you're all thumbs."

He pressed his thigh against hers. "Not quite."

Margaret's eyes flew open, all amusement fleeing as she felt the hard bulge at his groin pressing against her. What was she doing? What was she thinking of? A kiss was one thing, but this was more than a kiss, and she shouldn't even be kissing him.

This wasn't supposed to be happening! Never mind what his letter said. She couldn't really let it happen. But his hands kept moving, and it felt so good, so wild, her blood was racing and her mind was spinning away from her. She couldn't let this thing, these feelings, get away from her.

She opened her mouth to protest, but his fingers began to trace the sensitive flesh of her lips. Then his kiss claimed her mouth again before she could utter a sound, other than a moan of pleasure.

His words came back to her. He'd spoken of kisses burning like brandy on the tongue. This was more intoxicating than brandy. Brandy burned down into you, but the glow soon faded. The glow from his kiss, his touch, just kept growing and growing. It was driving her mad, out of control.

His hands moved, clever fingers working at hooks and lacings with a skill she'd overpaid her dresser for for years, completely freeing her breasts from the confines of the ill-fitting bodice.

"You don't understand," was as much as she managed to say when his lips moved from hers to suckle on one tightly hard nipple. The sensation running up from her breast hit her like lightning. Her back arched and she bit her lip to keep from calling out with unexpected pleasure. And she totally forgot whatever it was he didn't understand.

He'd said that if he was to see her again, he'd steal more than a kiss. This new sensation was far more exciting than his kiss. Or perhaps it was the hunger born in her by his kiss that made his hot, knowing mouth on her breast so delicious. His touch sent fire through her, fire that overwhelmed confusion, swept aside her good sense, sent head and heart reeling. It was all happening so fast, yet her body was telling her it wasn't happening fast enough.

Her knees were giving way, her hips were grinding

against his thighs. She couldn't keep her hands off him. She explored him, tentatively, restlessly, not quite able to gather the courage to brush her fingers against the hot shaft straining against her thigh. He'd said he wanted to draw her down on his bed and take her. Take her into his arms and himself into her. She wanted it too, ached to touch the most male part of him and be touched, to be taken and take. She'd never wanted anyone but Jamie Scott, and she wanted him now. The way he wanted her.

Jamie traced his tongue up the girl's breast, across the white column of her throat and down the other breast, flicking it across the hard pink bud. He kissed and nuzzled, reveling in her small, passionate moans, in her touch as her hands glided over his back and hips and combed through his hair. Then he took her mouth again, drinking in the sweet taste of her need. Her arousal stoked his.

She was so much more eager than the inn's older whores. She must be new enough to the game to still enjoy it, to know how to make a man feel appreciated. He knew she was sleek and hot and ready for him. Her easily heated little body sent a pulsing agony of desire through his groin. He wanted to bury himself in her with hard, slow strokes, to spend himself while he felt her shuddering and writhing beneath him. He ached to feel the helpless response of a lover rather than the pretended pleasure of a willing whore from the girl's soft-as-silk, beautiful body.

He picked her up. She clung to him as he took the few short steps to the bed pushed up against the far wall, her fingers working at the buttons of his waistcoat. He settled her onto the narrow straw mattress and paused long enough to finish the job she'd started. He stripped down to his shirt and breeches, then unlaced the back of his breeches and unbuttoned the front. His guns and belt had already fallen to the floor with heavy thuds. He snatched one up, putting it and his knife on the table by the bed, near at hand. About to burst from passion or not, he didn't forget where he was or that the constables had been on his heels not so long ago.

The girl lay still on the bed and watched him, eyes glinting like silver chips out of the shadowed corner of the room. She sat up, drawing her legs back when he climbed into bed beside her.

She'd gone all tense and stiff. He began stroking her, starting with her trim ankles, working his way up shapely calves and slender, satin-smooth thighs. He slowly peeled back the layers of skirts as he went, rumpling the material up around her waist. Eventually the warm juncture of her thighs was revealed to him, hidden treasure, uncovered, waiting to be claimed.

She was trembling beneath his touch. He could hear her breath coming in short, sharp gasps. She whimpered when he planted a kiss high up on her inner thigh.

Margaret hadn't been able to take her eyes off Jamie's hard-muscled back or the corded muscles of his long arms, outlined by the thin linen of his open shirt. There was no width to Jamie Scott. He didn't have the broad, hairy chest and narrow waist of some of the grooms she'd seen bathe in the pool outside Lacey House's stables. He was slim and hard, a light fuzz of brown hair tracing down his chest to his flat belly.

She liked him the way he was. He reminded her of the blade of his dagger, sharp and dangerous. His hands moved over her with sure knowledge, taking his time. She felt every defense being peeled away as he inched up between her slowly opening legs, exposing the aching core which was quickly becoming the center of her being.

She enjoyed looking at him, reveled in his touch, but it frightened her too. She'd never been alone with a nearly naked man. She'd never been nearly naked herself. She'd certainly never felt such an intimate, erotic touch before. It wasn't right. It couldn't go any further. Her mind knew it even if her body was putting up a strong argument the other way. It was telling her morality and self-possession and duty and propriety were nothing in comparison to this delicious, melting, total abandon.

Well, her body was wrong. What did she think she was doing? What did he think he was doing? This was going too far. She couldn't lose herself to erotic pleasure. Never mind that her insides were melting. Or that the desire thrumming through her like violin notes through crystal was going to shake her apart if he didn't do something more than just kiss and fondle her very soon now. Never mind all his promises about making love to her, they were just words she'd etched into her heart without realizing she'd done it. Those words couldn't become actions. Not between a duchess and the highwayman she hoped to reform. She couldn't let this go on. For both their sakes, she couldn't go through with it. It wasn't right. Not here, not now. He'd understand. He'd have to.

His hand came between her legs; his thumb stroked throbbing, hungry flesh while his fingers quested deep inside her. Her hips arched up involuntarily, welcoming the intrusion even while she tried to gain control over her senses.

She said, "Oh," then, "No!" as the probing caresses continued. What he was doing was sending her soaring, out of herself. She had to stop it now.

She tried to sit up, but the blasted, rumpled skirts piled over her weighed her down. She tried to close her legs. She tried to push his hand away. Tried to position her feet to push him back.

She said, "No," again. "We can't! I don't want—" as he

was suddenly looming over her. His suffused skin was slick with a sheen of sweat, his face that of a hungry stranger. She screamed.

The girl was ready, her insides sleek and tight. He positioned himself and thrust hard, sheathing himself with a moan of release in her hot velvet interior.

She cried out as he entered her. Then again, and he instantly knew why. Her hips bucked, her small hands pushed at his shoulders, movements of pain, not passion.

Dear God, the girl was a virgin!

Jamie was lost, poised over her and in her, desire still riding him and he didn't know what to do. She'd said no. He'd heard her but he hadn't understood. He hadn't much cared to understand, either. He could only be grateful he'd taken the time to arouse her so at least she'd been ready to be entered.

"You should have told me," he said, voice harsh with the strain of trying to control his raging body. The heat of her surrounding him was so delicious he couldn't make himself pull out, though his sense of responsibility told him he ought to. He should talk to her, find out what she wanted of him.

Her face was turned away. Her hands had dropped from his shoulders and were balled into fists. He couldn't tell if the drops of moisture running down her harlot's painted face were tears or drops of his own sweat.

"Too late," she whispered, to the wall, not to him.

She was right, it was too late. She was as forced into the life she'd chosen as he was. Whore and highwayman. Both had to start sometime. She'd have to make the best of it. He'd pay her well and be as gentle as he could. Better for her to start with him than that ham-fisted bumpkin she'd brought into the inn with her. Or any of the Red Bull's stinking, vicious patrons.

Maybe he'd keep her for himself for a while, ease her way into the hard, short life ahead of her. What was one more woman to look after when he already had so many to care for? It was a bloody, wretched burden, that's what it was. He needed some release from the tension. He needed it now.

His pleasure in the act was shattered, but he welcomed the oblivion of release as he pushed repeatedly into the engulfing core of the girl, trying to keep the rhythm as slow and gentle as he could. Trying to get it over with as quickly as possible without causing her more discomfort. She remained rigid and still beneath his thrusts. She made no sound, even when he collapsed on top of her. He was spent, exhausted, and wondered which of them felt more humiliated by the experience.

Margaret couldn't bring herself to move. For some reason she found herself stroking the taut muscles of Jamie's tense shoulders. It was almost like the thoughtless petting of a tired animal. His body was hot and heavy, they were both sticky with sweat.

She was . . . sad. Yes, the lethargic ache suffusing her was sadness. And disappointment. Sadness at her shattered illusions, disappointment that the heady buildup of excitement had led only to a moment of pain and several minutes of enduring the rest. She had thought his kisses, the arousal he had coaxed from her, would lead to something—some shattering, beautiful, fiery conclusion. Perhaps it would have, if it hadn't been for his words.

The pain of losing her virginity had been sudden, somehow unexpected. It hadn't been as bad as Maude and Grandmother and her Quaker governess had led her to believe. Once it was too late and the panic of what she'd allowed to happen had subsided, she'd thought the pleasure would sustain her.

Then he'd asked "Why didn't you tell me?" She'd heard the surprise, the almost-anger in his voice. She'd been too shocked and hurt to respond. All the fire in her had died.

What else would she be but a virgin? How could he have thought otherwise? "You're my first duchess," his letter had said. He should have known he was her first man. She hadn't known what to do. She had just lain there and let him take her and tried not to cry. Now she just wished he'd get up and go away. She wanted to crawl away from the Red Bull, run back to Lacey House, and never leave the safe confines of her home again.

He sighed and sat up. She kept her eyes closed and hoped he'd go away. Then he brushed his hands through her hair and dropped a kiss on her forehead. The touch of his lips burned her. She touched the spot as she heard him move around the room. She heard the sound of water splashing out of a jug. A few moments later a cool cloth was cleaning her thighs.

"It won't hurt the next time," he told her.

She knew the words and his care were meant as comforts. She appreciated them. She knew it would be easier next time. She'd been carefully instructed about the duties of woman and wife. But she wasn't anyone's wife, and there wasn't going to be a next time.

Jamie put away the cloth and sat down at the end of the bed. For a girl who'd started off as a lively piece of goods, she'd become damned unresponsive. Regretting her choices, he supposed. He didn't blame her, but he didn't like seeing her lying there, all limp and tragic and self-pitying. Like a spoiled, disappointed little girl, he decided. Well, he knew how to deal with little girls. At home, teasing was the favored treatment for such behavior. But somehow he didn't think verbal sparring would do much good with a tavern wench.

Her bare feet were near him. He picked one up. The toes were small and delicate. He kissed the tip of one and said, "You've got a pretty foot. He stroked a finger across the high arch. She made a noise and tried to squirm out of his grasp. "Ticklish." He chuckled.

When she would have snatched her foot backwards he held it firmly, cradled in his palm, intent on a bit of friendly torture. He wanted to hear the girl laugh. Jamie ran his fingers across the sole, enjoying the spattering of giggles she couldn't hold in. Good. She was relaxing. He'd be able to talk to her in a bit.

He started to continue the tickling, but found himself actually looking at her foot instead. Her skin was so soft. He'd noticed it before, but he hadn't paid attention. Soft and shell-pink beneath a coating of road dust. He explored further, looking at the soles, the heel, the neatly trimmed toenails. Not a callus or corn in sight. No scars or scratches or bruises or bug bites, just warm, firm flesh.

He turned back the skirts he'd so recently smoothed over her exposed legs and continued exploring. What he saw was beautiful, alluring, and completely wrong. There wasn't a sign of hard work or ill use or poverty anywhere on her lushly curved, totally unspoiled form.

He trailed his eyes and his hands from ankles to waist, like a horsetrader examining a thoroughbred colt. The girl suffered his touch in silence. Raising up on her elbows as he moved over her, she said and did nothing to stop him.

Suspicion and cold dread were growing in him as he looked up and met her eyes. Her finely lashed smoke-gray eyes. There was a proud tilt to her small, pointed chin as she met his gaze.

He rather regretted not having paid more attention to the girl's face before now. The fine bosom had been most distracting. The paint and patches and garish red hair had easily deceived an easy, unquestioning glance. What had there been to question? Why was he feeling so wretchedly foolish? What was there he should have guessed?

It couldn't be? He couldn't have bedded the girl he'd been dreaming about for weeks without even noticing. Could he?

No. Impossible. Nonsense. Ridiculous.

Jamie swallowed hard and said, "Margaret?"

7

"Margaret?" she repeated his question.

The amount of shock and suppressed anger the girl managed to put into one word amazed Jamie. But then, the whole situation amazed him.

"Margaret?" he said again, voice rising in pitch. He was quickly losing his grip on whatever the situation was. The whole day was turning out to be insane and farcical. First he'd lost, for who knew how long, a profitable livelihood he hadn't wanted in the first place. Then he'd lost his temper but won the fight. Then the victory celebration turned hollow, and now the girl turned out to be . . .

"You didn't know it was I?"

Jamie swallowed hard, but no answer came to his lips. For long, hideous moments, he just looked at the closed and hostile face of the duchess of Pyneham.

The silence engulfing them, spreading across the sordid, stale back room was as thick and tense as the air before a lightning strike. The soft smoke color of her eyes turned to hard flint. Margaret's eyes, certainly. His first duchess's eyes. Why hadn't he noticed sooner?

Jamie couldn't meet the accusation in them for more than a few moments before he looked away. He felt her stone gaze following him as he got up and finished dressing as quickly as he could. He avoided the patch of sunlight near the door, staying in the shadows as he covered himself from her sight. Several times he almost spoke. The words tumbled in his brain and choked in his throat. He was confused, suddenly out of his depth. He couldn't face her or himself or the situation. Whatever the situation was. Maybe she knew, but he didn't. All he knew was that he was feeling used and betrayed and toyed with.

God's death! Couldn't the girl have left him one illusion! One untarnished ideal of some perfect, pure thing.

Worse than the painful disappointment, worse than the suspicion that she'd used him as a plaything, was the guilt at how he'd taken her. She'd brought it on herself. She'd come to the inn in search of the dangerous thrill of bedding a highwayman, but she had realized her waywardness at the last moment. She had tried to stop him. She'd paid a high price for her wickedness. He didn't like being the source of her downfall.

The combination of guilt and anger kept him silent, drove him from the room. He had to get his emotions under control. Christ's blood, but he needed a drink!

There was a giant waiting in the hallway.

" 'Ere," the giant said, clamping a heavy hand on Jamie's shoulder. "What have you done with my lady?"

He recognized the large man now. "What was your lady doing with me?" he questioned.

"Playacting, of course," the oaf answered. He offered a half-witted smile. "She's going to be upset about my getting hit and all. I'm here to protect her."

The man was young, Jamie noticed, and seemed quite proud of his post as the duchess's protector. "You didn't do a very good job of it," he told the big lad. "What's your name? And what do you mean, 'playacting'?"

"Huseby, sir," he responded automatically to Jamie's imperious tone. "She's an actress, like. Her Grace, I mean. Takes after her great gran. My great gran tol' me her great gran did wicked things when she was on the stage before she became the king's whore and all. Playing amazons with naked breasts and such. It's in her blood, you see. No harm in it long as she's got someone to look after her.

"It's a lark. So she told Eloise—she's a real whore sir and very much to your taste, I'm sure—that she wanted her dress so she could live the role. I think she meant, Her Grace, I mean, not Eloise, she wanted to act the whore like in that play the villagers voted on as too wicked for good folk to see, but I went to in London once and it wasn't as bad as all that. My head hurts, and I think I want to throw up now, sir," Huseby added, turning toward the wall.

He proceeded to bend over and retch noisily. Jamie was stunned. Not by the retching, but by the flood of words that had preceeded it.

Act the whore? Live the role? Playacting? Huseby's explanation confirmed his suspicions, but Jamie still reeled from the words. How had the lass gotten to be so foolish? The duchess he held so dear in his memory had been a practical creature who'd known more about his business than he had at the time. Pity she didn't know anything about the reality of the world she'd provided the invitation for him to join.

Someone ought to teach her a lesson, he thought. Not

about lusting after dangerous illusions. She'd learned that well enough. No. She needed a good strong dose of what this life was all about. She'd led a life that was too safe and sheltered if she thought she could walk among his kind without coming to harm. Playacting, indeed! If she were one of his sisters he'd turn her over his knee.

While Huseby knelt against the wall, his panting background noise as he recovered from emptying his belly, Jamie stood and thoughtfully rubbed his long jaw.

The solution came to him so suddenly he threw back his head and laughed at the audacity of it. When he turned to look at Huseby, the big lad was still on his knees, staring at him foolishly.

"Your mistress is coming with me," Jamie told the boy. He had the mouth of a pistol resting lightly in the center of Huseby's forehead before the indisposed giant could struggled to his feet.

"How are you feeling?" Jamie questioned amicably. "Well enough to deliver a message to the dowager duchess, I hope? You'd better be well enough," he continued with deadly good humor. "If you want to see the playacting duchess again, you'll tell the dowager to . . ." Inspiration failed him for a moment.

Huseby was staring at him from beyond the barrel of the gun, eyes wide and mouth open.

Beyond the hallway Jamie could hear the boisterous sounds of the taproom as the inn's regulars went about their normal, unsavory business. He couldn't keep her locked up there. His cohorts would demand a share of the spoils. Whether she was a duchess or a new whore ripe for the taking, he'd have to fight the predators off eventually. Better to take her somewhere she could be safe and all his. There was only one place he could use as a refuge for a high-born hostage.

Mummy was going to freeze.

He'd worry about that later. Right now he had a ransom to arrange. "Does Her Grace have a house in town?"

"Uh . . . yes," Huseby answered.

"Good. Tell the dowager I'll send a messenger to the London house in two days' time."

The boy blinked in dazed confusion. "Messenger?"

"A messenger," Jamie repeated. "To discuss the ransom I'll name to return the duchess of Pyneham alive and unharmed."

"Ransom? You wouldn't harm her!"

Jamie didn't suppose he would, though he didn't know what he would do if he couldn't coerce a fortune from the Pynehams for the girl's release. He refused to entertain second thoughts.

"I won't harm her if you do as you are told." He took a pace back, gun still trained on the boy. "Get up," he commanded. "On your way, Huseby. Deliver your message—and heaven help the girl if you dare to say a word to the constables, or anyone but the dowager herself."

Huseby blinked stupidly, looked at Jamie, at the pistol. Then he stumbled off, hand pressed to his sore head, his heavy steps faltering but swift.

It looked as if Huseby, at least, believed his threats. Jamie sighed with relief, cast a quick glance back at the closed door of the bedroom, then hurried to the bar to fetch a bottle of blue ruin.

He didn't say a word before he left. He didn't, and she couldn't. The knowledge of how much of a fool he'd made of her and she'd made of herself left Margaret breathless and dumb.

Once Jamie Scott was well and truly gone, off to the

taproom to boast of his prowess, no doubt, Margaret finally stirred. She slithered off the thin straw mattress to the floor. Her lower body was sore, but she didn't think she'd have any trouble walking. She was determined not to have any trouble, for she was set on getting away from the Red Bull. She was going to collect Huseby, get to her coach, go back to Lacey House, go to her bedchamber— and never leave it again.

Which would not do Frances any good, of course, she knew. Or herself, if Lake truly meant to have her killed. Hadn't the original point of this ludicrous exercise in disappointment and humiliation been to get herself a bodyguard? How had she managed to lose track of her original purpose in a muddle of romantic nonsense and carnal . . . carnal . . . well, lust?

"Lust," she said, tasting the disagreeable dregs of the emotion. "I will never," she vowed, "open another letter from the likes of Jamie Scott." That, she added silently, was what she had servants for. "Servants. Jamie Scott. Bodyguard." She rubbed the point of her chin thoughtfully, and repeated, "Bodyguard."

She'd come here to hire someone to protect her. Now she knew that she should have sent her steward. Bartlett was more than capable of dealing with the scum who frequented the Red Bull. Not that a decent man like Adam Bartlett would set foot in such a sink of corruption. He would have set about the matter in a practical fashion and found a man as decent as himself to act as bodyguard for his mistress.

And he would have been wrong, she decided, slamming her palm down on the stiff mattress. Lake was too dangerous for decent folk to deal with. Her decision to seek a scoundrel was sound. Her method was in error.

Jamie Scott was still the best choice. She'd seen how

he'd handled himself in the fight, knew too well how masterful he was in getting his own way.

Though, she hadn't exactly tried to block his desires, not at first, she admitted, cringing from her own culpability. She forced herself to keep her attention on the original subject.

Admittedly, Jamie Scott as a protector was no longer a possibility. He certainly was not the man she wanted standing at her back now. No, most definitely not. Standing behind her, she realized, with feeble humor, he'd just use his great height to stare down the front of her dress.

Her attempt at humor only brought a hot blush at the thought of his eyes, or God forbid, his great thumbs ever on her again. She hastily tugged the tight bodice as high as she could, and wished for a fichu to cover the rest of her.

She wished Jamie hadn't scooped his weapons off the table before leaving. She supposed he wasn't fully dressed without them, but she'd have felt much more comfortable having something to defend herself with, just in case, when she went to collect Huseby. Not that she actually knew how to use a pistol, but just having one would be reassuring.

"Huseby!" She took a worried step toward the door. How long had she been with Scott? Was the poor overgrown footman all right? Was he wandering around in a daze looking for her? Concern for the footman replaced all her personal worries as she hurried to the door.

Only to have it bang open as Jamie Scott came marching into the room.

Her body flamed with emotions that threatened to overcome concern. Shame and hurt and indignation mixed with irrational joy at the sight of the highwayman. She knew very well she had no reason to feel joy at his return, but it was blended in with all her other feelings just the same. She cursed her fair complexion as she felt heat rising to her skin once again, from her cheeks down to her toes this time. She forcibly quelled every reaction but indignation as he came toward her. She noted the determination in his light brown eyes and the bravado in his stance, and chose to ignore both.

"Where's my footman?" she demanded with all the hauteur her shabby costume belied.

"Drink this," he said, holding out a blue glass bottle.

It was uncorked. She caught a whiff of juniper berries. "Is that gin?"

He looked at the bottle, then back at her. "Of course it's gin. We don't have much of a wine cellar at the Red Bull."

"What?" she asked bitterly. "No smuggled brandy?" She wished the words of his damned letter hadn't been burned into her memory.

"Do me the honor of drinking the bottle down," he said.

She took a step back. "Why?"

"To save me the trouble of pouring it down you."

She cocked her head to one side, more curious than afraid. "And why might you want to do that?"

He came inexorably toward her, backing her against the edge of the bed before he answered. "Because," he said, "I'll not have you screaming and making a fuss as we go through London."

"I'm not going through London," she informed him. "I'm returning to Lacey House."

He smiled, the gesture not reaching his eyes. "Eventually," he agreed. "Drink up."

"Where's Huseby?" she stubbornly questioned.

Jamie thought the girl could use a good fright, but apparently he wasn't the man who could do it. Not that he particularly liked being the one to do it. If he ever had the knack for threatening headstrong girls, his sisters must have worn it away years ago. Still, he had an abduction to get on with, and the day was getting late. Being convincingly threatening was part of his highwayman's stock-in-trade. Surely he could coerce cooperation out of one out-of-her-depth duchess long enough to get her insensible. The obvious weapon, the threat of more of the same bed games he'd already forced on her, he knew he would never use. He had another ace, though. He took another menacing step forward, intending to use it.

"Drink up," he commanded, "or Huseby's a dead man."

The girl's breath caught in an angry hiss. "What?"

"You heard me," Jamie answered, voice low and full of threat. "Cooperate with me or I kill the oaf."

"He's no oaf. He's a good lad!"

"Then take a good, long drink, sweet." He held the bottle to her lips.

Her eyes flashed at him, reminding him of dark storm clouds. "You're wicked!"

"I know," he agreed. "I'm famous for it. It's just the way you like me, sweet."

"Ha!" He tilted the bottle higher. She gave a great, angry sigh, and opened her lips for him.

8

"*Could you tell* me the name of a decent high-wayman?" asked the duchess of Pyneham. Her voice was slurred, partially muffled by her face being buried in his coat.

Jamie held her before him on the front of his saddle. He'd held her tightly on this precarious perch since they'd ridden away from the Red Bull. Despite caution, despite worry at being caught, despite the rain that had started an hour ago, Jamie was enjoying the ride. She was a softly curved, warm bundle in his arms. When the rain started he had unbuttoned his coat, wrapped her unresisting form in it, and drew her even closer.

She'd seemed unaware of him, except when he urged another drink on her. She had a third of the bottle in her when they started out and had finished the whole thing during the time on the road. Jamie wasn't sure so much gin was good for such a little thing, but was glad she made a quiet drunk. Or had until she asked her question.

She turned her head when he didn't answer, peering at him through rain and early twilight. "Fetch me a proper highwayman," she said, each word pronounced with careful, slow dignity.

He found himself brushing a hand through her wet hair. It came away stained with red dye. Rivulets of pink rainwater were washing down her cheeks, taking patches and face paint with them. She was drunk, shamefully dressed, thoroughly disreputable, but looking more like the Margaret he remembered with each passing moment.

"There are no such creatures," he answered her finally. "We're a wicked lot. You can't trust us."

"I know. I'm dizzy. And another thing," she went on, peering at him so closely her eyes were almost crossed. Jamie found himself tempted to kiss the upturned tip of her nose even as a raindrop splashed off it. He wondered if her neck hurt from the way she was craning around.

"What other thing?" he prompted, firmly ignoring such a dangerously tempting impulse as kissing her. Never mind that she was drunk and wouldn't remember. He would. He couldn't afford kissing the girl whether the gesture was bold or tender.

"What happened to your accent?" she questioned. "You don't sound Scots at all anymore."

He couldn't stop his lips from quirking in a brief smile. "What happened to yours?" he countered. "When we met at the Bull I could have sworn you were born somewhere in Cheapside."

"Thank you," she responded with a lopsided smile. "It is rather good, isn't it? Learned it from me wet nurse, I did.

Maggie Pyne of Cheapside at your service." Her whole body trembled in a fit of giggles.

Jamie shook his head. Drunk or sober, he didn't know what to make of the girl. A good lass, he wondered? Was she just spoiled and wayward and in need of correction? Or had she been born a strumpet and finally set out on the road to complete ruin? He regretted being the one who'd ruined her.

Whether she wanted to be redeemed or not, she was badly in need of a strong-willed man to take control of her and force her to mend her ways. Jamie both pitied and envied whoever that man might be.

Traffic on the road was thin this time of night. There were even fewer people going on foot. Jamie was alert to the presence of any footpads as he guided his horse toward home. The rain was keeping even the lawless element indoors. The occasional flash of a watchman's lantern drew Jamie's attention, but didn't cause him any alarm. No one in London paid any heed to the charlies, least of all the criminals infesting the streets of London. The watch was made up of tottering old men more anxious to avoid lawbreakers than catch them. Jamie'd heard rumors of the Bow Street magistrate organizing a force of thief takers, but Bow Street was far from the outlying roads where he practiced his craft.

It was a good long way from his house as well. The stories of his infamies had spread far and wide. Some of them he'd circulated himself on the principle that it didn't hurt to advertise when fear was such a strong element in his business. According to the stories, Jamie Scott never came near London proper; he was a gentleman of the heaths. James McKay, on the other hand, kept a home on Carrol Street and never ventured farther than his club.

He chuckled as he turned the horse into the alley behind

the town house. The weary animal picked up its pace, eager to be warm, fed, and dry in its own stable. Jamie looked forward to being warm and dry and fed himself, even if there was a family crisis to weather first. Crisis? He looked at the duchess as he pulled up at the stable door. Her appearance wasn't going to precipitate a crisis. It was going to cause a disaster. Possibly even a riot.

"This isn't the final edition of *Tom Jones* so I don't know if I should bother finishing it or not," Edwina said as she put the book down.

Samantha looked at the length of the low-burning candle and said, "I shouldn't worry about it tonight."

As she spoke, the sound of hooves clopping through the mud in the alley below their window could be heard. She and Edwina grinned at each other. "Jamie's home."

They rushed to the window. They'd grown used to their brother returning home at all hours. He usually spent quite a while in the stable tending the horse, then tried as quietly as possible to enter the house. She and Edwina always woke when he came home, and met him at the top of the stairway when he came in. Often Michelle and Alexandra joined them. They saw so little of their brother these days that any glimpse of him was welcome.

Tonight, however, was different. There was a shorter than normal interval in the stable and voices in the alley. One of them female and slurred with drink. Then not one but two sets of footsteps came up the short walk from the back gate. Samantha exchanged a puzzled look with Edwina.

By the time Jamie brought the girl into the house, Samantha and Edwina were on the stairs. So were their mother and Granny McKay. Apparently the noise had roused everyone in the house. Mummy was posed dramatically at the bottom of the staircase. Granny stood a few steps above Mummy. Michelle and Alexandra came crowding up behind her and Edwina on the landing overlooking the hall.

Jamie and the strange woman stood in a spreading pool of rainwater as it dripped off their clothes. Mummy glared in horror at them; everyone else just stared. The wet pair stood directly below the ceiling lantern left burning every night just in case Jamie decided to come home, so the woman's wretched state and obvious charms were in full view of the gathering. The woman blinked stupidly and waved.

Mummy let out a shocked explosion of breath, then stated what Samantha thought was most obvious. "She's a whore, isn't she? There's a whore in the front hall. A drunken whore! She reeks of gin and the gutter!"

The woman smiled stupidly. "Can't 'elp it," she answered. "Fell off the 'orse, didn't I?" She looked up at Jamie and nearly fell over in the process. Jamie hastened to steady her and left his hands resting on her shoulders when he'd caught her.

"Get your hands off that, that—"

"Whore," Granny McKay supplied.

" 'Ave you brought me to a brothel, Jamie Scott?" the woman asked, turning a sweetly silly smile on Samantha's brother. "It's not at all what I thought it'd be like."

"Hush, sweet," Jamie said, patting the woman's mostly bare shoulder.

Samantha almost smiled herself, more amused than concerned at the obvious affection between this unlikely pair. It was unsuitable and unseemly, of course, but it was rather sweet. She and Edwina exchanged looks while Mummy let out a shrill shriek.

"A brothel! Indeed! James, I demand you thrust that baggage out in the street!"

"But Mummy, it's raining." Samantha spoke up without thinking, and wished instantly she'd kept still as Granny McKay turned her basilisk stare on her.

"Get back to your rooms," she ordered.

Michelle and Alexandra squeaked like frightened mice and scurried away, night rails flapping around their ankles. Samantha and Edwina held their ground. This was too exciting to miss.

Below them Jamie squared his shoulders and announced, "The girl stays." He leveled a look on Mummy he'd learned from Granny. "And there'll be no arguing about it, madam."

"James!"

"There's nothing to discuss, ma'am," he added imperiously. "Come along, Maggie."

He took the woman's arm and guided her to the staircase. Mummy stood quivering in hurt indecision as the pair came toward her. For a moment Samantha thought she was going to stand firm and refuse to let Jamie and the doxy past. The moment fled on a flood of tears.

"Oh, James," she cried, and ran up the stairs ahead of the ascending couple. Granny and Samantha and Edwina hastily got out of her way.

From the top of the stairs she saw that Granny didn't try to stop the pair. "If you'll wait for me in the sitting room," he requested of the stern old lady, "I'll explain everything."

The bedraggled woman smiled at Granny. " 'Allo. I see you walk with a stick. So I wouldn't think of 'aving you curtsy, of course. I'd like to go to bed now, Jamie, as I'm very dizzy. I do so wish Maude was here even though you're so very clever at getting a girl out of her clothes."

It took Samantha a great deal of effort to smother the laugh that rose in her throat. Edwina wasn't so successful.

She giggled and cried, "She's foxed, Jamie!"

"Indeed," Jamie replied with a frown, and finished leading the woman up the stairs. "Samantha, Edwina, come with me," he commanded before taking the woman to his bedroom.

The girls hurried in behind them. Samantha heard Granny McKay struggling up the stairs after them, so she hastily closed the bedroom door before the old woman reached the landing.

Jamie struck a light, then settled the duchess on the room's only chair as his sisters came in. They looked from him to Margaret with the kind of wide-eyed attention best reserved for natural disasters. Margaret settled back in the chair and closed her eyes. Asleep, he hoped.

He began pulling some dry clothes for himself out of the wardrobe. He spoke fast, intent on getting the words out before they could ask any questions.

"I have to talk to Granny. I'll change in your room. I need your help." He jerked a thumb toward the duchess. "Take care of her. Don't let her out of your sight. Don't let her out of this room. Don't listen to anything she says." He looked intently at Samantha and Edwina. "Please believe that my *life* depends on keeping this woman hidden away. I'm putting us all in danger by bringing her here," he added.

Seeing his family had brought home to him just how dangerous this mad scheme was. He was painfully aware that he was risking more than his own life this time.

"I'm sorry," he told the uncomprehending girls. "I had to bring her to the only people I can trust. It's important she's hidden away where she'll be safe and unharmed."

He glanced at the unconscious duchess. She looked like

a small, sleeping girl, soaked to the skin, but soft and vulnerable. He found himself worried that she'd catch a chill, and not because his scheme required turning an unharmed hostage over for ransom. He didn't have the time to worry right now.

"Get her dry and put some brandy in her," he instructed. "That should take care of her. You will take care of her?" he pleaded. "Keep her out of the way? Keep Mummy from throwing her out on the street while I'm gone?"

"Of course we promise!" Edwina answered earnestly.

Samantha looked a bit more skeptical, but Jamie stepped to the door and was through it before the most clever of his quartet of sisters could bombard him with questions.

"James Scott McKay," Granny McKay said furiously, "just what to you mean by bringing one of your pox-ridden baggages into this house?"

She waved her cane under his nose. He decided to let her vent her spleen for a while before offering an explanation. From long habit he knew it was best to let her temper run its course. Unlike Mother, Granny was always pragmatic and reasonable after she'd had her say.

She waved her cane again, gesturing around the candle-lit sitting room. "I thought you intended to shelter your family from the life you've been leading. You've taken far too well to this highwayman's dissipated way of living. Don't think I haven't noticed, young man. When I told you to take the gold off the English I didn't expect you to fall in with the sort of low crowd you've been frequenting."

She stumped angrily up and down across the threadbare

rug. Jamie sat very still. He rested his gaze on a single candle on a nearby table while he waited her out.

"You should be ashamed of yourself. Consorting with common criminals is one thing, but this! Bringing a drunken slut home . . . Do you expect to install her as your mistress? In your own house? I'll not have her sullying my clean bed linen, spreading her filth and corrupting your sisters. Are you mad? James, are you listening to me?"

"Yes."

The old woman reacted to his calm answer by taking the chair opposite him, folding her hands on the head of her cane, and asking, "Well?"

Jamie tugged thoughtfully on his ear, pulling on the gold-and-topaz earring. Her earring. His knightly token, or so he'd come to think of it. What foolishness! Never mind sentiment. Time to set his plan in motion. Who better than Granny McKay? The old besom was the most ruthless person in Britain. He was proud to call her kin.

"The girl's no common slut," he said. He touched the earring again. Where to start? "She didn't come here voluntarily. I've abducted her."

Bright eyes peered suspiciously at him from out of her wrinkled face. "You've stolen a doxy?" He nodded. "Pray tell, why?"

"She's not a doxy."

"No?"

"No."

Granny McKay thumped her cane on the floor impatiently. "Don't be mysterious with me, lad. If you've a reason for bringing her here, spit it out."

"I'm holding Maggie for ransom. Margaret. I mean, she's the duchess of Pyneham."

"Just how much have you been drinking, James?" she asked with cool sarcasm.

"God's truth, Granny," he replied solemnly. "This is no joke. I haven't touched so much as a dram today, and the girl is the duchess. She was the first person I robbed. This is her earring that I kept. I wrote her a letter once when I'd had a bit too much. I'd promised her a letter, you see. And she came to the tavern I think I must have mentioned in the letter to find me. To find a silly, sordid adventure with a highwayman, at least," he added in a low murmur to himself. "When I recognized her I saw a chance to make our fortune by selling her back to her family."

Granny McKay's expression had shifted from skeptical to annoyed.

"I haven't got any other choice," Jamie hastened to explain. "I know you and the duchess's grandmother were friends when you were young. I grew up on your stories. I recognized her name when we first met. She thought I was talking about her great-grandmother, which was just as well since I was supposed to be in disguise."

"You're babbling, lad."

Jamie threw up his hands in exasperation. "Everyone else I've talked to today does, I thought I might as well join in."

She gave him an admonishing look. "Just explain what you're up to so I can help."

He took a deep breath, calmed himself down, and went on. "As I said, I recognized the girl. It's time I retired from highway robbery. Abduction's as much a hanging offense as the crimes I'm already wanted for. Name a crime that isn't a hanging offense to the property-loving English, from stealing stale bread to stealing a woman."

"Hanged for a penny or a pound. Aye, I know. So you got her drunk and brought her home?"

"Hardly safe to leave her at the Red Bull. She's a fool-

ish little thing, but I won't see her harmed. And, and . . .
I . . ."

His words trailed off, and he felt himself blush. He had
to tell someone, and Granny was the only one he could
trust with certain, delicate, intimate truths. "I bedded
her," he confessed. "Took her maidenhead. It was an
accident."

She cocked her head to one side, her nightcap tilting
dangerously close to falling off. "An accident?" she asked.
"A duchess's maidenhead is a highly prized commodity,
James. They don't usually lose them accidentally. What
did you do?"

"I didn't know . . . It was . . . Never mind, it doesn't
matter."

"It might to her. I think it does to you."

Jamie wished he hadn't brought up the subject. "I don't
have time to let it matter. What's done is done. Its' not
important," he said. "It's ransoming her that's important.
Our arranging for the family to leave the country is important. Taking care of the family is all that matters. I need
your help. I need you to go to the dowager to negotiate the
ransom."

"If you've taken her maidenhead, a ransom might not
be the best solution. There's an easier way to deal—"

"Please go to the dowager," he pleaded. "She'll talk to
you. You're old friends."

"And I've been known to drive a hard bargain or two
in my time." She rubbed the silver head of her cane
thoughtfully. "It's going to take some hard bargaining to
settle this mess properly."

"You can do it, Granny," Jamie acknowledged. "The
dowager's to come to the Pyneham London residence. Will
you meet her there?"

The old woman sighed and thumped her cane loudly on

the floor one more time for emphasis. "And when is this meeting supposed to be?"

Jamie grimaced and spoke apologetically. "I thought two days might give her time to reach London."

"You're keeping the girl here?"

He shrugged. "Where else?"

"Your mother? The girls?"

"It can't be helped. You'll do it?" he pleaded.

Granny McKay gave a harsh, cackling laugh. "Do I have a choice, lad? If we're ever to recover from your mother's fit of the vapors we have to get your drunken duchess out of the house."

9

The dowager duchess of Pyneham was tired. Her bones ached from hours of rattling across the countryside on muddy roads to get to London. She was worried to the point of illness from waiting for the promised messenger from the highwayman. And now, as if the day wasn't complicated enough, the ambassador of Schlewig-Halzen was taking up her time, a good portion of the dining room, and most of the meal she'd ordered for herself. Since he'd come from the king, the most she could do was sit in grim silence while he was served plate after plate from the dishes on the sideboard.

While he ate and tried to wheedle an agreement out of her, she could do no more than scrape her spoon around an untouched dish of soup. She didn't even know why she'd ordered food. Why hadn't she taken to her bed as soon as she got from her mud-splattered coach? Why had she agreed to see anyone who came to the door?

Because she was expecting someone other than a messenger from King George, that's why. Where was Scott! What was he waiting for?

"His Majesty is most displeased," the ambassador repeated for the fifth time, distracting her from her greater worry. He downed another glass of wine. "Most displeased."

Six. She ticked the number off on her fingers. "Yes," she said. "I know. But there's nothing anyone can do. The girl will marry where she will. It's English law."

"Bah," he said with derision. He leaned across the table, shaking a fat forefinger at her. "A girl should do as she's told. So should a young man. It is for those older and wiser to make proper marriage alliances. You should see to it, madam. You will see to it. Your own king desires you to see to the girl's marriage.

"I," he went on, "am charged to see that the duchess of Pyneham is settled with Count Ernest." He offered a none-too-convincing smile. "The king wishes to let the young duchess know that she will only please him by marrying. Once she is married she will be welcome at Court again, and all will be well between your duchess and her king. Yes. We will have a new duke to sit in your House of Lords. Yes. A closer alliance between your house and the royal family. Yes. And all will be pleasant and beneficial. Yes? Yes."

He nodded his head so firmly it set the tail of his bag wig bobbing. He then offered her a superior smile, as though they'd just sealed the marriage agreement.

"No."

Heavy brows lowered over piggy eyes. "What?"

"I meant," she elaborated, "that it is not for me to decide. There's nothing I can do."

The girl could be dead, the dowager wanted to scream at this interloper who was trying to tell her how to manage her family. This foreign interloper from a foreign king ordering the life of a descendant of the royal Stuarts! It galled the dowager's Jacobite sensibilities.

And while he talked, her girl, her dearest, wayward, foolish, beloved Maggie could have had her throat cut by that scoundrel Scott. Did the ambassador really think she'd bargain her away to his impoverished, dissipated toad of a master? Did he think Margaret was no more than lands and titles to be transferred into greedy hands? The dowager would sooner see her wed to her blasted Scots highwayman! Get out! she wanted to scream at the ambassador. Get out of this house!

While her thoughts raged, she kept a vague, polite expression on her face. She'd spent too many years at Court herself to ever give her true emotions away. "I'm sorry I can't help you," she said, lying. "Would you care for some port?"

"No." The ambassador snapped out the word and rose ponderously to his feet. "The king will be most displeased if your granddaughter does not marry soon."

"I'm sure he will," she answered solemnly.

"There will be repercussions."

"A pity." And I'll worry about them when and if I get her back, she added to herself. "Good-day," she added. "The butler will show you out."

The ambassador left with angry strides that shook the china as he passed. The butler came back seconds later and handed her a note.

The dowager opened it with trembling fingers, mouth dry with fear. She read the neat script anxiously, only to be disappointed at the message. "Sophie Thorne McKay? This is from Lady Sophie?" While it was true that Sophie was a lifelong friend she hadn't heard from for several years, this was hardly the time to renew their acquaintance. The butler, however, was waiting for her reply. "She's in the hallway?"

"Yes, Your Grace. The lady is most anxious to see you," he added. "She mentioned having news about a mutual acquaintance of yours named James. Said the message was too privy to put in writing."

James. James Scott? Could her old friend be a messenger from the highwayman? Could it be? It had to be. No one knew about Margaret's abduction but herself and the fool footman who'd brought the news. She'd threatened to have him whipped and transported to the colonies if he ever breathed a word about what had happened. Somehow Sophie McKay must have been coerced to act as go-between for the cur who'd taken Maggie.

Her thoughts raced, but she kept her voice calm. "Then I will see her. Bring her to me in the book room."

Lady Sophie looked old, old and threadbare, but as proud as ever. She marched into the book room, supporting herself with a cane, and took a seat opposite the dowager without waiting to be asked.

She rested her hands on the silver head of her cane and leveled a frank look at the dowager. "Hello, Arabella," she said conversationally. "Let's discuss our foolish grandchildren, shall we?"

The dowager breathed a tight sigh of relief. "Do you know where Margaret is?"

"When I left the house she was in Jamie's bed. I imagine she's still there," was Sophie's blunt reply. She shook her head sadly, but went on while the dowager was too taken aback to reply. "She's ruined, Arabella. I'm sorry for it, but it couldn't be helped, apparently."

"Couldn't be helped!" the dowager burst out indignantly. "Are you telling me she's been ravished by a common criminal?"

Sophie McKay lifted her head proudly. "James Scott McKay is not common at all, as you well know. I'll grant you Andrew McKay was no duke of Pyneham, but his family's as good as yours." She shook her finger at the dowager. "You had your cap set for Andrew as much as I did. Don't try to deny it."

The dowager didn't. She remembered too well her youthful attraction to the man Sophie'd married. She had trouble not sighing fondly at the memory while Sophie went on.

"My father was an earl, and Jamie's mother is kin to the Buccleugh Scotts. So it's good old blood you'll be getting in my Jamie."

"What?" The Dowager narrowed her eyes suspiciously at her old friend. "Sophie, what are you getting at? What about Jamie Scott the highwayman? What about the ransom?"

Sophie didn't answer immediately. She took her time and gazed at the book-lined shelves around them. This library was much smaller and not as well stocked as the one at Lacey House, but Sophie seemed to like what she saw.

"I've been cursed with scholarly grandchildren," she said. "All five of them. This will suit nicely."

The dowager wasn't interested in anyone's grandchildren but her own. "You ever were a tease, Sophie. Tell me in plain words what you're getting at."

So she did.

"My grandson James is also Jamie Scott. He became a highwayman to support his family, like a dutiful lad. He's dangerous and notorious and that does attract the women. There's more at stake here than a ransom. It's become a matter of honor. Your Margaret ran off to meet him and they've ended up lovers."

Sophie thumped her cane. It came down with a dull thud on the flowered French carpet. "Lovers," she repeated. "It's been going on for days now. I'm only frightened the scandal will get out. It'll ruin the girl's reputation, infuriate the king."

The king was already infuriated enough with Margaret, but the dowager wasn't going to mention it to Lady Sophie. A duchess tumbling with a highwayman could only be more disastrous for the family's precarious position. Her tumbling with James McKay was, perhaps, marginally better.

The dowager folded her hands in her lap and said, "I see."

Sophie leaned forward conspiratorially. "I'm glad you do. The question," she continued, "is what are you and I going to do about Margaret and James?"

"I think she must be awake again."

"Perhaps we'd better let her stay awake this time."

The voices spoke in whispers that sent a pounding through Margaret's head, a pain unlike any she'd ever felt before. Each word fell on her with the force of a hammer blow. She groaned and tasted bile. She wanted to die, but couldn't call up the strength to pray for it.

She'd been ill. She knew she'd been ill because she remembered the whispers telling her she was ill, that above all else she must be quiet. She remembered dizziness and nausea and one loud argument over a chamber pot. She threw it at someone's head, she believed. Then she sang very loudly for a while and ripped down the bed curtains. She'd been dreaming of fire. Must have been fevered. She didn't know how long the fever had lasted. She did remember gentle hands and voices that continually urged her to drink.

The medicine she dutifully swallowed burned going down her throat. It didn't help the dizziness any. It did warm her insides amazingly well and kept sending her down into deep, dreamless sleep.

Sleep she wished would come and cover the pain now. The pounding in her head demanded too much attention, there was no sleeping through this. It didn't help that she could hear the faintest rustle of the girls' skirts as they moved closer to the bed. She could hear them breathing. She prayed they didn't start whispering again. Her head couldn't take that much noise.

"We better get her up, Edwina. Granny said the duchess wants to see her right away."

"You shouldn't have given her so much brandy, Samantha."

It seemed God was not going to grant her any favors this morning. She tried burrowing her head under a pillow, but she could still hear them speaking.

"It was to fight off the chill," the one called Samantha said defensively.

"And to keep her quiet."

"It worked."

Someone touched her shoulder. The pillow was snatched away. "You have to get up now." The voice belonged to the one called Edwina.

Margaret reluctantly opened an eye to find herself being

looked at by a brown-haired girl with extraordinary almond-shaped eyes. She'd never seen her before.

"Where's Maude?" Margaret asked. Her tongue felt as if it'd been stuffed with goose down. "Fetch Maude," she commanded the new maid.

Instead of obeying, Edwina cast a puzzled look at the other girl. The other girl stepped into Margaret's line of vision. She was a fresh-faced blonde in a faded pink satin dress. She shook a finger under Margaret's nose. Margaret vaguely remembered that this was the one she'd thrown the chamber pot at.

"We'll have no arguments from you, my girl." She shook the finger again.

Margaret stared at it in pained fascination. She ached all the way down to her toes; the last thing she needed was a dictatorial nurse. She sat up slowly. It wasn't an easy process. Touching her fingers to her aching temples was an even harder task, but she managed it. There were long strands of tangled hair lying on her cheeks and shoulders. It felt filthy. She needed to bathe. A cup of hot cocoa might help her head. Food was out of the question. Her uneasy stomach lurched even at the thought of cocoa.

"Fetch my maid," she ordered. "Then leave me."

"Fetch your—" Edwina gave Samantha a shocked look.

"You're an impudent one," Samantha said cheerfully, then grabbed Margaret by the shoulders and hauled her out of bed.

Margaret was standing barefoot on the threadbare carpet before she noticed that she wasn't in any bedchamber she recognized. Had she become sick at a house party? Become sick and been taken to a stranger's house.

Or been forced to drink an entire bottle of gin by that cur Jamie Scott before being dragged off to a brothel.

"I'm being held prisoner!" she announced loudly as

memories came rushing back. "Doxies!" she declared, staring at the girls in horror.

"Where?" Edwina shouted, looking around frantically.

The noise sent a shaft of pain straight to the center of Margaret's brain. It left her breathless and quite helpless as Samantha took her hand and led her from the room.

Jamie Scott was just setting foot on the first-floor landing as they came out of the bedroom. For an instant Margaret was overjoyed to see him. Her heart raced and her aching head was forgotten as his wide brown eyes looked sympathetically into hers. For just that instant his presence offered shelter and stability in a situation that made no sense. Then she remembered what happened, what they did, how little he thought of her, and how she'd come to be his prisoner.

Where? This house full of women must be a brothel. The girls flanking her weren't housemaids but whores. Bringing her to such a place proved once and for all that Jamie Scott was no savior and no gentleman.

She hated him and knew he saw it shining in her eyes. He took a step toward her, then looked away. Her headache came back with a rush, and she tried not to listen to him as he spoke.

"Whose coach is that outside?" Jamie demanded of Samantha. He pointed at Margaret. "I thought I told you to keep her out of the way. Why don't you listen to me?" he ended. It sounded petulant and childish, and he didn't blame his sisters one bit for the hostile glances they gave him.

The instant he'd seen Margaret he'd feared she was sick. She looked lost and lonely and genuinely ill. There was a gray pallor to her fair complexion and dark circles beneath her eyes. When their eyes met he almost went to her, but the expression on her face changed quickly, blocking him out.

"Granny sent us to fetch her," Edwina told him. "There's a duchess here to see your doxy."

Jamie couldn't resist the urge to goad his wayward prisoner a bit. "The doxy is a duchess," he said. His lightly spoken words got him a look of hatred from Margaret.

"I only know what Granny said," Edwina answered him. "She came back in the coach with a grand lady who's waiting in the sitting room to see . . ." She trailed off, turning a disapproving look on the bedraggled girl. "Her."

"And Mummy's still in her room with the megrims," Samantha added tartly. "It would have helped if you'd explained what's going on before disappearing for days. You're always doing that. Just going off without saying a word. Granny's not at all happy with you this time, Jamie. She's waiting for you in her room," she added.

"You needn't look so pleased about it," Jamie complained to his sister.

"It hasn't been easy keeping her quiet," Samantha answered. "She's a lively jade, and filthy besides."

"Pity the chamber pot was empty." Margaret's voice came out as a rasping croak, but the bitter sarcasm in it was enough to make Samantha blush.

Jamie decided it was wiser not to ask how the girls had accomplished the task he'd set them. It was probably best to deal with the emergency at hand.

"Granny brought the dowager here?" If it was true, he feared they were all going to hang. His sisters nodded. "What was she thinking of?"

The man didn't shout, but his voice was loud enough to stab into Margaret's head. She'd been trying to ignore him, but the meaning of his words struck her as hard as the sound. She found herself looking at him, allied with him in a fit of terror. "The dowager?" she said desperately. "I don't want to see her!"

Jamie gave the girl a sympathetic look. He didn't particularly want to see his grandmother either. "We're for it, I fear," he told her. "You and I."

Her bloodshot gaze dropped from his when he spoke, but he did see her bottom lip quiver. He feared a tear was going to roll down her lovely cheek any moment now. He was feeling wretched enough already. If she started crying, it was going to be damnably difficult to keep from taking her in his arms and promising to take her right home.

10

Samantha was not sympathetic to either her brother or the strange young woman he'd brought home. She didn't mind mysteries, or making herself useful, but she liked being kept informed of what was going on. She had a suspicion Jamie had been up to quite a bit she didn't know about lately, and she didn't like it at all. "Come along," she said to the woman. "Can't keep a duchess waiting."

The woman turned a baleful look on her. "I have, you know," she croaked. "Frequently."

Jamie watched Margaret go from the edge of tears to snappish annoyance and decided it was best for the two of them to get on with the family confrontations. He wasn't happy about his grandmother's bringing Margaret's to the house when the dowager could have as easily brought the watch with her. That she'd come alone must be a good sign. Her presence must mean the ransom negotiations had gone well. If not, he supposed he could hold both Pyneham ladies hostage if he had to.

He'd spent the last two days arranging to take his family down to Romney where some smuggler friends of his would get them out of the country. All that remained now was for him to dip deeply into the duchess's fortune and get his family away. Once he was out of England he could try to put the last few months behind him and start over.

He stepped forward, taking Margaret's arm. She flinched but didn't try to pull away. He suddenly realized what must be the matter with her, how the girls had kept her quiet. He groaned in sympathy.

"Gin doesn't mix well with brandy," he said. She neither answered nor looked at him. He had to agree that they were beyond conversation. "I'll escort you to the sitting room." She sighed, and suffered his touch as he took her down the hall and opened the door.

A stern old voice announced, "What the devil have you gotten yourself into, gel?" as Margaret went inside.

He closed the door quickly, leaving Margaret to deal with her family dragon. He turned on his heel, squared his shoulders, and strode to Granny McKay's room, bracing himself to deal with his own.

Samantha looked at Edwina after Jamie disappeared into Granny's room. "I had better find out what's going on soon," she announced.

"We deserve to know," Edwina agreed.

"Right," Samantha concurred with a firm nod. "You listen at Granny's door. I'll take the sitting room."

* * *

Margaret found a chair and sat down. The dowager got up from a window seat and came purposefully toward her. Margaret tried to pretend she wasn't there. It was harder to do when her grandmother shook a finger under her nose.

"Just what have you gotten yourself into, my girl?" she demanded. "I told you to hire Jamie Scott as a bodyguard, not throw yourself into his bed. You've ruined yourself, girl! Running off to a place like the Red Bull! Acting like a common slut! You'll be the laughingstock of the country if this ever gets out!"

Margaret winced. "You know about that? About all of it?"

"Indeed I do. The shame!"

Humiliation mixed with the pain and discomfort, making her head pound even worse. "Who told you?"

"Sophie told me," the dowager answered. "And well she should." Margaret's eyes crossed as the finger was shaken at her some more, closer to her nose this time. "What if the king finds out? Worse yet, what if Lake finds out? Lake would latch on to this scandal as an excuse to get himself named your guardian. He's got friends at Court, girl. Friends in the government. You have neither. Or have you forgotten?"

Margaret wanted to shrivel into a small ball and hide under the chair. "No, Grandmother," she whispered instead. She wished someone would offer her something for the pain, at least. She felt she could cope ever so much better if she had a strong dose of something to dull her senses. Dulled into oblivion would be nice. Instead she was being shouted at. Next she would be asked to think.

"I'm sorry, Grandmother," she offered.

She was. Very sorry. Never mind the scandal, she was just sorry life wasn't at all like playacting. The few minutes during which she had actually forgotten just how serious life really was had led to a monumental disaster. Stupid of her to pretend anyone really cared for her. "I'm never going to open another letter."

"What? Have you been listening to me?"

"I'm sorry, Grandmother," Margaret repeated.

"Sorry! You'll be sorrier before this day is over."

"Yes, Grandmother."

"I wish I could beat you."

"Yes, Grandmother." Margaret wished she could too. It might take her mind off the headache, and the lecture.

"Beating would be altogether too good for you. What possessed you? I suppose he's a handsome devil," she went on before Margaret could offer any explanation even if she'd been planning to. "The McKays have charm, I'll grant."

"McKay?" The only McKay she'd ever heard of was her grandmother's old friend, Lady Sophie. The one whose tart, amusing letters the dowager used to read aloud as evening entertainment for her granddaughters. What did Lady Sophie have to do with Jamie Scott?

The dowager was standing before her with folded arms. Margaret made an effort and peered anxiously at her grandmother. "McKay?" she repeated. "I don't understand. What are you doing here? Why am I being kept prisoner in a bawdy house?" She looked around. The room was shabby, but seemed respectable enough. If not in a bawdy house, then where was she?

"McKay," the dowager said, ignoring her other questions. "James *Scott* McKay. The young devil you gave yourself to turns out to be Sophie's only grandson. So at least you won't be marrying too far beneath you. Better a McKay than a fat German." She wagged her finger under Margaret's nose again.

"And it will be a fat German if it isn't McKay. The king's determined to see you married, my girl, never mind your rights. He's the king, and he can get a silly girl married to his cousin if he really wants to. You best make the choice before he makes it for you."

"But . . ." Nothing made sense. Her head hurt. She was lost, confused, her senses reeling. What did fat Germans and kings and marriage have to do with Jamie Scott who wasn't Jamie Scott, and she wasn't Maggie Pyne, and this wasn't a bawdy house. "But . . ." she repeated.

The dowager studied her granddaughter with far more sympathy than she showed. The girl looked terrible. It wasn't just the ragged clothing or the obvious aftereffects of too much spirits. She looked like a girl who'd had her heart broken. What had she and James McKay really gotten up to? Had it been a fling on his part and true love on Maggie's? It had been obvious the girl had wanted the highwayman ever since they met on the road. The dowager had watched the obsession carefully, hoping it would die down, half-glad the fool child had finally given her heart to someone, even if it was only a scoundrel. Well, it hadn't died down. Maggie'd run off to find her hero-scoundrel instead.

And, the dowager had to admit, she'd pushed the girl into it. Perhaps she'd hoped for a bit of a hero in the highwayman herself, someone to protect the child from Lake. Lord knew she needed the protection.

Perhaps James McKay hadn't turned out to be the hero Margaret had envisioned. Well, it didn't matter now. She'd had him, and he'd had her. It was time the girl settled down. Time to think of securing the family.

"What if you're with child?" she questioned.

"What?" Slowly, the expression in Margaret's eyes

went from dull confusion to bleak terror. "What do you mean, with child?"

God's blood, but the girl was an innocent fool! "You've bedded with the man, haven't you?" the dowager demanded.

The greenish pallor of Margaret's complexion suffused a slow, deep red. She hung her head. "Yes, Grandmother."

"Well? What did you think could happen? Or were you thinking that it's all right for bastards to run in the family?"

Margaret swallowed hard and said, "Oh, dear." She rubbed her aching temples. "I think," she told her grandmother, "that I've made a complete ass of myself."

"I think, my dear," her grandmother answered, "that you are marrying James Scott McKay as quickly as a parson can be found."

Margaret tried to think. Unfortunately, the conclusion she came to was that she had several good reasons for marrying Jamie Scott. Nothing and no one was that they seemed, and she'd made a complete fool of herself. The freedom she'd thought she had was at the mercy of the king. Embroiling herself in scandal gave her unscrupulous brother-in-law an opening, and she'd fall into his power if she wasn't careful. Somehow the prospect of life with the highwayman seemed to be the slightly lesser evil. Allying herself with the king's cousin was out of the question. It had always been out of the question, even if she had to marry someone else quickly to avoid that trap. Most disastrous, she might be carrying Jamie Scott's child.

She was a fool. An utter and complete fool. She had no choice but to make a marriage of convenience with a common outlaw—or an uncommon Scottish noble disguised as an outlaw—she still wasn't sure how the McKays came into it. All she knew was that she was in a trap. It was of her own making. She didn't want to see Jamie Scott again let alone be married to him. And she had no choice.

She rubbed her temples again. How she wished the headache would go away! "I think," she said unhappily, "that you should fetch the parson."

"You want me to what?" Jamie shouted at his grandmother. "Are you out of your mind? What have you and the dowager been up to? Marrying the girl's not in my plans. It's all arranged. You were supposed to ask twenty-thousand pounds for her release and then we were—"

"Twenty-thousand is a good dowry for a duchess," Granny McKay interrupted the boy. "The dowager agrees as well. The marriage contract is being drawn up as we speak."

"What?"

She folded her hands on her cane and looked steadily at the lad. He was standing by her window, looking stubborn and haggard and confused. He wasn't as handsome as her dear Andrew had been, that long jaw had come from the Scott side of the family, but he was well favored enough. More important than his looks was his sense of honor and duty, not to mention a strong dose of Presbyterian conscience. He was a kind lad, as well. A kind, sober, honorable, dutiful, handsome young man. What girl could ask for more? Personally she thought the duchess was getting the best of the bargain.

The problem was, Jamie was also stubborn. Once he made up his mind about something he made a complete and thorough job of it. Look how he'd taken to being a highwayman, for example. Taken to it so well he was having trouble thinking like a man of his own class. Fortunately, as always, he had her to guide him into the proper course of action.

"Making a good marriage is just the thing you need to recover the family fortunes."

"That wasn't your original plan," he reminded her.

She noted just how stubbornly his jaw was set and the tense line of his slender body as he stood in profile to her. "I didn't think it was likely, I'll grant you. You've done the best you could, Jamie, but it's time to move on. Time to save yourself from the hangman, lad. You put your life at risk for the family, but that's over now. You can come home, be yourself again. You've had an amazing stroke of luck. Use it while you can."

"Luck? Luck?" He laughed harshly. He was looking out the window and not at her as he spoke, clearly wrestling with some sour memories. "The girl came looking to be tumbled by a highwayman. Was that luck? And the highwayman was happy to tumble her. I didn't even stop to ask her name. I've grown callous and cynical. I live in a wolf pack, and there are times when I like it."

He turned a bleak gaze on her. "I'm one of them, Granny. How do I give it up?"

She thumped her cane on the floor, and stated the obvious. "You stop robbing the road traffic," she instructed, "and start being the duke of Pyneham. That's how you give it up."

"You don't under—"

"Hush. What I understand," she said coldly, "is that you made love to a duchess and you are going to marry the woman. Those facts are clear to me. Are they clear to you, James?"

He spread his hands helplessly. "It's not as easy as all that."

"Of course it is," she countered. "It's all arranged. You

only have to show up at the wedding. You bedded the woman, she can take the consequences."

"But . . ."

"Think of the family. Think of your sisters. Me. Do you want us to rot in poverty? For Samantha to become a governess, or worse? You have to take care of them."

"I know. I've been taking care of them."

"You've been managing to put food on the table," she replied. "You've done your best lad, and we're all grateful. Now you have a chance to do more. You must grasp the chance before it slips through your hands. As the duke of Pyneham you can provide lavishly for the girls."

"Aye," he agreed, rubbing his long jaw. He was looking thoughtful at last. Always a good sign with Jamie. Jamie could always be counted on to do the right thing. "But what about Margaret?" he wondered.

"What about her?"

He gave her a fierce look. "The woman should have some say in this," he pointed out.

"She ruined herself," Granny McKay pointed out. "It's up to wiser heads to salvage her reputation now. Marrying you is the price of her good name. The dowager agrees to that. She'll see that the girl agrees as well. I've no doubt on that score," she answered firmly. "The dowager will see to the good of her family. I'll see to the good of mine. And it will be to the advantage of both."

But . . . Jamie thought the word, but didn't say it aloud. There was really no use arguing with Granny McKay at this point. Marriage was better than swinging from the end of a rope, he had to admit. Marriage to a duchess was all any ambitious young man could hope for. He could have property, place, power. Perhaps he should have thought of this solution himself. Perhaps he'd been half-dreaming of marrying a duchess when he wrote Margaret the damn fool letter that brought her running to her ruin.

Well, if he had been dreaming of marrying the woman, he hadn't realized it. He'd only written what was in his heart to the woman he'd thought she was. He'd been wrong about her. She'd turned out to be a foolish adventuress. It was right that she pay for her escapade.

Pay, yes, but with her future? Her happiness? Not that marriage was supposed to make one happy. It was just a duty, like any other. He didn't even consider his own happiness. How could he? He had to think of his responsibility to his family first. What could be better for them than his making such a brilliant marriage?

He had to do it, didn't he? Had to spend the rest of his life with Margaret Pyne of Pyneham. Silly, foolish, wanton, willful, lovely Margaret. His first duchess. The prospect wasn't as bad as all that. The lass was less upright than he'd thought her, but he was no model of rectitude himself. Bedding her would be sweet. Had been sweet . . . until . . .

She'd said no. He couldn't get the memory out of his mind. She'd tried to save her virtue, halfheartedly perhaps, but she had tried.

A no was a no. From a duchess or a whore, it shouldn't matter. He should have listened. He was at fault for taking her as he did. He owed her something for taking her maidenhead without her leave. Damn the family. Damn the fortune. He owed Margaret Pyne an offer of honorable marriage.

Never mind that there was no love on either side.

"Very well," he told his waiting grandmother. "Fetch the parson. I'll marry the woman."

* * *

Edwina and Samantha met midway between the sitting room and the bedroom doors. They looked at each other with astonishment and wonder.

"She's a—" Edwina began.

"Duchess," Samantha finished. "He's—"

"A highwayman," Edwina finished. "They made . . . had . . . relations together—"

"I know." Samantha blushed.

"There's going to be a wedding. What does it all mean?"

I'm not sure what it means to them," Samantha answered. She couldn't hold back a delighted laugh. She hugged her sister. "Edwina," she announced happily, "we're going to be rich again."

"Mummy's probably going to faint," Edwina replied. "But at least now we can afford smelling salts," she added pragmatically.

11

"*The wedding dinner* is going well," the person to her left said brightly. "Considering how quickly all was assembled and the guests invited."

Margaret did not look up from contemplating her wedding ring to acknowledge the words. She was vaguely aware of the man seated next to her. Aware in an odd, detached way, more aware of bits of him than of the complete person. She could deal with the fact that Jamie Scott—McKay—was dressed in silver brocade. That cream lace cuffs spilled across the back of his long-fingered hands. One hand held a crystal goblet as he accepted a toast from someone much farther down the long table. The other covered her own right hand, disguising the fact that her fist was clenched around a bunched-up span of table linen. The warmth and texture of that hand weighed heavily on the rest of her senses, but she refused to think about it as anything other than another object in her dining room.

She looked at the table service, the silver and china gleamed with appropriate grandeur in the warm glow of candlelight. A trio of musicians played in the hall outside the dining room, adding a gentle background accompaniment to the conversation.

A dish of peas dressed with butter was set before her. She found herself able to appreciate their color without feeling the least urge to eat them. She hadn't had the least interest in food all day, though she felt a vague appreciation for the hasty efforts of the kitchen staff to provide an instant feast.

That morning she'd woken up in her townhouse bedroom, and thought that perhaps the last few days had been a disastrous dream. Then the sisters had shown up, along with a maid and a dress suitable for the wedding, and all appetite had fled. At least the headache was gone. Which was a relief, considering how much the sisters talked.

The sisters. She shuddered in horror at the thought of the sisters.

Jamie Scott—McKay—hadn't lied when they first met. The highwayman had four sisters. She'd spent much of her time since leaving the McKay house in the company of the sisters. The two young ones kept their noses in books, contenting themselves with only the occasional curious glance toward the madwoman who was doomed to marry their brother.

The elder pair, Samantha and Edwina, were the talkers. They'd chattered incessantly while they acted as guard dogs in the coach and in her house while she was stripped and bathed and put properly to bed. She couldn't help but listen to their chatter. Mostly it was about books. The most pressing topic had been whether or not a new edition of some book by Henry Fielding would be better than the latest edition and what a pity they would have to wait so long before they could read it, but at least now they could afford to buy it properly bound instead of with blue paper covers.

The conversation had continued that morning while Margaret dressed, in the coach during the short ride to the church, and, in whispers, while they played bridesmaids, preceding her and the groom up the aisle to the waiting minister. They'd discussed Utopian philosophy on the ride back from the wedding. They were still talking now. She could make out their voices if not the actual words, even though their places were halfway down the table from where she sat.

At least they hadn't asked her opinion of anything. In fact, the only person who had addressed her at all today was the vicar, and then only to ask the traditional questions. She'd given him the two-word answer he required with hardly any hesitation. Having agreed to this farce she was determined to carry it off with all the self-possession she'd been trained for. She couldn't recall anything else. Except for a brief instant when Jamie's lips brushed hers, surprisingly chaste and awkward.

The voice of the ambassador from Schlewig-Halzen offering a grudging toast brought her out of her reverie. His presence at the feast reminded Margaret just who the alternative to the bridegroom might have been. Anyone, even a lying, thieving, whoremongering Scotsman, was better then the foul-tempered, foul-smelling autocrat the king had wanted for her. So, she concluded as her attention drifted back to the recent comment, the wedding dinner was indeed going well.

"Very well," the person next to the person on her left

said, echoing her thought. "It was a fine wedding as well."
This voice belonged to Granny McKay, she realized, and
the first speaker was her own grandmother. "The minister
gave a lovely sermon."

"And so he should have," the dowager replied, "considering how much Margaret has spent on repairs to St. Martin's, not to mention the parish poor fund."

Jamie watched his wife while the old woman talked.
Maggie Pyne was gone, washed away by a good scrubbing,
he supposed. The duchess he remembered was back,
dressed in blue, her gold hair lightly dusted with powder.
She wore a diamond necklace. He wore her topaz earring.
He tugged on it, wondering if he should give it back,
wondering what to do with Margaret now that he had her.
Putting her back on a pedestal and worshiping her from a
far was out of the question. He though it might be a good
thing if he could think of something to say to her.

He'd been searching for a topic of conversation all
through the meal, something that wouldn't touch on any
of the awkward memories they shared. He wanted to tell
her she looked lovely, but the crowded dining room, with
every eye and ear turned their way, was a far too public
place for such words. Besides, if he was going to mend her
ways, it was best not to feed her vanity.

He wanted to tell her how uncomfortable he felt. That
a quick trip to a tailor might have helped him look the
part, but he hardly felt like a duke. But he couldn't afford
to show her how vulnerable he felt, not when it was now
his duty to care for her.

Her hand had been cold when he'd placed his over it.
The gesture had seemed correct, an outward symbol of
their joining. She hadn't moved, or acknowledged his presence in any way. Her skin had warmed beneath his touch,
but she hadn't relaxed one bit. Public or no, it had been on

the tip of his tongue to ask if she was still annoyed about the gin, to see if she'd react. Fortunately, their grandmothers started talking, and he latched on to their subject instead.

"It's a fine entertainment," he said. He leaned his head closer to his wife's and said, "I'll be glad when it's over though."

Both of the old women cackled as Margaret raised her head stiffly. To his right, his mother said, "Jamie!" and tittered. Mummy had been in unusually good spirits since discovering she was going to be a duchess's mother-in-law.

"Ready for the wedding night so soon?" Granny McKay asked gleefully.

He hadn't meant it quite that way. Yes, he was anxious to retire with his wife, but that was so they could have some privy conversation before they got on with the bedding part. Not that he didn't welcome the chance to claim the real Margaret Pyne instead of the doxy from the Red Bull. Margaret turned her head to look at him just as a reminiscent smile came to his lips.

"You rutting swine," she whispered, the annoyed words spoken so low they reached only him.

"I?" he whispered back in amazement. "It wasn't I who—"

"There will be dancing in the reception rooms," Margaret announced, turning to speak to their guests.

"And theatricals in the music room, Your Grace?" a young man's voice questioned from the end of the table. "I so enjoy your little theatricals. Marchmont and I have been rehearsing some speeches from *The Modern Husband* to gratify the company and celebrate your good fortune."

Jamie looked down the table at the speaker, a bewigged young fellow in mustard brocade and too many face patches. If he wasn't mistaken, the speaker was Lord Edgware, from whom he'd taken a gold watch and twenty guineas on Finchley Common no more than a week ago. The realization of his change of station hit Jamie with the force of a pistol ball, but he forced himself to ignore the sudden feeling of disorientation.

"There will be no theatricals," he announced. "My wife has given up that useless and debauching form of entertainment." His tone was harsher than he had intended— the sort of tone he had used when he demanded a victim to stand and deliver. His words produced a brief, embarrassed silence among the diners as the servants cleared away the final course.

He stood, and Margaret followed his lead, as did the guests. He took his wife's arm, but left it to her to guide him upstairs to the reception rooms while the rest of the gathering followed in a brightly dressed knot of forced conversation.

Margaret's heart sank further as her husband pronounced her punishment for all the world to hear. Her life was going to be pointless and cheerless from now on, wasn't it? No more theatricals. No more plays. No more acting. A small spark of anger at his unfairness began to burn away some of the numbness that had covered her senses in the last twenty-four hours. Useless, he'd said. Debauching. If she was debauched just who was it who'd debauched her? Fine way for a man who'd been roistering and rioting not a week ago at the Red Bull to be acting.

"Hypocrite," she whispered, pulling away from him as they entered the first of the house's two connected reception rooms.

Jamie let her go without answering her charge. He took up a place by the room's gilded fireplace and watched his wife move with a kind of automatic grace through the group of guests. Her one-word accusation scratched at his conscience.

She was right, he had to agree, he was being a hypocrite. Of sorts. He was determined to reform both her and himself. He wasn't quite sure yet what was going to be necessary to make them over into the sort of people they should be. He needed time to think on the subject, to experiment and relearn the concepts of right and wrong. Until he could find some balance, he intended to be a strict watchdog for both of them. Perhaps this must seem like a hypocritical way for a highwayman to behave, but it truly was for the best of reasons.

Margaret paused and spoke and paused again to listen. It was all habit and she was thankful for it. Habit, and the talent for acting which her husband so deplored. Around her she heard everyone discussing just how the marriage had come about. She managed not to flicker so much as an eyelash when she heard that she and Lord James McKay had known each other for years. That their grandparents had been urging the union since they were children. That they'd met again after years apart and had decided to marry instantly. It was, people were assuring each other, a love match. She smiled at everyone's good wishes and didn't feel reassured at all.

The crowd spread out, some into the larger reception room to dance, some into the music room to play. Margaret remained where she was, in the same room with Lord James McKay. It wouldn't do for the loving bride to stray too far from her adoring bridegroom.

She was not by the door when the newcomer arrived, but she heard the stir caused by his entrance and turned immediately to see who had entered.

Lake had never been handsomer, more commanding. He shined in the candlelight, a tall figure in black and

silver striding purposefully toward her, his gold hair a
burnished, silky crown. His full lips were curved in a smile;
the expression in his eyes was deadly. Margaret froze at
the sight of him, but she stood her ground. Her attention
was so focused on the enemy that she forgot anyone else
was in the room.

They met in the center of the room. He went through
the motions of a perfect bow and kissed her hand. She
smiled, and said, "Greetings, brother," with a parody of
warmth.

He kept her hand clasped in his. His grip was not gentle.
"It seems I'm to wish you happy," he said. In a whisper he
added, "Do you know what you've done, Maggie?"

"Thank you," she replied. Groups of chatting people
surrounded them. A footman appeared. Lake took a glass
from the tray he held and the servant moved on. His eyes
locked with hers, his hatred and fury pouring over her.

"Where is my sister?" she asked as she had asked so
many times before. Tonight she dressed the words in the
guise of polite inquiry. "Could she not attend?"

"Your sister is unwell," he answered as he always did.
"And what?" he whispered, "does this wedding mean? Do
you mean to cheat me out of the dukedom? Whose mad
idea was this? Do you know what you've done?" he repeated. The words rang out as an ominous threat.

"I've done nothing but my duty to Pyneham," she answered.

Lake's smile turned malicious. "Has he filled your belly
already?" he asked, the words uglier for being whispered.
"Is that the cause of your haste?"

It was possible. She knew by the sound of Lake's low,
evil chuckle, that the thought showed in her face.

"You're not certain, though, are you?" She shook her

head, too upset to control the gesture. "Pray there's no babe to replace your sister as heir, Maggie."

She swallowed hard, confused and afraid. She looked into his cold eyes. "Why?" she asked, knowing the answer already.

"As your heir Frances has some value," he pointed out. His smile chilled her as he continued. "Your bearing a babe would render Frances's existence useless, wouldn't it?"

"Now there's a black cat set among the pigeons," Jamie said as he noticed the tall, blonde man enter the room. The pair to whom he was talking, Jeffrey Edgware and Harry Norris, chuckled at his comment. When the man made a beeline for his wife, Jamie asked, "And just who is the black cat?"

"Your brother-in-law," Norris supplied easily. "General Sir Charles Lake."

"Impressive, isn't he?" Edgware asked, a gleam of wicked amusement in his eye.

"General Lake? I've heard of him," Jamie added admiringly. Who hadn't heard of Lake? Of the battles won, the decorations, the field promotion to general at the age of twenty-five, the wounds and early retirement to stand for Parliament. The man was a hero, as well as active in politics.

"He games," Edgware added. "When he's not whoring."

"Hmm," Jamie said. His attention more on the pair standing in the middle of the room. "I suppose it's time to meet my new brother."

For all his old blood, education, and wealthy relatives, Jamie had never spent any time among the upper ranks of the English nobility. His time in London had been spent

surviving, not joining the correct clubs. He had never as-
pired to belong to this exalted social circle, but found the
present company very amiable.

He left Edgware and Norris and approached his wife.
The whole time he'd been getting acquainted with the
young men, a large part of his attention had been on
Margaret's blue-clad form. He knew that Samantha was
taking part in the dancing. Mother and Edwina were in the
music room. Michelle and Alexandra were far too young
to be out in company, so they were safely tucked away
with some new books. And the grandmothers were getting
tipsy together over by the massive silver punch bowl. He
was aware of all his womenfolk, but his wife's where-
abouts interested him most of all.

He'd watched her be a gracious, if somewhat distracted,
hostess. She'd moved dutifully among her guests. The blue
satin of her panniered gown shimmered in the candlelight.
Her jewels glittered, her pink cheeks and shining lips were
bright spots in the pale oval of her face. He had watched,
hoping she'd make her way to his side once she'd spoken
to her guests—for form's sake, if nothing else. He had
refused to trail after her, or to command her presence.

Whether she had intended to join him or not, it was his
duty to go to her now. He had a smile and friendly greeting
ready for Lake as he came up to the trim, black-coated
man.

But his smile froze when he saw the look in Margaret's
eyes. There was a fixed, pleasant grin on her lips, and no
tension was betrayed by the way she stood. But her eyes
held the bleak hopelessness of a trapped animal.

Without thinking, Jamie's arms went protectively
around her shoulders as he stepped behind her. He pulled
her to him, enclosing her in a protective embrace. Her
slight shudder vibrated against his chest as she settled

against him. He wondered if it was from distaste or relief, as he met Lake's eyes over his wife's head.

The hot malevolence of the other man's stare didn't bother him. Jamie had faced down many a brave man on the road, knowing it wasn't just the brace of pistols he carried that made him a formidable foe. No, he wasn't bothered by the hatred, but he found the jealousy deeply disturbing.

He ignored any stirring of misgiving and quirked his lips into the semblance of a friendly expression. He said evenly, "Welcome, friend. Or should I call you brother?"

Lake looked him up and down, his open contempt raked Jamie from the top of his head to his scarlet shoe heels. "Brother?" The word came out cold and sharp. "I call no Jacobite Scotsman brother," he announced, voice ringing loudly in the now-hushed room.

Jamie absorbed the man's hatred and offered him a coolly controlled smile. "Then you should call me brother," he replied. "For I'm no more a follower of the Stuart pretender than you are. I've never worn a plaid or stolen a sheep, either," he added, glancing with an inviting smirk at the silent listeners.

A wave of mild laughter rippled around the room. The response was enough to remind the sneering general they were not alone. Lake stepped back and made a small bow, apparently deciding to mind his manners for the moment.

"Welcome, then . . . brother," he said, biting off the last word with icy precision. He turned his attention back to Margaret. "I'll convey your loving greetings to my lady wife."

"And my greeting to your wife as well," Jamie added. "Lady—?"

After a moment's hesitation, Margaret said, "Frances. My sister's name is Frances."

He wondered why Margaret hadn't mentioned having a sister before now. Then he remembered that they hadn't exactly had a chance to hold a normal conversation yet. "I'm sorry she missed the wedding."

"She is ill," Lake said.

Jamie felt Margaret's shuddering sigh and held her a bit closer. "I'm sorry to hear it."

Lake gave the barest of nods. Margaret said nothing.

From inside the circle of Jamie's arms Margaret felt lost, unsure of how to react to either of the men. Jamie's words and actions confused her. The moment Lake appeared she'd actually forgotten her bridegroom was in the room. When Jamie came up behind her, enfolding her in a warm, possessive embrace, she'd felt relief so intense it left her physically shaken. She recovered her senses as Lake transferred his anger from her to a new enemy, and Jamie easily took up the cat-and-mouse power game.

Of course, she realized, her fortune meant everything to Jamie Scott. He'd defend his right to it against all comers. She trusted the highwayman to recognize a threat when he saw it. Still, he didn't know who the true pawn was in the game. It was Frances she had to defend.

She found her voice and said to her brother-in-law, "I pray your lady wife will remain well."

Lake gave her a thin smile. "I trust you'll do everything in your power for her, my dear?"

Jamie loomed over her. His strong arms circled her. Wiry muscles clad in soft brocade pressed intimately against her back. The warmth of his breath tickled her ear. He was her husband. She already knew he was strong and forceful and lusty. She didn't know how she was supposed to deny him her bed. Besides, the damage might already be done—else there would have been no wedding today. Still, she could do nothing but nod her agreement to Lake's demand.

"Then I'll bid you good-night," Lake said.

Jamie seized the opportunity presented by Lake's words. "I think," he announced, moving to take Margaret by the hand, "that it is my lady and I who will bid the company good-night."

A raucous cheer went up from the company, everyone but Lake joining in the sudden hail of bawdy jests. Many people in the room made for the door.

Jamie frowned at the thought of taking the leading part in a bawdy traditional bedding. "Alone," he said firmly to the smiling, snickering guests.

He gave the crowd a look that dared anyone to follow, then turned and led his bride from the room. His last sight was of Lake, standing still and menacing; it was as though the angel of death had walked into the wrong party by mistake. The dowager's voice rang out behind them as they left, ordering the guests to let be and attend to the dessert tables instead.

Once in the hall, Jamie ignored the footmen loitering in every possible corner and inquired of his wife, "All right, where do you keep the bedroom?"

Margaret found herself almost amused by the man's consternation. The look of plain curiosity on his long face tempted her out of some of her rancor. "I don't have a bedroom," she answered honestly, "I have a state chamber. The room's the size of a meadow but the marble floor's too cold to attract any sensible sheep. The bed's behind a carved rail like a gold altar suffering from an excess of cherubs and could probably sleep six. And it's not very comfortable," she added.

Jamie smiled and put his hands on his wife's shoulders. It was going to be hard being a stern husband when he kept being charmed by her. "I didn't ask what it was like," he reminded her, rubbing his thumbs sensuously along her collarbone, beneath the shining stones of her necklace. "I asked where it was."

His hands were a heavy weight; the gentle stroking motion across the base of her throat was shockingly distracting. Pleasurable. She couldn't allow either emotion to enter into her dealings with this man.

His fingers trailed from her shoulders to her throat, then down to touch her necklace. "I hope you got your topazes back, though diamonds are nice."

"I got my necklace back," she answered sharply, "but these aren't diamonds." All her best jewels were locked away at Lacey House. "This is a paste copy. About as genuine as our love match," she added, still angry about the reception room conversation.

Jamie just smiled. "We'll see what's genuine," he said, and kissed her. Her mouth opened in shock, and his tongue was inside before she could stop it. His breath mingled with hers, wine flavored, the taste and touch intimate and coaxing. She made some sort of noise, and his hands moved. One came around her waist pulling her nearer, the other came between them. It sketched the outline of her tight-fitting bodice. The kiss deepened as he cupped her breast.

Sensual heat was trying to flood her senses, to wipe away resentment and anger with mere sensation. Passion, she realized, was easy. She didn't want to be tempted by him. For Frances's sake, she didn't dare. For her own self-respect she didn't dare. He hadn't recognized her, she reminded herself sternly. His only interest was a body to spend himself in.

His mouth moved to the base of her throat, the caressing of her breast became more daring.

"No thumbs," she said, pulling out of his grasp. "Definitely no thumbs."

Jamie took a step back, aware that fondling his wife in the hallway was an outrageous thing to so. He put his hands behind his back, all the while looking into her fine gray eyes. They'd gone smoke color, and were bright with both anger and desire. "You like my thumbs," he pointed out, unable to resist teasing. "It was you who came looking for me, lass. There's no need to be shy now."

Annoyance replaced the unwanted sense of pleasure from his touch. Her answer was passionate, but with outrage. "Yes, but did you ever bother to ask why I came looking for you?"

Jamie was taken aback by the question, but before he could get any words out she went on, "You'll not share my bed, do you hear me? I won't be humiliated like that again." She pointed down the hall to the wide staircase. "There are plenty of bedrooms on the second floor. Pick one and sleep in it."

He crossed his arm. "But I don't want to sleep."

She mirrored his gesture. "Then I suggest you take yourself off to Molly—"

"Lucy."

"—at the Red Bull. Or go and write some other fool love letters. Or go to the devil."

"I'd rather go to bed with my wife."

"That, sir, is the one thing you will not do."

Jamie drew breath for another angry retort, but stopped himself just short of shouting at the fool woman. He wasn't sure what to make of Margaret's determined fury. He did know the hallway was no more a place to be having an argument than it was to be making love. Never mind the ever-present, listening servants. There was too much chance of their being overheard by the guests. From the determined look on Margaret's face and the flashing anger that had replaced the more tender emotion in her eyes, it was obvious she wasn't ready to give in any time soon. He was tempted to sling her over his shoulder and simply carry her off.

But such thoughtless behavior had led to disaster the last time. He had no intention of making a disaster of this marriage. Damn it, she was lovely! And, damn but he wanted her. But he wasn't about to make a fool of himself a second time. It was only one night, he told himself. She was still feeling ashamed over what happened. He'd give her time. There'd be plenty of other nights. Let her have this one to herself, wedding night or no.

He got hard control over his anger and his frustration. He drew himself up to his full height and gave her a small, stiff nod. Just as stiffly he said, "Very well, madam. Tonight you are free to sleep alone. But," he added warningly, "don't expect me to be so lenient tomorrow. Good-night, wife." He turned and strode away.

Tomorrow? she thought, feeling herself go pale with the rush of apprehension as he disappeared up the stairs. She'd have to fight this battle again tomorrow, wouldn't she? Not just against him, but against herself. For she had to admit that the lean, handsome Scotsman still attracted her even though she knew he'd only used her out of lust and greed. She didn't like to admit to either surprise or disappointment at his leaving her alone without very much argument.

Tomorrow, she repeated unhappily, and tomorrow and tomorrow. The words were a frantic litany as she made her way to her state chamber with its big, uncomfortable, lonely bed.

12

Margaret didn't rise until nearly noon the next day, which was normal enough for someone keeping city hours. She would never think of staying in bed so late at Lacey House. Of course, if she'd stayed safe at Lacey House, she thought as she was attended by a pair of maids shocked at her husband's absence from the bridal bed, she wouldn't have had cause to lie awake most of the night wondering where her husband might be.

She took her morning chocolate and some toasted bread in the alcove by the window in the dressing room. In the country, she recalled, all she had to worry about was having her bed burned out from under her.

To take her mind from the memory of the fire she glanced out the window. It was raining. The street below was full of mud and a snarl of slow-moving coach traffic.

A goodly number of those coaches were vying for space in front of her house. Favor seekers and hangers-on come to wish the duchess well and beg for bits of her fortune and influence. They appeared with vermin-like persistence to loiter about the house whenever she was in London. Their numbers rose and fell depending on how she stood in favor with the king, but they never completely disappeared from the premises. There seemed to be an unusually large number of callers waiting about for her to hold a levee this morning. Which she had no intention of doing.

She went back to her toast and discovered she had an appetite. She was considering ordering some food when she heard a knock on the bedroom door.

"The sisters!" she gasped, appetite immediately fleeing. She rose to her feet. Perhaps she could hide in one of the clothes chests. Her panic was stilled a moment later when a maid led Mrs. Gribbons, the housekeeper, into the dressing room.

Mrs. Gribbons marched up to her, planted her stout form before her, and announced without preamble, "The sisters, Your Grace. What's to be done about His Grace's sisters?"

Taking her seat once more Margaret contemplated the worried expression on the elderly woman's face, and said, "Personally, I'm in favor of drowning."

Mrs. Gribbons was not amused. She went on relentlessly. "I need to assign ladies' maids to the elder ones, and a governess must be found for the younger pair." She shook her head. "I don't know why they didn't bring their own people to attend them, but the lack has thrown my household out of order. I've thought of consulting His Grace's mother." Mrs. Gribbons rushed on while Margaret was still drawing breath for a reply. "But she seems most ineffectual, if you'll pardon my saying so. And Lady

Sophie always seems to be closeted with Her Grace, the dowager. Not that this is something to interest the dowager, who's nursing a frightful head this morning, I'm told," Mrs. Gribbons added disapprovingly. "Of course it seemed best and proper to consult your wishes in the matter of the sisters before any arrangements could be made."

"Perhaps not drowning," Margaret murmured thoughtfully as she gazed out the rain-spattered window once more. "Perhaps we could just lock them in the book room and feed them once a month or so."

Mrs. Gribbons ignored her solution. "I need to know what sort of arrangements need to be made for the young ladies."

And you're looking to me to see that your orderly household is set to rights, Margaret added to herself. Well, she supposed, if the sisters were kept in luxury they might keep busy enough to leave her alone. "Find them maids," she ordered. "And have their bills sent to my man of business." The housekeeper didn't looked pleased. Margaret didn't understand why. "Yes?"

"Those girls . . ." The woman's lips drew together in a tight line. She shook her head despondently, then bobbed a curtsy. "As you wish, Your Grace."

The woman was not happy when she left, even though Margaret had made the decisions she'd asked for. Margaret didn't like this disruption in the Pyneham household, either. She couldn't toss the talkative young women out on the street. They were, after all—and she gritted her teeth with frustration at the thought—her husband's sisters. "If he wants them here," she said between those gritted teeth, "then here they stay. All must be made comfortable for my husband's plague of loc—family."

She briefly considered going back to bed rather than

facing the rest of the day. In the end she decided getting out of her stiff, tightly laced finery would be too much effort for everyone involved. After some minutes' contemplation of the rain and her growling stomach, she decided to find out where her kitchen might be kept and to eat her way through the pantry. Surely the sisters would never think of looking for her belowstairs.

She was perfectly prepared to ignore the crowd in the hallway when she left her chamber. What she was not prepared for was the sight of her long-limbed husband leaning casually against the marble banister at the top of the staircase. Or the fact that the crowd's attention was concentrated on him. Very few eyes shifted to her as she stepped into the corridor. All the visitors, she realized with half-amused annoyance, had come to see what sort of pickings they could wheedle out of the new duke.

"I should have expected it," she said. She hadn't but then she hadn't been thinking much at all the last few days. Not since she received the letter from the man at the head of the stairs.

"Gaming's not to my taste," Jamie said as he watched Margaret move through the crowd. She glided with regal grace, looking neither right nor left, barely acknowledging a score of fervent well-wishers. She wore sapphire-blue today. Almost somber enough for widow's weeds but for the cream lace and pink-ribbon trim, he thought, disapproving. She looked well rested, which was more than he could say for himself. He didn't know how she managed to ignore the crush of people, but he admired the ability greatly. He was holding a handful of petitions and his ears ached from all the syrup-laden pleas he'd already listened to. Thank goodness Edgware had arrived to offer felicita-

tions and decent conversation while he waited for his wife
to put in an appearance.

He supposed he should have expected people to come to
him looking for a patron. Lord knew there'd been times
when he'd been tempted to go begging hat in hand to his
better off relatives. Now, he realized with dreary certainty,
his relatives would be calling on him.

"You must come," Edgware insisted, touching his arm
but unable to draw Jamie's attention away from Margaret.
"Never mind the gaming, Pyneham. Everyone of interest
frequents my club. People you should know, and who
should know our new duke."

Jamie glanced briefly at the young man. The lad was a
fop, but Jamie could sense a good-natured intelligence
beneath the paint and patches. "Aye," he agreed. "You're
right about that." Perhaps he could even come across a few
eligible fools willing to take the girls off his hands at this
club of Edgware's. "Tonight," he agreed.

He nodded to Edgware's pleased smile, then stepped
away from the balustrade as Margaret reached the spot
where he waited. He handed the petitions to the waiting
butler. He was sure Margaret intended to pass him without so much as a nod of greeting. That would never do.
Not with so many eyes watching and tongues eager to wag
over their slightest move. So he snagged his arm around
her slender waist and drew her into an embrace, kissing
her before she could offer any protest. Let the tongues wag
over this, he thought as he fully appreciated her soft lips
and gasp of surprise.

She snatched her head back. Her eyes were wide, her
cheeks flaming. "Wh-what?" she sputtered.

"We're newlyweds," he whispered quickly, trying not
to chuckle at her discomfiture. "It's expected."

Margaret looked around her and saw a sea of grinning

faces. How kind of Jamie not to disappoint his audience, she thought bitterly. And he'd given her to believe he didn't approve of playacting!

She eased out of his grasp and into her part with a charming smile. "Good morrow to you, too, my lord. You're occupied," she added, glad for once of the crowd. "I'll be on my way."

He held his hand out to her instead. "Walk with me," he commanded. He gave a dismissing look to the hangers-on as she reluctantly gave him her hand.

"Just how," he asked when they were downstairs, away from the crowd, "do you deal with those vultures?"

"Peremptorily," she replied. Adding with more honesty, "Mostly I refer them to my secretary, or man of business."

"Ah," he said. "Just what I want to talk to you about."

Of course. She should have expected this. It was a wonder he hadn't discussed finances over the wedding dinner. She was, after all, his golden cow. "Milk away," she grumbled. Ignoring his puzzled look, she directed him to a sitting room whose windows overlooked the back garden. The frail-looking chair she chose all but disappeared beneath her wide skirts as she sat. She folded her hands in her lap, looked up at her husband, and said, "Yes?"

She'd been prepared for him to loom. She was used to being loomed over by the likes of Lake and her father. She wasn't prepared for the disarming sight of having him settle on the chair opposite her in a loose-limbed sprawl. Or for his relieved sigh.

"It's my feet," he said, light brown eyes twinkling. "The cobbler didn't get the fit of these things quite right."

Her gaze dropped, past a pair of well-turned calves sheathed in white silk stockings, to her husband's feet.

They were long and narrow, like the rest of him. They were clad in a pair of red-heeled, jewel-buckled confections in the latest style.

"We must all suffer for fashion," she remarked primly.

"I'd rather get a new shoemaker," he replied. "Which," he added, "is the first practical thought I've had in days."

When Margaret did not respond, but looked past him to a clock on the mantle, Jamie stroked his jaw thoughtfully. She wasn't eager to respond to his friendly overtures, and he didn't blame her.

He leaned forward in his chair. "About your property," he began.

She reeled off a long list of the houses and investments she owned, finishing with, "The steward at Lacey House manages the estates. Mr. Carruthers manages everything else. You will find their service satisfactory." Her face was set in an emotionless mask as she spoke, her words were without inflection. The combination spoke volumes. She knew what she was worth, at least materially, and thought the material was all he was interested in. Which, he supposed, he should be. Rubbish.

"I've spoken to your man of business," he told her.

"I see." Two words, spoken with cold contempt.

"Early this morning," he went on. "He had papers for me to sign." She showed no curiosity. "Papers requiring me to give up my name in order to assume the Pyneham titles." He sat back and steepled his fingers. "It appears my name is now Pyne. I've given up my birthright."

She mirrored his gesture and looked at him calmly. "And taken mine. It's a more than fair trade."

Jamie didn't try to argue with her. Not when it looked as if she might start crying at any moment. She was looking like the vulnerable, hurting girl he'd first met on the road. He didn't like being the cause of her pain. He was stung at giving up his name, but he wasn't so proud that he thought the McKay name meant everything. That his children would be called Pyne wouldn't make them any less his. He'd love them whatever they were called. Besides, they'd make his claim to the title more valid. Despite his title as duke, and power to control his wife's property, her sister Frances remained the Pyneham heir until a child was born to Margaret. This was to keep the title in the blood royal.

"I had to sell my family's falling-down rock pile of a castle across the border to pay my father's debts," he admitted. "I've decided to buy that property back." He saw her disapproval, but she didn't argue. So he told her the rest of the plan. "I'm going to gift it to our second son."

"Second son?" Margaret nearly slid off the narrow chair. Her heart raced, her thoughts reeled. "What do you mean, second son?"

The man went unconcernedly on. "Or third. Whichever one has a bit of sense and doesn't mind changing his name to McKay to inherit the land."

"Third?" The word came out as barely a squeak. Did the man think she was a brood sow? Didn't he understand about Frances? No, a quiet, reasonable voice in the back of her head reminded her. He doesn't.

"Unless I can find a McKay cousin willing to marry Sammie."

His wife responded with a muttered sentence that might have been, "He'll have to be deaf."

Jamie diplomatically chose to ignore this comment. He also chose to ignore that she'd gone pale and wild-eyed at the mention of children. He didn't blame her for fearing sex after what happened at the Red Bull. He'd just have to gentle her over the fear. Perhaps it hadn't been wise to leave her to her memories and fancies last night.

He decided it was time to change the subject. Remembering the Red Bull reminded him of another subject. He steepled his fingers again, realized that the gesture made him look as sanctimonious as a parson, and stood, jamming his hands in his pockets.

"Why?" he wondered, gazing down on the pale and lovely girl. "Why did you come to the Red Bull?"

He was looming at last. It was such a masculine way of showing power. She had quite a way to look up his long, lanky frame to meet his gaze, but she didn't let the distance stop her. The problem was, what was she going to tell him? It was one thing to seek a highwayman out as a bodyguard, quite another to involve a stranger in her family problems. Of course, she had to admit, James Scott McKay Pyne now was the family problem, as well as head of the family. And he was waiting for an answer.

And Margaret, being more honest than cunning, told him, "I'd been having trouble with some vandalism at Lacey House. I was seeking some professional protection." It was the truth. It just wasn't all the truth. "By the way," she added as he gazed down on her with incredulous curiosity, "General Lake won't like having you for a relative. He doesn't much like having me for a relative."

His heavy, straight brows came down in a puzzle line, his wide eyes narrowing. "What about the playacting?"

Margaret sighed. He obviously hadn't taken her admittedly obtuse hint about Lake. "I was in disguise."

"Why'd you let me take you to bed? Was it because of that fool letter?"

She felt herself color. Her hands fidgeted in her lap. "I don't wish to discuss it."

"You could have gotten killed. I should never have written that letter," he added.

"I know."

"You had no business paying any attention to it."

"I know," she said again. "You didn't mean a word of it."

What? How could she say that? Jamie thought, stung by the bleak hatred in her words, by the way her body tensed when he spoke. As though his words had hurt her. He supposed, in a way, they had. His one bout of romantic idealism had sent her off looking for a protector. Or so she claimed. The footman had said she was just there for a lark. Then again, he found himself adding with chagrined reasonableness, she hadn't necessarily told the servant her true reason for looking for him. Which was something that should have occurred to him at the time. He'd still been angry, in a tearing rage at Taggert, at life, at the world, and at himself for what he'd become. He was never reasonable when he was angry, especially not when he was angry at himself. It was always so tempting to find excuses, someone else to blame.

His silence was not reassuring. The flashes of emotion crossing his face were confusing. She didn't know whether to tell him to go to the devil or ask if he was feeling all right. The best she could manage was to tentatively say, "My lord?"

"Jamie," he said. "My name's Jamie."

She shook her head. "Oh no," she answered, a poignant memory of a conversation on a dusty road with a masked man brought an ache to her heart. "It was too much familiarity that got us into this situation."

He laughed sharply, throwing his head back. "God's death, it was indeed."

Her cheeks burned with embarrassment as it became evident to her that he'd misunderstood her words. She rose, summoning up every bit of dignity at her command. "Have I leave to go, Your Grace?"

She didn't want to talk to him anymore. She was being dramatic. And from the sober look of her she hadn't been thinking about sex when she'd spoken of familiarity. Perhaps he had a talent for misconstruing her meanings. Best to withdraw from the field for now and let her have a bit of a sulk. A few hours of seriously feeling sorry for themselves generally did Samantha and Edwina a world of good when they were annoyed with him. Once they were over it they'd throw a few things, there'd be a great deal of shouting from him as well as his sisters, then the air would be cleared. He and Margaret could have a proper shouting match tonight and get all this nonsense cleared up. He'd leave her be for now.

He swept her an elegant bow. "Don't bestir yourself, madam. No need for you to face half the populace of London in your own hallway. I'll deal with them while you rest easy here."

Margaret gasped with anger at the effrontery of the man's words. Rest easy? He'll deal with people. First a catalogue of her possessions, then an easy dismissal. Relegated to her own sitting room was she? Typical male. Just like Father.

She sat, and forced an acquiescent expression onto her face. "Yes, my lord." And master, she added to herself as he turned and walked from the room. What would he want next? Sons, she knew. Oh dear.

Jamie rubbed the spot on the back of his neck where his wife's eyes had burned into him as he'd left the sitting room. He'd thought of those eyes as smoke, but had just learned they could flash pure fire. Problem was, he wasn't sure what he'd done to offend her at the last. Whatever it was had upset her more than anything else that had passed between them. He was tempted to go back to her, but Samantha and Edwina came down the stairs as he hesitated by the door. When they saw him they called out and hurried to join him.

"You're looking grand, Jamie," Edwina greeted him.

"Jamie, Your Grace," Samantha said bluntly. "We need our own coach."

"Why?" Jamie asked. "What do you need a coach for?"

"We want to go to Bath. Or at least Ranelagh Gardens. We haven't been anywhere in ages. And we should have a ball," she added. "Mummy would like us to have a ball. We could meet proper suitors then."

"There's so much to see and do," Edwina added, gazing at him hopefully with her uptilted brown eyes.

"Hmmm," Jamie said, enjoying their open exuberance. He looked at his eager, happy sisters, and recalled the unhappy, confused woman he'd just left. Margaret, he decided, could use a bit of cheering up. "I think you should spend some time with my wife," he told them. "Get to know her."

Their happiness changed instantly to appalled dread. Edwina clasped her hands before her dramatically. Samantha merely looked as if she'd tasted something bad.

"Oh, no, Jamie," Edwina cried. "Must we?"

"Don't tell me she needs guarding again," Samantha complained. "All she does is look sour and sickly and pretends we don't exist."

"And her a fallen woman," Edwina added righteously. "Mummy says she'll be a bad influence on us." When Jamie frowned at her thunderously, she added, "Besides, I feel like a fool around her. I don't know what to say to a duchess, so I natter on like an idiot. Samantha does too."

"I do not."

"You do."

"She doesn't like us, Jamie," Samantha insisted. "Or want anything to do with us."

He folded his arms and looked them over, taking note of their pretty new dresses. "You seem to have a great deal to do with her," he pointed out. "You weren't wearing brocade before meeting her, as I recall. It's her fortune you want to spend, her coaches and houses and servants."

"They're yours now," Samantha insisted. "You're the duke of Pyneham."

"You will be kind to her."

"It's only a marriage of convenience," Edwina said.

"Granny McKay says—"

"The devil with Granny!" Jamie cut off Samantha. He raked them with a commanding look. "It's what I say that matters in this household. I will not be disputed with."

They looked at each other and rolled their eyes, but neither of them chose to argue further. "Yes, Jamie."

He pointed toward the sitting room. "Go in there and be nice to your new sister," he ordered.

"Yes, Jamie."

"Right now."

They made faces at him. Samantha stuck out her tongue. But they went.

When the sisters entered she knew he'd sent them. Like a punishment from God. She sat very still and pretended to ignore them. The girls stood by the door and talked to each other, an argument in easily overheard whispers.

"I say we tell her about the earbob," Samantha insisted.

"It's Jamie's secret," Edwina answered.

"It's all right. In fashionable marriages people understand these things. The duchess and Jamie were only having a fling. Granny said so."

"And his secret love is of a much longer standing," Edwina agreed. "She has first place in his affections.

You're right, Sammie," she concluded. "We must tell her."

"Keep her from interfering with his happiness," Samantha added beligerently.

"Quite right. You do it."

Margaret didn't know what they intended, but she stood to face them as they approached. Both girls were taller than she was, though Edwina wasn't much taller. Not that she had any intention of being intimidated by any more McKays just at the moment. When they reached her she looked at them haughtily and spoke coldly. "I believe a curtsy is due me." Better to go on the offensive, she concluded.

"Well!" Samantha declared, but she did bow. Edwina followed suit.

"I don't recall requesting your presence."

"Jamie sent us," was Samantha's truculent answer. There was a definite change in the duchess today, Samantha noted. More like the drunken doxy who'd tossed the chamber pot than the block of stone they'd spent the last two days with. She was being haughty, but at least she was also lively. "His Grace says we're to be kind to you," she informed the angry young woman.

"The pox take His Grace," the duchess responded. "You may withdraw."

"He doesn't love you!" Edwina blurted out.

The girl's cheeks colored as though Edwina words had struck her. Interesting, Samantha thought. "Love isn't the issue," she reminded her sister. "She's a romantic," she explained to the duchess. "So's Jamie, for that matter."

"The point is," Edwina said, earnest and breathless at once. "He loves another. He has for ever so long. Weeks and weeks. He wears her token. Sometimes. At least," she rushed on, "I haven't seen him wear it for ages but he wore it yesterday. At the wedding. That had to be symbolic. Didn't it, Sammie?"

"Indeed it does," Samantha agreed. "The point is," she went on as the duchess stared at them, pale and wide-eyed, "we don't blame you for lusting after Jamie. It's natural, I suppose. He's sweet though a bit thin-shanked for my taste, and his jaw's a bit too long—"

"He's dashing and handsome!" Edwina spoke up loyally. "And it doesn't really matter if you have a grand passion for him, because his heart's given elsewhere," she told the duchess. She knew she preferred having her cherished brother in love with someone she didn't have to share him with. A secret love who was far away was much better than a resident wife. She didn't want Jamie's wife changing things between her brother and his sisters. "You don't even have to live together. It isn't fashionable."

Token? Margaret thought. He wasn't wearing any token yesterday. The only thing he'd been wearing besides a fine suit of clothes was her earring. The one Jamie Scott had promised to keep, and did. What has he been telling these silly magpies? That he loved the girl who gave him the earring? That he wrote love letters to her?

"Love token? Heart already given?" She laughed. "Your brother," she said harshly, "will tumble anything in skirts."

"That's not true!" Edwina shouted.

Samantha shrugged. "He's a man, isn't he? What's sex got to do with love, Your Grace?"

"Sammie!"

"The point is," Samantha said, "aside from a bit of normal whoring, his heart is given to the lady who gave him the earring."

It could have been true. He might have loved the memory of his first duchess. The words twisted in Margaret, but she couldn't deny the possibility. It was possible—not likely, but possible—that Jamie had meant every word of the letter at the time he wrote it. It was her pride, she chastised herself, that wanted her to believe in love. To want him to truly love her. Perhaps, she countered the realist. But if she must live with him, it might make things easier if he loved her. If he loved his duchess perhaps he might someday feel something kindly for the real her. Did she love him? No, she answered honestly. Not now. But, perhaps . . .

For Frances's sake, she couldn't let herself think beyond perhaps. Meanwhile, the sisters were looking at her as if they expected some sort of response to their revelations.

"I gave you leave to withdraw."

They looked at her steadily, with a stubborn determination she recognized as a McKay trait.

"You're not going to go away, are you?" Margaret questioned, with a kind of inevitable calm. People had this way of not doing what she told them.

She supposed that if they weren't going to leave, she could. So she smoothed her skirts over the wide panniers that supported them and sailed past the McKay sisters. At the door she threw them a cold, threatening look. She raced for the back stairs before they dared to follow.

She wanted very much to be away from McKays. Especially the McKay who expected her to provide him with sons. It was an inevitable consequence she simply had to avoid for as long as possible. Edwina was correct about fashionable marriages. She was almost grateful the girl had brought up the subject.

"Gone?" Jamie asked as he dabbed blood off his forehead with a silk handkerchief. The cut wasn't serious but it hurt like the devil. He glared at the butler. "What do you mean Her Grace is gone?"

"She left for Lacey House earlier this evening, Your Grace," the stone-faced butler informed him. "She said she wished to be away from your sisters."

"What?" Jamie demanded. He brushed some dirt off his coat. Not that the dust mattered. The coat was ruined, spattered with someone else's blood. "She's traveling at night?" What had those fool girls said to her? Or were they just an excuse to be away from him?

"Yes, Your Grace."

"God's death! Doesn't she know how dangerous the roads are. It's a hunter's moon out there tonight. Easy pickings."

"The roads are dangerous?" Edgware piped up. He was seated on the staircase. He'd staggered over to it and plopped down after he and Jamie had dashed the last few yards to the house, a pair of ruffians on their heels. "The *roads* are dangerous?" he repeated, a bit wild-eyed. "Lord, man, the streets aren't exactly safe. I never thought I'd be attacked in Mayfair. It's as if those bully boys were waiting for us. They certainly seemed intent on more than robbery."

"Yes." Jamie rubbed his bruised jaw, paying little heed to Edgware. His mind was on his wife's leaving.

"Clever of you to keep a knife up your sleeve, Pyneham," Edgware went on admiringly. "Pistols do ruin the set of a man's coat. Too bad I lost m'sword gaming. Odd sort of wager, I told Lake, but he said he wanted the thing. Odd to see him at my club at all, and playing for such low stakes. Trying to get on the good side of his new brother, I suppose. Won your sword, too though, didn't he?"

"What?" the distracted Jamie asked. "Yes. Yes, he did. No matter, I'm not very good with the thing." Lacey

House, eh? Damn. How was he supposed to get the girls married from some mouldering ruin in the country? Well, there was nothing for it, he supposed. He looked at his disheveled young friend. "Go to bed, Edgware," he commanded. "Find him somewhere to rest," he told the butler. "Then report this to the watch."

"Yes, Your Grace."

He considered the cut on his head, the bruises and the soreness in his side that might very well have been a cracked rib. He and Edgware had been accosted by at least a half-dozen serious villains meaning business. That lot had wanted blood as much as money. It was a good thing several stout footmen had appeared on the scene to chase them off.

Jamie put the incident out of his mind, more concerned with Margaret's flight. He knew he shouldn't have stayed out so late. He should have stayed with her tonight. He should have put his own marriage in order before worrying about his sisters' prospects.

It was two in the morning and Jamie was tired and sore from the fight. The romantic thing to do would be to jump on his horse and ride after his wife. He wanted a hot bath and a good night's sleep. He'd go after his wife in the morning.

13

"*I won't ask* why you felt compelled to marry so suddenly," Adam Bartlett said as Margaret took a seat in his office.

It was early in the afternoon. She'd arrived back at Lacey House late the night before. She'd been dreading questions from Bartlett, but if he wasn't going to ask for explanations, she decided not to give any.

"But." He rested his hands on a pile of papers and peered at her with the bemused amusement which reminded her of the Adam she'd grown up with.

It coaxed a smile from her. "But?"

He gestured with a twitch of his firm chin. "But why is Huseby following you around like a beaten puppy. A beaten mastiff puppy?" he added.

Margaret glanced behind her to where the big lad, his

wrists poking out of his ill-fitting livery, lingered by the office door, looking repentant and watchful.

"I'm sorry, Your Grace," he proclaimed, not for the first time. He'd followed her to her chamber door when she stepped out of her coach. He'd been waiting outside it for her this morning. He was, indeed, following her like a mastiff puppy. She hadn't the heart to send him away.

She nodded reassuringly to him and turned back to Bartlett. "It's a long and complicated story," she told the steward.

"With some connection to your marriage, I think," he said. "There was quite a bit of excitement here a few days back. The dowager told me to mind my place." His expression reverted to its usually closed mask, but he let the mask slip for a moment more when he said, "I was worried for you."

His words warmed her, made her long to throw her arms around him and draw out the boy she remembered. The boy her sister loved, who was brave enough to love a duke's daughter. Unfortunately there was no place for that boy in the world they lived in. So she only acknowledged his concern with, "Thank you. I've had adventures, but all is well now."

"And His Grace? Is all well with him?"

It was Huseby who replied, stomping forward to announce, "His Grace. Ooh, he's a wicked cove she's married, Mr. Bartlett. Wicked. When word came from London she'd married 'im, I knew right enough it was my fault. I never meant for Her Grace to— Ouch!"

Margaret had gotten up and kicked the young giant in the shin to get his attention. "Hush," she ordered, ignoring her aching toes. "You mistake who I married," she told Huseby, speaking slowly and firmly. "You're confused because the names are similar. You will not speak about my husband as if he was a—"

"Highwayman," Huseby supplied before she could think of a more diplomatic word.

It was a struggle to keep from kicking him again. She couldn't fault the lad for his honesty and devotion. But for the sake of the Pyneham title, if nothing else, Jamie Scott's past had to be buried.

The devil with the title. She couldn't stand the thought of any man doing a brief dance at Tyburn Tree for the sake of a few pounds despite the laws of church and state. As for Jamie's crimes against her . . . she'd brought them on herself, and she'd work them out with him herself. Somehow. Or at least keep herself at such a distance from him he'd soon forget her existence.

"Enough. Peace, Huseby," she said. "His Grace is *not* a subject for discussion." Her glance took in Bartlett as well. "Understood?"

Bartlett shuffled papers. Huseby limped back to his spot by the door. Neither attempted to pursue the subject.

"Good," Margaret acknowledged their obedience placidly. She took her seat once more. To keep up her facade of calm she studied the painting on the wall behind Bartlett's desk. It was of an autumn hunt scene, full of horses and dogs and piles of storm clouds on the horizon. Frances, she recalled, loved riding to hounds. She, on the other hand, always felt sorry for the foxes, useless vermin though they might be.

"Will the duke be taking up residence at Lacey House?"

Bartlett's neutral voice brought her attention back to present concerns. "What? I don't know. I doubt it," she said. "No. Definitely not. He prefers town life. I'll be saf— staying here."

"I . . . see." Bartlett made some notes. "Does General Lake approve of this marriage?"

She couldn't stop her sarcastic laugh, or the acrid, "What do you think?"

Bartlett looked at her with concern in his dark blue eyes. "I think," he told her, "that you have transferred the danger from yourself to your new husband."

Margaret's heart sank at hearing one of her secret fears spoken aloud. "I know," she said. "I didn't mean to." She'd gone off with an ill-formed notion of finding a protector and created a more volatile situation instead. She wasn't sure what to do about it. Except . . . she did have one idea. "What if," she suggested, "we play the game by Lake's rules for once?"

Bartlett leaned forward. Voice low, he asked, "And what rules might those be?"

"Why, with no rules at all," she answered with grim humor, but her voice equally low. She trusted Bartlett, and she trusted Huseby, but she'd had all too much proof of spies in her own house in the past. Speaking softly, she went on, "I'm sick of being civilized, Adam. I'm sick of being worried to death. Of being bullied and blackmailed, as well. I'm finally determined to do something about it."

Bartlett cocked his head, curious, but offering no comment.

"What if," she suggested, "we plant a spy in Lake's household?"

"A spy?"

"An informer." She nodded emphatically. "If he can do it, so can we."

There was a thoughtful silence, before Bartlett said. "I know. I already have."

"Really?" she asked, delighted at Bartlett's show of cunning. "When?"

"When you disappeared, of course. I thought Lake was involved at first. I sent off someone I trust to seek employment in the Lake household, but I haven't heard back as yet."

Margaret wanted to talk about Frances, to share her hope that they might soon hear from her sister. But, of course, she couldn't discuss Frances with Bartlett. Despite Lake's treatment of her, Frances was his wife. She would always be Lady Frances, and Adam would always be a servant. The gulf was vast and deep, and there was no need to remind Adam of it.

She rose instead. "Let me know the instant you hear anything."

"Of course, Your Grace," he replied, blank-featured and formal.

She gave him a polite nod and went out, Huseby trailing behind. In the hallway she was nearly bowled over as the butler rushed up to her.

"Your Grace." Dominick was breathless and flushed with excitement. "There you are!"

She grabbed the butler's arm. "What? Another fire?"

"Your Grace, His Grace has arrived, in a coach! The dowager in her coach. Womenfolk . . . everywhere!"

"Oh," she said, heart sinking. No more than a few hours in her home and here were her problems already catching up with her. All of them, sisters included. She sighed, and said, "Gather the household in the rotunda to meet His Grace. "I'll join you there."

"We have to be nice to you," Edwina said as all four sisters followed her along the first-floor gallery. "Jamie said so."

Margaret pressed her lips together and ignored the comment. Samantha, usually the most talkative of the pair, hadn't spoken so far. Margaret supposed she should be grateful. Except that the blonde girl kept looking at her in thoughtful, brooding silence instead of at the family portraits hung in gilded frames along the gallery walls.

Upon his arrival Jamie had given her one sad, puppy-like, reproving look, ushered in his whole clan, and settled down to chat with each and every servant. Margaret waited for a few minutes before trying to slip away, nursing emotions that ranged from odd pleasure at the sight of her husband's slender form to annoyance at the sight of her husband's slender form. She'd hoped he'd callously take her money and leave her in peace. She didn't know what to make of his sudden appearance. Whatever his purpose in coming to Lacey House, she did her best to unobtrusively get out of his sight as quickly as possible.

Jamie's attention had been on her the instant she moved to leave the room. He broke off his conversation with Bartlett to signal the girls. She was immediately surrounded by young McKays. "They'll keep you company," he told her. "We'll talk later."

She smiled stiffly and quickly decided having the girls with her wasn't such a bad idea. "I'll show you the house," she'd told them.

So far, the tour had been less than a social success. Lacey House, built in the Palladian style by her grandfather, was the pride of the Pyne family. The McKays, however, weren't acting as though they were particularly impressed by all the ducal grandeur. The McKays, she supposed, were too busy nursing hostility toward their Jamie's doxy to be impressed. And probably tired from the journey, as well, she decided.

She ignored the hostile older sisters to concentrate on the younger pair. She found them casting furtive glances of mixed awe and apprehension her way. The combination unnerved Margaret. She knew she wasn't an awe-inspiring sort of person. She supposed the girls must think she was some sort of evil witch who'd put a spell on their brother and disrupted their lives.

As she realized that the McKay girls were probably more confused about the recent doings than she was, all her resentment at them melted away. After all, she wasn't the only one affected by her marriage to James Scott McKay. It was high time she stopped feeling sorry for herself and did her duty by her new family. If there was one thing she was good at, she knew, it was being dutiful. If she concentrated on fulfilling her responsibilities to other members of the McKay family, it might help her keep her mind off her near-panic about having to deal with Jamie sometime in the near future.

She moved forward, putting a hand on each of the younger girls' shoulders, trying to put them at ease. "I have a book room," she told them.

Michelle looked up worshipfully. "A book room? Really?"

"A big one. Would you like to see it?"

"Oh, yes," Alexandra said enthusiastically. "Please."

Chatting amiably about schoolrooms and about calling her own Quaker governess out of retirement for them, Margaret guided the girls downstairs and along the hallway to the library. The older girls trailed silently behind. Within minutes Michelle and Alexandra were happily ensconced on a window seat, with thick leather-bound volumes on their laps.

Margaret said, "I'll have tea sent in to you later," and turned to leave. She hoped the other girls would take the book bait as well, but they followed her out of the library.

She didn't know what to do about them. She didn't feel

like walking a sulking pair of young women over the rooms and grounds of Lacey House. Besides, if anyone was entitled to have a good sulk at Lacey House it was herself and not the McKay girls. She decided on tea and cakes, so she took them to the morning room and rang for the butler. Samantha and Edwina lingered at the memento case beneath Great-Grandmother Margaret's portrait.

When Dominick arrived, she said, "Tea and a light meal, please. The young ladies are tired from the journey. Have my and Lady Frances's old rooms prepared for them." When Dominick looked shocked at her orders, Margaret couldn't help but give a hollow laugh. "Those rooms are hardly shrines. Tell your missus to give them a good airing so they can be put to use."

Dominick did his best to wrestle his features to impassivity. "Yes, Your Grace. And the others? The dowager and Lady Sophie have decided to spend a few days at the dower house," he added helpfully.

Margaret nodded at this information while she considered other household details. "We've plenty of spare bedrooms. The Blue Suite for my mother-in-law, of course. Michelle and Alexandra seem a bit old for the nursery, but I remember it having a lovely view of the gardens and the windows giving plenty of light. If they must read constantly there's no reason for them to go blind from it. Tell Mr. Bartlett to have the rooms decorated to the young ladies' tastes."

She didn't want to discuss Jamie's living arrangements. She didn't want to think about them, though she assumed he'd claim the grand bedchamber next to her own. Reserved for the ducal spouse, it was connected to her suite by a shared dressing room. She supposed ordering the connecting doorways bricked up might be something of a conspicuous gesture, though she had no other idea about how to deal with her husband's presence. She was left brooding about living arrangements as the butler left.

"She's being nice," Edwina whispered to Samantha. "Why is she being nice?"

Samantha didn't have an answer for her sister's question. She watched as the duchess dismissed the servant, then took a deep breath, squared her shoulders, and turned to face them. She was a beautiful little thing, Samantha observed as she looked past her preconceptions to study the woman her brother had married. It wasn't just the fine clothes or the detached, regal manner of her station that made her a beauty. In fact, she didn't have much of a regal manner, not most of the time.

Samantha was beginning to suspect that the duchess of Pyneham was regal and aloof because she and Edwina hadn't given her a chance to be anything else. She had to admit they'd been nothing but hostile toward Jamie's wife, thinking of her as a combination of doxy, duchess, and rival. It had seemed better to think of her as simply a source of income rather than as a person. Better to use the excuse of 'Jamie's secret love' as a shield against this intruder than to acknowledge that Jamie had brought a stranger into his life, and theirs. Jamie had a wife, and Samantha admitted to herself that she was jealous.

She admitted it because Jamie had made her. The coach ride from London had not been pleasant. When Jamie wasn't silently fuming, he'd lectured them. When he hadn't been lecturing, he'd been asking uncomfortable questions, such as where had their manners, good sense, and intelligence gone. When he hadn't been lecturing or questioning, he'd been issuing orders to treat his wife with the respect she deserved.

The object of Samantha's scrutiny went to sit on one of the yellow brocade chairs near Edwina.

"The painting," she said, uncomfortable under Samantha's steady gaze, "is of the first duchess. It's a bit shocking for a sitting room, I suppose," she went on, trying to make polite chatter. "But we're a shocking sort of family. *She* was, at least." A flicker of amusement crossed Samantha's features, enough to sting Margaret into adding, "I seem to be following in her footsteps. Of course, the gin was His Grace's idea. And the brandy was yours. It was brandy, wasn't it?" She looked placidly at Samantha, daring the girl to comment.

Samantha was a naturally pink, robust girl. Margaret got quite a bit of satisfaction in watching her pink cheeks go bright red. "Well . . . actually . . . yes. Jamie had said to keep you warm and . . . quiet." Samantha moved to the chair opposite her and took a seat. "Just exactly what was going on between you and my brother?" she questioned curiously. "It all seems so—"

"Shocking," Edwina contributed. She ran her fingertips along the top of the memento case beneath the painting. "What are these things?" There was a torn shirt, a pair of soiled gloves, and a lock of hair, and a cask of buttons, among other things.

"Not now, Eddie!" Samantha commanded with a sharp gesture. "I'm speaking to the duchess."

Edwina planted her hands on hips. "I'll ask questions if I like!"

"But mine are more important."

Edwina responded to Samantha's reasonable tone instantly. "Yes, I suppose they are. Do explain about the gin, Your Grace."

"Those things," Margaret replied, choosing to enlighten Edwina first as Dominick and a maid brought in trays with teas and plates of food, "are some souvenirs from King Charles's day. Love tokens and such," she explained. She pointed at the portrait. "She was the king's mistress and never let anyone forget it. My favorite," she added, "is the cracked royal seal on the bottom shelf." Edwina leaned down to look as Margaret went on. "It apparently got lost in the sheets one night. History is mum on why King Charles had it with him or what they were doing with it. A new one was made before this one was found. Great-Granny kept it as a memento."

By the time she finished speaking, the servants had left. Edwina came to sit by her sister. Margaret took her cup while she considered how to answer the elder sister's question. The girls were now talking to her instead of around her, which was an improvement, she supposed. She found herself tempted to fall into more than just surface conversation. Loneliness and isolation had driven her to all sorts of insane behavior lately, but sharing confidences didn't come easily to her no matter how tempting it might be to unburden herself to someone. Still, she felt she owed Samantha an explanation of some sort.

"Well," she said after taking a sip of tea, "I met your brother early in the spring on Hounslow Heath. It was—"

There was a knock on the door, and Dominick entered without waiting for permission. "What?" Margaret asked him.

"His Grace, Your Grace, wishes to see you immediately. In your bedchamber."

Margaret could feel all the blood drain out of her face as her heart gave a frightened lurch. Jamie? In her bedchamber? What did the man want with her in her bedchamber? Why hadn't she sent for the bricklayers when she'd first thought of it? "Dominick?"

He bowed and left before she could say another word.

As though, perhaps, Jamie had told him not to linger long enough for her to send a refusal. Which, she admitted as she stood, she would have done. Could still do, what with all the footmen loitering in the halls waiting to be useful. She hesitated, biting her lip nervously, until Samantha spoke.

"You best go. It wouldn't do to keep him waiting. He's been in a fearful temper these last few days."

Margaret sighed, acquiesing. She understood about men's tempers. There was no use making this any harder on herself and her household than it had to be. When her husband called, it was her duty to answer. No use getting a servant beaten because he brought the master an answer he didn't like. She nodded to the girls, then left them to their tea while she obeyed her husband's summons.

"Jamie in a fearful temper?" Edwina asked incredulously after the duchess left. "Our Jamie?"

"He's been in a temper with us," Samantha reminded her.

"You made it sound like he was going to beat her."

"Nonsense. Try some of this cold meat pie, it's delicious."

"She looked frightened. Odd. You're right, the pie's delicious. You know, there's something about that painting . . ."

Samantha glanced behind her. "A Lely, I think. Wonder if she caught a chill while posing. I would if all I was wearing was a bit of scarf and some jewelry."

"Jewelry!" Edwina put down her plate with a clatter. "That's it. It's the jewelry. Sammie, look at the earbobs! Don't you recognize them?"

Samantha was almost afraid to look. From Edwina's

tone she knew what she would see when she looked at the first duchess's ears. "God's death," she muttered, Jamie's favorite curse, when she did take a look. "Just what is going on between those two?"

"It's his token. She's wearing his token."

"I can see that," Samantha said irritably. "But why? How'd she get it? I mean, how'd he get it?"

"Maybe he stole it from her!" Edwina suggested in wide-eyed excitement.

"Stole it?"

"He's a highwayman, remember? What if," Edwina went on in a rapid whisper, "they met on the road. He robbed her, but she won his heart. He kept her earring as a good luck token. She couldn't get him out of her thoughts. He wrote her a letter. I think I overheard something about a letter. She went to him in disguise, but he didn't recognize her and, well, you know what happened. Then of course he had to marry her, but how could a highwayman marry a duchess? He had to abduct her and keep her hidden until Granny could arrange a wedding. It's all terribly romantic."

"It's the most ridiculous thing I've ever heard."

"It could have happened," Edwina defended her theory. "Just look at the painting. It is her topaz earring he's been wearing?"

"Then why didn't she mention it when we were on at her about his secret love?" Samantha couldn't remember everything they'd said, though it must have been enough for her to be mortified if the duchess ever brought the conversation up again, she was sure.

"Maybe she didn't think it was any of our business. Besides, they've been quarreling. A lover's quarrel," Edwina ended decisively.

"Of course it's our business. We're his sisters."

"And she's his secret love. Though I don't think she knows it at present," Edwina added sadly. "Jamie's been miserable for the last few days. I finally realize it's because of a misunderstanding with the woman he loves. And we'd better do something about it," she added, before Samantha could.

Annoyed at being upstaged by Edwina, Samantha said, "Eat your nuncheon."

14

As usual, her bedchamber was populated by several people. Unusually, one of them was a tall, slender male in buff coat and breeches.

It was the sturdily built figure of her maid Margaret chose to approach as she entered the room.

"You've laid out one of my formal riding habits, Maude," she said distastefully. "Why?"

Jamie, stepping between her and her maid, answered. "So you can come riding with me." He offered her a winning smile mixed with a no-nonsense lowering of his heavy brows. "It's a fine afternoon. I thought it would be good to see some of the estate. Your stablemaster was telling me about the fine bloodstock you keep. I wish to try them out."

Riding? In a habit and sidesaddle? Not to her taste at

all. She hadn't been riding in months. Not since having to attend a pheasant-hunting party with the Court last autumn. She didn't ride often at home; when she did she considered it a very private pursuit.

"Riding, Your Grace?" she asked, hoping she had heard him incorrectly. He was certainly dressed for riding, his light brown hair unpowdered and tied away from his long, narrow face.

"Riding," he said firmly. "I'll wait for you to change."

There was no point in arguing. If the new duke of Pyneham wanted to survey his property from horseback, she was the best guide he could have. He probably wanted her to present him to the tenants and estate workers as the new master of them all. She exchanged a resigned look with Maude, gestured, and the maid followed her back into the dressing room where the dresser was already waiting.

"You should have told me you don't know how to ride," Jamie complained as he lifted Margaret onto his horse.

"I can ride," she answered as he climbed into the saddle behind her. He gathered up the reins, putting his arms around her to do so. His reply was an annoyed grunt. She supposed his opinion of her might have been higher if the blasted animal she'd been perched precariously on hadn't dumped her into the shallow water of Holborn Brook as they were crossing the ford, then run off toward the stable. Blasted sidesaddle! And blast her own favorite mount for having a sore leg today!

"I can," she insisted. "Just not very well. Ouch," she added as the horse started off at an easy walk.

The day was sunny and warm, and the countryside was

green and full of birdsong and the droning of insects. She'd
acted as guide as they rode for several miles along paths
between bountiful fields, through woods, and across pas-
turelands. She explained everything she knew about her
lands as they moved along, including history, the neighbors, the village, and the nearby towns. Jamie asked intelligent questions, but spent much of his time praising and
testing the glossy black mare he'd chosen for himself from
the stable. While he'd enthused over his mount, she'd
clung for dear life to hers, and pretended it was the easiest
thing in the world.

Her mount had been a bit restive, but the ride had not
been really unpleasant until they reached the stream that
formed the border of the estate with the village common.
She didn't know what set the fool animal off, but one
moment she was guiding it across the brook, the next she
was in the brook, and she'd hurt her leg being thrown out
of the blasted sidesaddle! Now there she was, wet through
and in Jamie Scott's arms once more.

"You're making a habit of this," he said, as though
reading her mind.

She threw him an aggrieved look over her shoulder. "At
least this time I'm not drunk."

"And I'm not in a temper," he answered mildly. He
reached around and stroked damp hair off her forehead.
"How do you feel?"

"I'm fine. I really can ride," she added sheepishly, turning forward again. "Just not very well."

"I've noticed. I've been terrified you were going to fall
for the last hour."

Oh. She hadn't thought he'd been paying any attention
to her struggles to control her horse and her perch. "It's
just been a while since I rode like that."

"Foolish of you," he chastised her. "You should take a

more personal interest in the stables. I thought your head groom looked a bit surprised when we rode out. We'll be starting riding lessons as soon as your leg is better," he added.

His tone was so authoritative she didn't try to protest, just grimaced distastefully. He put an arm around her waist to steady her. She felt the warmth and strength of him at her back, through the soaked material of her riding habit.

"Relax," he suggested. "I'll have you home in no time."

She was soft and small, a fragile porcelain creature filling his arms, damp but not in the least uncomfortable to touch. Jamie held Margaret against him, appreciating her presence far more on this bright afternoon than he had on the long, farcical ride from the Red Bull. He appreciated not just the beauty of the girl, but the chance to play protector instead of villain. He wished she'd told him she didn't like to ride before they set off, but he admired the stoic stubbornness that kept her in the saddle longer than he'd expected.

They rode in silence for a while, covering the ground between the ford and the main approach to Lacey House at an easy walk. As the minutes passed slowly Margaret gradually relaxed into the rhythm of the ride and into his embrace. He didn't want to unduly tire the horse or break the mood, so he kept the pace as slow as possible. He didn't know what his new wife was thinking, nor did he ask. He simply decided to enjoy the presence of a lovely woman on a beautiful afternoon.

Eventually they entered the long drive up to the main house. The white stones thickly paving the drive crunched under the mare's hooves. The sound roused Margaret out of her reverie. She'd been very nearly asleep. Far from being perturbed by her husband's very masculine presence she'd been . . . comfortable.

"I've been thinking," he said. The sudden sound of his voice made her jump.

Jamie had to tighten his grip to keep her from taking another tumble. "I've been thinking," he repeated over her slight gasp. "About properly reforming both our ways."

"Reforming?" she said, voice full of confusion. She shot him a suspicious look over her shoulder. "Have I married a nonconformist, then? The vicar won't like that. We're strictly high church in Holborn Lacey."

"Reforming as in changing my ways," he went doggedly on. "And yours."

"My ways? I'm not the one who, well, you know, robbed people," she added in a very small whisper after first checking to see no one overheard.

He was gratified at her concern for his reputation. There were people nearby now that they'd reached the point where the roadway split. One branch led to stables and other outbuildings, the other to the Palladian portico that was the main entrance to Lacey House. Grooms from the stable were approaching, as were several people from the main house.

He leaned forward and whispered in her ear. "I'm not going to rob people anymore. What I thought I might do," he continued in a normal tone, "is set up a fund to help those who've been robbed, administer it out of your St. Martin's parish in London. Pay back a bit of what I've taken, give it to the deserving poor. What do you think?" he asked, hoping he didn't sound as hopeful for her approval as he thought he did.

Bartlett and Huseby were very nearly even with them as Jamie reined in the mare. Margaret could only look around in consternation at her husband as the others drew within earshot. She didn't know what to think or what to say. Or what he wanted from her for that matter. She couldn't disapprove of any charitable impulse. Nor had she realized his conscience was hurting him. Did he have a conscience, then? What did he mean by reforming *their* ways? She'd only been wicked once.

"I'm paying for being wicked already," she heard herself say bleakly, before she could stop the words from coming out.

Bartlett reached them before Jamie could answer, but she saw the hurt look in his eyes as he released his hold on her.

Bartlett reached out to steady her as pain lanced up her leg, both surprising and inspiring her. She fell into the steward's arms, hardly noticing her husband quickly dismounting.

"Your Grace, are you all right?" Bartlett asked worriedly.

Jamie tossed the reins to the big footman as his eyes met the steward's Jamie hadn't been too disconcerted by the look of intense concern on the man's face as Margaret had clutched at him. But the hostility he saw as they stood with Margaret between them did nothing to endear the man to Jamie. Bartlett's attitude toward his wife, Jamie thought with hostility of his own, was far too familiar for a servant. Margaret's hands clutched the cloth of Bartlett's coat front, her weight leaning against him. The man held Jamie's gaze for only a moment before concentrating on the lady.

"What happened, Your Grace?" Bartlett asked Margaret.

Jamie stepped forward before she could answer and scooped her into his arms. "A simple fall," he said tersely, starting purposely forward. Bartlett kept pace with him as he carried Margaret into the rotunda.

"Shall I send for the doctor, Your Grace?" Bartlett asked.

"Call for her maid," Jamie replied, knowing the question was not for him but answering it anyway. "She needs a hot bath and a good night's rest, nothing more."

The man didn't answer, but he did hurry up the stairs ahead of them, willing enough to obey an order once it had been given. At least he does as he's told, whether or not he likes the teller, Jamie thought as he followed after the steward.

Margaret didn't seem to notice his exchange with Bartlett. Her eyes were closed tightly, and she was biting her lower lip as though to keep from making any sound. Perhaps the fall had given her more than a few bruises? Jamie stroked her hair comfortingly as he took her into her bedchamber. A large group of women had already gathered to care for their injured duchess. He set her down carefully on the bed and the women scurried over to her instantly, getting between him and Margaret. He stepped backward toward the door and told himself he was leaving her in the best possible hands.

He'd witnessed her fall. She'd seemed all right on the ride back. This could be no more than a momentary weak spell. She was going to be fine, he told himself.

He was concerned for Margaret's safety, of course. But he also knew, as he turned and made his way to the long gallery that ran the length of the first floor, that he was once again going to be spending another long night alone.

"I'm sorry, Your Grace, but Mrs. Wendall insists on seeing you."

Margaret looked up eagerly at Maude's apologetic announcement. Her maid obviously didn't understand that any diversion was welcome at this point.

Samantha looked up from the book she'd been reading aloud and asked, "Who?"

"The vicar's wife," Margaret explained. She looked back at Maude. "Show her in. No, wait! Show her to the morning room. I'll meet her there presently."

"Are you sure you should get up?" The question came from Maude—and Samantha, Edwina, Michelle, and Alexandra. All four sisters were present at her bedside. The elder girls were seated on chairs, while the younger pair were perched at the end of the large bed. Their mother had left to take a nap only a few minutes before.

"Yes, yes. I'm sure I can make the effort," Margaret assured them, throwing off the covers. "It's time I tried my legs."

After four days in bed, Margaret wished she hadn't exaggerated her injury quite so much. If Jamie hadn't looked so hurt at her remark about doing penance, if she hadn't felt such a strong urge to reach out and comfort the man, she wouldn't have needed to make such a fuss when Bartlett showed up to help her off the horse. At the time it had seemed like a good idea. She needed to find ways to keep her husband out of her bed. The fact that she was feeling the urge to throw her arms around him and cuddle him was certainly of no help.

So she played the invalid. She'd almost become an invalid after seeing the local doctor Bartlett had insisted on calling the day after the accident. He examined the livid and genuinely sore bruises on her legs and backside and decided a cupping would help them fade. She was nauseated and weak from the loss of blood well into the next day. More penance, she told herself, for avoiding her conjugal duties. And more excuses, though Jamie didn't ask for them as she had expected him to.

What she hadn't expected was for her new family to rally around her to keep her company and cheer her up. The grandmothers, at least, left her alone, sending an occasional note of advice from the dower house.

She was used to being isolated and lonelier than ever during bouts of illness. The dowager disliked illness, always keeping her distance from sick people. The McKays, she soon learned, had no truck with isolation. They didn't even have much concept of privacy, and respect for her exalted station was a foreign concept to the girls. They were, after all, her loving sisters. It seemed they'd decided while she and Jamie were out riding that she wasn't a wicked monster. So they read to her and talked to her and fluffed her pillows and fetched her embroidery and made her laugh. She felt guilty for deceiving them, but was grateful for their company.

She was even more grateful for the shield they provided during Jamie's visits. With the girls around her like mastiffs dressed as maid of honor, she and her husband had no chance for private conversation. They also had no time for awkward, honest confrontation. Whenever he came, she always asked to be read to. The girls loved it, and it kept conversation at a minimum. The closest they'd gotten to communication, let alone any physical contact, in the last four days had been the assessing, discerning looks she occasionally caught in his eyes while she pretended her attention was totally caught up in Samantha's reading.

He'd visited first thing that morning and told them he was going to spend time visiting tenants today. With Jamie out of the house, she felt safe in getting out of bed to meet Mrs. Wendall downstairs.

She dressed quickly in a green-patterned sacque-backed

morning dress, then said to the girls, "Come with me, why don't you? It's time you were introduced to the neighborhood." The girls were eager to become involved in local society, seeing as they were "exiled from the *real life in town*," as they'd dramatically pointed out to her. They came with her gladly, probably as happy to be out of her bedchamber as she was.

Mrs. Wendall, usually that soul of courtesy, didn't bother with a curtsy when Margaret came into the morning room. Instead she shook a finger at her and proclaimed, "You've missed more rehearsals than I can count, Your Grace. I know you've been busy being married and all, but this neglect of the fete simply cannot go on. Young Alfred Huseby's insisted we use his sister, Eloise—though I wouldn't mind so much since she's sworn to mend her ways, if only she could act—as your replacement. Surely, Your Grace understands that we simply can't have Eloise playing Titania at the summer fete!" She stamped her foot on the floral-patterned carpet.

"Really?" Margaret echoed. She stared in awe at the vicar's mild-as-milk wife. "Mrs. Wendall, is that you? Replacement for what?"

The woman gestured sharply. "The play, *A Midsummer Night's Dream*. Your part, the queen of the fairies? How could you have forgotten?"

Margaret wanted to reply, *I've been raped—more or less—kidnapped—more or less—married—more or less—injured—more or less—and I am constantly threatened and blackmailed by a member of my own family. Do you really expect me to remember some stupid play?*

Instead she answered, "Oh. I'm sorry. I've been rather preoccupied recently."

"A play?" Alexandria piped up. "Really?"

"A summer fete?" Michelle chimed in. "May we go?"

"Shakespeare?" Edwina questioned enthusiastically. "I do so love Shakespeare."

"Titania?" Samantha asked thoughtfully. "Are you playing the fairy queen, Margaret?"

"I was," Margaret said. "But apparently—"

"Of course she's playing Titania!" Mrs. Wendall spoke up. "Who else?"

"Quite right," Samantha said soothingly. "Mrs. Wendall, is it? I hear you're the vicar's wife. Her Grace has been too indisposed to introduce us, but there's no need to stand on formality." She quickly made the rounds of the room getting everyone identified before going on. "Tell me, who's playing Oberon in this splendid little production of yours?"

Mrs. Wendell sighed at the question. "For lack of anyone better, Mr. Wendall has volunteered to play the fairy king." She threw a long-suffering look at Margaret. "You know what he's like."

The man was as kind as the day was long, Margaret knew, but he delivered his lines the way he did his sermons, stiff as a board and stodgy as pease pudding. "Yes," she agreed unhappily, "I know."

"I'm sure we can find someone more suitable," Samantha said sympathetically. "The thing for now is to get on with these rehearsals. Her Grace must just play catch-up while we all do our best to help."

Mrs. Wendell looked at Samantha gratefully. Samantha looked fondly at Margaret. Margaret looked suspiciously upon the girl's sudden helpful enthusiasm. Samantha was sincere, she thought, but she detected the gleam of cunning in her eyes as well.

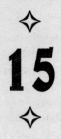

15

"*I'm going to* have her out of bed and on horse-back before the day's over," Jamie declared determinedly as he walked along the gallery toward Margaret's bed-chamber. From now on it was going to be his room as well, he'd decided. He'd done a great deal of thinking on his morning ride. He and his wife were going to have it out, he'd concluded, and they were going to have it out today. He'd been letting her hide from him in her room for quite long enough.

Along the way to Margaret's room he passed the por-trait of the last duke of Pyneham. He paused to look critically at the picture. Margaret's father had been a hand-some man, but there was no softness in his painted fea-tures. He looked both proud and headstrong. "You were a right bastard, weren't you?" Jamie murmured. "I've been talking to the servants, laddie, about how you raised your children. And no one has had a kind thing to say. My father might have been a wastrel and a fool, but at least he didn't scare his children to death."

While he was chastising the portrait of the dead duke he noticed Maude coming toward him down the long hallway. He turned to his wife's maid with a smile and doffed his hat. "Good-day to you, mistress."

The woman blushed, returning his cheerful greeting with a quick, bobbing curtsy. "Your Grace."

He bowed in response and watched her expression change to one of surprise. "I'm not nearly so graceful as your lovely mistress," he said. "Except when she's in the saddle, that is. Convey my greetings to her, will you, Maude? And tell her I'd like to see her in the stables in half an hour."

"Half and hour, Your Grace? In the stables?" The woman's expression was now one of confused concern. "Her Grace just told me she'd be spending the rest of the day in rehearsal."

"Rehearsal?" Anger at the girl's easy defiance flared in him. When he continued, his voice was deathly quiet. "What sort of rehearsal would this be?"

The woman blanched. "The play for the midsummer festival, Your Grace," she answered quickly. "Mrs. Wendall said that—"

"Theatrics!" Jamie slapped the flat of his hand angrily against his thigh. "She knows what I told her about playacting." He pinned the frightened maid with an angry look. "And just where might I find my wife?"

She gulped and pointed toward the opposite end of the gallery. "In the ballroom . . . Your . . . Your Grace."

Jamie turned and marched toward the ballroom, his hopeful, indulgent mood shattered by quickly growing annoyance. Wicked jade, he thought as he reached the ornate, gilded double doors of the ballroom. He'd drag her away by the hair if he had to!

He could hear voices beyond, masculine rumbles declaiming some sort of fancy speech. A play was it? And how many of the characters were handsome lads playing to a pretty duchess's vanity? Aye, vanity all right, and all the wanton tendencies he was determined to keep in check. They'd have no playacting in this house, he vowed in silent fury as he pushed the door open. Nor a disobedient wife.

He strode in and called angrily, "Margaret!"

She was sitting on the polished wood floor on a pile of velvet pillows, with Alfred Huseby's shaggy head in her lap.

She looked up, eyes wide with fright, as Jamie took in this odd scene. Huseby jumped with lumbering nimbleness to his feet to stand protectively over the seated girl.

Huseby?

The notion of having just caught his wife in a compromising position with her adoring oaf of a footman was ludicrous. So ludicrous Jamie's righteous anger was halted in its tracks. Not only halted, but run over in a stampede of bemusement.

"Margaret?" he questioned in a far quieter tone.

Looking around in complete confusion, he saw that the wide, high-ceilinged room was full of people holding blue-bound chapbooks and openly staring at him. All four of his sisters were in the room. Jamie had spent the last several days getting to know his neighbors and the prominent people of Holborn Lacey. Many of them were in the ballroom, including the vicar, his wife, and the doctor who'd looked at Margaret's injured leg.

Margaret did not stir from the pile of cushions. She stiffened her spine and dared her husband's reproof with a defiant look. *I will give you my property,* she thought. *My body if I must, is also yours. But this I will not give up. I will have my plays, and you may go to the devil if you don't like it. Go ahead,* she would have said had the room not been full of people, *beat me if you like. I won't compromise on this.* For all her bravado, inwardly she waited for him to shout, to strike out, to drive everyone away and make her the laughingstock of the county.

Instead, Samantha sailed up to him and said, "Oh, good, Oberon at last."

"Oberon?" at least a half-dozen voices questioned, including Jamie and Margaret.

Samantha, well aware of her brother's confused annoyance and her sister-in-law's stubborn reaction, had no intention of letting the situation get out of hand. She'd been watching the pair of them for days. She'd seen puppy-dog eagerness shining out of Jamie's eyes when he was looking at Margaret. She'd seen reluctant interest in the way Margaret avoided Jamie's presence. She was ready to admit that Edwina was correct in her theory about the newlyweds. Christ's blood, someone had to show a little sense.

"Oberon," she said, thrusting a copy of the play at her brother. "Who better to play Oberon and Titania than the duke and duchess of Pyneham?" He looked at the chapbook, then at her. As if she were mad. She hastily put herself between her brother and the rest of the room. "Shakespeare," she said. *"A Midsummer Night's Dream.* We need someone to play Oberon. The vicar's just awful. It'll make Margaret happy if you do it," she whispered. "And if you don't do as you're told, James Scott McKay Pyne," she whispered even more softly, but very fiercely, "I'll know the reason why!"

But for the cane and wrinkles, Samantha looked and sounded just like Granny McKay. Jamie couldn't keep the smile from his lips. "What was Huseby doing in my wife's lap?" he whispered back.

"He's Bottom."

"It wasn't his bottom, it was his head."

"He's playing Bottom. The one who gets turned into an ass," she explained in exasperation.

"Couldn't happen to a more deserving fellow," Jamie replied. He recalled the play now. It was the one about humans with romantic complications running around lost in a fairy wood where the king and queen of fairies were having a marital spat. The whole thing was about as nonsensical as the way he and Margaret were acting.

He shrugged good-naturedly and took the blue-bound copy of the play from his sister. He heard Margaret's nervous sigh of relief.

Samantha turned and had a few words with the vicar and his wife. The next thing Jamie knew the vicar had taken his hat in hand and left, throwing him a grateful look on the way out, and he was standing next to a man named Jordan. The red-haired Jordan had the role of Oberon's mischievous fairy accomplice, Puck. Huseby took his place back in Margaret's lap. Mrs. Wendall showed Jamie the spot where he was supposed to start reading, and the rehearsal began again.

Margaret ran her hands nervously through Huseby's hair, keeping her head bent over his prone form as Jamie began to speak. His voice was light and easy on the ear, tinted with irony and without the awkward pauses to be expected from someone unfamiliar with the play. But then she already knew the McKays were a disgustingly well-educated lot. And he'd been disgustingly polite the last few days. Polite and concerned and well read and responsible and guilty over his past crimes. Of course, now he could afford to be guilty, now that he had her money to support his family.

The thought rang falsely in her mind. It sounded petty. One didn't find fault with a man for taking care of his family. Unless, of course, she reminded herself, the man resorts to robbery and coercion to do it. Lake no doubt considered his actions as taking care of his family interests. Elevating one's family to a dukedom was certainly an admirable thing, even if cruelty and violence were necessary to achieve such a goal. One does what one has to do. Remember that, Margaret, she thought, as Jamie's voice played along her nerve endings in a most distracting, strangely enticing way.

People moved and spoke, reading lines over and over. Jamie was thoroughly bored with the whole rehearsal process within minutes. He and the rather truculent-sounding man playing Puck went over their speeches several times before Mrs. Wendall was satisfied.

"Once more," she finally said. "Then Titania and Bottom."

Margaret nodded. Her fingers continued to play through Huseby's hair as he and Jordan gave their lines. Jamie couldn't keep his eyes off the unthinking sensuality of the movement of her small, graceful hands. Her skirts, without stiff panniers to hold them out, billowed around her on the floor. The deep-cut neckline of the green and white dress was covered in a lace fichu, leaving only a demure hint of bosom showing. She looked innocent, but hardly otherworldly. Not like a fairy queen at all. Not like a duchess, either, and certainly not a common doxy from the stews of London. Who she was, he wasn't sure. What she was, was imminently desirable.

She also looked like a young woman with a great deal

on her mind. Her expression was far too somber for some-one merely concentrating on remembering her lines.

In fact, when it came time for her to speak, she had no trouble rattling off the words from memory while every-one else needed the script. She looked at Huseby and spoke earnestly of love and longing and besotted passion. The crowd held its collective breath at her words. Huseby looked worshipfully up into her eyes and sighed.

Dialogue from a play or not, it was more than Jamie could take. "We're going riding," he said, stepping for-ward to lift his wife up by the elbows. Huseby's head hit the floor with a thud.

Margaret turned a frightened look on him and said, "What?"

Jamie ignored Samantha's chuckle and Huseby's groan. "Riding," he repeated, hustling his wife to the door, her hand firmly clasped in his.

"But . . ." she began.

"Right now, Madam."

If there were shocked murmurs and sisterly laughter in the room behind them, he ignored the sounds. Privacy, he thought determinedly. His wife and he were going to have some privacy if he had to drag her to the middle of a barley field to find it.

"Riding?" Margaret asked as they entered the stables. "In this dress?"

"It's as good a dress as any," her husband replied shortly. He pointed at a groom. "Saddle my mare, and something gentle for—"

"Saddle Mushroom," Margaret cut him off. She pulled her hand from Jamie's grasp, sick and tired of being tugged about as though on the end of a leash.

"Mushroom?" Jamie asked.

"Mushroom?" the head groom asked at the same time, in a tone much more dubious than Jamie's.

Margaret lifted her pointed little chin stubbornly. Ignoring her husband she spoke to the groom. "He's my horse, isn't he?"

"Yes, Your Grace, but—"

"And I'll have my saddle as well."

The groom cast an alarmed look at Jamie, who was taking in the scene with his arms folded and his mouth slightly ajar. "*Your* saddle? The one you use when you ride alone?"

Margaret nodded emphatically. "It has been mended, I hope?"

"Oh, yes. Good as new."

"Then fetch Mushroom and have him and the duke's mare saddled."

The groom bobbed his head respectfully, though Jamie noticed that the older man then shook it worriedly as he walked off.

He looked at his wife. He was rather happy to see the bright stains of color in her cheeks and the defiant glint in her fine gray eyes. "Mushroom?" he asked again.

"It's his color," Margaret explained. "A sort of off-white raw-mushroom tint."

"I see." And he did as a big horse was led from one of the stalls. "Your saddle?" he inquired further.

Her saddle. Margaret almost shuddered as she remembered why it had needed mending, that Lake's spy had tampered with it to do her injury.

"It's not a sidesaddle," she confessed, and waited for her husband's reaction. He didn't say a word. He showed no signs of outrage, so she went on.

"It's not that I can't ride very well," she explained. "It's just that I've never mastered the sidesaddle." She looked down, scuffing her feet on the sawdust-covered stable floor. It stirred up memories as well as the warm wooden scent. "Frances was always wonderful in the saddle, but I never have gotten the hang of it—and it's not as if I haven't tried for years. But I liked to ride, so Adam—"

"Adam?"

"Adam Bartlett. The steward. Only he wasn't the steward when we were young." She gestured toward the silver-haired head groom who was supervising the saddling of the horses. "That's Bartlett's father. Adam taught me to ride. Not properly because I couldn't, and can't, but like a boy."

She looked back at Jamie, daring him to deny her use of any saddle but a proper, feminine, uncomfortable sidesaddle. The sort she'd fallen out of a few days before. "He doesn't approve now that I'm grown of course. No one does. So I try to ride properly for Adam's sake if nothing else, but mostly I don't ride at all."

"I . . . see." It was all he could think of to say on the subject.

It was the fondness in her voice for Adam Bartlett which disturbed Jamie, not her unconventional means of riding. He'd heard years of companionship and understanding and complete trust in the undertones of Margaret's voice. He remembered the steward's concern when he brought Margaret home from her fall. He recalled Margaret's eagerly leaning on Bartlett for support, and the man's hostile glance toward him. He wasn't jealous, not exactly. How could he be? It was a friendship of years, an inappropriate attachment left over from childhood, nothing more.

The horses were led out. Margaret gave him another of her furtively defiant looks as she bundled up her full skirts into a sort of pantaloon, then let the head groom help her onto her odd-colored horse. Jamie shrugged and vaulted gracefully onto his own spirited mare. They rode toward the woods in silence. Jamie soon stopped worrying about whether Margaret was going to keep her seat and began to enjoy himself.

At least he enjoyed the warm if slightly overcast weather and the fine animal he rode so skillfully. All his thoughts centered on the girl riding silently, but with far more assurance than last time, at his side.

"You're surrounded by people," he said at last, not one to keep his worries to himself for too long. "People who know just what to expect and what you expect from them." She didn't offer any comment. "You're good at this," he went on finally. "Though I must say, I don't like it."

"As long as no one sees me no one will know," she answered.

"I wasn't talking about riding, but your talent for not talking." He took time to rub his thumb along his jaw, studying the protective hunch of her shoulders before he went on. "You use silence to hide, Margaret."

Stung, she looked at him sharply. "Do I?"

He nodded. "Aye. That and playacting. It took me a few days, sweet, and a few gossipy servants," he admitted. "But I see through you now. I'm told it's how you hid from your father's black moods. And now it's how you're hiding from me."

"I . . . see." She couldn't deny his words, though they devastated her. She wasn't much good at denying truth, just ignoring it. All she could do was try not to show any fear even though she was suddenly stripped of her only defenses. The question was, what would Jamie do with the knowledge?

The one thing she could do, she did. She turned Mushroom around and headed back toward Lacey House and people. He was right about her being surrounded by people as well. All she could think of was to use as many people as possible to shield herself from encounters with her husband.

The woman was panicking, quietly, stubbornly, but panicking just the same. Jamie didn't understand her reaction. Why couldn't she simply talk to him instead of running away? He'd given her a perfect opening in a perfectly private spot. She'd reacted by turning tail and running.

"Oh, no you don't," he declared, catching up to her. He grasped Mushroom's bridle and brought both horses to a halt. They sat in the middle of the road, looking at each other as he blurted out, "Margaret Pyne what is the matter with you? Can't a man get a decent argument without you haring off like a frightened rabbit?"

"Why would anyone want to get into an argument?" Margaret shot back before she could stop the words. "Decent or otherwise? Tell me what you want and I'll do it. What more do you want from me?" she asked helplessly.

Mushroom nickered nervously. Jamie's mare dropped its head and began to nibble on grass grown up between the ruts in the road. The clouds shifted slowly overhead while they looked at each other in charged silence.

"What do you want from me?" Jamie asked finally.

"Never to have seen your face," she answered, surprised at how deep the anger was in her; surprised at how much the words needed to be said. She was even more surprised at how easy it was to look into his eyes and reveal the pain her heart was carrying.

"To have the memory of your letter without the knowledge that you're no better than any other man," she told him, almost choking on unshed tears. "To have my maidenhead and my freedom back would be nice as well." Though she wasn't sure what use she'd been making of either when she'd had them. "You can't give me any of those things, but that's what I'd have if you could give me anything."

"And I'd have you back safe on the pedestal I'd put you on if I could have my way," Jamie admitted. "But what's done is done, and we have to learn to live with each other." He held a hand out toward her. "Stop running from the facts, lass, and come be my wife."

The earnestness of his words, of his open expression, tempted her—to know him, to be with him, to trust him. Perhaps she could build some sort of life with Jamie, since he seemed determined to force himself and his family on her. Perhaps he and his family were just what she needed to free her from the devastating weight of her isolation. Perhaps, but how could she work on finding a measure of happiness for herself while Frances remained in danger? Until her sister was safe how could she ask anything for herself? She had to be responsible, to do what was right for *her* family.

Aware of the romantic futility of his gesture, he dropped his hand. He wished to God he'd never kept his promise to write the girl a letter. He wished he hadn't fallen into the low ways accepted in his former profession. He wished he hadn't acted like the low-living, desperate scoundrel Margaret had every reason to hate. He tried to think of some way to make peace.

"You can have your bloody playacting," he said at last. "I've given in on that already, you may have noticed."

She ducked her head, then looked up at him through thick golden eyelashes. "Yes," she admitted. "I noticed." When she spoke he smiled at her. His smile drew words out of her against her will. "Thank you."

"You might as well know now that I can be talked in to almost anything. And," he added, gentle and serious,

"I'm not sorry I wrote the letter, Margaret, just for what happened afterward. If we could start again, I'd gladly go back and do so."

Don't do this to me, she wanted to beg him. Don't charm me. Don't make this worse by making me care for you. Oh, Jamie, she thought desperately, please let me keep your tarnished image to hate instead of making me see you as a man I could love.

Instead of answering him, or lingering in the roadway to hear more, she nudged her horse in the sides and set off again. He kept pace with her.

For a moment, when she'd thanked him, she hadn't looked haunted. There had been a smile for him in her eyes. And more words wanting to get out, he was sure of that. She held back and rode on instead, trying to avoid him again. He decided not to push her further right now. He hoped she'd think about what he'd said. He'd let her have her silence for the rest of the ride. He'd have words with her, and more, when they were finally alone in bed. Tonight.

16

The woman standing on the top stair of the entrance portico looked as if she were frozen in place, eyes staring in blazing anger. It was Jamie's mother. Margaret shot a confused glance at her husband; all she got was an amused smirk in reply. No footman was nearby, probably driven away by the wrathful McKay woman.

"Hello, Mummy," Jamie said, doffing his hat politely. "You're looking—"

"Well!" the woman interrupted stridently "Well, indeed! I'm mortified." She swiveled her angry gaze to Margaret. "Simply mortified. Have you no decency? None whatsoever? Showing your ankles to the countryside!"

"And her husband," Jamie added, looking down at Margaret's foot. "It's a very nice ankle, Mummy."

"And wantonly pressing your thighs against the flesh of a—"

"Horse." Jamie hastily cut the tirade off again. "It's all right, Mummy," he added. "Mushroom's a gelding." His words came out in a laconic drawl.

Margaret saw the imp of mischief dancing in his big brown eyes when they looked at each other. It wasn't possible to stifle her answering giggle.

"Well!" the frigidly stiff woman on the stairs said. "Well! If the master of this house countenances such loose behavior, I've no idea what will become of my girls. No idea at all."

Margaret didn't know what to say. Not that she had a chance to say anything, as Jamie's mother ended with, "Really!" and gave a huffy toss of her head. She stomped toward the wide doorway at the top of the stairs.

Margaret stared after her in consternation as Jamie leaned close and said, "Welcome to the family."

She met his conspiratorial smile. "Is she always—?"

"Always." He nodded. "But only with people she cares for. She's accepted you as her daughter, Margaret. God help you," he added with a teasing grin.

"I'm glad," she answered sincerely as a warm glow radiated through her.

She scarcely remembered her own mother. Her relationship with her father had been formal at best. Jamie's family was certainly anything but formal.

His brown eyes sparkled with an amusement that warmed her. She said, "Your mother's very—"

"Odd," he finished for her. His mare tossed her head restlessly. He stroked her neck, running his hands soothingly along the sleek, muscular neck.

Margaret's gaze was drawn to the movement, fascinated by the gentle strength in his big, bony hands. The man fascinated her. He fascinated and confused and amused her and complicated her world. It was rather like being in love, she supposed. She didn't want to act as if he weren't there. She was torn between wanting to run away and wanting to invite him into the morning room for a cup of tea and a long chat. Or . . .

She attempted to close her mind off to any other possibility and looked away from Jamie. She tried to deny the pang of longing for him before it caused her to behave like a rational woman in love. Life wasn't rational. Their situation wasn't rational. She knew she had no business wanting him, no business thinking they had a chance for a normal marriage. What was a normal marriage, anyway? Perhaps she should ask Frances's opinion of the subject if she ever saw her sister again. She must think of Frances. But she knew with sudden clarity that she had never stopped wanting Jamie. She was terrified by the knowledge. She had no idea what she was going to do about it.

As she modestly gathered her skirts around her and dismounted, she caught sight of Adam coming down the steps toward her. His presence offered her distraction from the things she couldn't have. She left Mushroom with a groom and hurried up the stairs to meet him.

Jamie's heavy straight brows drew down in annoyance at the sight of the approaching steward. A moment before, Margaret had been smiling at Jamie in a distracted, fond, almost hungry sort of way he didn't think she realized she was doing. He'd found her regard disturbing. It was as if they were drawing close to each other, if only for that brief moment.

Now she was gone again. Bartlett again. The steward, the doings of Lacey House, too easily drew his wife away from his side. She was proving a difficult woman to court, he thought in exasperation. Tonight, he vowed, as he watched Bartlett sketch a bow, then escort his wife into the house. Tonight there would be no one but him in her bed to offer any distraction.

With Margaret out of sight, Jamie rode away from Lacey House. His intent was to give the horse some proper exercise; his mind was on the future.

"You've heard from Frances?" Margaret asked anxiously as soon as they reached the privacy of Bartlett's office.

His voice was as bland as ever when he answered. "Heard? No, I haven't heard from Lady Frances."

Margaret was sorry for the way she'd phrased the question, but knew it was better to let it go. "What have you heard, then?" she asked.

He passed a piece of paper to her. She unfolded it and read the message aloud.

"Have arrived at Lake residence, your honor, having been hired as replacement to head footman. Have yet to come into contact with the lady of the house. Must proceed cautiously with inquiries. Am writing, your honor, with intelligence of General Lake's current disposition. Which is, sad to say, ugly. His mood is as foul as his language and his treatment of his servants. His habits are lewd and scandalous, even behind the closed doors of his own dwelling. But it is not of his licentious behavior that you have charged me to report. I fear the man is plotting still against Her Grace the duchess, though I have no proof of what such plots might entail. I have seen him in furtive company with several of his cronies and other persons of low character and estate. I fear the worst.

I charge you, sir, have a care for Her Grace's safety at
all times.

  Your obedient servant,
  John Lodge.

After wading through their spy's formal spate of words,
Margaret looked back at Bartlett. "He has a future as a
novelist."

Her words brought an amused twinkle to Bartlett's
dark blue eyes. "Of the more lurid sort," he said. "I trust
his loyalty," he added. "And his powers of observation."

Margaret tossed the letter on the steward's desk. "I
wish he'd observe my sister. Where is she? How is Lake
treating her?"

"Give the man time, Your Grace," Bartlett said soothingly. "And have a care for yourself," he added. "Lake's
not through causing trouble. Lodge made that plain
enough."

Margaret sighed. "I know." She considered telling him
about the threats Lake made to her in London, but found
it was too personal to share with anyone. "I know," she
went on, "that you're keeping a close watch on all the
staff. I'm satisfied to trust to your vigilance and John
Lodge's information."

Bartlett frowned. "Pretty, reassuring words, Your
Grace, but I'm not the one in need of them. I don't believe
my vigilance will do you a bit of good if Lake's really
determined to harm you."

She stamped her foot, a most satisfying petulant gesture. "Adam Bartlett, I'm attempting to soothe your—"

"I know," he cut her off. The steward had disappeared
momentarily; it was her friend who went on. "You've
spent your life making sure no one shoulders any worries

but you. Does His Grace know about any of this? Does he know why you went looking for him in the first place?"

She glanced away from his worried face. As she twisted her fingers together nervously she answered, "Yes, of course. Some of it. A little. I don't—"

"You don't trust him, do you?"

She looked down at the floor and sighed. "You need a new rug, Adam. This one's terribly worn."

"Maggie!"

"I don't know! Perhaps. A bit." She brought her gaze back to Adam's. "I don't know."

He shook his head, and his face changed, expression going blank again. "Be careful, Your Grace," he warned. "You're in as much danger as ever. Be alert, protect yourself."

Margaret nodded at his grave advice. "Don't worry," she replied, an idea occurring to her as she spoke. "I know at least one thing I can do to help myself."

The woman was driving him mad. Insane, Jamie thought. He rode along the edge of the home woods, letting the horse and his mind wander without much guidance.

The day they met, he remembered, he didn't think either of them was ever going to keep quiet enough to get on with the robbery. Now he couldn't get two words out of her.

"I'm trying to be patient," he said aloud to any birds or trees that might have a mind to listen. The black mare's ears flicked attentively at the sound of his voice. Besides the dusty thud of her hooves on the well-worn path, Jamie's irritated voice was the only sound. "Do you think," he continued, at least having the horse's attention, "that I would have chased after her from London with the entire family in tow if I didn't mean to make a proper marriage of it? Has the silly wench considered me for a moment? Have I ranted at her for running away? Have I forced my attentions on her? Have I told her even once that I care for her? Well, no, I haven't but I've been rather hoping she'd notice." He ran a hand down the length of his long jaw. "Perhaps if I tried talking to her with a scarf wrapped around my face she'd pay more attention to me," he concluded. She'd certainly found it easier to communicate with a total stranger than she did him. He'd been safer to her as Jamie Scott.

"The woman's a lackwit," he complained. "A scared silly lackwit with the most beautiful face and form I've ever seen."

No, not a lackwit, but she was scared silly. And not just by the idea of being wed against her will. There was something more she was hiding—he could feel it. She'd run to him because of some threat. There was a reason behind Bartlett's blank-faced protectiveness. A reason behind Huseby's and Dominick's and Maude's doting anxiety for their mistress. They were a wary lot, not yet willing to take their new master into their secrets. Oh, he could pry a few facts about the past from the underservants, but the ones who knew anything really useful were loyal to no one but their little duchess.

And Margaret herself? Where the devil did her loyalties lie? Not just with herself, he was willing to wager. But would her loyalties, her affections ever belong to him along with her person and properties?

As he mulled over this sticky question, the path emerged from the woods. From this point it led through ripening fields and pasture land to several of the estate's larger tenant farms. The day—a hot one despite being gray and overcast—was growing late. A large barn loomed up to his left beyond a stand of young apple trees. He heard the drone of bees in the air, and saw the busy insects at work among the yellow and white flowers lining the edge of the path at irregular intervals. Jamie took in the quiet scene and found it relaxing.

The first shot took him by surprise. By the second, he had a pistol in his hand while his eyes searched for the telltale puff of smoke. The shot had come from nearby. Poachers, he thought riding cautiously back toward the woods. Bold, brash poachers to be after Lacey House's game in the middle of the day. He was wondering how many they were and what sort of weapons they were using, when a third shot rang out from behind him. The musket ball hit him in the head before he had time to turn.

"His Grace has not returned yet," Dominick told Margaret as she came down the last steps from the grand staircase into the rotunda. It was long past nightfall. The earlier clouds had been blown away. Stars shone through the windows set in the domed ceiling far above where they stood.

Margaret had dressed very carefully for dinner. Her dress was lavender brocade and silver-shot lace, carefully designed to show her small waist and the creamy globes of her breasts to perfection. A dusting of rice powder had been added to her breasts to make them seem even creamier. She wore her topaz necklace and pearl bracelets. Her hairdresser had worked for two hours to turn her hair into a high, spun-gold confection. Her face was as carefully and subtly painted as if she were attending a Court function. She didn't normally keep such formal state at Lacey House, but she'd responded to an impulse to look beautiful tonight. She'd sent word to all the girls to dress for dinner, and she'd been especially careful with her own toilette.

She knew why she wanted to look beautiful tonight. It was a foolish thing to do, and she fully expected to be teased by her sisters-in-law. She more than half-hoped her appearance would please her husband. She wanted him to think she was beautiful, and be damned to the consequences.

"I'm afraid His Grace will not be home for dinner," Dominick added apologetically. "Though he has sent no word."

Disappointment twisted around her heart. Twisted so hard she could hardly breathe, just stand and stare at the butler.

His Grace will not be home for dinner. How often had she heard those words when she was younger? And how often had she been relieved to hear them? It hadn't bothered her in the past to know the man in charge of her life was out hunting or whoring or drinking throughout the neighborhood. Or was off at the stirring of an itch for diversion, for months at a time. It hadn't hurt her in the past, why did it leave her aching and angry now?

Lord knew she was used to it. Why should a man stay at home when the wide world held all its pleasure for him to sample? Jamie had a taste for whoring. Her body had been remembering it all afternoon. Samantha and Edwina had told her how he left the family alone for long, worrisome stretches while they lived in London.

She raised her head proudly and looked Dominick in the eye. "His Grace will not be home for dinner? I see. He doesn't know what he's missing."

The butler's eyes swept over her, a faint smile tugging at the corners of his mouth. "No, Your Grace. He doesn't. Perhaps he lost his way riding," he offered hesitantly.

"When he's spent every moment he's been here on horseback?" Margaret countered. "I doubt it."

"As you say, Your Grace. However, The dowager and Lady Sophie have arrived from the dower house," he went on. "They've already been seated in the dining room."

Sweet Jesus! she thought. Not them. Not when I'm dressed for seducing my own husband and he doesn't bother to put in an appearance. Grandmother will tease. So will that crafty old besom, Lady Sophie, if half of what the girls say about her is true. She would have run her hands distractedly through her hair if her hairdresser hadn't stiffened the structure too much to make the gesture worthwhile.

"If they're there we best not hold dinner up any longer."

"That's probably not advisable, Your Grace," Dominick agreed. "The other ladies have also—"

"Fine," she interrupted. "You may begin serving. Tell them I have a headache," she added. She walked away without waiting for his acknowledgment.

She went to the book room and stood before a glass-fronted case along one wall. Enough moonlight shined in through the tall windows for her to see. She'd been meaning to visit this cabinet since her conversation with Adam. Despite her preoccupation with her looks she'd remembered to bring the key with her. She opened the cabinet and brought out a slender cherrywood case. She took it with her and returned to her room, putting it under a stack of pillows on her bed before calling Maude and the others in to undo all their careful handiwork. She would wait until she was alone before she opened the case.

There was a gun room in the house, of course. Blunderbusses and fowling pieces and a large assortment of other hunting guns were locked securely away in specially built cabinets. Margaret knew how to use a hunting rifle, but somehow it didn't seem practical to keep one next to her bed at night. She'd promised Adam to have a care for her own safety. And she certainly wanted to protect her privacy. What better weapon to have to hand, she'd decided, than one of her father's dueling pistols.

Once alone in bed with them she'd be safe. Safe from Lake's minions. Safe from anyone who might consider venturing in through the connecting dressing room as well, she thought grimly. Just let anyone, assassin or wandering husband, try to enter my bedchamber tonight.

"Let the bold highwayman see what it's like when someone sticks a pistol in his face," she grumbled angrily beneath her breath. "He'll be in for a shock."

Having a gun in her hands made her feel safe. It would certainly look formidable. She should have thought of keeping a pistol by her pillow long since. She would keep one there from now on.

Tomorrow, she vowed, she'd start learning how to use it.

17

Jamie had only a vague memory of struggling through a moonlit field as he followed his horse to an empty shed. It was an odd memory to wake up with, though he did wake up in the shed at the first light of dawn, with the black mare nuzzling him anxiously.

"Couldn't you have gone for help, lassie?" Jamie asked as the mare's velvet muzzle butted his shoulder.

He sat up and touched the aching spot at the edge of his hairline. A bit of crusted blood flaked off on his fingertips, but there didn't seem to be any real injury. His hard landing upon falling off the horse probably caused him more damage than the near-spent rifle ball.

He climbed cautiously to his feet, but soon found that he had no more injury than cramped muscles from sleeping on the hard earth of the floor, a slight headache, and a

powerful urge to answer nature's call. He'd felt worse after
many a night at the Red Bull or being chased across the
heaths by a band of constables.

He led the horse outside, relieved himself, then
mounted and rode slowly back toward Lacey House.

Margaret tucked the cherrywood box under her arm and
stepped into the gallery. Huseby stood across from her
door. As the big lad came smartly to attention, she
couldn't help but notice he looked a bit worse for wear. He
had a bruised cheek and a nearly-swollen-shut black eye.

"Sweet Jesus, lad, what happened to you?"

The footman looked both sheepish and pleased by her
concern. His fair skin blushed bright red as he said, "It's
Eloise."

"Your sister hit you?"

"Oh, no, Your Grace! We were at the tavern in the
village last night, and, uh . . ." He faltered.

"Well?"

He hesitated. "Uh, well, you see . . ."

"Did you get into another tavern brawl?"

He grinned. "Yes, Your Grace."

"Defended Eloise's honor, did you?"

"Dubious though it is," he responded. "There were
some gentlemen stopped in—a bit in their cups already.
Tried to hire Eloise's services, and a fine price it could have
brought her. But she wasn't having any of it. She's determined to be a good girl."

Margaret noticed the footman sounded a bit regretful at
his sister's reformation. She made a mental note to find the
girl some decent employment that would help with the
family income. "Yes?" she urged Huseby to continue.

"There was a bit of a dust-up," he reported proudly.

"Eventually the toffs declared they'd had a 'demmed fine brawl' and took themselves off elsewhere."

"Thank goodness for that." She would have hated to have her people accused of attacking a group of gentlemen. The facts had little influence on the law where members of her own class were concerned.

"Yes, Your Grace." By the look of satisfaction in the lad's good eye she could tell he'd given as good as he'd gotten last night.

She shook her head and said with indulgent affection, "Get some rest. Recover from the adventure a bit."

He bobbed his head obediently, and she left him in the hallway. She met Jamie on the stairs. It was obvious from his disheveled appearance what he'd been up to as well.

So, her husband had been among the group of carousing gentlemen, and Huseby had spared her feelings by not telling her. His rumpled clothing and bruised forehead told her all she needed to know.

"You swine," she said, raking her eyes coldly over the duke of Pyneham.

Jamie could see how Margaret might have the wrong idea about his appearance. "Swine?" He rubbed his stubbed chin. "I spent the night in something like a sty," he admitted wryly.

"Of course you did," she agreed, cool as ice.

Before he could get out another word, she raised her chin proudly and walked past him down the marble staircase.

Jamie let her go. He hurried on to his rooms, passing a battered-looking Huseby as he went. He got a quick explanation out of the big lad. It certainly explained Margaret's jumping to an obvious conclusion. He'd get cleaned up and then explain what really happened to him.

It was only as he reached his own door that what she'd

been carrying registered. "A pistol case?" He glanced back toward the staircase. "What the devil would the woman want with a pistol case?"

Margaret pointed the gun at the cabbage rose twenty feet away and fired. The lead ball went far wide of its mark, and the puff of smoke made her cough. The blasted pistol was heavy, and her arms ached from holding it steady against the recoil. She remembered the casual way Jamie Scott had waved his pistols about when he'd stopped her coach. He'd made it look easy.

He was a swine, she reminded herself as she set about reloading first one, then the other, of the brace of silver-inlaid pistols.

A carousing swine. A brawler. A . . . a . . .

"A man," she complained and raised the gun again.

Changed, shaved, and refreshed, Jamie followed the erratic sound of pistol shots to the bottom of the rose garden. There, surrounded by an acrid cloud of gunsmoke, he saw his wife. This end of the garden held a low brick-rimmed fountain and a trellis arbor twined with red and white roses. Margaret was standing with her back to the fountain. From where she seemed to be aiming, Jamie deduced she was attempting to do some lethal damage to a group of red blooms arching out from the right side of the trellis. Either that, or she was firing blindly into the woods behind the garden. What she was doing was surprising enough. He was more interested in why.

As he approached her, boots silent on the springy summer grass, he noticed the dress she was wearing was shimmering, sky-blue satin. He stopped to take in the incongruous scene for a moment. Lord, but she was lovely, with her pink cheeks flushed and her golden hair gleaming in the morning sunlight. With the white gunsmoke floating around her like a fairy veil, she seemed like a vision out of a dream.

A dream with a gun. He chuckled to himself. He'd dreamed of the girl in blue often enough since their first meeting on the road. The dream was his now. The reality was far stranger than anything his dreams had conjured. Stranger and more enticing. Reality was also in need of a few shooting lessons before she hurt herself with those blasted pistols.

Margaret didn't drop the gun when a pair of long-fingered hands settled around her waist, though it was a near thing. She gasped from the startle, but the touch was too familiar to cause panic. Warm emotion rushed through her, momentarily chasing away all thought.

"Hello," Jamie said, lips close to her ear. "It's the swine."

"Mmrr?" was her incoherent reply.

Having Jamie's arms around her was familiar, oddly comfortable, and stimulating, even without the horse. It was better, actually, without the rocking motion of the horse or rain or wet clothes. It wasn't so distracting. Or perhaps it was more so. She didn't mean to relax back against the firm support of his chest, or to make a sound that was a cross between a purr and a contented sigh. It just happened.

She came to her senses almost immediately and straightened to stiff-backed attention. His low chuckle informed her he'd noticed her lapse.

"Swine."

"As I said. I really did mean to come home last night," he added. "Huseby told me about the fight. I wasn't there."

"Ha!" She knew she should let the subject go. Where he spent his time was his business. She told herself she was just outraged at his profligate behavior. She had only herself to blame if she'd dressed for him and waited for him and hoped . . .

"I . . . fell off my horse."

"Of course you did."

"Even the best of riders have the occasional accident," he reminded her.

Before she could pull away, Jamie dropped his hands and the subject. He asked, "What have you got there?"

She didn't bother with the obvious answer as he plucked the pistol from her hand. "Hmm," was all he said after a brief examination of the sleekly curved weapon. After a drawn-out silence while she watched him warily over her shoulder, he added, "You're standing wrong."

"What?" Margaret asked, spinning to face him, annoyance forgotten.

"And a dueling pistol's made to be used one-handed."

"I know that," she answered. "It's heavy."

He nodded. "A dueling pistol should be custom-fitted for its owner. This ten-inch smoothbore is a work of art, but hardly suitable for a woman."

"I know. I've used fowling pieces which are perfectly proper, but . . ." Her words trailed helplessly off while he continued to look at the pistol.

He touched the silver mounts and filigree work on the stock. "Bit fancy for a dueler. Distracting."

He ran a finger down the length of his jaw while she waited for him to demand just what she thought she was doing. His reasonable, professional attitude was more worrisome than the outrage she expected.

"Can't have you using this."

"I—"

"I'll order something to fit your hand from my gun-smith."

"What? You will?" she blurted out in surprise at his unexpected offer. "You'll give me a pistol?"

The faintest of smiles quirked up his wide lips as he nodded. "Something suitable for a lady."

An odd, affectionate warmth spread through her. It was the first offer of a present from her husband. A gun. How nice. It was the practical sort of gift she could really appreciate. "Thank you."

His expression was serious, his brown eyes questioned her, though he didn't ask for any explanation. "We'll work with what we have for now, shall we?" He handed the gun back. "Hold it with only your right hand. Like that. Yes. Let's begin, shall we?"

"A shooting lesson?" Margaret asked, flushing with pleasure. "You're going to give me a shooting lesson?"

"If you want it."

"Yes, please," she responded promptly, her smile wide with eager delight. Odd, she thought, that I find the man disarming in the presence of firearms.

Jamie had his suspicions about why his wife wanted to learn to use a pistol. He connected her sudden interest in guns to yesterday's 'poacher,' and stories he'd heard of burned bed hangings, and the reason she'd come looking for him in the first place. He didn't yet know why danger surrounded her, or who was responsible. She'd mentioned vandals, not assassination attempts, the one time he'd asked for an explanation.

He suspected Adam Bartlett knew all. But the girl

trusted her steward and didn't trust her husband. He knew it was time he did something to build trust between them if he ever hoped to get the truth out of her. He was going to need the truth if he was going to protect her properly and stop the people responsible before they hurt her.

So he swallowed his curiosity for now and moved closer to her. "Pistol shooting's a bit different than hunting."

"I've noticed," she grumbled.

"But the skills are the same," her reassured her. "First." He put his hands on her waist again. After a moment of relishing the simple act of touching her, he turned Margaret so she was standing sideways from the roses she'd been shooting at.

"You want to present the smallest possible target to an opponent," he explained.

"I do?"

"Yes. In your case that's not a very large target at all, my pretty little duchess." She felt the brush of his lips as he kissed the top of her head. This slight touch sent a shiver through her. "A dueling pistol," he went on, "is made for accuracy at fairly close range without having to worry too much about sighting. It's built for speed."

His hand slid down her right arm until his fingers circled her wrist. He guided her arm up and helped her hold it at the proper angle and support the weight of the heavy pistols. Every slight movement brought them closer together. His every movement made her more aware of his presence, large and male and commanding. For once, knowing that a man was in control of a situation didn't bother her. Well, it bothered her, but not in the usual ways. Instead she was fascinated by the feel of the lean muscles of his forearm stretched next to hers. She was so fascinated by the sensations spreading through her from every point where they touched she hardly noticed the weight of the gun.

Jamie's forefinger rested on the pulsepoint of Margaret's wrist. He stroked the spot with an almost imperceptible movement and felt her blood quicken. For a moment he forgot exactly why he was holding her in such an odd fashion. He just knew he liked it.

Margaret blinked. Why was she staring at a cabbage rose through the sight of a gun? Why was it so hard to breathe? What were his fingers doing? What were his thumbs up to? One of them was rubbing her stomach, wasn't it? It felt good.

"Gun," she said, desperately trying to pull her mind back to the reason they were standing so close together in the rose garden.

"Gun?" he asked. His breath tickled across her ear.

"Mmmp," she answered. Margaret's voice was strained to a squeaky whisper in the effort to concentrate. "Wh-what happens next?"

Next? Next? Jamie wondered frantically. Take her in your arms and kiss her until you're both wild with need. Shouldn't that be what happens next?

"What?" he said. "Next?"

The hand on her waist slid up to rest just below her breast, tantalizing by not quite touching. The heat radiating from his palm seared through the material of her dress, through boning and undergarments, leaving her skin sensitized, aching to be set free to his touch.

"What do I do?" she asked. "With the gun?"

He didn't give a damn about the gun, but a lesson was a lesson. He bent his head until his lips brushed her ear. She let out a breathy gasp as he said, "Don't hesitate. Don't think." Sweet Margaret, this is no time to think. "Just point and shoot."

She rested against him, tender, soft, pliable, her lush little body a perfect fit with his. He was acutely aware of her every breath, every movement, the scent of her sunwarmed hair, the irregular rise and fall of her breasts, the change in tension of her arm and shoulder. He almost didn't notice the roar of the pistol when she fired it.

A fat red rose exploded in a crimson shower of petals. Its dying scent mingled with the acrid reek of gunpowder. Jamie and Margaret stood in silence for a moment while the echo of the gunshot faded away.

Then they laughed. Together, full of pleasure and surprise, they laughed all their grievances away.

She dropped the pistol on the ground. He turned her, enveloped her in his arms. As their lips met, a voice in the back of Margaret's head implored her to stop, to remember Lake's threats. But she couldn't stop. Passion came in this unexpected place and time and she refused to fight it. The setting was incongruous, but the emotions were not. She was dying inside, weighed down by too much guilt and responsibility. Jamie's touch, Jamie's kisses took her out of herself, offered her respite and healing and life. With Jamie it wasn't playacting; everything about him was so real.

His hands moved over her back, down her sides and up again. She trembled beneath his touch, soothed and aroused all at once. Their mouths joined over and over, tongues playing together, then parting. His mouth found the pulse in her throat and the tender spot where her breasts swelled above the neckline of her dress. She ran her hands through his hair, tugging out the ribbon holding it at his neck. She tangled her hands in its soft brown waves and brought his head back up. She looked him in the face—saw passion and hunger and hope all reflected in his great, wide eyes. She kissed him with sudden possessiveness, gently on the lips at first, then the hollows of his prominent cheeks, his eyelids and temples, even the length of his heavy, straight brows. His face was freshly shaved, smooth to the touch, all length and angles.

"Jamie." She whispered his name between one fiery kiss and another.

"Ah, Maggie," he answered. "My Maggie."

She touched him, hands fumbling blindly through layers of brocade waistcoat and linen shirt to the taut-muscled flesh beneath. "I want to see you," she confessed. "To know how a man is made. Now," she pleaded. Before responsibility and uncertainty caught up with her again.

He held her face in his big hands. Her eyes were bright and devouring, flashing from quicksilver to storm cloud intensity.

His own control was slipping fast, but he found the will to ask, "What? Here?"

"Yes," she answered eagerly.

His eyebrows shot up in surprise. "On the lawn?"

"Why not?" she countered. "It's our lawn."

He cupped the soft globes of her breasts in his palms. Weighted under satin he still felt their response. He was growing hard and needful, willing to abandon caution at her urging. She hooked her arm around his neck. Drawing him closer, she rubbed against him, her nipples hard against his chest, pressing herself against the pulsing heat at his groin. The searing contact rocked most of the sense out of him.

"All right," he agreed, fumbling with a lacing on her gown. "Right here and now if you like." But caution and seemliness warred with eagerness a moment longer.

He looked around, squinting in the glare of sudden bright sunlight. The rose arbor was nearly as public as the lawn. A nearby stand of oak trees surrounded by a trimmed boxwood hedge caught his attention. Private enough, he decided.

"What's that?" he asked.

Margaret drew her attention away from the burning need coursing deep inside her long enough to answer. "That? It's called the Dance. Grove's been there forever."

He ran his hands over her, slow and sensual. A husky, pleased sound was drawn from the back of her throat. The Dance, he thought, willing to wager the village youths had met there to dance on May Day since time began. They wouldn't be the first couple to lie together in yon grove. "Come on." He led Margaret hastily toward the trees. "We'll have shade enough to keep our bare bums from burning in the sun."

Margaret giggled at such a practical consideration. She showed him the gap in the ring of bushes and the small grass-and-moss-covered patch near where a spring bubbled up in the center of the oak circle. "It's called the fairy ring."

She giggled again as she undid buttons and laces with shaking fingers. "Fairies," she said to his hot, questioning look. "Oberon and Titania."

"What nonsense," he muttered, but there was laughter in the sound. "You are a fair queen of fairies," he said when her clothing was at last a blue puddle at her feet. Her hair tumbled unbound around her shoulders and down her back. "A gold and perfect creature." He reached out to touch her on breast and throat, smooth thighs, and the golden mound between. The touch of his tracing fingertips was both intimate and tentative.

She shuddered with pleasure. She reveled in the dual sensations, both achingly sharp and meltingly warm, brought by his touch.

"I, on the other hand," he said as he stepped away from

her, "am no Oberon. More like a skinny mule, perhaps?" He held out his arms and turned around, fully naked, thoroughly aroused. "Don't tell me you like what you see?" he asked once he'd finished his turn and caught sight of her flushed, enthusiastically smiling face.

She nodded. "Indeed I do." In fact, the rush of pleasure at seeing him sang through her senses. He was so slender, his rangy form dappled in sunlight and shadow, his wavy hair stirred by an errant breeze. She felt wanton and totally unashamed to be naked in front of him. Perhaps her behavior was wrong, perhaps all this nakedness was improper, but it felt right. She was so sick of hiding her true self behind masks on top of masks. She hoped Jamie felt the same. He obviously saw no beauty in his long, lean, wiry form. He was more vulnerable than she. Hence, he was braver to reveal himself to his wife's judgmental stare in the full light of day.

She said, "You'll do fine for me. Jamie." She stepped closer to him across the scented grass. "My Jamie." Kind, patient, astonishingly upright, slightly dour, but hot-headed, hot-blooded. And romantic fool enough to risk highway robbery and passionate letters as well. "My Jamie."

His chest was lightly furred, a paler shade than the rich brown of the hair on his head. She ran her hands over him, shyly at first. His eyes closed slowly, his breathing grew ragged and his skin more flushed as she progressed farther down his torso.

"Do you like this?" she asked. "May I touch . . . you . . . there?"

"Oh, yes." He moaned. "Please."

She did. Her fingers circled stiff flesh. It was hot velvet, pulsing a little, responsive. His hips jerked convulsively as she stoked rhythmically from brown-furred base to sensitive tip.

"You like it," she declared happily. "Shall I do it some more?"

Jamie's eyes snapped open. "No."

As he drew her hand away her expression changed from shy delight to disappointment. He lifted her hand to his lips, kissed each finger in turn. Then he drew her down on the ground. The scents of moss and clover rose up around them. He lay beside her, caressed her hair, her face, moving with a sense of wonder "I like your touch," he whispered. "But I don't want your hand, love. I want you."

Margaret's hands landed on his shoulders. The nails, neatly trimmed to fine points, bit into his bare flesh. "Me? Specifically . . . me?" she questioned. She was aching with wanting him. Aching and on fire, and he was her husband. There was nothing she could deny him. Nothing she wanted to deny him, but she had to know. Did he want to spend his passion with the first woman who came to hand? Or was it her he wanted? The question hadn't troubled her when they had come into the oak grove, but it did now.

He was panting, holding hard on to the last shreds of control. He kissed her, hard and possessive. "You," he ground the words out fiercely. "God's death, woman, how could it be anyone but you? You're my wife."

He touched the tensed silken muscles of her thighs, coaxing, easing her legs open. He watched her face, full of need and acceptance as he raised himself over her. "It won't hurt," he promised. "I swear it won't hurt."

It didn't hurt. The sensation as he slid deep inside her was exquisite. It was the complete opposite of pain.

He wants me, she thought. The words burned away, her other senses demanded she leave thought behind.

She was aware of the earth beneath them, yielding,

fragrant, cradling their straining bodies. Light mixed with shadow moved across them. Bird calls and the scratch of branches tossed by the breeze blended with the rising urgency of their breathing. Jamie filled her, moved inside her with sleek, insistent power. She held on to him, rising to every demanding stroke. She felt as if she were racing toward the sun, seeking consuming fire. She pulled his head down to her, captured his mouth with hers. Their tongues joined, small, passionate sounds passed between them, intimate gifts, lifegiving as air.

When Jamie's hard-muscled body tensed, then ground in quick, hard jerks against her, she felt herself mingling with him and the pure engulfing fire of the sun claimed them both.

18

"It didn't hurt, did it, love?" Jamie asked anxiously.

Margaret's eyes focused slowly on Jamie's face. "No," she answered in a stunned whisper. "Not at all."

"Good." He kissed the pink tip one breast. It was still ripely swollen and sensitive. She made a small, shocked noise. "Oh, no," he said, addressing the peaked nipple. "I'm not starting anything now. I couldn't if I tried."

"Oh, good," Margaret said. He heard her yawn. Jamie yawned in turn. The temptation to cuddle with her under a tree for a nice long nap was strong.

He closed his eyes and lay with his head on the lovely soft pillow of her breasts. He yawned again. Lovely girl, he thought as her fingers combed through his hair. Lovely day. Lovely, sated, delightful. It never felt this good before.

He sighed contentedly.

She said, "The midges are going to start biting if we don't move soon."

"Hang the midges," he mumbled into her breast.

"I'm supposed to see my secretary this morning."

"Hmmm." He held her closer.

After a short interval, during which he nearly dozed off, she said, "We have to rehearse . . . it's only a few days until—"

He sat up and glared down at her. "Are you always so *damned* dutiful?"

Her eyes took on a familiar, wary expression. "Yes."

He sighed and helped her up. "So am I. Loads of nonsense, really," he added, "taking the world so seriously." He went to their piled clothes. He pulled on breeches and shirt, then began passing bits of clothing to Margaret. It took a great deal of lacing and tying and pinning to get her looking halfway decent.

"You've the talent to be a lady's maid," she said as he straightened the tight-fitting bodice over her straining breasts. "Something you learned from your sisters?"

Jamie snorted. "Ah . . . no," he admitted without meeting her eyes.

"Somehow I didn't think so."

Was that a note of jealousy for a lass he barely remembered in her voice. He rather hoped so.

She was just one of . . . hundreds . . . dozens . . . a few . . . hundreds of women, she thought. She shouldn't have done this. She was just one of . . . No. He said he wanted *her*. It was her he wanted. And she wanted him. She'd ignored her sister's safety, perhaps her life, because she did what *she* wanted. She wasn't responsible at all. She'd let lust . . . If she was truly conscientious and caring she wouldn't be hungering after carnal relations with . . . with her own—

"Husband," she said and sniffed.

Jamie smiled down on her. "Yes?" he answered agreeably.

"And children," she added, almost oblivious to his presence as a sudden revelation almost overwhelmed her. It shaped itself into words and she said, wonderingly, "I want children."

"So do I, love."

"I'm two and twenty," she went on. "Of a good age to be a mother."

"Twenty-three is not too young for a man to be a father," Jamie added. "Let's try for as large a crop as my parents managed, shall we, love?" He started to take her in his arms, but she jumped out of his reach.

"No! I can't! I dare not! You don't understand!"

His first reaction was annoyance. Then he saw the fear, even as she tried to mask it. What did she fear? Childbirth? Lord knew it was a frightening enough experience. But if a ninny like his mother could . . . Or did she fear having his children? Did she fear diluting her near-royal bloodline with his. No. The look on her face reflected an old, deep terror.

Something to do with her vandals, he'd wager. With attempted murder and her furtive conferences with the steward?

He took her by the shoulders. "Now, lass," he began, "I need some answers from—"

The sudden rustling in the hedgerow behind sent Jamie spinning to face a possible enemy. Damn! He'd come to the grove without a weapon. "Who's there?" he called. His muscles tensed, ready to spring forward to attack. "Stand and de— What do you want?"

Bartlett appeared at the opening in the hedge. The dark-haired, somberly dressed steward reminded Jamie of a rather diffident crow as he stood before him, head cocked slightly to one side. Bartlett held a large folded square of paper in his hand. Huseby loomed up behind the steward. The footman peered toward Margaret, all curiosity and loyal protectiveness.

"What do you want?" Jamie asked them.

"A letter, Your Grace," Bartlett replied, holding out the cream-colored square of paper. It bore a heavy, red wax seal.

"A letter?" Margaret moved swiftly around Jamie. "From Frances?"

"For His Grace," Bartlett said, handing the letter to Jamie. "From the king."

"From the king," Margaret repeated. Her ridiculous surge of hope died in confused disappointment. Of course it wasn't from Frances, she chastised herself bitterly.

Jamie stared at the royal seal. "For me?"

"For the duke of Pyneham," Bartlett summed up succinctly. "The messenger said you were to comply immediately with His Majesty's instructions."

"It took us some time to find you," Huseby chimed in. "We were a bit worried, what with finding the guns and all, but then I remembered the Dance and how it's a nice private place for a couple to have a bit of—"

"Huseby!" Bartlett, Jamie, and Margaret shouted as one.

The thin, embarrassed silence was broken by Margaret, asking, "What would the king want with His Grace?"

Bartlett looked significantly at the letter. Jamie broke the seal and fumbled the stiff sheet open. He read through the flowery, formal language, then gave them the gist of it. "I'm summoned to Court. To Hampton Court Palace.

Today. I'm to present myself tomorrow afternoon at the latest."

"You'll have to ride like the devil to do that," Bartlett said.

Jamie chuckled. "Well, if Dick Turpin could make it to York . . ." But then, some highwaymen were more legendary than others, he added to himself. And Turpin was hanged in York, wasn't he?

"You?" Margaret blurted out. "You're summoned to Court?" He nodded. "Just you?"

He gave her another nod, though this time his brows lowered with annoyance. Her disbelieving tone rankled.

Margaret was so upset by the implications of Jamie's singular invitation that her wits scattered for a moment. She'd done as the king wished. She'd married. Not his cousin, true, but she had married. She was still out of favor. Lake was not. If she was out of favor how could she ever influence anyone to help her against her popular brother-in-law?

"Damn," she muttered. "I should have married the king's cousin."

"What?" Jamie stepped closer, eyes glinting with anger. "What?" he repeated.

Margaret moved instinctively away from danger, closer to Bartlett. "I meant . . ." She fumbled. "if the king wants to see you, and alone, and I'm to stay here . . . I . . . he must—"

"Still be displeased with Her Grace," Bartlett filled in for her. "The king's ill will preys on her mind. Being exiled to the country is difficult for a lively young woman. She meant no offense, Your Grace."

Jamie glared at the steward. He misliked Bartlett's loyally stepping in to defend Margaret's incautious words. He misliked the lurking watchfulness of both steward and footman, as if they were alert to any sign of violence toward their precious duchess. And what would they do, pray, if he chose to discipline his wife for her foolish tongue? Or even to politely ask her to explain herself? He could feel the late duke's ill-tempered ghost hovering behind their attitude toward him, and he misliked the comparison most of all.

Margaret cast an annoyed glance at Bartlett. Adam knew she infinitely preferred life in the country to the Court. She should be the one to defend herself from her own stupid words instead of letting him lie to try to protect her.

Jamie gave her a demanding look, but she held her tongue. She had no intention of discussing her personal problems in front of the servants. She especially had no intention of bringing up a subject Adam Bartlett found painful while he was present.

"We'd best return to the house," she said. "His Grace has much to do in a short time. "Huseby," she added as she walked past Bartlett—out of the Dance, away from intimacy, back to dutiful reality. "Inform the duke's valet he'll be leaving for Hampton Court within the hour."

Within the hour? Jamie thought, watching his wife walk briskly away. He looked around him in confusion, hardly able to believe their closeness had shattered so quickly. Could the royal favor be that important to her? He found that hard to believe.

"What is wrong with the woman?" he questioned in fierce frustration. Today. Within the hour. He would have to leave without having it out with Margaret. The summons was clear about the king wanting his new duke at Court sooner than immediately. Any delay would be noted with Germanic displeasure. The day he met Margaret, Jamie recalled, the king had made her cry. He couldn't like anyone who made her cry, but he'd best go dance attendance and try to charm on the man. It was his duty, for Margaret and Pyneham's sake, to make King George and all those in power his bosom companions and trusting allies.

"Within the hour," Jamie agreed as he followed after the others. "Aye. Get it over with. Then come home swiftly and find out what's eating at your wife."

The garden in moonlight, white stone walks easing down to the silver ribbon of the Thames, was beautiful. Jamie strolled along a lane dotted with topiary figures and wished he had Margaret by his side. He wondered what she thought of Hampton Court. The old palace wasn't as grand as her own Lacey House and wasn't in very good repair, but Jamie liked the gardens. They held a sense of history as well as river views and numerous turnings and niches suitable for any activity from solitary contemplation to privy conversations to full seductions. His mind was more on conversation, since his companion of the moment was not his lovely wife, but Lord Jeffrey Edgware.

It was Midsummer Night, and a full palace revel was in progress. A masque was being performed in the audience chamber. A fireworks display was competing with the moon to light up the night. The colorful blossoms of light were lovely, but Jamie didn't think they could do much to upstage the moon.

"I wish I were home," he said to Edgware as they stopped by a low wall overlooking the riverbank. He'd been there earlier in the day, accompanying the king on an expedition to feed the swans while discussing politics.

"Missing your delightful duchess, are you?" Edgware asked.

"Yes." Midsummer Night. He wondered how the village play was going. He imagined Margaret's lovely form in a beautiful, diaphanous gown, her gray eyes bright, her whole being transformed by the part she played. At least, he thought with some satisfaction, Reverend Wendall could be trusted not to appreciate her charms, even if his Oberon was less than satisfactory.

"I miss her too," Edgware said with a laugh. "Unsuccessful as my suit was, I hold no grudges."

Edgware one of Margaret's suitors? It dawned on Jamie that she must have had innumerable suitors. A faint stab of jealousy gnawed at him. Had she cared for any man but him? He'd heard about the death of her betrothed at the battle of Culloden. Did she resent him because he was Scots? She'd never shown resentment of his ancestry.

The king had, at first. His Majesty had quizzed him on his relations and his loyalties. Thankfully his branch of the McKays was free of any hint of Jacobite leaning. It didn't hurt that Granny McKay was from a fine old English family, or that he'd had a completely English education. Seeing the chance for preferment from a duke, many a relation of Granny's spoke on his behalf. These were, of course, the same relations he'd not dared turn to when his family were in dire straights hardly a month before.

"The king favors you," Edgware said, interrupting Jamie's sour thoughts. "He smiled at the mention of your name today. I heard him say you were a sensible, well-spoken young man."

"Did he?"

"Yes. Damn, but I'm glad my tutor beat the German language into me."

"It comes in handy at Court," Jamie agreed. "I'm just glad you were here when I arrived."

"Hardly an accident," Edgware admitted. "Heard you were sent for, so I popped in to keep you company."

"Thank you."

"And to ask for your sister. The one with the fine eyes. Plays harpsichord."

"Edwina."

"Saw her at your wedding. Thought I might like to see her at mine. As the bride."

"Oh?" Jamie questioned with tight, brotherly suspicion.

Edgware went blithely on. "Suppose I should pay my respects to the cunning-looking blonde lass as well."

"Samantha."

"Man should make sure he has the right sister before making an offer."

"Really?"

"Oh, yes. I've set my fancy—honorably, I assure you—on Edwina. But I'm not one to rush into serious romance."

"I'm glad to hear it," Jamie drawled, relaxing a bit at Edgware's claim of serious intentions. He was supposed to *want* to marry off his sisters, after all. Edgware was swiftly becoming a good friend. He was sure Edwina could do far worse.

There was the sound of laughter and approaching feet on the loose stones of the walk. They turned from companionably watching the reflected lights on the river to wait for the approaching party. Five courtiers accompanied by servants bearing lanterns on long poles came into view. Jewels sparkled in the lamplight; satin and brocade mirrored the flash of fireworks overhead. Jamie recognized the tall, well-made figure of his brother-in-law as the group came to a halt twenty feet from the wall where they stood. The two ladies seated themselves on a marble bench and began exclaiming over the fireworks. The trio of gentlemen ranged themselves elegantly around the bench.

Edgware made a small, annoyed sound. He plucked at

Jamie's sleeve, urging him farther into the shadows. "General Sir Charles Lake," he said, using Lake's full title even though he sounded none too happy about seeing the man.

Jamie waited in curious silence and eventually Edgware continued, "Lake's a fine example of a man who chose the wrong sister."

"Is he?" Jamie asked, peering, with no great liking, at his brother-in-law. Lake was engaged in leering lasciviously down one of the lady's low-necked gown. She didn't appear to object. "Which one's Lady Frances?"

"Neither."

Jamie wasn't surprised. "Lake's a fashionable husband, I see."

"Of which you don't approve. I'm glad," Edgware added. "Her Grace deserves better than Lake. Even if he doesn't think so."

A prickling of danger raced up Jamie's spine. "Tell me," he said, voice low and edged with hard suspicion.

Edgware pitched his voice equally low as he answered. "Lake's hungered after Margaret since she was fifteen. Her father was a second son who met Lake in the army. When he unexpectedly inherited the title, he brought Lake home with him. Lake watched the girls grow up and took a fancy to the elder. She wouldn't have anything to do with him, so he took the younger girl. Funny thing is, Frances is the more beautiful of the pair, and far more biddable. But it was Margaret Lake wanted. And still wants," Edgware warned.

"Indeed?" Jamie's terse question held a world of threat.

"I doubt your lady is aware of the man's continued attraction," Edgware told him. "But it's common knowledge in every gaming hell and bawdy house he gets drunk in. I suppose he'll see sense now that she's wed. He was friendly enough to you that night we gamed in London.

The betting book at my club had favorable odds for his challenging you to a duel before then."

Jamie rubbed his jaw. "Really?" He pushed himself away from the wall and out of the shadows. He approached the group, moving with a loose-limbed, predatory stride. He wasn't surprised when Lake glanced up and looked as if he'd seen a ghost.

He didn't suppose he could shoot Lake in the garden of Hampton Court Palace. He wasn't carrying a gun. He probably wasn't as good with a sword as Lake, and he saw no reason why the odds should be in the other man's favor.

The bastard had tried to kill me—twice if those coves in London were sent by Lake. Certainly the "poacher" was his doing. Jamie could see that much in his face. Lake's assassin hadn't lingered to see more than that his victim had fallen from the horse. Lake must have been gleefully awaiting the announcement of his demise while putting in an appearance at Court.

Jamie seethed with cold fury and indignation as he moved inexorably forward. Anger boiled up in him, but more for Margaret's sake than his own. Lake's seeing him as a rival and enemy he could deal with. It was the sure knowledge that Lake was also behind the "vandalism" at Lacey House that fueled his rage. This man had frightened his wife, he fumed. Frightened the woman badly enough to drive her into the arms of a wanted criminal.

Edgware's hand clamped around his arm like a band of iron. "You look like death on horseback," he whispered fiercely in Jamie's ear. "Move softly, Pyneham. Jealously is out of fashion."

Jamie turned his head at Edgware's warning. There was a ghostly quality about the young man's moonlit face. His intent, shadowed expression reminded Jamie of images of Death, and the hangman.

Be a pity to escape Tyburn for thieving only to end there for a case of just retribution. Imagine the fit Mummy would have. The errant thought, sounding very like Samantha's sensible sarcasm, intruded on his murderous plans. A permanently frozen mother-in-law would be a hell of a thing to leave his widow, he had to admit.

The image brought a calming balm of humor. There were more efficient ways of destroying a man than outright killing him, he reminded himself. He was, Jamie recalled, a duke. A slow, satisfied smile formed on his lips as several possibilities came immediately to mind.

"That's better," Edgware said as Jamie's smile became wider. "You've won the game. No need to get angry over the past."

As far as Jamie was concerned the game was just beginning, but he made no such comment to his companion.

By the time Jamie had himself under control, Lake's expression had warped back to bland neutrality. Jamie was sure they were equally aware of mutual animosity, but he stepped forward and said cheerfully, "Well met, brother!"

Lake's response was equally effusive. "Pyneham! I'm overwhelmed at the sight of you!"

I'll wager you are, Jamie thought. How much did you pay the fool who botched shooting me?

"Do you know Countess Laudale and Lady Ellis?" Lake gestured gallantly toward his companions. "Colonel Tolvere and Lord Haywerd?"

Jamie bowed over the ladies hands and murmured compliments.

"Oh, we've met the duke," Tolvere said.

"Well, I have not," Lady Ellis said. "But I've heard he's been brightening this dull place for *days*, Sir Charles," she added with a giggle.

"Ah," Lake said. "I'm behind on the gossip, being just arrived. Came to make your bow to his majesty, did you, Pyneham?"

"And a pretty bow it was," Haywerd replied for Jamie.

"He's been charming everyone," contributed Tolvere. "Amusing fellow."

"Becoming quite the royal favorite, aren't you, Pyneham?" The foppishly dressed Haywerd asked, with just a hint of malice.

"One strives to be pleasant."

The countess gestured coquettishly with her fan. "So pleasant that we shall be devastated when His Grace leaves tomorrow."

"Leave?" Lady Ellis asked in a high-pitched squeak. "Oh, surely not!"

"You've been here scarce a week," Tolvere said.

It felt more like a month to Jamie. All he wanted was to go home and resume the courtship of his wife. Resume protecting her as well, he realized with a cool glance toward Lake. For some reason, Edgware's hand landed heavily back on his sword arm. He forced a smile. "Good evening, brother."

"A moment," Lake said as Jamie started to leave.

Jamie tensed further as he saw the glint of calculation in the man's icy blue eyes. "Yes?"

"I'm holding a house party at Rishford Abbey starting the beginning of next week," Lake told him. "I'd relish your company, Pyneham. Time I got to know you better."

"I'd enjoy that," Jamie lied.

"Then you'll come? And you as well, Edgware?" he added, though his intense attention was all for Jamie's answer.

"I'll consider it," Jamie replied—and did, for all of three seconds. All he wanted was to get home and stay there, not walk into the lion's den. "Good evening," he said again, bowed to the ladies, and faded back into the shadows of the garden.

"Or so Mrs. Metford assures me," the dowager answered shortly.

"Henry Fielding will be at Metford House?!" Samantha crowed delightedly. "I can't believe it!"

"I just told you it's so," the dowager snapped. "What's the matter with you, gel?"

"*The* Henry Fielding!" Edwina gushed.

"He's only a magistrate. Come down for the assizes, I should imagine."

"He isn't *just* a magistrate," Samantha informed the dowager. "He is an *author*."

"Oh, *that* Fielding," the dowager scoffed. "Wondered why Lady Metford was having a ball in a magistrate's honor. Seditious rascal. Isn't he the one whose plays caused such a flap, Maggie? Maggie? Margaret, are you listening to me?"

Margaret was listening. She had noted every word of the conversation. She just wasn't particularly interested in the social life of the neighborhood at the moment. She stood by the morning room's garden door while lively conversation went on around her. She gazed toward the boxwood hedge and oaks of the Dance, and remembered her and Jamie's brief, timeless time beneath the sheltering trees.

"Yes," she finally answered her grandmother's strident question. "He must be the same one."

"How'd that scoundrel become a judge?" Granny McKay wondered.

"The usual way," the dowager replied. "Learned how to fawn over the proper duke."

"Of course," Granny said.

"Well," Edwina said. "I think he should spend more time writing. *Tom Jones*—"

"No!" Margaret spun around. "I don't want to hear another word about— Wait a moment . . . that Fielding . . . big, gouty fellow with a tree-stump nose . . . is the magistrate?"

"Yes," Samantha answered. "Do *you* know him."

"Met him once," Margaret said slowly. Her sisters-in-law were suddenly looking at her worshipfully. "He was with the duke of Bedford, I think." She cocked her head curiously as the girls continued to stare. "If I had a pet poet on staff, would I get more respect out of you?"

It was Alexandra, looking up from a book, who answered. "A resident poet might have helped the midsummer fete."

"Nothing could have helped the midsummer fete," Granny McKay declared.

"If only Jamie could have been here for the play," Samantha sighed. "Instead of the dreadful Reverend Wendall."

"Well, he wasn't here," Margaret snapped. She turned back to the window to continue her brooding.

She'd discovered she wasn't pregnant the day after Jamie left. She had ached with loss at first because she truly wanted Jamie's baby. Then she'd reviled herself bitterly for considering her own needs. Then she'd realized that her rush to marry an unsuitable outlaw had been in fear over nothing.

Only he wasn't unsuitable, he was wonderful. She'd lost her freedom, but she'd also lost her loneliness, but . . . The confusion had left her inarticulate with misery for days. It was very difficult to perform Shakespeare when one was inarticulate. She wished Jamie had been at the midsummer fete. She wished he was home now. She wished he would at least write.

The thought of a letter brought her out of her self-pitying reverie. There was correspondence on her desk her secretary could not take care of for her. It was time she resumed her duties.

When she turned from the window she discovered she was alone in the morning room. Both grandmothers and all four sisters had disappeared. A glance at the mantel clock told her she'd been sunk in gloomy staring for at least an hour.

"I don't suppose I'm very good company," she acknowledged. She went to her writing table and rifled through a stack of letters. Before she could sit down, the door opened. A servant would have knocked. She looked up sharply, hoping it was only a relative, as she reached for the pistol in her deep skirt pocket.

"Jamie!" she cried, abandoning the firearm to run to the slender man framed in the doorway.

Jamie gathered her up in his arms and kissed her so thoroughly she was prepared to drag him down on the flowered carpet by the time he was done.

"You missed me," she declared.

"A little," she said as his hands did things to the front of her deep-cut bodice.

Sensation left her breathless as well as warm and wanting, but she made herself speak. "The king."

"Loves me." He kissed her again. "Do you love me?"

"Well—yes, actually," she admitted as his hands continued to roam. "I do." He reached her hips.

"What's this?"

"It's a gun. I keep one under my pillow as well." He

drew away and looked at her strangely. She floundered for an excuse as his expression darkened with annoyance. "I've been practicing."

Jamie's joy at knowing his wife loved him clouded with sudden worry for her safety. And recrimination for having left her alone. Why hadn't he at least charged Bartlett or even Samantha to look after her?

"I saw our dear brother at Court," he told her. Did it reassure her to know that Lake was nowhere near by? Or did she even suspect the source of her troubles?

Margaret forced a smile. "Lake is hardly 'dear' to me."

"Good," he said with a decisive nod. He reached into her pocket and took out the pistol. He put it down on one of the yellow brocade chairs, then pulled her closer. "Wouldn't want anyone to get hurt," he said as his hands went back to caressing and exploring through layers of fabric.

Margaret would very much have liked to give over to the tingling, sharp, and melting sensations coursing through her. Instead she summoned up all her concentration and said, "Was Lake alone?"

"He was with friends." He buried his face in the fragrant spun gold of her hair. He heard the faint *tick-tick* of hair pins hitting the carpet. "I love your hair."

"Thank you. Just friends?"

The woman was relentless! "Yes!" Jamie shouted. He stepped away. He'd felt the heat of her skin beginning to flush with desire, but her reaction to his shout was a look of cold pride. It was the look of someone waiting to be struck. He wanted to groan in several different kinds of frustration. Instead he told her, "Lake invited me to a house party."

Her cold fear disappeared, replaced by a look of crafty pleasure. "An invitation? To Rishford Abbey?" She clapped her hands together. "How wonderful! I haven't been there in years."

"He invited me. He wants to—"

"We must go!" She grabbed his hands. "Jamie, please. We must go! Say we can, if only for a day or two. It would mean so much to me to see Frances. Oh, please, please!"

Her silvery eyes were shining with feverish hope. Her open pleading touched him deeply. He sensed underlying currents, things about her family relationships she wasn't telling him. But there was a beginning of trust, of needing him. He couldn't help but respond to her need. He knew he wouldn't dare to crush the hope, her pain would hurt him too much.

"Very well," he agreed. *"We'll* go to Lake's house party."

Her reaction was so swift he was taken completely by surprise. Her kiss was so passionate and compelling there was only one way he could react. By letting her drag him down on the floor and have her way with him.

19

"Here? In the coach?" Margaret giggled. Jamie's clever hand crept higher under her skirt, toward the center of growing desire. "But we're almost there."

The coach was comfortably upholstered, its confines were intimate, the swaying motion held sensual promise. The idea seemed wicked, forbidden. True, they were man and wife, alone, with the curtains drawn—but the coachmen and postilions were only a few feet away.

They were approaching Rishford Abbey. Margaret hesitated, but only for the length of a deep, exploring kiss. While their tongues were erotically entwined, Jamie's hand crept higher up her satin-smooth thigh.

"Yes, Jamie. Now!"

Jamie's chuckle was low and triumphant. His subsequent actions were more than obliging. The positioning grew awkward, and their lovemaking was accomplished in fits of mutual giggles at the contortions needed to satisfy passion, but the emotions were intense.

At a rather critical moment in the proceedings Jamie muttered, "Have to . . . get a . . . bigger . . . coach."

Margaret wrapped her legs around his narrow hips, threw her head back against the cushioned seat, and exploded with amusement and soaring, shattering release. She was being reckless with all this lovemaking. Jamie's touch consumed her, released her from fear and constraints. She hadn't been able to keep her hands off her husband since he'd returned home from Court.

Minutes later, when they'd managed to straighten their clothing and regain a measure of decorum, Jamie raised the window shade to look out. "We're approaching a gatehouse," he told her.

Her heart raced, but she made no answer. The glow of sated pleasure centered deep in her being ebbed away like a receding tide. Reality and a sense of danger and her desperate reason for this journey reasserted themselves. Margaret clung to the hope of soon seeing Frances.

The coach stopped briefly at the gate, then proceeded swiftly up the drive to the main house, a U-shaped brick building dating from the Tudor era. Much of the material for the house had been taken from the destroyed abbey which had stood on the grounds since medieval days. Having spent some time there as a child before Lake acquired the property as part of Frances's dowry, Margaret knew the place well.

Margaret tried to compose her thoughts and her features. She must soon face her enemy. She was not welcome at Rishford Abbey, but her husband's invitation would buy her time and a measure of courtesy. She must use the time to find and speak with Frances. She had a half-formed, wild plan to spirit her sister away. She was hoping Jamie would help her defy another man's God-given rights over his wife, but hadn't quite worked up the courage to broach the subject to him. As the coach came to a halt before the lantern-lit door, she reached for Jamie's hand.

She'd been playful, happy, feverishly exuberant through the trip. As they reached their destination, Jamie felt Margaret grow tense. The hand that clutched his was cold. She was worrying about her mysterious, sickly sister, he thought. He was grateful she was leaning on him for a bit of reassurance. He raised her hands to his lips, lingered warmly for a moment, and then helped her from the coach.

A butler registered their appearance in the entry hall with calm efficiency. "The duke and duchess of Pyneham. Sir Charles is away at the moment, but we've prepared a room for you, Your Grace. I'll show you there."

As he and Margaret followed the servant up a circular stair, Jamie said, "Will your master be away long?"

"Sir Charles is entertaining his guests at the abbey ruins tonight, Your Grace," the butler answered. "Melodramatic theatricals in a suitably eerie setting."

Jamie cast a wry look at Margaret. "Theatrics. Does it run in your family?"

She didn't seem to hear him. "Is Lady Frances at the ruins also?"

"Lady Frances?" The butler's face went even blanker, if that was possible. "Lady Frances is indisposed."

"Oh." Margaret was silent until they stopped before a door. "Please inform Lady Frances her sister is here."

The butler opened the door. "Lady Frances is not to be disturbed."

"Oh."

Jamie watched, desperate with pain for her, as the hope in her clear gray eyes died. She looked bereft and bruised and utterly exhausted. Jamie put his arm around her and drew her into the room, toward the warmth of a fresh-laid fire. The warmth was welcome, for the late June night was cool. A cold supper waited on a table near the fire.

"Thank you," he said over his shoulder to the butler.

A pair of footmen came in with their bags, and a red-haired maid hurriedly followed them. Jamie waved the girl back out. "In the morning," he said. "Attend us in the morning."

Margaret sank into a chair as the door closed behind the servants. "Did the maid look familiar to you?" She passed her hand wearily across her eyes. "I must see Frances."

"Of course," Jamie agreed. He went to the bed and turned down the covers. "It's rest you need, sweet." He spoke with soothing confidence. He wasn't confident at all. The depth of her disappointment had left him shaken.

The butler's stone-faced refusal to allow Margaret any communication with her sister hinted at an answer to one of the questions he had had about his wife's relationship with Lake. Besides the matter of inheritance the only item that had not been negotiable in his and Margaret's marriage settlement had been her generous allowance to General Sir Charles Lake. He'd wondered why. So, he concluded now, Lake was holding the sister hostage against Margaret's continued generosity.

Jamie shook his head in sympathy. He knew he'd do anything to protect his sisters. He cursed Lake for putting Margaret through even a moment's pain. He vowed again that something would be done about Lake.

He went to Margaret and took her hands. "Come. Let's to bed."

She jerked away. "No! I can't! I should never have—!"

"To sleep," he soothed. He took her in his arms,

stroked her gently, as he would any panic-stricken creature. "Just come to bed to sleep, sweet. All will be well tomorrow."

Margaret clutched at Jamie's back. He was all sinewy muscle beneath thick velvet, like a reassuring rock. Yes, sleep would be good, she thought. Oblivion. A time without worries. She rubbed her forehead against the lace of his neckcloth. She felt his fingers working at the back lacing of her dress. "Clever lad," she murmured, reassured by his presence.

"Oh, aye," he agreed. "Give me a hand with my waistcoat, sweet."

They undressed each other. Jamie found them nightclothes in the piled baggage. But once ready to sleep, Margaret gazed at the bed in consternation. She looked from the bed to Jamie then back at the bed. "I've never slept with anyone," she admitted. "How does one go about it?"

Jamie swallowed the urge to laugh. She looked so solemn he feared she'd take amusement for mockery. "I've shared a bed a few times," was all he said. "It's a comforting and congenial experience. Or can be," he added with a warm smile. "In the right company. You, sweet wife, are the perfect company." It wasn't just flattery; he longed for the simple conjugal privilege of holding her in his arms through the night.

She dug her bare toes into the hearth rug. "I've always wondered what it would be like—cuddling and such."

"Pleasant." He picked her up and tossed her onto the soft feather mattress before she could hesitate longer. He blew out the candles and climbed in beside her. Once the bedcurtains were closed and the covers pulled up around them he said, "If you have cold feet I'll toss you back out again."

She turned on her side and put her head on his shoulder.

The touch was light, her attitude experimental. He gathered her closer, kissed her forehead, and said, "Goodnight."

Jamie's long, lean form relaxed against hers, limp and heavy with sleep almost instantly. She found odd how well his masculine body fitted so well against her. It was warm where they touched. The texture of his skin was . . . nice. The sound of his deep, steady breathing had a soothing effect. She hoped he didn't snore. What if she did? Would he mind?

All these new thoughts and sensations distracted her for quite a while. She tried to sleep, to keep her mind off Frances. But she was too close now to drift off to sleep with just the hope of seeing her sister the next day. She'd made it as far as Rishford Abbey; she knew she must exploit the moment before Lake sent her packing.

She edged away from Jamie slowly, missing the newfound comfort of his presence even as she abandoned it. It was only for a little while, she promised herself. She would explore for a bit, try to find Frances's room, or at least the man Bartlett had sent to spy for them. Then she'd come back to bed, to sleep, to Jamie.

Jamie mumbled and turned over when she finally slipped out of bed, but he didn't wake. She put her light travel cape over her nightgown for decency's sake, then cautiously made her way out into the hall.

The hallway was still lit at long intervals by candles in wall sconces. She surmised that either the hour was earlier than she had thought or that Lake's guests had not yet returned from the expedition to the abbey ruins.

She wasn't sure whether to be grateful for the light or not as she glided silently on cold, bare feet along the parquet floor. The problem was, though she knew the layout of the house, she hadn't a clue as to where Frances might be. So she cautiously tried every door as she came to it. Meanwhile, she was alert for the appearance of servants or returning guests.

She found nothing but locked doors near her own room. So when she came to an intersection, she turned left and found herself heading toward the circular curve of the stairway that led to the main floor. The maid who'd come in with the baggage appeared at the top of the stairs just as Margaret reached them.

"You!" they said together.

Margaret recognized her now, Janet Cole, the servant who'd fled Lacey House after the fire. "You tried to burn me in my bed," she accused the startled red-haired woman.

"I've told the master about you!" the woman shot back. She touched a livid mark on her cheek. "You've roused his temper, you have. You'll be sorry."

Margaret saw fanatical devotion to Lake burning out of the woman's eyes. She wondered why, but didn't want to delve into the reasons. "Where's my sister?"

"Silly creature," the woman answered. Margaret didn't know whether Janet referred to her or Frances.

She didn't care. She grabbed the maid by the shoulders and pushed her against the wall. The woman was bigger, but Margaret was too angry to consider anything so trivial as her own small size. She was perfectly prepared to beat the information out of the murderous maid. "Where is she?" she whispered. "And recall, my fine trollop, that I could have you hanged for what you tried to do to me!"

"But she won't."

The sound of Lake's voice held the shock of a whip crack. Margaret couldn't breathe for a moment. She hadn't heard him approach.

He grabbed the back of her cape, pulling her away from the maid. Janet came after her, spitting fury, her hands extended like claws toward Margaret's face. Lake swatted the woman away. "Go."

Janet gave him a miserable look and fled, sobbing, out of sight. Margaret stared after her until Lake pinned her against the wall.

"Well met, little sister," he said. There were spirits on his breath, and his expression was bleary. "How nice to see you in your nightie." He kissed her.

Margaret's knee came up automatically. Hard. "I've been brawling in taverns lately," she told the gasping, bent-over figure. "It changes one's perspective." She wiped the back of her hand contemptuously across her lips.

"Bitch," he snarled as he straightened.

She reached for a brass statue on a nearby table and held it like a club. She didn't know why she was behaving so aggressively. She did know she was utterly calm, and quite enjoying herself. Perhaps she'd just been under Lake's crushing thumb for one moment too long and had finally broken.

"I'll crack your skull if you come one step closer," she declared. He didn't look as if he believed her.

She was saved from having to prove her point, as the sounds of people coming up the stairs distracted them both. A trio of young men approached from below. They were well dressed but looked mussed and windblown. The pair in the lead didn't look any more sober than Lake. She recognized neither of them. The man bringing up the rear was Lord Jeffrey Edgware, former suitor, fellow amateur thespian. His expression was thoughtful and a bit disapproving.

"Hello, Edgware," she said loudly, to get his attention. "How nice to see you again."

Lake stepped back, and she edged away from the wall

as the three men joined them in the hallway. She put the statue down, but not too far from her hand.

Edgware bowed very formally to her. "How lovely to see you, Your Grace," He handed back her cape as he rose. She hadn't known she'd lost it.

"Pretty piece you've got here, Lake," said one of the young men. He was tall and very large, the flesh covering his big form undecided as yet whether to run to muscle or fat. His mouth and eyes were too small for his wide face. His nose and cheeks were red-veined from too much drink too often.

"Mind your tongue, Bonham," Lake ordered.

"She's the duchess of Pyneham," the other stranger told his friend. "I'm Graeme Dalworthy, Your Grace," he told her. "I served with your betrothed's regiment at Culloden." He was thin and sharp-featured and looked ready to weep with sentimentality.

"Betrothed? Oh, yes, Edward."

"A good man, cut down in his prime by a stinking band of rebels. Scottish bastards," he added, weaving drunkenly as he made an obscene gesture. "How you must grieve for your loss."

"She's pretty," Bonham said. "Lake always finds pretty ones." He belched loudly. "Cool night. My arse is still—"

"You poor suffering lass," Dalworthy cut him off.

"Yes. Of course. Terrible loss," Margaret agreed with the sentimental drunk. She backed slowly away from the group. She kept a careful eye on Lake as she moved, but he seemed content to remain hunched and sulking in the middle of the group.

When he woke alone, Jamie understood where Margaret must have gone. What he didn't understand was why he found her on the edge of a group of belligerent men. One of the men was Lake. Jamie hurried forward. The last person he wanted her to see without him was Lake.

He came up behind her swiftly and wrapped his arms around her. "Walking in your sleep, lass?"

She craned her head back to look at him. "Was I?"

He couldn't help but drop a kiss on her forehead. "Why's he got his hands on her?" a truculent voice questioned. Jamie threw a glare into the group of men; a general response to the specific statement.

Lord Edgware touched the large man's arm. "Because she's his wife. Go to bed, Bonham, you're too foxed to think."

"Married?" a tall, narrow-faced fellow asked. The man looked affronted at the information. "Married? The girl's barely had time to recover from her loss."

"Recover?" Edgware scoffed. "Culloden was four years ago, Dalworthy."

Dalworthy struck a dramatic pose. "Not in my heart. Damn Scots."

Jamie could barely suppress his frustrated groan. "Time to go," he said to his wife. She nodded.

As they turned to leave, Lake spoke up. "Surely you know the duchess's husband is a Scotsman?" Lake's voice was strained, as though he was fighting off pain. But there was no mistaking the malicious intent of his words.

"Scots! No! The bastard!"

Jamie sighed. He could see it coming. The next moves were inevitable, farcical. General Lake was finding others to fight his battles, which was a reasonable thing for a general to do.

He gently set Margaret aside a moment before the heavy hand landed on his shoulder. "Keep your hands off her. She's an English woman!"

Jamie turned slowly, shaking off the drunk's hold. He refused to argue with the man. He met the other man's bloodshot gaze and waited.

"Leave off, man," Edgware said as he rushed up to them.

"He's a Scottish pig," was Dalworthy's furious answer.

"He's an English duke," Edgware pointed out. "Mind your tongue."

Out of the corner of his eye Jamie saw Margaret reach for a vase and heft it like a weapon. "Lass," he warned before she could start a battle.

"Listen to him!" Dalworthy sneered. "Ordering a *lady* as though she were his dog!"

"Bastard," Bonham spoke in agreement. "Mounts her like one too, I'll wager."

Jamie marked down the big man's insult for later reprisal and switched his gaze to Lake. Something ailed the general, all right. There were lines of pain marring his ruthlessly handsome face. But the discomfort didn't disguise the pleasure he was taking in his guests' behavior. Lake obviously expected trouble and wasn't going to try to stop it.

"Pig!" Dalworthy repeated, and spat. Jamie sidestepped the contemptuous gesture, but he didn't try to avoid the slap in the face which came next.

"Fine," he said in the tense silence that followed. "Pistols at dawn." He gave a small, polite bow. "Good-night to you all. Come along, sweet." He took Margaret by the hand and led her back to their room. He heard Lake arranging for the other men to act as seconds as he opened the door to their room. There was no mistaking the glee in the man's tone.

"You could have let me hit him over the head," Margaret complained as they got back in bed.

"Why waste a perfectly good vase. Get those cold feet off me, woman."

She settled down beside him with her feet tucked up under her nightgown. Her original purpose for leaving bed was pushed to the back of her mind. Her new concern was concentrated on Jamie. "You shouldn't have—"

"I can't let your fine English nobility bully me because I was born just over the border," he told her. "It was bound to come to this. Best sooner than later."

She couldn't help but agree with his reasoning, though she hated the circumstances. "Dueling's illegal. You could get in trouble. Or killed." Lake would like it if Jamie got killed. For the first time she realized that she should have warned Jamie that Lake wanted his title. "This is all my fault," she said. "I've gotten you in trouble."

"I'll only get in trouble if I kill the fool."

"Will you?"

"No."

"What if he kills you?"

"He won't."

"How can you be sure?"

"Because he'll have a gargantuan headache come morning. I doubt he'll even be able to see me, let alone shoot me. Go to sleep," he ordered. "We both need the rest."

Before Margaret could say more, he turned on his side. They were soon lying together spoon fashion while Margaret searched her tired mind for a way to protect her husband from the folly she'd brought on him. Nothing occurred to her immediately, and Jamie seemed so confident that all would be well. He did need his rest, and she was so tired. The intimacy of simply lying beside him filled her with wonder, fogged over her worries, and soon lulled her to sleep.

* * *

"Of course I'm coming along," Margaret insisted.

"You're not," Jamie repeated. He finished buttoning his coat. Margaret stood. He gently pushed her back on the bed. She sat stiffly. Nothing in her attitude was meek or obedient this morning. He quite liked her this way. Still . . . "No," he said firmly. "I forbid it. Ladies do not attend duels."

"What about witnesses?" she demanded.

"Our seconds will be there, Edgware and Bonham. And Lake, probably." He yawned and stretched as much as the tight sleeves of his coat would allow. "Why did I say I'd shoot the idiot at dawn?"

"It's traditional." So, she thought, Lake and two of his friends with guns would be there. Lake wouldn't waste an opportunity to rid himself of a rival for the title. She had to arrange a way to protect Jamie from Lake's mischief. It was all her fault, she railed at herself. She should never have gotten anyone else involved in her problems. Her thoughts raced feverishly as she tried to think of a plan. Then she jumped to her feet.

"Excuse me." She ducked past Jamie and out of the room.

Margaret was pounding on the door next to theirs by the time Jamie got out in the hall. She then hurried to the next, shouting, "There's a duel! Wake up, you louts! Do you want to miss the show?"

Doors opened, sleep-drugged faces peered out at the shouting woman. Curious then excited conversation began among the rudely wakened guests.

"What?"

"A duel? Where?"

"Who's fighting?"

"Dalworthy," Margaret told the gathering crowd.

"What? Again?"

"Must be a Scotsman in the house," a fellow in a night-cap contributed.

"Oh, yes," Margaret said. "The duke of Pyneham."

"Pyneham?" a woman in a nightshift sheer enough to reveal overripe curves asked eagerly. She licked her lips. "I've heard of him."

Jamie was gratified at the stinging glance Margaret shot the woman's way. He leaned in the doorway with his arms crossed and watched his wife stir up a hornet's nest of enthusiasm over the duel. After a few minutes she came up to him with a smug look on her face. Doors were slamming, servants were being called.

"Everyone else is going," she told him. "May I?"

He gave her shoulders a slight shake, a cross between reproving and affectionate. "You're a scoundrel," he informed her. "A scamp, and a rogue as well."

"Yes. May I go? To defend your honor from Lady Pilbourne, if nothing else."

"Very well." He kissed her soundly. "I'll see you on the field of battle," he added as Edgware came up the hallway carrying a tooled leather pistol case. "I'd best go."

Margaret looked at the crowd of people hastily assembled in the fountain court in front of the house. Dawn was just turning the sky pink and pale blue. She gave a slight nod, grimly satisfied that any mischief her brother-in-law might have been planning was neutralized by the eager crowd of witnesses. She was sure he had been planning something. She could tell by the annoyed expression that spoiled his handsome features as the combatants and their seconds joined him in the center of the red-brick courtyard.

Jamie looked annoyed as well, his heavy brows lowered. Dalworthy, on the other hand, looked pale, disheveled, and completely at sea. Margaret doubted the lout even recalled what he was fighting over.

"Provincial Scots bastard," he said as Edgware presented the open pistol case to them.

Apparently he hadn't forgotten. She wondered if he'd been up all night. If he was sober. If his being drunk would affect his aim. For all she knew the man was the finest shot in Britain. She wondered if she should be worried for her husband's safety. What if Lake had somehow tampered with Jamie's gun? What if it misfired? It could blow up in his face. Dalworthy could—

The gathering was awash in buzzing conversation. Bets were being laid among the gentlemen. Ladies were tittering and speculating and giving her jealous, sideways glances. Margaret had managed to ignore all of it until this threatening whisper materialized out of the babble.

"I'm watching you," a wasp-vicious voice spoke quietly beside her.

While the men selected weapons and began pacing off the firing distance, Margaret turned to face this new threat. Janet Cole was standing beside her. The woman was no longer dressed as a servant. She wore a gray silk gown cut low enough to suit fashion for a courtesan or a Court lady. Her hennaed hair was heavily powdered, and she wore enough face paint to cover any bruises Lake's fist might have raised. She looked at Margaret with open hatred.

"What are you doing here?" Margaret demanded.

"I'm here to be your maid of honor," Janet answered. "To be your companion in the master's house."

"I don't need a companion," Margaret told her. "You're dismissed."

Janet's smile was malevolent. "I take my orders from the master. He's set me to watch you. Watch you I will," she added with an emphatic nod.

"I see," Margaret said as the sound of double pistol shots roared out behind her.

The sound, sudden, somehow unexpected, sent a shock of terror through her.

"Jamie!" She whirled just as applause and cheers erupted from the avidly watching crowd. One man was lying on the bricks. Two other men knelt beside the still figure, hiding him from Margaret's view. The other combatant stood on the opposite side of the courtyard, tall and slender and still. Sunlight gleamed off his shining brown hair, but didn't seem to touch the matte-black surface of the dueling pistol he held at his side. Their eyes met. He gave her a reassuring smile.

"Oh, Jamie," she said, trembling with relief. She ran to his side, engulfing him in the hardest hug she could manage.

"Point and fire," he said, as though reminding her of her lesson. "Nothing to it."

"You're alive! You're safe! You didn't . . ."

"A graze," Edgware said, coming up beside them. "Well done, Your Grace."

Jamie let the pistol drop to the ground. "Glad he's going to be all right."

Edgware laughed. "A scrape on the arm isn't going to bother him. The galling part's losing. He's one of the finest shots in Britain. Drunk or sober." To Jamie's scathing look he added, "Didn't seem wise to warn you beforehand. Didn't want to make you nervous."

"Thank you," Jamie said sarcastically. "I appreciate that very much. Where's breakfast?"

Margaret tugged on Jamie's sleeve. "You might," she

suggested, matching his sarcasm to Edgware, "have a care for your wife's nerves. Say something manly and reassuring, at least. Dour Scotsman," she grumbled.

"Dour?" he said, and kissed her. Sweet Jesus, how he kissed her! It was a torrentially demanding, branding, engulfing sort of kiss that left her melting inside, weak in the knees, and breathlessly, achingly dazed.

"Manly enough for you?" he inquired.

She leaned her head back on his arm and gazed up at the sky. "Um, yes."

He caressed her throat. "Now I'm not sure whether I want you or breakfast first."

"I think our host might insist on breakfast," Edgware commented.

Margaret heard someone approaching across the brick pavement, but she didn't pay any attention until Lake said, "Is this a private entertainment or spectator sport?"

Margaret heard the vicious insinuation in Lake's lightly spoken words. She slipped out of Jamie's embrace in reaction.

Before Jamie could ask for the gun back, Lake clapped a brotherly hand on his shoulder and gave a hearty laugh, clear indication to all onlookers that his comment was a joke. A man couldn't be called out for joking. Pity.

Jamie knew it had been a mistake to come there. They were leaving, he decided. As soon as Margaret had a chance to visit this sickly sister of hers, they were leaving.

"The doctor's been summoned for Dalworthy," Lake said. "All is well." He gestured toward the house. "A victory celebration is now in order."

Jamie wondered if their host was going to serve poisoned porridge, but supposed a communal meal was safe enough. "Come, sweet," he said to Margaret. "Let us go in."

The guests were returning to the house, and Janet had come to stand at her side. Margaret's rapturous reaction to Jamie's kiss had ebbed to a cold ache in her belly. She felt ridiculous, and the situation seemed hopeless. "I'm not hungry," she said. "I have a headache." She shot an annoyed glance at Janet. "I'll return to our room."

"You've hardly slept. Take a nap," Jamie advised. "Join us when you've rested."

She nodded. Jamie watched her walk away. The red-haired girl followed after her. So did Lake's hungry glance. The man's undisguised lust made Jamie's blood boil. He didn't know if Lake's manner was meant to show contempt toward him or if he simply didn't realize how he looked. Jamie didn't much care what was going through Lake's head. He managed to hold his tongue and his temper and accompanied Lake and Edgware in to breakfast.

20

She could tell it was afternoon by the angle of the sunbeams slanting across the end of the bed, warming her feet. Margaret supposed it was the sun on her feet that woke her up.

Woke her up?

She sat up with a wild jerk. How could she have fallen asleep? She'd only meant to pretend, to distract Janet who absolutely refused to go away. The woman had stood with her back to the door and hadn't let Margaret leave once they'd come in. Janet reminded her that her husband had told her to take a nap. So she had lain down and kept a wary eye out for any movement from the woman. Wary and tense Margaret might have been, but, somehow, she was also fatigued from all the earlier strain. Her body demanded rest. The bed was comfortable. She apparently gave in to the seduction of sleep.

"What a traitorous, foolish thing to do!" she chastised herself as she looked anxiously about the room. She was alone. She got up, made herself presentable, and went to the door. Janet was seated just outside.

"Ah," the maid said, jumping to her feet. "The master has work for you. I was going to fetch you soon."

"Work?" Margaret bristled at Janet's attitude. "Fetch? Just whom do you think you're talking to?"

"The duchess of Pyneham." Janet bobbed her a mocking curtsy "An uninvited guest in my master's house. And a would-be murderess," she added. Her eyes shone with fanatical hatred.

"I?" Margaret pointed at Janet. "You—"

"You were going to hire a man to kill the master. The dowager said so! He set me to watch you, and good thing. I was there to stop your plotting!"

Margaret vaguely recalled the look of panic on Janet's face the night the dowager proposed hiring Jamie Scott. The redhead had run from the room. Margaret had supposed it was in fear of the dowager. So the woman had tried to kill her to save Lake, and Margaret had fled into the arms of Jamie Scott.

"That'll teach us to gossip in front of the servants," Margaret said.

It was obvious the girl was in love with Lake. Margaret couldn't imagine why.

"Come with me," Janet commanded.

Margaret noticed a pair of large footmen lingering attentively near them in the hallway. She wanted to scream in frustration. She was as much a prisoner in this house as her sister was. She'd thought it would be easy to speak to Frances once she got inside Rishford Abbey. It was proving to be impossible instead.

She *must* find John Lodge, she decided. The spy was her

only possible source of help. But what the devil did the fellow look like? Bartlett had said he was thin and fair and inconspicuous. That description was apt for many of the servants in Lake's household. She couldn't march up to every footman she saw and start demanding names. She couldn't draw attention to him. She could only trust he'd find a way to contact her.

"Come along," Janet insisted, tugging her arm. Margaret shook her off.

"Where's my sister? Take me to Lady Frances immediately."

The hovering footmen came a few steps closer. Margaret eyed them nervously. Just how far had Lake authorized them to go? Would she be bundled off somewhere and locked away? Thrown down the stairs and said to have met with a fatal accident? Where was Jamie? And why had she put herself in such danger? They wouldn't dare harm her. Would they?

Neither Janet nor the two large men reacted to her demand to see her sister. The trio just looked at her with sullen, stern determination.

At last she sighed and capitulated. "Just where am I supposed to go with you?"

Janet smiled triumphantly. "You're to act as hostess at an afternoon salon. The ladies are waiting to take tea with you."

"Hostess?" Margaret asked. "Lady Frances is mistress of Rishford Abbey."

"But you're the highest ranking lady present," Janet countered. "The honor falls to you."

Hostess, she thought with disgust. At a tea party. How charming. How clever of him to make her the center of attention. It would be more difficult to sneak away from a gaggle of ladies than one fanatical, jumped-up maidservant.

"Bastard," she muttered. Then she gave a bitter smile and said, "Lead on."

"How was your day?" Jamie asked as his borrowed valet helped him into a silver brocade coat embroidered in black.

Margaret emerged from behind a screen where she'd been dressing for dinner. The redhead followed close behind her.

Margaret was dressed sumptuously in white satin, trimmed in gold lace and ribbons. "I wish I'd brought Maude," she said as she sat down at a dressing table. The maid began arranging her hair. She moved efficiently, but looked angry and resentful of her work.

"Your day?" Jamie asked his wife again.

"I drank tea," she answered shortly.

"Did you see your sister?"

"No."

"Why not?" he asked, irritable at the thought of having to spend another day watching his back in Lake's company. Still, he thought, it was better to keep Lake's attention centered on him rather than Margaret; it was safer for her that way. She didn't answer his question. He noticed her hands clenched tightly together in her lap and decided not to press an issue that obviously disturbed her. Not in front of the servants. He turned to his dressing table instead. His valet had packed a suitable amount of jewelry in a velvet-lined case. He chose a ring, then picked up the topaz earring and turned back to Margaret.

"What do you think?" he asked. "Shall I be conservative or dashing tonight?"

His question coaxed a smile out of her. Her gaze swept over him, in his brocade and lace. She nodded her approval. "Dashing," she said. "I definitely prefer you dashing, Your Grace."

He put on the earbob, then bowed to her. "At your service, Your Grace."

The maid finished with Margaret's hair and moved away. Margaret stood and said, "Let's go to dinner. I'm famished."

He took her hand and kissed the soft center of her palm. "So am I. But I suppose we have to have supper first."

She giggled, but pointed firmly toward the door when he would have lingered for a kiss.

Never mind what she'd said earlier, she wasn't the least bit hungry. All Margaret wanted, as she sat at the dining room table, was to find out which of the servants moving around the spacious room was John Lodge.

Overhead a chandelier blazed with the gold glow of candles set among crystal. Candle stands along the table and on sideboards added more light and heat to the already warm room. Margaret looked about her, well aware that the mellowing effect of candlelight was the only thing that softened the cold, predatory expressions of most of Lake's guests. Except for their fashionable clothes, this crowd could have fit in at the Red Bull. Many of the people she'd encountered at the highwayman's tavern actually smelled better. She'd heard reports of the worldly, debauched crowd Lake preferred for his private entertainments, but hadn't quite understood what was meant by the veiled, drawing room tidbits of scandalous gossip until today.

The ladies had spent the afternoon tea time gambling

and bickering and anticipating tonight's entertainment at the abbey ruin. There'd been a great deal of snickering over costumes and roles and partners, but Margaret had been more intent on gossip than on theatricals for once. She'd been desperate to discover any word the women might have on Lady Frances Lake. Instead she'd ended up with an earful of information about who was sleeping with whom. No one seemed to be involved with her own husband. She'd learned about several interesting cures for the pox. The whole experience left her longing for her sisters-in-law and their tedious discussions of books and philosophy. It had also left her with no appetite for another meal in this lecherous company.

Not that she had any choice. Her duty was to sit at Lake's table, to play out her role, and hope for contact with her spy. The food, meanwhile, was excellent, despite her lack of taste for it. Lake had a famous chef, as she well knew, whose equally famous salary came out of her privy purse.

She picked at a piece of cold fish in aspic, and wished once again she could cut off Lake's allowance to get her sister back. That threat hadn't worked. No threat worked. All was lost. Perhaps she should just give up.

A hand touched hers. A voice whispered under the hubbub of voices around them, "Why so sad, sweet?"

She looked up at Jamie. She remembered concern shining out of his eyes even when they'd looked at her from above the edge of a concealing red scarf. She'd always longed to trust the man who owned those eyes. But what good was trust when everything was so hopeless?

I should tell him, she thought. I will tell him. Quietly, right now. Lord knows there's enough of a din in here for a private conversation to go unnoticed. He smiled encouragingly at her and rested his hand on her shoulder.

She opened her mouth to speak, but before she could a surly voice across the table from Jamie spoke up. "Do you always paw your wife in public? Bad form." Bonham continued loudly. "Man should paw someone else's wife if he doesn't want to be thought a fool."

Jamie threw a disdainful glance down the length of the table. "So I've noticed," he observed.

There was an uncommon amount of laughter at his comment. He recognized the sychophantic nature of the noise and gave the attentive company a cynical smile. It wasn't easy being a duke. There were a great many eyes on him tonight. Most seemed to be shining with a feral glow in the glare of the candlelight. His host, seated at his side, was still and watchful as a snake. Bonham, full of wine and himself, was a hostile pig.

The day had been spent gaming. Jamie had sat with his back to the wall, sharing a table with Bonham, Lake, and Edgware. Groups of onlookers gathered around them from time to time. There had been little conversation. Jamie had won more than he had lost, mostly from Bonham. The big man had started out the day furious over Jamie's besting Dalworthy. His attitude only grew more surly as the day went on. Jamie judged the man was just below the boiling point at the moment, and he didn't much care. He did wonder how Lake planned to use Bonham against him, however.

"My wife," Jamie said, stroking Margaret's shoulder gently, with the back of his hand, "takes up my entire attention."

"Hmmph." Bonham snorted.

"Newlyweds," Lake said. "Charming, isn't it?" he added, a touch of delicate malice in his voice.

There was a weak wave of tittering from some of the

ladies around the table. Edgware held up his glass and called out jovially, "A toast to the newlyweds, then."

As glasses were raised, the crystals catching ruby fire from wine and the light, Jamie turned his head to salute his blushing wife. They shared a brief smile.

The moment of communion was shattered once again by Bonham's truculent voice. "Nasty, unmanly, French fashion," he said. "Men in earrings. Bah!"

Margaret watched as Jamie touched the sun-gold jewel dangling from his ear, then turned cold eyes on Bonham. "A present from my wife."

Bonham jeered. "Wife." And swilled down another glassful.

"Thought the earring looked familiar," Lake said. "One of the famous stolen pair, isn't it?"

Margaret jumped at the reminder. She'd forgotten what a laughingstock she'd been over her intense interest in Jamie Scott.

Bonham lifted his head from his glass to stare at Jamie's ear. "I've seen that before," he said after a long deliberation.

"And where is that, pray tell?" Lake wondered. "I don't recall your having prior acquaintance with our lovely duchess."

"Not on her. Him!" Bonham scratched his heavy jaw and several chins with bovine thoughtfulness. Margaret lost sight of him for a moment as a servant replaced her fish with a custard-and-fruit dessert. A folded square of paper dropped silently into her lap.

Her glance shot up to the footman's face. She focused on fair, nondescript features. Lodge? He spared her the most minimal of nods before moving into the background once more.

Margaret cautiously unfolded the paper and read,

"Grave news. I shall await you at the entrance to the maze at midnight. Your guard will be too occupied to follow. Take the greatest of care to come alone. J.L."

Drama. Margaret thought as she read. Sweet Jesus, more drama. Couldn't the man just tell her where Frances was? She refolded the note and slipped it in her pocket. Damn drama!

"I've got it now!" Bonham proclaimed, jolting Margaret's attention back to the dinner conversation. "Jamie Scott!"

Jamie folded his hands on the table linen and looked Bonham squarely in the face. "Who?" he inquired as a ripple of questions spread around the table.

The questions exploded into silence as Bonham said loudly, "The highwayman Jamie Scott. He was wearing that earring when he stopped me on Hounslow Heath. Scared him off with a well-aimed pistol ball. But not before I saw that earring." Bonham eyed Jamie suspiciously. "He was a skinny, ugly Scotsman."

"Like the duke?" Lake asked jokingly.

Jamie gave Lake a sour look as he tried to recall any time he'd been scared off from a robbery. He couldn't recall any. He must have relieved Bonham of his valuables at some point in his short career on the road, though, from the man's accurate description of him.

"His Grace is *not* skinny," Margaret spoke up.

"Jamie Scott," Edgware said, leaning around his buxom dinner companion to give Jamie a friendly perusal. He laughed. "There is some resemblance," he agreed. "The man robbed me of a watch, once. I remember his accent."

"And the earring?" Lake questioned.

Jamie thought the general looked to be possessed of another bright, dangerous idea. It didn't help dampen

Lake's enthusiasm when Edgware answered, "Oh, yes. I remember the earring."

"Jamie Scott," one of the women said admiringly. "I've heard he's a handsome, daring rogue."

"And a dead shot with a pistol," someone else added.

"As is our duke," Lake reminded everyone.

"How'd you get Scott's earring?" Bonham demanded. He leaned forward, peering, narrow-eyed, at Jamie's face. "Brown eyes." He pounded a hammy fist on the table. China rattled and nearby candles flickered as he announced, "Scott. By God, you're Scott!"

"Nonsense," Edgware called. "He's the duke of Pyneham."

"Ah, but who was he before he was the duke of Pyneham?" Lake wondered. The general's voice was calm, amused, pitched low enough so only those nearest him heard. Margaret, Jamie, Bonham.

"There's a five-hundred-pound reward for Scott," Bonham said. He rubbed his jaw. "Maybe I should turn you in to pay off my gambling debts."

"Scott's never been seen unmasked," Lady Carswell said. "He's rumored to be dangerously handsome."

"All highwaymen are dangerously handsome," Mrs. Lawson said. "Until they're hanged."

"Isn't there a man who told the constables he could identify Scott?" Lake asked.

"One of his accomplices," Edgware said. "I heard something about Scott avoiding a trap the accomplice set. Then he disappeared. Been lying low for a few weeks, I expect. Sensible chap."

Jamie avoided glaring angrily at his friend. If he were sensible, he thought, he'd hit Edgware over the head to shut him up. He and Margaret exchanged an uncomfortable look.

"How did you come to have Scott's earring, Your Grace?" Lake asked. Bonham continued his belligerent staring.

"Sweet Jesus!" Margaret spoke up suddenly. "As if everyone didn't know that old story." She waited until all eyes were firmly turned to her before she went on.

"It's not Scott's earring, it's mine." She kept her contemptuous attention on Lake. "Scott stole my jewels. I pawned them back, but he kept one of my earbobs. That's how Scott acquired his famous topaz." She turned a loving smile on Jamie and called up all her acting skills as she made up her script on the spot.

"His Grace already told you it was a gift from me. So it was. On our wedding day. The topazes have been our family's love tokens ever since King Charles gave them to Great-Grandmother. It didn't seem right that a rascal like Scott should have one—as though he'd stolen my love—and my dearest bridegroom should not. So I presented him with the remaining earbob."

She looked around her audience and lowered her voice conspiritorially. "Though he wasn't so pleased when I had to take an embroidery needle to his ear so he could wear it."

"I yelped like a kicked dog," Jamie admitted to help increase the laughter.

When the merriment at his expense died down, Margaret stood, officially ending the meal and the discussion. As everyone else rose she said, "Come, ladies. Time to leave the gentlemen to their brandy."

As she marched out at the head of a small female procession, she reflected that sometimes being a duchess wasn't such a bad thing. Especially when she got to make dramatic exits.

* * *

"Now, where," she wondered as she made her way down a tree-lined path, "is this maze? I don't remember a maze in the garden when I was little."

The moon had faded to a dim sliver, but the starlight shed enough light for her to traverse the wide path with ease. The problem was that she didn't know where she was going. She hadn't wanted to ask anyone in the house, especially not when she was afraid of being stopped by the servants. So she'd blundered out the first door she'd found unattended and trusted to luck. She felt lucky that Lake's female guests had been eager to return to their rooms to prepare for the upcoming entertainment at the ruins. Janet had not reappeared at her side so she had a few minutes of freedom at last. All she had to do was find the blasted maze and John Lodge. She really wished Jamie was with her.

The path led gently uphill, away from the neatly groomed lawn behind the house. She followed it to the top of the hill where the path divided. A bowl-shaped valley stretched out below. The ruins of the fourteenth-century abbey began a few feet to her right. Broken walls and a square tower loomed out of the landscape. Torches lit the base of the tower, picking out worn carvings in the tumbled stonework. A knot of people waited in the ragged shadows of the walls. A wide smear of dark ivy climbed in a perpendicular swath across the front of the tower. The empty doorway was bracketed by torches, one of which had set the nearest ivy leaves smoking.

Margaret had expected to see a small stage set up in front of the ruin. What she saw instead was a sort of altar. A naked girl with rouged nipples and a chalice on her belly was spread-eagled on top of the altar.

Margaret took a hasty step back as she took it all in.

Oh, dear, she thought, not really surprised, it was one of *those* sorts of parties. Even out-of-favor duchesses heard rumors of the latest excesses in fashionable circles. It was the sort of hideous nonsense she should have expected from Lake. And the company he kept.

Lake's guests, she noticed at last, as they took their places in a half-circle around the altar, were garbed in monks' and nuns' robes. Another glance at the naked girl confirmed Margaret's suspicion of just where Janet Cole was spending her evening. At least Lodge was correct about the girl not interfering with their meeting.

She took another step back as a shout went up from the congregation. A man stepped out of the tower doorway. He was naked but for a scarlet hood covering his head. Magnificently naked, muscular, gold-pelted, and fully aroused. Margaret gulped at the sight of him, swallowed a shocked gasp, and quickly fled back the way she'd come.

Lake of course. She'd thought she was sophisticated enough, just jaded enough to deal with the notion that the people she'd had dinner with were about to take part in a full-dress orgy. Yet she found as she raced back down the path that she was afraid and heartsick at the implications of what was going on at the abbey.

He was a monster, she thought. A sick, lecherous fiend. Did Frances know about this? Did she have to deal with it? Did he force her to watch? To participate? Oh, God, please no. Not that.

Tears blinded her. She paused to dash them away and glance back to make sure she had not been seen or followed. When she turned to hurry on again, she ran straight into a wall. The impact sent her flying backwards. She fell to the ground, stunned. The wall grunted. She looked up, then up some more, and realized she was looking at a tall, broad figure in one of the monk's robes. She had been followed! No, he'd come from the direction of the house.

"Late for the orgy, are we?" she wondered, and didn't realize she'd spoken out loud until he pulled back his hood and said, "Yes, but you'll do well enough."

She was not particularly impressed with the menacing bravado of Bonham's answer. Nor was she surprised at his plopping down on his knees beside her. "Don't even consider touching me," she warned.

He reached for her.

Jamie marched up the path, not sure whether he was annoyed or concerned. Margaret was not in their room or anywhere in the house. He hated to think she'd left for the evening's entertainment without waiting for him to escort her. He didn't know why no one had told him where these ruins were or what time to be there, not that he wanted to attend theatricals, but Margaret . . . All Edgware would say was, "Not our sort of thing. Think I'll go to bed."

It hadn't helped Jamie's mood to find Bonham in conversation with a groom in the front hallway. The pair gave him furtive, malicious looks, then hurried out the door. Bonham was definitely up to something—instigated by Lake, no doubt.

"Devil take Lake," he grumbled. "I want to find my wife."

He found her a few moments later, around the next bend of the path. She stood there, her white dress frosted by starlight, and pale hair haloed her face. A dark figure writhed and whimpered at her feet.

"I told you not to touch me," she said. "Are you going to be all right?" she added sympathetically. Jamie hurried forward.

The man on the ground struggled to his knees. Even in

the dim light he had no trouble recognizing Bonham's jowly face.

Sudden rage blazed through Jamie. "You touched my wife?"

The question was asked in a quietly dangerous voice. He lashed out. His booted foot connected with the man's kidneys, sending him sprawling across the path. "No," he said to Margaret. "He is not going to be all right."

"Jamie!" She put a restraining hand on his arm. "I already kicked him. Please, No more violence. I just want the man out of my sight," she added in disgust.

The man was nothing but a drunken bully, Jamie thought. Giving him a good thrashing might be satisfying, but he'd still be a drunken bully tomorrow. Jamie bent and hauled Bonham up by the armpits. The lout weighed about as much as a horse, but Jamie had no trouble managing him. "What's the fool wearing?" he asked as he took in Bonham's costume. "Some sort of papist nightgown?"

"Ah . . . no." Margaret cleared her throat. She wasn't quite sure how to word an explanation. "Oh . . . they're having a bit of a bacchanalia down at the ruins. An orgy," she explained at his questioning grunt.

There was a brief silence before Jamie said, "Oh." He shook Bonham hard. "You'll be leaving Rishford Abbey tonight," he commanded. "Ride or walk or take a coach, but get out of my sight." He shook him again, then pushed him away. Jamie took no more notice of Bonham as the man backed silently away.

Margaret watched his retreat and saw the hatred and the flash of cunning in the last glance he gave them before he disappeared around the turn of the path. There goes trouble, she thought. They hadn't seen the last of him yet.

21

"*Orgy?*" *Jamie said* in disgust. He took her arm. "Bonham isn't the only one leaving. We'll not be a part to such nonsense. What are you doing out here?" he added. "You weren't invited to—?"

"No!" She tried, unsuccessfully, to pull away from him. "Jamie, I can't leave. I have to find Frances. You don't understand!"

He heard the note of fear in her voice, and the desperation. It was enough to make him forget his outrage over orgies and Bonham's behavior. He drew Margaret into his arms. She came to him and held him tightly. He could feel her quivering, with tension, fear, and suppressed rage as well, he thought. He just held her for a while, trying to give silent comfort while his thoughts swirled with questions.

He didn't understand anything, did he? Just what game

were she and Lake really playing? And the stakes? Life and death? And whose life was really in the balance? Margaret's? His? The mysterious, missing sister's?

"Frances," he said. He drew Margaret deep into the shadows beneath the trees. "Tell me," he urged as her pale face turned up toward his. "Tell me about Frances."

Margaret stood very still. She felt encircled, not just by Jamie's arms but by his concern as well. It was as though he was a protective wall between her and the world. She felt safe. She'd never felt safe before and didn't know what to do.

"Frances," he repeated, relentlessly drawing her out. "This is all about Frances, isn't it? The attempts on my life, threats to you, all of it comes back to Frances. Doesn't it?"

She nodded, but added, "Yes," in case he couldn't see her response in the dark. "Always. Everything. Did he try to kill you as well?" she asked, belatedly taking in the fact. She saw his answering nod clearly and let out a long sigh. "I thought he might. I didn't know he had. I should have warned you. You should have told me."

"And worry you?" He laughed softly. "I need to know what you haven't been telling me."

It was not just about her sister. It was about Lake wanting Margaret too, Jamie added to himself. But she didn't see it, and he wasn't going to burden her with that added knowledge. "Tell me." He felt her hands draw into tight fists against his back.

"I'm at my tether's end," she said. "There's nothing I can do."

Tether. What an awful way of putting it. As though she were some trapped animal. "Margaret."

"It's my fault," she rushed on before he could say anything more. "Father forced her to marry him when I wouldn't. She said she didn't mind. He's so handsome, after all. So famous and popular. I hoped it would be all right. But then Father died, and nothing was left to Frances. Lake only got her dowry and the income from Rishford Abbey. It should have been enough for any man, but he wanted more. He wanted me to become his mistress."

"What?" The word came out as a low growl as Jamie pulled her closer. So, she did know, but her next words showed that she didn't truly comprehend.

"He wanted to control me, my fortune. He wants the title, you see. I couldn't do it, not even for Frances's sake. I'm selfish, really, but I truly didn't think it would help her. She'd still be his wife. He controls her completely—whom she sees, where she goes, whom she can write to. At first he would only let me see her for a few minutes at a time and he was always present.

"He made her ask me for money. I argued with him, so he stopped letting me see her at all. But he sent letters he dictated—awful things in Frances's handwriting, such as how she didn't mind if I became his lover and worse. Or he delivered them himself sometimes."

"When he wanted money," Jamie guessed.

"Yes."

The darkness was warm around them. It was an earthy, fragrant summer night. Sounds of revelry intruded faintly from the direction of the ruins. Jamie held his wife close. He also kept hard control on the dangerous anger growing inside him. "Go on," he urged her.

"I . . . I put up with it for a while. But when the letters stopped and only the demands for money remained, I tried to do something. No minister would talk to me . . . they're all his friends. So I appealed to the king." She gave a deep, shuddering sigh.

"I was told not to interfere between husband and wife

and that I should be a good girl and get married myself. To his cousin. *Perhaps* he'd have helped me if I'd married his cousin. But if I lost control of my fortune, how could I help Frances? So I threatened to cut off Lake's allowance. He didn't like that."

"Called your bluff, did he?"

"Yes. And then . . . there were . . . He . . ."

"He tried to frighten you into submission? Or kill you, perhaps? There were accidents? *Vandalism.*"

"Yes." Her voice was barely audible.

"You were desperate. And you thought the fool who'd stolen your jewels might help you?"

"I . . . had hopes. But then . . . you . . . and I . . . and things happened. And Lake said . . . And I've only made things worse."

"Lake said . . . what?"

Margaret heard the angry threat in Jamie's voice, felt the wiry muscles of his back grow hard with tension. He'd calmly shot someone this morning. She didn't want him to end the day with the murder of his brother-in-law. But she wanted to tell him, needed to explain, because in Jamie she'd finally found a man she didn't want to hide from.

"Well?" Jamie asked in the same low, threatening tone. Margaret almost smiled, knowing the threat wasn't for her. She went cold when he added, "Does Bartlett know this secret? Does Bartlett know everything?"

"No." She reacted to his jealousy. "Some things are too private to discuss with Bartlett."

"Or with your husband," he added.

She heard his pain. Her heart went out to him, but she was annoyed as well. "Are you feeling sorry for yourself, Jamie McKay?"

"Yes." He kissed her cheek. "You sound just like Granny McKay. I like it."

"Oh, lovely," she replied. "I've been trying to act like an obedient little wife when what you want is a dictator."

"Well, not a dictator. Just someone who'll speak her mind now and again. What is it even Bartlett doesn't know?"

Margaret considered evading the question until she could get Jamie away from Rishford Abbey, but she didn't think he'd be diverted that long. "Promise you won't do anything?"

"Why?"

"Because if you kill him you'll be hanged. Being rid of you both would solve all my problems," she added tartly. "But it's not what I want. I want to be your wife."

"Thank you. Tell me."

"Promise first."

"I promise."

Pain grew around her heart at the memory of the threat. Anguish and defiant anger propelled the words out of her. "He said I mustn't have a child. That I dare not replace Frances as my heir. If I had a baby he'd have no more use for her. He would kill her. He didn't say so—exactly—but I knew he would. I had to choose between my sister's life and being a wife to you."

"I'm going to kill him," Jamie said, cool, rational, and determined.

"You promised!"

"Not tonight," he agreed. "But he is going to die."

She made no attempt to dissuade him. "I didn't try very hard to obey him. My baser instincts kept getting the upper hand. I'm playing with Frances's life, but I . . ." She held him tight and whispered in his ear. "I love you, Jamie."

Jamie had been trying hard to sort through his own emotions. He tried not to be angry or indignant or hurt. He tried not to let his own pride get in the way. Fortunately her words were a balm to his spirit. He still said, "Why didn't you tell me? Trust me?"

Margaret looked up, past Jamie, to the stars visible through the still branches of the trees. "Sweet Jesus, Jamie," she told him. "I wish it was just a matter of trust. It's not trust, it's me."

She leaned against her husband's slender but rock-solid form. Stars wheeled above them as she recalled all that had happened since he'd demanded her coach to stand and deliver. Deliver? She'd delivered herself into his hands, and her heart as well. And the process had hardly been painful at all.

"Not trust," she repeated, sensing his hard-held patience. "I trusted you even when you held a gun on me."

"If not mistrust, then what? Lord, girl, don't you know I love you?"

The confusion in his first question and the passion in the second rocked Margaret out of herself. Her world shifted faster than she could keep up with it.

"Wh-what?" She blinked on sudden tears. They stung her throat as well as her eyes. She thought the tears were from sheer relief and pleasure, but she was so confused she wasn't sure. "Do you? Love me?" she asked, uncertainty making her shy.

"Of course."

There was a significant pause. Margaret waited while the air between them crackled with impending revelations. She held her breath.

"Damn," he said at last. "I've never told you I love you, have I?"

She let her breath out in a sound that wasn't quite a laugh. But she wanted to laugh, with joy, with rapture, with Jamie. For years and years. More than anything she wanted a long life spent constantly with Jamie.

"I love you," she told him, joyous with the chance to express an honest, unguarded emotion. "In truth I fell in love with you because of the red wool scarf you wore as a mask. It seemed so—domestic."

"It itched." He laughed softly and ran a finger across her cheek. "You weren't one bit frightened of Jamie Scott. You were so—sweet and understanding and helpful. How could I not fall in love with you? You got me in such a state, I wrote the only love letter of life. But." He stepped away from her. "No romance until you tell me why you've been going through hell all by yourself. And just what you're doing out here other than assaulting Bonham?"

Margaret smoothed her satin skirts. She wondered if she looked as foolish as she felt. She wondered if the starlight could pick out the embarrassed blush burning on her cheeks and throat. "You think I should be like your sisters—tell you everything and shout and say what I think. But I can't be like that. You can't be like that and be a duchess."

"Can't see why not?" he grumbled.

She shook her head. "But you see . . . I'm not real." No, that didn't make sense. She tried to be a bit more specific. "A hundred people look at me every day and they make me what I'm not. I'm not saying this correctly!"

She paced back and forth then faced him and tried again. "Surely you've begun to feel what it's like. I'm responsible for everybody. They depend on me. I answer petitions and make decisions and take care of my tenants and my retainers and relatives of my relatives. I must be kind and generous and confident and soft-spoken and gracious."

She took a deep breath and added, "I can hardly wait

for the day when I can be nasty and crochety and high-handed like the dowager."

"In the meantime," Jamie added for her, "you wouldn't know how to confide in a flea."

"Precisely." So he did understand. "I wasn't trained to delegate."

"Responsibility." He put his arms around her again. "We're very alike, sweet. Both too damn responsible for our own good."

She rested her head on his chest. He took the way her forehead rubbed against the lace at his throat as an agreeing nod. "By the way," he added. "You didn't notice his approach, but someone's been spying on us for the last five minutes."

The man who had sneaked up the path to lurk nearby had moved cautiously and nearly silently. Jamie had noticed him all the same. He'd kept part of his attention on the listener, judging him less important than hearing Margaret out.

Margaret, instead of being startled at his revelation, lifted her head and said sharply, "Lodge?"

"Yes, Your Grace?" a thin tenor voice answered. "I have the honor of being, in your service, John Lodge."

"Right." She stepped out of Jamie's arms and marched up to the newcomer. "What are you doing here?"

"I waited by the maze, Your Grace," Lodge explained. "Well past the time allotted. When it came to me that you might be lost or detained, I thought it best to try to find you."

"You found me. Where's Frances?"

Jamie grasped her by the elbow. "Who's he?"

"A spy," she answered. "Where's my sister?"

"A loyal servant, Your Grace." Lodge's head darted furtively from side to side. "We must take care."

The man reminded Jamie of a frightened rabbit. "We're alone," he assured him. "He gave Margaret an admiring look. "Planted a spy in Lake's household, eh? Good, lass."

"Thank you. Where's Frances?" Take me to her."

"I'm sorry, Your Grace," Lodge answered. "I have grave news."

Margaret gasped. "She's dead, isn't she? He killed her?"

Jamie heard the beginnings of heartbroken panic in his wife's voice. "Explain quickly," he ordered the informant. "I'm not very patient."

"She's not dead!" Lodge reassured hastily. "She's been sent away. To Bethlem Hospital."

"Bethlem Hospital," Jamie repeated slowly. "Where have I heard that name before?"

"Bedlam!" Margaret exclaimed. "That's Bedlam."

"Yes. I remember now. Oh, Margaret—"

"He's locked her up in a London madhouse!"

"Monstrous," Lodge contributed. "A most fiendish application of his spousal—"

"I'm going to kill him!" Margaret raged.

Jamie tightened his grip on her arm. "Now, Maggie—"

"Vile," Lodge said. "Wicked. A lecherous fiend."

"You're not helping any," Jamie told Lodge while Margaret struggled to get away. "Calm down, Maggie. Be logical."

"No."

Satin ripped and Margaret bounded away. He jumped after her, grabbed her around the waist from behind, and held tight. She kicked backward. Her slippered foot connected hard with his shin, but Jamie didn't budge.

"No," he said, and repeated the word over and over until her struggles died down somewhat.

"Why not?" she asked, sounding petulant but rational at last.

"If I can't, you can't. Not tonight. You'll not go near Lake. Promise me."

"But—"

"Promise, Margaret."

While she'd been fighting him, he'd been making plans. "There's nothing you can do," he told her.

"Oh, yes, I know," she said, voice raw with bitterness. "A wife is a husband's legal property."

"True," Jamie acknowledged. "But what's the use of having laws if we can't break them now and again?"

"Jamie," she said, her voice soft and hopeful. "We're going to break Frances out of Bedlam."

"No, of course not. But we will get her out and safely away from Lake."

He looked around. Lodge still hovered, ghostlike and anxious, in the shadows. "You," he said. "Have our coach readied. Now."

As Lodge scampered off Jamie gave Margaret a reassuring squeeze. "Let's get our things." He urged her down the path.

"Why? Where are we going?"

"London," he replied. "Where the duke of Pyneham can find a magistrate and a minister or two to bribe."

Jamie kicked the snoring man in the seat across from him to wake him up. "Glad you came with us, Edgware," he said. He raised the coach's window shade. It had rained during the night, and fresh mud in the rutted road was slowing their progress. Margaret, curled in the crook of his arm, sighed and opened her eyes.

"Glad you pounded on my door and invited me along," Edgware replied. "Not my sort of country party at all. Only accepted the man's invitation thinking you might show up. Glad we left before Lake returned. Would have been awkward explaining why we were leaving."

It wouldn't have been awkward, Jamie thought. It would have been fatal, promise or no promise. He smiled into the storm-gray eyes of his wife. He wasn't sure which of them would have attacked Lake first.

Margaret wished she hadn't slept, even if it had only been for a little while. She'd dreamed of dungeons and chains and cries for help in the night. Bedlam. Her sister was in Bedlam. People went to that madhouse to look into the cells and laugh at the caperings of the poor, mad souls chained to the wall. She'd dreamed of laughter. Of Lake, glorious and golden, arrogantly naked, standing over a mad creature chained in the dark. His friends had been with him, cackling, cruel wraiths in the background. The woman trapped in Lake's chains had not been Frances.

"Why did he do it?" She rubbed her forehead against her husband's shoulder. "How could he be so cruel?"

To punish you, Jamie thought. She'd twitched restlessly while she slept. He didn't know the details, but could imagine the horrific direction her nightmares had taken. Lake was going to pay for every moment of pain he'd caused Margaret and her sister.

Edgware produced a small case from his coat pocket. He brought out a comb and mirror and set about straightening his appearance.

"You're a fop," Jamie told him.

Edgware cast a boyish smile at them. "I know. Edwina will admire me all the more for it, I'm certain. Why did General Lake do what, dear duchess?" he inquired. His next question was aimed at Jamie. "And just how are we going to set about destroying him. For I can see by your evil glower that you intend to do nothing less."

"A melodramatic fop," Jamie countered. He rubbed his stubbly jaw. "Edwina's in for a treat, I see."

"Edwina?" Margaret asked, pulled out of her misery by their enigmatic references to Jamie's sister.

"Edgware fancies himself in love with Edwina. He'll change his mind once they've met."

"Oh." Margaret didn't feel up to pursuing the subject. "I'm hungry," she said, surprising herself at feeling such a mundane sensation.

"We'll stop at the next inn," Jamie told her. "Wait out the rain for a bit and refresh ourselves." He called up orders to the coachman, then answered Edgware's question about Lake. "First I'm going to get an order naming me his wife's guardian."

"You can't do that," Edgware said. "No court's likely to interfere between a man and his wife."

"Not for long," Jamie said in agreement. "But all I need is a writ to free her from him long enough to hide her safely away somewhere."

"Hmmm," Edgware answered. "Once Lady Frances is safe, that's only the beginning. Am I correct?"

"You are," Jamie said grimly. "There's his allowance to stop. And his seat in Parliament to take away."

"How?"

"Finance his opponent in the next election." Jamie assessed the other man. "How'd you like to stand for Parliament?"

"Be proud to," Edgware responded promptly. "That's a beginning, but Lake's still popular in all the right circles."

Jamie gave a soft, dangerous laugh. "More popular than an active Whig duke? I think not." He stroked Margaret's hair. "Brace yourself, sweet," he said. "You're about to become a political hostess."

Margaret gave her husband an admiring look. He'd just outlined a thorough and civilized way of beginning to destroy the public life General Sir Charles Lake so mightily relished. It wasn't the only revenge Jamie intended, she was sure of that, but it was a clever way to start.

"You read law at Cambridge, didn't you?" she questioned.

"A bit. Don't tell Mummy," he said. "She wouldn't approve."

Margaret chuckled. She felt cheered despite her worries. She looked at him, knowing love and hope shone in her face. She remembered their making love in the coach not so long before, and wanted to repeat the experience. She wanted to give herself to the man she loved then and there, with complete trust and honesty heightening the experience. She and Jamie shared one long, burning look before directing scathing glowers at the third passenger.

Edgware gave a roar of laughter. "Oh, dear. I seem to be interrupting a tryst."

Margaret blushed hotly at her thoughtless wantonness. A look at Jamie showed his cheeks flaming brightly as well.

She was distracted a moment later as the coach pulled in to a busy innyard. She and the men alighted and hurried inside through driving rain. They were settled in a private parlor with a hot meal before them soon after.

Margaret ate quickly, without noticing what she ate. She'd been left more exhausted than refreshed by the sleep she'd gotten in the coach. She didn't bother asking to be shown to one of the inn's bed chambers. As soon as the dishes were cleared away, she moved to a well-padded chair, put her feet up, and promptly fell asleep.

* * *

She woke to the sound of men shouting and a hand shaking her shoulder. Before her the embers of a banked fire glowed in a small fireplace. Rain pelted angrily at a narrow window to her left. A stranger's portrait looked down at her from over the mantle.

"Where am I?"

"There's trouble, I fear," a voice she knew said quietly. She looked up and recognized Edgware standing by her chair, an anxious expression on his face. Margaret began to rise, and discovered she was covered with a gentleman's silver brocade coat. Memory came back. She smiled, thinking of Jamie draping his coat over her for comfort. Dear, tough, tender, dangerous, darling Jamie.

"Nonsense," Jamie said sternly from across the room. Several voices answered him as at once.

Margaret stood and turned to see what was the matter as another man spoke up. "The voice is all wrong. But I recognize the cow-eyed whoreson, all right. That's Jamie Scott."

Margaret knew that voice. She looked at the short, balding man who'd spoken. Taggert. The man from the brawl at the Red Bull. She gasped and grabbed Edgware's arm for support. "Sweet Jesus, he's taken," she whispered.

"You must speak to these men, Your Grace," Edgware said, his words cut through her frozen fear. "Tell them it's a mistake."

Margaret looked at the other men. She wasn't surprised to see Bonham. He stood with his arms crossed, his large bulk blocked the door. He was looking at Jamie with an expression of malice and triumph. Taggert stood between two other rough-looking men. Both held pistols. Jamie was directly facing a soberly dressed older man in a bag wig. He held his hat in his hand and looked officious.

"These are grave charges, Your Grace," he said. "Grave and serious and you must answer them."

"I'm afraid they're trying to arrest him," Edgware told her. "It seems Bonham hunted us down and brought a witness and constables with him. Mean-spirited bastard," he added as he brought Margaret forward. "This is a poor idea of a joke," he spoke angrily to Bonham.

"No joke," Bonham replied. "You're going to dance with Jack Ketch, Scott."

Jamie ignored Bonham, though the reference to the hangman made his throat itch. This was his worst nightmare come true, but he wouldn't allow himself to show any fear. He put his arm around Margaret's shoulder and said calmly, "Sorry to disturb you, my dear."

Margaret took her cue from her husband and lifted her head defiantly. "I don't appreciate your sense of humor, Bonham." She waved a dismissing hand toward the constable and his men. "Take these fellows and get out of my sight."

The constable flashed a nervous look at Bonham, but he merely sneered and said, "Remember the reward. Do your duty."

The constable gave a decisive nod. "Now, then, sir," he said to Jamie. "I'm arresting you for the capital crime of highway robbery."

"He's a slippery cove," Taggert warned. "Take him now while he's unarmed."

"He's a duke," Edgware spoke up. "Bonham, you'll make yourself a laughingstock if you go through with this."

"Put him in irons," Taggert suggested.

The intruders moved forward. Jamie was surrounded, and Margaret got pushed aside. Bonham raised a pistol, aiming it at Edgware as he took a step forward. "No," he said.

"No," Jamie agreed. There was no getting out of this, he realized. Bonham was determined to have him arrested. The men with him were complying with the eagerness of the well bribed. No show of arrogant superiority on his part was going to get him out of a trip to Newgate. If he resisted there could be violence. Bonham was perhaps hoping there would be violence.

"Very well," he said as he was herded toward the door. "I shall come peacefully. You'll see it's all a mistake soon enough."

Margaret followed after Jamie. Edgware came with her, his hand on her elbow as though she needed support. "I'm coming with you," she called as Jamie was hustled past the staring onlookers in the taproom.

She caught up to Jamie at the door, worming her way past his guards. He turned and took her in his arms. "You're going back to Lacey House," he said.

"But—" she protested.

"I'll be home in no time," he assured her as he was pulled away. "Edgware, see that she gets home," he called as he was hauled out into the rain.

Horses were waiting in the innyard. After his hands were tied behind him, Jamie was helped into a saddle. Bonham took the horse's reins. Jamie turned his head as the animal was led away. Through the pounding rain he saw Margaret standing rigid in the doorway, Edgware's hands clamped firmly on her shoulders. Her hands were clenched in fists at her sides, her expression was tightly controlled. He knew she was fighting tears, fighting not to show anything, not to let the world know she was terrified.

His own terror was bone deep and fatalistic. He should have known this would happen, been prepared to pay for his crimes. Guilt assaulted him as he was taken away, as Margaret disappeared from view. He had a terrible premonition he would never see her again. He loved her. He had vowed to help and protect her. He'd failed her. She was suffering now, and it was his fault.

As he was taken along the road to London, drenched to the skin and spattered with mud, reviled and laughed at by his captors, gaped and jeered at by gathering crowds, all he could think of were his failures. He'd failed his family, Margaret's family. He'd failed his wife. This scandal was going to destroy her. Lake was going to prey on her. Damn and damn and damn. He should have protected her somehow. He should have seen this coming.

He deserved what he was going to get.

22

"Don't worry, everything will be all right."

If he pats my hand once more, I shall bite him, Margaret thought. She knew she was being unfair, and this just added to her guilt. Edgware meant well, but his words were no comfort to her.

Her fault, she thought again. This was all her fault. The words had rolled around in her brain with every revolution of the coach wheels. As the hours passed and they drew closer to home, she fell deeper into crushing depression.

What could she do? If only she hadn't insisted that Jamie visit Rishford Abbey. If only she hadn't angered Bonham. If only, if only . . . She sighed and rubbed her fingers against her aching temples.

"We'll be there soon," Edgware said. "Another mile or two at most."

His soothing tone grated against her ears. The man was treating her like a bereaved widow. *I've barely begun to be a wife,* she thought. *I'm not ready for widow's black yet.*

As the thought surfaced, Margaret lifted her head sharply. "I'm not ready to be a widow." Instead of pain, the words brought a cold, clarifying anger.

"Why am I always blaming myself for everything?" she asked. She didn't expect an answer. Edgware didn't disappoint her. The handsome young man merely looked at her in surprise.

She went on, not really talking to him anyway. "I am *not* going to take to my bed to weep and wail while my husband rots in Newgate." She thumped the coach seat with the flat of her hand. The dull thud of the padded cushion added emphasis to her determined words. "Something must be done."

"Of course," Edgware said, placating her. "It's all a horrible mis— oh, we're here."

She didn't miss the tone of relief in his voice as the coach came to a stop beneath the portico of Lacey House's main entrance.

Margaret didn't wait for anyone to help her alight. She jumped down and ran for the house, skirts flying. "Dominick!" she called, even as the butler opened the door for her. "Dominick, I need a plan!"

"A plan, Your Grace?" the butler asked, a startled expression replacing his hard-held butler's calm. "I beg your pardon?"

"Yes. A pardon would do nicely."

Edgware came pounding in behind her. He and Dominick followed as she paced into the rotunda. Edwina and Samantha were just coming down the grand staircase. The girls were smiling, obviously rushing to welcome them home.

"We must talk," Margaret announced sternly.

"Grave news," Edgware added.

Margaret gave him a poisonous look. "Yes."

"What?" Samantha asked as she rushed to Margaret's side.

"Where's Granny McKay? And the dowager?"

"In the library with the girls," Edwina replied. "Alexandra's reading *The Decameron* aloud. Shocking."

"The old girls are loving it," Samantha added. "Mummy—"

"Never mind your mother," Margaret said. "It's our grandmothers I must talk to. Fetch them," she ordered Dominick. He hurried off. "And Bartlett," she called after the butler. "Send them to the morning room.

"Come along," Margaret said to the others. She led them off to the morning room, determinedly ignoring questions until everyone was assembled.

"Jamie's in Newgate?" Granny McKay shouted.

"Frances is in Bedlam?" the suddenly pale Bartlett said above the angry thumping of Granny's cane.

Margaret didn't intend to repeat any of her explanations. There wasn't enough time to coddle them until they were used to the news.

"Infamy!" the dowager exclaimed. "The king must be informed. He won't countenance this sort of prank. A Pyneham in Newgate. Absurd!"

"My thoughts exactly," Edgware spoke up.

Margaret turned to look at Edgware. He was hovering behind Edwina's chair, his hands held just above her shoulders, as though he wanted to touch her but a barrier held him back. Propriety, she thought, and almost laughed. Propriety meant very little to her at present.

"You're popular at Court," she said to Edgware.

He bowed. When his shadow crossed Edwina, the girl jumped as though she hadn't noticed he was there. Dominick and a footman entered with laden tea trays.

"We'll have some brandy to go with this," the dowager informed the butler. He hurried out.

"Huseby, stay!" Margaret rapped out when the footman would have followed. A grin spread across his face, and the big lad took a spot by the door.

"Popular." Margaret returned her attention to Edgware. "You must go to the king. Tell him about this foolishness. Convince him it's only a joke."

"Certainly," he agreed. "I'll do my best."

"What are you waiting for?" Margaret asked as Edgware lingered to accept a grateful look from Edwina. She gestured toward the door. "Time's wasting. Go. Now. Huseby, see that he has the best horse in the stable, then get back here."

"Yes, Your Grace. Come along, my lord."

"Adam," Margaret said as the pair left, sidestepping Dominick as he brought in the brandy decanter. "Send word to my London solicitor, just in case the king can't be persuaded."

She accepted a glass of brandy from the butler and downed the fiery drink in one gulp. It affected her not at all as she started pacing. She stopped by Samantha's chair and exchanged a worried look with her eldest sister-in-law. "We need time," she said to her. "And I fear we haven't any."

"Why?" Samantha asked quietly.

"What about Frances?" Bartlett demanded, raising his voice for the first time Margaret could recall.

"*You* never mind about Lady Frances," the dowager ordered harshly. "Such insolence."

"The duke is safe," Adam went on, ignoring the dowager. "We'll buy him out of Newgate quickly enough. Frances is in a madhouse. What are you going to do about it, Margaret?"

"Jamie isn't safe," Margaret countered. "I know it in my bones. He isn't safe. Lake's caught him in a horrible trap."

"He's done worse to your sister," Bartlett reminded her. "For years and years and years."

Margaret wanted to cover her ears at the adamant fury of his words. She barely recognized the fierce man before her. His control was gone. Adam the boy was gone. Adam the man was dangerously angry. He'd taken as much as he could from his 'betters.'

Margaret's heart went out to her friend. But at the same time a part of her saw clearly that here was a weapon. Was it one she could use? Or one that would turn on her? The last thing she needed was for Adam Bartlett to hare off to Bedlam to the rescue. He'd probably end up locked away himself.

She might end up locked away before this was over, she thought. With good reason. Frances, Frances. What was she going to do about Frances?

She paced and thought and looked from one family member to another, hoping for some helpful suggestions. All she saw were eyes, watching her, like troops awaiting her command. She found herself in front of Great-Grandmother Margaret's portrait. She looked up at the smiling face so like her own.

What would you have done, you clever old doxy? she wondered. The painted lips just kept smiling, but a clear thought popped into Margaret's head. It was so lucid she wasn't sure whether it came from her fevered, exhausted mind or was a message from the first duchess. Deal with one crisis at a time, it said. Decide who's in the most danger and get them out. Be as ruthless as the great-granny who clawed her way out of the gutter to put you where you are today.

Jamie, she decided instantly. Jamie was in the most danger. She turned to face the watchers, the grandmothers, the sisters, the steward, the loyal footman who'd returned without her noticing. Her troops. Oh, Lord.

She concentrated her attention on Adam Bartlett. "Lake can't kill Frances," she told him. "As long as she's my heir he needs her alive."

"I know. But—"

"But he needs to kill Jamie. Jamie is his most dangerous enemy. It's a race for time—before I have a child, before Jamie destroys him. Lake must dispose of Jamie." She crossed her arms and looked around at her rapt audience.

"Never mind trials and the hangman. It'll never get that far. What better place to arrange a murder than in a prison? He can be killed in his cell by a paid assassin. Jamie must be freed immediately."

"Because you love him more than your sister?" Adam said.

Margaret was struck dumb with pain at his accusation. All she could do was look at him, helpless tears in her eyes. She felt paralyzed as Adam Bartlett came toward her. He was a large man, not so tall as Jamie, but broad at the shoulders and sturdily built. Desperate anger crackled through his every movement. She was afraid lightning was going to strike when he took both her hands in his.

"Don't cry, Maggie," he said. He bent forward and kissed her cheek. "Just tell me what I can do to help."

She heard the dowager sputtering indignantly in the background and the shocked gasps from the girls. She didn't care. She'd lost her steward and gotten her friend back. Somehow, she knew, everything was going to be all right. They smiled at each other, with fear and tension, it was true, but acknowledging hope as well.

"We'll get them back," she promised. "Both of them."

"How?" he asked, letting her hands go.

She looked at the gawking crowd. "What I need," she quoted her husband, "is a magistrate I can bribe."

While her audience considered this statement she went to her desk. After looking through a pile of papers she'd hidden in a drawer she said, "Ha. The reward isn't for five hundred pounds, but six." She tapped a sheaf of paper slowly against the desktop. "Well, we can up that ante a bit. Huseby."

"Yes, Your Grace?"

"Do your remember the Red Bull? I want you to go there," she went on before he could reply. "There's a girl named Lucy who works there. She's Mr. Taggert's inamorata."

"What?"

"Doxy. I want you to convince her that she and Mr. Taggert will be much happier living in, say, Jamaica. It's warm there, I hear. And with a thousand pounds to live on they should do well."

"What are you doing?" Bartlett asked.

It was Granny McKay who answered. "Getting rid of the only witness willing to turn king's evidence. Clever girl," she added admiringly.

"Clever enough, and easily enough arranged," Bartlett said as he eyed the footman. "But sending Huseby . . ."

"True," Margaret said. "Take Eloise with you. She'll know how to talk to the girl." She's the one with all the brains in the family, she added to herself. She pointed to the door. "Hurry. Report to me the instant you get back." Huseby nodded and bowed out.

The door banged heavily shut behind him. Margaret turned to the dowager. "I want you in London," she told her grandmother. "We've Edgware to deal with the Whigs. You can stir up the Tories. Talk to your Jacobite friends. Get them in an uproar over this affront to the Pyneham title. We'll need popular support to weather this scandal. Spend whatever it takes."

"Aye," the dowager agreed after a short, thoughtful silence. "I suppose you have the right of it. Wouldn't be good for the family if your highwayman was hanged. Don't look at me like that, gel, it was a jest."

Margaret glanced out the glass-paneled garden doors as the dowager followed Edgware and Huseby off on her assigned part of the rescue mission. Rain had given way to watery sunlight. A look at the mantel clock told her it was still midmorning, just a little before ten o'clock. Where was Jamie right now? Was he manacled and helpless? Did Lake know he was in Newgate yet? Surely Bonham would have run back to the abbey to gloat with his friends. She had to protect Jamie, help him. So much more she needed to do. If only . . .

"A magistrate." Samantha's voice brought her out of her reverie. She turned as the girl went on. "A magistrate to sign a writ to get Jamie out of Newgate?"

"Precisely," Margaret replied. "I think Jamie had someone in mind to help Frances, but—"

"Would Henry Fielding do?" Edwina spoke up.

"Justice Fielding," Samantha added, looking displeased that she'd been upstaged by her little sister.

Fielding? Down for the county assizes. Margaret recalled the conversation. Fielding, well connected but not well off. Yes, she decided, he would have to do. "Where was he staying?"

"He's staying at Metford House," Bartlett answered. "Unfortunately."

Margaret nodded in disgust.

"Unfortunately?" Samantha asked.

"Metford is a friend of Lake's," Bartlett explained. "A very good friend."

"I will not have Lake finding out what we're doing," Margaret declared. "He'd figure a way to counter any plan we make."

"Just send for the man," Granny McKay suggested. "Tell him you want to read his book."

"Good idea. No," Margaret changed her mind instantly. "I can't bring him here. Lake might still have spies in the household."

Granny McKay thumped her cane on the floor. "Well, if you won't go to him and he can't come to you, what are you going to do?" she demanded loudly. "Kidnap the man?"

"Of course!" Margaret rushed forward to hug the old woman. "You're brilliant! That's exactly what we'll do!"

"I wish you'd let me take care of this alone," Bartlett said as they moved their horses from the cover of the woods to get a better look down the hillside. Margaret gazed down at the road from over the top of a bush. The clank of harness and hoofbeats could be heard in the distance, but the carriage was yet to be sighted.

Margaret fidgeted with the red wool scarf she'd tied around her neck. "You wouldn't know how to go about it," she told him. The third member of their party rode up as she spoke.

"And you do?"

She ignored Bartlett's sarcasm. "At least I've been robbed."

"By an expert," Samantha said proudly. And giggled.

Margaret glanced fondly at the other rider. Samantha was seated on Jamie's black mare, wearing a groom's borrowed clothing. Margaret had been delighted to find that the girl could not only ride, but that nothing could keep her from sharing in this escapade.

"I'm glad you came," she told Samantha. "But I wish your mother hadn't made such a fuss when she saw how we were dressed."

Samantha shrugged unconcernedly. "You know Mummy. I hope that's Fielding's coach."

"Has to be," Margaret said. It was near sunset, though with the way the clouds had moved in again, rain threatened, and it seemed much later. "The assize court would have dismissed by late afternoon. The way to Metford House isn't much traveled. Anyone heading that way has to take this turn just after the ford."

"If the coach doesn't turn this way after it crosses the stream," Bartlett explained further, "we'll—"

"Wait for the next one," Margaret said grimly. "It'll be this coach," she added with inarguable certainty. Please, God, she prayed silently, let it be this one.

The coach came into view. It was a fat, lumbering old vehicle with horses to match. Margaret noted happily that there was only the driver to deal with. She hoped there was no rifle propped on the seat beside him in this peaceful stretch of countryside.

The stream was a bit rain swollen, but not so much that the coach had any trouble splashing across.

Samantha touched her arm. "Here it comes."

Margaret clamped down on a surge of excitement as the old coach, still shedding water, made the turn they were hoping for. She shared a look and determined nod with her companions.

"Like I told you," she said, and adjusted the red scarf over her face. Adam and Samantha followed her lead.

Pistols drawn, the three of them rode swiftly down the grassy hillside. Bartlett rode toward the lead horses. Samantha cut off retreat, leading the saddled horse they'd brought for their prisoner. Margaret rode boldly toward the coach.

She called out, "Halt." She held up the pistol to show the driver she meant business. The heavy weight of the weapon in her hand reminded her of rose gardens and lessons in love as much as it did her encounter with the highwayman Jamie had once been.

As the coach slowed she got a close look at the coachman's terrified face. It made her go cold at the realization that she was responsible for frightening the poor man. But she didn't dare let her resolve stumble, not for a moment. She'd make all this up to the people involved later.

The coach came to a halt. She caught Adam's menacing movement as he brought his hunting rifle up to his shoulder. The driver's gaze shifted forward at the sight of the long rifle. She left Bartlett to make sure the man made no move and rode up to the coach door.

The door opened from the inside. A deep voice rumbled from within. "The gout's acting up, my good fellow. If you expect me to *stand* and deliver, you are chancing grave disappointment."

"I do need you to stand," she answered. "In fact, I need you out of the coach this instant."

"A lady bandit, I perceive," the voice responded. "You'll hang just the same, you know." The voice sounded rather sad at the prospect.

"Perhaps I'll have a sympathetic judge, Mr. Fielding."

She pulled the door all the way open and peered inside. The big man looked vaguely familiar. She wasn't sure if his paunch or his nose was the more impressive, but both were certainly oversized. There were papers spread out on the seat around him and others in his hands. His bandaged foot was propped up on the seat opposite. He eyed her with a look that said he wasn't one to be intimidated.

"You know my name, do you?" he asked, one bushy eyebrow cocked at a curious angle. "Perhaps you've passed through my court at Bow Street?"

"No. Get out, please."

"Now, my esteemed brother has a remarkable memory for voices, but I can't say I recall yours, lovely and melodious though it is. With some education, I think." He rubbed at his massive jaw. "Perhaps I would recall the face."

"Later," she said with a smile in her voice. "I promise. Please get out of the carriage. Or I will shoot your gouty foot," she added, growing impatient with his lack of movement.

"Would you, indeed?" he wondered. It perturbed her that he sounded more curious than worried.

Margaret fired her pistol into the coach. Fielding jumped and howled as his foot slammed hard on the coach floor. Margaret winced sympathetically. She tucked the empty pistol into her belt and drew out her second gun.

"Please get out of the coach now, Mr. Fielding," she requested calmly. "I'm quite done with the warning shot nonsense. Next time . . ." As her voice trailed significantly away her prisoner gave her a furious look, gathered his papers into a case and hobbled to do her bidding, bringing the case with him.

Samantha brought up the extra horse at Margaret's signal. Bartlett cut the traces on the coach and drove the carriage horses off, while Margaret and Samantha helped

Fielding, who clutched his writing case in his arms to mount. The whole operation took only a few minutes. They were soon riding back up the hill with their prisoner, headed for their selected hideout as darkness closed in on the woods.

"All is in readiness," Edwina informed them as they entered the cottage. Fielding was pushed through the door first. "Let me take that. I'll get a cushion for your foot," Edwina said as the big man dropped into the first chair he came to. She put his case on a nearby table.

While Edwina bustled about solicitously, making the prisoner comfortable, Margaret looked around the cottage. It belonged to a tenant who'd recently gone missing. A rascally old fellow whose disappearance had brought local poaching reports to an all-time low. Her gamekeepers certainly didn't miss the man, and Bartlett hadn't yet decided on what to do with the property. It had seemed the perfect, secluded spot to bring a prisoner.

Edwina had taken charge of provisioning the hideout. As she looked around, Margaret saw that the girl had laid a fire, unpacked a basket of food, and lit the room with candles brought from Lacey House. She and Samantha exchanged an amused look.

"She likes to be useful," Samantha said as she took off the flowered silk scarf she'd been using as a mask.

Margaret untied the woolen scarf. Jamie was right about it itching. She came to stand before Fielding while Bartlett made the introductions.

"Duchess of Pyneham?" Fielding said skeptically. He looked her over. With an expert eye, she thought, as she noted the smirk of appreciation on his bulbous lips. Far from being offended, she found something charming in the ugly man's regard.

She shoved aside a candlestick, Fielding's case, and a writing case Edwina had brought from Lacey House. She perched on the space she'd made. Samantha stood on the other side of the table. She immediately started looking through Fielding's papers.

"Young woman—" he began indignantly. He started to rise, but Bartlett put his hands on his shoulders and pushed him back in the chair.

"My apologies for all this drama," Margaret said, claiming the prisoner's attention. "But we are reacting to a dangerous situation with desperate measures. We need your help." She gestured around the one room cottage. "Since I cannot be assured of a privy conversation in my own house—"

"Which is?" he quizzed her.

"Lacey House. Six miles east of your host's home. We met at the duke of Bedford's levee six month's back. I wore blue, you wore a wine-stained coat thanks to the offices of a clumsy footman. When the duke offered to have him thrashed, you said you'd rather sentence the man to eternal infamy in your next book." She cocked her head to one side and asked, "Do you remember me now?"

"No," he answered. "But it is a good tale."

"Thank you." She smiled. "I made it up. When we met at Bedford's you were in your cups. I doubt you recall any details of the evening."

Fielding laughed. It was a big, boisterous sound that filled every corner of the room. "Such cheek," he declared. "If you're not a duchess you ought to be."

"I am." She took off her gloves, flashing her bejeweled and manicured hands. "Note the seal ring."

"Ah." He nodded. "Very well, *Your Grace*. What is

this dangerous situation you wish to discuss?" He folded his hands on his wide belly and peered intently into her face.

Margaret responded easily to the powerful gaze. "You must prepare a writ to release my husband from Newgate," she told him bluntly.

"No," he replied with equal bluntness.

"You must!" Edwina spoke up. She opened the writing case she'd brought, having pushed Samantha aside to get at it. Whatever it was Samantha was reading, Margaret noticed with annoyance, her attention was no longer on their plight. While Edwina purposefully unpacked paper and writing implements, Margaret took a deep breath and launched into an abbreviated version of how Jamie had ended up in Newgate Goal.

When she was finished, Fielding repeated, "No."

Bartlett swore. He paced the room angrily as he declared, "Tell him all of it. Tell him why."

Margaret followed Adam's movements with her eyes while her thoughts raced. "I'd rather offer him money," she said after a few moments' contemplation.

"A bribe?" Fielding questioned, expression bright and alert. "You're assuming I'm corruptible?"

"Oh, yes," Edwina said. "We've read your books."

"Young woman," he responded gravely. "My characters are meant to represent the moral state of the populace, not reflect my personal character."

"I was thinking more in terms of patronage than bribery." Margaret explained. "It could do you no harm to have the duke of Pyneham as your friend."

Fielding stroked his massive jaw. "But what if the man's guilty?"

"Nonsense!" Margaret said quickly, too sharply. "It's clearly a prank."

"Then why are you so afraid, my girl?"

It was Bartlett who answered. "Because the duke will be dead before he can stand trial. They're victims of a conspiracy, don't you see? There's murder plotted against them both, and Lady Frances as well. She'll die in Bedlam. I know it."

"Bedlam?"

Margaret would rather not have muddied the issue with their other pressing problem, though it was preying on her mind. "My sister's husband—"

"Sir Charles, that would be."

"Yes."

"I know him well," Fielding went on. "What? Has he had her clapped up for a troublesome wife?"

"Isn't it horrible?" Edwina questioned.

"It is," Fielding explained, "perfectly legal. A man is supposed to decide what's best for his wife."

Edwina stomped her foot. "It's vile and horrible."

"I agree," Fielding said. "But it is the law."

"We all know it's the law!" Margaret snapped. She was so frustrated she felt like tearing her hair out. Or running screaming out into the night. Instead she said reasonably, "I'm not interested in the niceties of the law. I'm interested in bending the law a bit until my husband is safe." She gave Fielding her most steely, determined look. "You will give me what I need. Now."

"No."

"God's death!" She slammed her fist against the tabletop. "Why doesn't anyone ever listen to me?"

"I cannot help you get the man released from Newgate."

Margaret jumped down from the table, almost overturning the candlestick in her haste. Samantha gave her a reproving look as she steadied the candle. The flame guttered for a moment, casting wild shadows across the papers in Samantha's hand.

Margaret said, "What the devil have you got there?"

Samantha looked at the pages she held. "A manuscript. In his handwriting." She cast an adoring glance at Fielding. He acknowledged her look with a smile and nod.

Edwina was at Samantha's side instantly. "Really? The final edition of *Tom Jones?* Is that it? Here?"

"Pardon me," Margaret said loudly. "But I *thought* we were trying to save your brother's life!" She snatched the pages from Samantha's hand.

"I'm sorry," Samantha said, "but it's enthralling. So much of it is new, I scarce recognize the story."

"Indeed," was Margaret's disgruntled reply. Nevertheless she took a look at what she was holding.

> The world hath often been compared to the theatre; and many grave writers, as well as the poets, have considered human life as a great drama, resembling, in almost every particular, those scenical representations which Thespis is first reported to have invented, and which have since been received with so much approbation and delight in all polite countries.

"It has some merit, I suppose," she concluded.

"Some merit?" Fielding looked indignant. Once more he started to rise. Once more Bartlett pushed him back down. "It is my finest work to date," he declared.

"It is," Edwina said in agreement.

Margaret feared a literary discussion was about to ensue, but everyone's attention was drawn to the cottage door as a loud knock sounded. Samantha grabbed a pistol and hurried forward. The door opened before she could cross the room. Huseby, followed by his diminutive sister, Eloise, came in out of the rain.

After breathing a sigh of relief, Margaret demanded, "Well?"

Huseby grinned. "Taggert's taken care of, Your Grace." He patted his sister on the head. Or would have if the short girl hadn't been making a curtsy to Margaret. "You were right about Eloise being able to deal with such ruffians."

"Well done," Margaret said. "Thank you." She dismissed the Husebys from her thoughts. She looked back at Fielding. "Help me."

He looked sympathetic. "I cannot."

She thrust the manuscript toward the candle flame in a fit of pure, unthinking anger. She didn't heed the gasps from the girls, Fielding's shout, or his vain attempt to rise. Bartlett held the big man in the chair as smoke curled up from the edge of one of the sheets of paper.

She met the author's anguished gaze and demanded, "Is my husband's life worth as much to you as this *damned* book!?"

A tiny lick of flame caught at the corner of the bottom sheet. Fielding's eyes widened in horror.

"No!" he shouted. "It's the only copy!"

"Good," Margaret said coldly. She was beyond compassion at this point, beyond civilized behavior. She only knew she needed help.

"I'll do what I can!" Fielding promised. His superior confidence was gone, lost in a panicked croak.

Margaret slammed the papers on the table, crushing out the tongue of flame with her hand. If it burned she didn't feel it. "The writ," she said. "My husband."

Fielding ran his hands over his face. "Woman," he said

at last, voice strained with anguish. "I *cannot* do anything for your husband."

Margaret grabbed up the papers again. "But I can help your sister!" he rushed on frantically. "Bedlam is within my jurisdiction."

Margaret and Adam's gazes met, sharing sudden hope.

"How?" Samantha asked. "Can she be released without her husband's permission?"

"We can always forge that," Edwina piped up. When Margaret and everyone else turned their attention on the girl, she blushed and shrugged.

"Why didn't I think of that?" Margaret wondered.

"Granny McKay says one needs to be Scots to be truly devious," Edwina answered helpfully. "Could we," she continued, addressing Fielding, "forge General Lake's permission to release Lady Frances to a physician's keeping? And you write an official order also releasing her?"

"I was going to suggest that," Fielding said. "Though it won't look very official without my magisterial seal."

"Oh, we've thought of that," Edwina said. She produced wax and the old royal seal from the first duchess's memento case.

Margaret laughed. "If it was official enough for a king, it'll do for us. The keepers at Bedlam probably can't read anyway."

"But what will we do about a physician?" Samantha asked. "Surely Dr. Clark won't—"

"Oh, Mr. Bartlett will play the physician," Edwina explained. "He looks quite serious and proper enough for the role."

"Yes," Bartlett said with a decisive nod. "I'll do it. It will work."

"Fine," Margaret agreed. "Do it."

"I'll go with him," Samantha offered. "As a nurse for poor Lady Frances."

Margaret nodded to her. "But what," she demanded of Fielding, "about my husband?"

The magistrate looked woefully at the manuscript she clutched in her hands. Margaret sighed and put the paper on the table. Fielding relaxed considerably as she did so. He steepled his fingers together on his massive belly.

"It is not within my power to remand or release prisoners from Newgate. I am not the magistrate in charge of the case. If I were at my own district office in Bow Street I might be able to bring the man out for questioning. Though that is rarely done, and how I would explain my interest in the case, I do not know. I cannot simply order the man released before he has even been charged with a crime. Not without proof of his innocence, or a royal or parliamentary decree.

"I could, perhaps petition for his transfer to the Tower, since he is a duke. But since he is charged with highway robbery, and Newgate is the prison to which highwaymen are sent and has held many a nobleman in its time, transferring him would also prove difficult. I will do what I can within the law, which is very little.

"And," he added, "I will not have the stink of corruption hanging about what I'm trying to do at Bow Street. If this means watching you burn my book, I will likely watch while you burn my book."

"Oh, the devil take your bloody book," Margaret said. "The devil take the 'stink of corruption.' What about good old-fashioned patronage? Is the reputation of the Bow Street magistrate above a little help from a duchess's privy purse?"

Fielding gave her a worldly smile. "Patronage, yes, corruption, no. I said I'd do what I can. But we're talking about the bloody duke of Pyneham, remember. It's in the hands of the Lord High Justice, or Parliament, or King George himself to get him off, not a lowly magistrate."

"We'll have the king's pardon in a few days," Margaret said as she began to pace restlessly around the small, crowded cottage. She stopped at the hearth and stared into the fire. A log collapsed in on itself, sending up sparks as the flames ate into its heart. No time, Margaret thought desperately. No time. Lake would send a murderer for Jamie soon. What was she to do?

From behind her, Fielding said, "You've been foolish enough, girl. I'll not hold your actions concerning myself against you. I know people do mad things for love." He gave a deep, rumbling chuckle. "I might find a story out of this nonsense. But," he went on seriously, "if it is a case of mistaken identity or a prank, leave the case for the king and courts to deal with. It will only be a few days before all is set right. You've said so yourself. Don't lose your head."

"It runs in my family," Margaret said with a bitter laugh. She looked over her shoulder at Edwina. "On the Scottish side." She turned from the fire. She looked at each staring face, while her mind groped for a plan. She was half frozen with fear and hopelessness, but it was too late to simply trust to the law to save Jamie. She had to save him. She was the only one who truly understood the danger he was in. She had to do something.

An idea hit her as she spotted the pair by the door.

"Eloise," she said, stepping forward. "Take off your dress."

"But, Your Grace," Huseby spoke up immediately. "She doesn't do that anymore."

"No, no," Margaret said. "It's nothing like that. I need to borrow it."

"Borrow it? But why?" Samantha asked.

Margaret turned to her sister-in-law. "It occurred to me," she explained, "that if the duchess of Pyneham can't save Jamie, maybe Maggie Pyne can."

23

"*The Lord sends* you into fire . . . damnation that you so richly deserve. You are lost, sinners damned to burn for all time. Yet, there is great joy to be found in your eternal punishment."

The Ordinary of Newgate smiled up from his pulpit, straight at Jamie, as a chorus of jeers and chain rattling went up from the convicts ranged around him on three sides of the chapel.

Jamie's response to the fawning look from the Ordinary was a bored yawn.

The man standing next to him in the chapel's upper gallery leaned over and confided, "He gave the same sermon the last time we had a hanging."

"Give us something new," one of the four condemned men seated before the pulpit demanded. "Man deserves some entertainment before his trip to Tyburn."

The Ordinary ignored the other prisoners. He had eyes only for the duke of Pyneham. Perhaps he thinks I'll make him my chaplain, Jamie thought.

The Ordinary continued his sermon. "For while you whoreson scoundrels are doomed to die, your passing serves the living as an example of dread fear and—"

Jamie yawned again. Lord, but it was hard to stay awake in the presence of this preacher! He scratched his ear, then flicked away one of the many persistent flies buzzing around the overheated chapel. He looked up at the ceiling, counted four rats on the ceiling beams, then looked at his feet rather than at his fellow prisoners. From not too far behind him he could hear the sounds of steady, fleshy thumping and heavy breathing as a pair of inmates took advantage of the chance for male and female prisoners to have social—of a sort—intercourse.

Just because a girl's in jail doesn't mean she shouldn't make a living, Jamie thought with wry amusement. And thank God, he added fervently, Margaret is spared the horror of knowing what goes on in this place.

He was treated well, had his own private cell with an outside window, and could afford a mattress and food. He was well off, but the lot of the common prisoners left everything to be desired. He especially pitied the many poor souls who had been thrust into Newgate without a penny to their names. Without money to bribe the guards for the simplest necessities, life was harsh and vicious and frequently short. Money brought food and spirits inside, bought bedding and a guarded place to sleep. Complete poverty meant bug-infested slop, darkness, and common cells where the strongest men and women preyed on the weak. Everything in Newgate was bought. Even affection, Jamie was reminded as the nearby thumping ended in a deep growl of satisfaction.

Someone muttered, "My turn," as the Ordinary lifted his voice in song. The choir joined in, their voices as ragged as their clothing.

"Wat?" another voice snarled. "Get off 'er. It's my turn."

"No, me."

"Now, lads," a breathless woman spoke up.

Heads were turning. People shoved closer as an altercation seemed about to break the monotony of the holy service. Jamie found himself being pushed back, away from the gallery rail, deeper into the crowd.

"I'll take 'Enry next," the woman said.

"Why?" one of the customers demanded.

" 'E's already on top of me, that's why."

A ripple of coarse laughter moved through the crowd. Jamie couldn't help but smile at the woman's practical acceptance of her situation. An elbow poked him in the ribs. He turned his head to nod agreeably to the man beside him. And saw the knife.

It was clenched in the fist of a bald, grinning, toothless man. It was aimed straight for Jamie's guts.

Eluding the thrust in the crush of pressing bodies wasn't easy, but Jamie was thin and lithe. He managed to turn aside just enough to avoid a fatal stab, but the sharp blade still slid across his stomach. It sliced through shirt and skin, leaving a line of blood and fiery pain. A flesh wound, Jamie thought, while the choir began another hymn.

People saw the knife and moved quickly away. Within a flash of a second Jamie and his attacker had some room to maneuver. Jamie was unarmed. He was thankful he was only made to wear leg manacles in his cell. In the chapel, with the freedom to move, he could kick.

Kick he did as his attacker lunged for him again. They both missed. People were shouting, and guards were pushing their way through the crowd. Jamie knew all he had to do was wait.

He danced away from another lunge and slipped on the sticky floor. He fell on his back. The bald man landed on top of him. For a moment Jamie thought the man's breath might be more lethal than the knife. He spat in the aggressor's eyes. At the same time Jamie's hard fingers closed around the man's wrist.

The brief distraction gave Jamie time to gain a bit of leverage as he twisted the man's wrist with all his might. Jamie heard bones grind. The knife clattered to the floor as his attacker gave a strangled cry of pain.

The guards arrived just as Jamie judged the danger to be over. The attacker was dragged off him and soon bludgeoned senseless, beyond any chance of questioning. The knife disappeared into an unknown pocket. Jamie was helped to his feet.

"Lord help us, Your Grace," one sneering guard exclaimed. "Never thought to see a lord fighten' over a whore."

Jamie checked the cut on his stomach. It wasn't deep, and the bleeding was already slowing. He looked around him at ragged strangers. Their stench filled his nostrils; their excited, greedy faces, the predatory gleams in their eyes, closed his mouth on what he'd started to say to the guard.

Jamie knew why the man had attacked him. He was probably already guilty of a capital crime, as were most of the men and women in Newgate. One more hanging offense meant nothing to this desperate lot. The lure of gold they could drink and whore away while they lived would be enough for almost anyone here.

If he were to say 'someone is trying to have me killed',

the answer would not only be 'who?', but 'how much is he paying?'.

Jamie just shook his head rather than comment to the waiting guards, and let them escort him back to his cell. He knew now that Lake wasn't going to stop until he was dead, and that he was alone.

"What?" the skeptical voice asked loudly. "You're for His Grace?"

Jamie awoke from ugly dreams at the man's voice outside his cell door. The distraction was welcome. He got up from the narrow bed, moving carefully to ease the aching cut on his stomach. He moved to look out the wide, barred window set in the middle of the heavy wooden door. The turnkey stood in the poorly lit corridor outside, blocking the half-visible form of a woman. Jamie caught only a glimpse of a soiled blue skirt and a hint of yellow hair.

"I'm here to entertain the duke," the girl said, her accent as thick as the Thames by the London docks. "I'm sent as a present by 'is friend, Lord Edgware."

"Go on," the turnkey said. "Off with you. Only ladies of quality visit His Grace."

"Quality." The girl gave a disgruntled bark of laughter. "I'm 'ere to tumble 'im, not take tea."

"So were the others."

"Oh, really."

Jamie rubbed his jaw. He wasn't sure if he was more annoyed, at Margaret's setting foot inside Newgate, or amused, at her cold reaction to the knowledge he'd been visited by other ladies. Anyone could get into Newgate for a price during visiting hours, after all. Jealous, Margaret? He half-hoped so.

He stepped closer to the grill and called, "Maggie Pyne. What are you doing here, girl?"

Margaret stepped around the turnkey. "Come for you, love," she said, tossing her head. Her eyes blazed at him, but her voice remained jokingly cheerful as she added, "Perhaps my services won't be wanted if your lady friends are keeping you tired out."

"Who says I let them in the door?" Jamie stuck his hands through the wide iron grate. She took them, and he tugged her closer. "I've become a wonder and marvel for bored ladies, but it's my Maggie who has my heart."

Margaret smiled, with her warm gray eyes as much her lips. "I hoped as much. Now," she went on briskly, turning her head to address the turnkey. "Can't stand here all day. My work's inside." She held up a silver coin.

The turnkey came hurrying up. Even as he pocketed the silver he asked suspiciously, "You know this trollop, Your Grace?"

"Most biblically," Jamie affirmed. He watched Margaret blush from her hairline all the way down to the nearly completely exposed globes of her breasts. She'd been borrowing Eloise Huseby's clothes again, he saw. "Carnal knowledge," he went on deliberately. "She's a lusty, lithe-some—"

"Let me in and I'll show you just how lusty a wench I can be," she promised before he could say another word.

"Let her in," Jamie ordered, producing a second coin for the turnkey.

Once the door scraped shut behind her, Margaret wasn't sure whether she wanted to kiss her husband or strike him. He solved the problem by kissing her instead. She ended up clinging to him, breathless with passion, her reason for being in Newgate momentarily forgotten.

Jamie winced as he pulled Margaret into a tight embrace, but her softness, the sweet, heated scent of her skin, drove the minor pain from his mind. He didn't know whether to shake her or kiss her again, he was so caught between exasperation and joy at seeing her. "Is there some reason?" he inquired in a soft, sarcastic tone, "why my *wife* couldn't visit me?"

" 'Spose she could've, love," Margaret whispered, "But duchesses aren't much good at breaking people out of prison."

Jamie's brows came down in the thunderous way that made him look like he had a very annoyed caterpillar crossing his forehead. Margaret brushed her fingertips across them lovingly. "Now, Jamie," she coaxed. "Let me explain."

Still frowning, Jamie drew her to the narrow bed. She shuddered as the chain hobbling his legs clanked with each movement. She'd imagined finding him chained in some dark, rat-infested hole. There was a wine bottle on the table, and the bed had clean linen. He had a chamber pot, and the floor looked to have been recently swept. But he was still in chains. And she hadn't missed the bloodstains on the front of his neatly mended shirt.

"You're hurt," she said.

He rubbed his stomach. "What? No, sweet. Just made the mistake of going to church without my coat on. It was a rough sermon for an Anglican service."

She put her hand over his. "Something to do with mortification of the flesh, was it?"

"Something like that."

Margaret did not like the way Jamie's gaze darted away from hers as he spoke. "Jamie?"

He pushed her back on the bed. "Jamie!"

"Hush!" He kissed her throat, then whispered in her

ear, "If you're going to pretend to be a trollop, act like one. We might be watched."

"I think you're trying to distract me. Get your thumb off that."

Jamie sat up, but he kept his palms splayed across the soft mounds of Margaret's breasts. Her nipples were hot, hard points pressing against the centers of his hands. His fingertips rested on the smooth, pink skin below her collarbone. "I think," he said, "I'm the one getting distracted."

He looked toward the door, but didn't see even a shadow of movement. Just to be sure, he reluctantly got up and shuffled across the narrow room to have a look out the grate. By the time he was satisfied that they had enough privacy to talk, Margaret was seated at the table, her bodice up and her hands folded primly in her lap.

"Very well," he said, and took the chair opposite her. "No more distractions. What are you doing here? Dressed like that."

"I told you. I'm going to help you escape."

"I don't need any help to escape."

Her face lit with eagerness. "You have a plan?"

"No, I do not have a . . . I don't need to escape."

"You do. Before Lake kills you."

"You heard about that?" Jamie got to his feet. "It was only yesterday."

Margaret jumped up. Her arms went around Jamie. "He tried already? I knew he would. I'm so glad I'm not too late. Are you all right?"

Jamie held his wife and swore under his breath. With a few words he had just negated any reasons he might give for not trying to escape. He already knew he was in danger from the other prisoners. He dared not trust any of his noble visitors. He knew Lake was bound to try again. While he was imprisoned Margaret was even more vulnerable than before. He needed to be with her to protect her. He needed to get out of Newgate to protect himself.

Margaret was trembling in his embrace. "I'm fine," he reassured her. He shifted his feet, rattling the chain on his manacled legs. "Just how do you propose I escape?"

Margaret had come prepared for an argument. When it became apparent she wasn't going to get one, she needed to take a few calming breaths before she could get her thoughts on the actual plan.

She stepped away from Jamie and pulled up her skirts. While he looked admiringly at her legs, she began emptying the contents of various pouches hanging from a belt at her waist. From a litter that included fresh clothes for Jamie, a black wig, a small makeup case, and a heavy money bag, she picked up a ring of keys.

"Mr. Fielding was very difficult about some things," she said. "But he was kind enough to provide me with the name of the locksmith who supplies all the prisons. He assured me one of these will work."

Jamie crossed his arms. "I see." He kept most of his attention on the door as Margaret knelt and began trying keys. "What happens once the manacles are off?"

She waved a hand toward the clothes. "Disguise."

"I see. Warts and wig and an eyepatch?"

She grinned up at him through a fall golden hair. "Precisely."

"God's death," he muttered.

There was a soft click. It sounded as loud as a pistol shot to Jamie's ears. "Ah," Margaret said. She moved to work on the second lock.

He curled a finger around a strand of her hair. "Then?"

"We have to wait until sunset."

"When visiting hours are over. We've about an hour, then."

"Yes. There, you're free. Change clothes."

"Watch the door. Once we're out of Newgate—"

"I have a coach waiting."

"Of course. And?"

"And then we flee into hiding, well ahead of the hue and cry."

"Why don't we just go home?" he inquired mildly.

"What? But—"

"It's Lake we're running from, lass, not the law. We're a duke and duchess," he reminded her. "They know where we live."

"I don't suppose hiding is feasible," she agreed reluctantly. "By the time we get home you'll probably be officially free, anyway. You just can't stay here where Lake can get at you."

Jamie stroked her cheek. "Sorry to spoil the drama for you, sweet. How do we get out of the cell?"

"Ah." She sighed. "That's the trickiest part. We'll have to lure the stair guard and the turnkey in here and . . . well . . . hit them over their heads?"

"Hmmm . . ."

"Perhaps if we left them a great deal of money they wouldn't mind the headaches so much."

"And how do we lure them in here?"

"Well." She cleared her throat. "You're a generous fellow." She looked at the floor. "I thought perhaps—"

"Yes?"

The words rushed out in a breathy squeak. "You could offer them a tumble with Maggie Pyne."

Samantha didn't know which was worse—the human stench, or having almost every footstep down the dark corridor punctuated by screams and raving shouts. This was hell, she concluded as she tried to keep her eyes on the officious little demon leading the way. Or on Bartlett's tense, straight back. She wanted to look anywhere but into the cells as they passed them.

The madhouse was permeated by a damp chill, despite it being a warm summer day. The sun slanted only faintly through the narrow, barred windows at the end of the corridor.

The windows flanked a staircase leading up to the next floor. When they reached the stairs, the attendant leaned into the light and read the documents again. The papers had passed from hand to hand to hand since their arrival more than half an hour before. While no one had actually questioned their authenticity, no one at Bethlem had been particularly helpful, either.

The attendant pursed his mouth and gave Adam a grudging look. "Her keep's paid through the end of the year. Along with the salary for her nurse."

"We will not want the fees reimbursed," Bartlett assured the man.

The man gave a sharp nod. "There's nothing here about Lady Frances's keep."

"It isn't important. Consider the money the general has already paid to be a charitable contribution for care of another poor soul."

"As you say, Dr. Bartlett. We've treated Lady Frances well," the man went on. "Better than most."

"I'm sure," Bartlett answered. Samantha watched as several coins passed from the steward's hand to the attendant's. "For your personal service."

The coins disappeared without comment. The attendant unlocked the stairway door. Samantha shook her head in disgust, gathered her skirts, and followed the men up the narrow steps.

The room at the top of the stairs was barred on the outside. Once the door was unbarred and unlocked it creaked open on loose hinges. An old woman in a black dress and stained white apron and cap sprang to her feet as they entered. By the woman's clothes and quick movements, Samantha was instantly reminded of a magpie. The magpie held a thin leather strap in one hand.

"She's been a good girl today," the old woman said to the attendant. She looked to the other person occupying the room. "We might let you eat tomorrow if you stay a good girl."

Samantha seriously considered strangling the woman with her bare hands. She didn't want to know what Adam Bartlett might be thinking behind the neutral mask of his face. She had to force herself to look at the silent figure seated, no, bound, to a chair in the center of the room.

Samantha made herself note details rather than take in the whole picture immediately. Otherwise she thought she might be ill. First she noticed the gray dress, dirty and torn at the shoulders. Then she saw the wraith-thin form the dress covered and the dirt and faded bruises marring her fair skin. She saw a tight braid of dirty hair that might possibly have been blonde originally. Then she looked at the woman's face.

What she saw was a ravaged version of Margaret. All life and emotion was bleached from the girl. Frances didn't even acknowledge the presence of anyone else in the room. She simply stared ahead, unblinking. If she heard or saw, she gave no sign.

Samantha could only admire Bartlett's self-control as he pretended not to see Lady Frances either. "Your charge is now under my care," he told the magpie. "Release her and prepare her for a journey."

The old woman looked curiously at the attendant. "Do as Dr. Bartlett says, Mrs. Finch."

"Well!" she said, and went off to undo the bindings holding her victim in the chair. While she worked, she said ingratiatingly, "You'll be wanting a proper nurse for poor Lady Frances, I trust? I've been good to the poor creature, and I know her ways."

She finished unfastening the bindings. As she wound the cord around one hand she smiled fondly at the still woman. "She's quiet now. That's my doing. She's a sly one, she is. But I've kept her tame."

Samantha watched Bartlett's hands ball into tight fists. His answer was a calm, "I'm sure."

Mrs. Finch gave him an eager look. "You'll be wanting me to come with you, Dr. Bartlett?"

"No." The word came out as a disdainful command. Bartlett gestured to Samantha. "I've brought my own nurse. You're dismissed, Finch." He waved Samantha forward.

She took great pleasure in shoving the horrible magpie out of her way as she went to Lady Frances. It was no effort to help the emaciated woman to her feet. Samantha put an arm around Frances's shoulder for support. When she took a step, Frances moved automatically with her. She walked where she was led, with numb acquiescence. Samantha swallowed the tears and denied the urge to share a pitying look with Bartlett. She guided Margaret's sister forward. The attendant led the way, with Bartlett following behind them.

The little procession moved in silence back through the corridors of Bethlem Hospital. Going in, Samantha had refused to look at the horror of the place. On the way out she simply didn't notice. They were at the coach door before she even realized they were outside, and Bartlett was the only other person with them.

He touched Samantha's shoulder. She happily released Frances into his arms. He scooped the thin woman up and entered the coach. Samantha swiftly followed. She found him seated, with Frances held tightly on his lap. Bartlett was crying. Samantha called for the coachman to drive on.

Once the coach was moving, Frances's stiff form relaxed. She turned her head, her gray eyes suddenly focused and alert. She looked first at Samantha, gave the faintest of smiles, then tenderly touched Bartlett's face.

"Is it really you, Adam?"

Samantha watched in surprise while Frances wiped Bartlett's tears away. She kissed his cheek. "It is really you," she repeated, voice tired but full of wonder.

Bartlett's hands clutched convulsively at Frances's tiny waist. He drew her into a short, fierce kiss. Samantha was too delighted to gasp in shock.

"You're all right!" she exclaimed instead. "You're not—"

"Mad," Frances interrupted. She laughed. A little wildly, it was true. "Oh, no," she went on. "I saw at once it was an escape attempt and did my best to help my rescuers." She stroked Bartlett's cheek. "I'm so sorry for frightening you, Adam."

He laughed, faintly. "Lord, girl," he said, beaming with joy. "I'd forgotten there were two actresses in the family." He kissed her again. "You're safe, now. I'm taking you home."

Samantha had no doubt "home" meant being with him forever and ever. It was so wonderfully romantic. What a pity Edwina wasn't there to share the experience.

✳   ✳   ✳

"You're annoyed with me, aren't you?"

Jamie acted as though he hadn't heard Margaret's question. He continued to stare moodily out the coach window. He'd scarcely spoken a word since they'd left London. They'd stopped only to change horses on the trip back to Lacey House, sleeping in the coach and taking quick meals while the horses were changed.

It had not been a pleasant trip. It was made worse by Margaret's anxiety to find out if Frances was safe. Jamie hadn't seen fit to disclose the nature of his brooding preoccupation. As the coach drew up before the doors of Lacey House, Margaret decided she was tired of sharing the company of a dour Scotsman in need of a bath.

"Are you annoyed with me?" she repeated.

He ran a hand along his long, stubbled jaw. "What?"

"Annoyed. Because I rescued you? You're having a fit of conscience, aren't you?" she guessed.

"I don't want to talk about it." Her words had hit a nerve that had been bothering him for days.

"I see."

She didn't. After all they'd been through, he didn't want to talk to her? He was dismissing her from his private councils. She was, after all, an unimportant female. She was only his wife. Typical male. She looked out the window, tried to ignore her confusion and hurt, and began drumming her fingers on the window casement.

"Stop that."

She jumped at Jamie's irritated snap. "What?"

"No. You shouldn't have rescued me."

She hadn't expected him to answer her earlier question.

The coach stopped. A footman hurried forward to open the door. "I didn't think you wanted to talk about it," she said.

He helped her to the ground. "I don't."

"Oh." They went up the stairs and into the rotunda.

"I am guilty," he said miserably.

A crisis of conscience. Just as she'd suspected. And the last thing she needed right now. "So?"

Jamie had never before heard such an irritated edge in Margaret's voice. He came to a halt in the exact center of the great entry hall, beneath the arch of the gilded dome.

"So? So? So perhaps I deserve to hang," he told her gloomily. "To put your life at risk for a criminal. I don't deserve—"

"No," she said, voice rising. "You don't."

Completely taken aback by her hostility, Jamie replied in kind. "I don't deserve what?"

"Sympathy."

"I wasn't asking for sympathy. I was trying to explain—"

"Explain, what? That you're an evil, damned wretch? Were you looking forward to the trip to Tyburn?"

She planted her fists on her hips. There'd been too much fear, too much worry, tension and reckless adventure. Margaret's emotions were strung too tight, and her control had grown precariously thin. She felt she could laugh herself into madness, or scream until she was mute. Shouting irrationally at her husband came as a welcome relief.

"You ungrateful swine! How dare you moon over moral dilemmas when I'm trying to save your miserable life!"

"Ungrateful am I?" Jamie shouted, his dour worrying transformed to fiery anger. "Ungrateful? Am I supposed to fall at your pretty feet like a slobbering—"

"No! But you can leave off moralizing constantly."

"Moralizing? Madam, I'll have you know that I—"

"That you what?"

"That I'd like to finish a sentence!" He shook a finger

at her. "And another thing. I'm sick of your adventures. You near frighten me to death daily and I—"

"I got you out of prison!"

"You could have been killed. You—"

"I was frightened for you!"

"I was frightened for you! So—"

"So? So?"

"So . . ."

"So as I was saying," Granny McKay told Mrs. Wendall. "Her Grace generously offered to have her physician care for Justice Fielding when the attack of gout struck him so severely on his return from the county assizes. Everything else is a pile of nonsense. The driver made up the whole tale."

"I thought as much. Her Grace is so generous," Mrs. Wendall said admiringly. She turned a friendly look on the large man seated in the room's most comfortable chair. "I'm sure you must be enjoying the amenities of Lacey House, sir."

"Oh, indeed," Fielding answered amiably. His swollen foot was propped on a soft cushion. He was swirling a glass of fine brandy in his hand. He looked Granny McKay in the eye. "And the duchess is *so* generous. Such a dear, kind, young woman. Her offer to refurbish my Bow Street offices is most welcome."

Granny McKay shared a smiling nod with the shrewd magistrate. She was quite satisfied that she and he were dealing with the situation to the satisfaction of both.

She was delighted the vicar's wife had dropped by for a courtesy call. Respectable, talkative Mrs. Wendall was the perfect person to squelch the rumors of bandits and kidnaped authors flying around the neighborhood. She'd been invited to tea and an introduction to Mr. Fielding. Now she was getting ready to leave with the story of a demented coachman and the duchess's good deeds well settled in her mind.

She was getting ready to bid the good woman farewell when the butler entered. Dominick was flushed with agitation. Shouting could be heard from the direction of the rotunda as he hurriedly closed the door behind him.

"Yes?" Granny McKay asked.

Dominick glanced worriedly over his shoulder. "Their Graces have returned, Lady Sophie."

"Good." Granny McKay grabbed her cane and hurried to the door. Once in the hallway, however, she paused. The shouting could be heard as distinct, angry voices from out there. She cocked her head and listened for a few moments. Then she turned and went back into the morning room, closing the door firmly behind her.

She resumed her seat and folded her hands on the silver head of her cane. "They're fighting," she placidly informed the curious guests. "Always the sign of a strong marriage with the McKays."

"So I don't need your permission to have adventures!"

"So I don't need your permission to regret my sins!"

"Sins? Sweet Jesus, Jamie, isn't the charity fund you've started at St. Martin's repentance enough? You're already paying back to the poor what you took from the rich."

"Oh." After a significant pause, he said, "I'd forgotten about that."

"Hmmph." Margaret snorted and flounced angrily up the stairs.

Jamie watched the provocative sway of her backside

with riveted interest. As his temper cooled, other drives kicked in.

"Vixen," he said as she disappeared from view. "I need a bath," he added. "Then I'll show her who's husband here."

24

The first person Margaret saw as she entered her room was her maid. She was holding a pistol. Maude's plain, serious features cracked into a wide smile when she saw Margaret.

"Thank God you're home safe, Your Grace." She held out the gun as she pointed to the pistol case on a nearby table. "I was just wondering whether these things should be returned to the library."

Margaret remembered that General Lake had still to be called to an accounting. She shook her head. "Oh, no. Leave that just where you found it. I may yet have need of it. Put it back under the pillow."

Maude's lips pursed in disapproval, but she answered dutifully. "Yes, Your Grace."

Margaret had more important things on her mind than weapons. "Is Frances here? She is, isn't she? She's safe?"

"Oh, yes, she's safe," Maude told her. Tears welled in the maid's eyes. "Safe, but she's so . . ." She wiped her eyes with the back of her hand.

"Where is she?" Margaret demanded. "I must see her!"

"Oh, no, Your Grace. Not now! The poor lamb's sleeping."

"Where?"

"The Lavender Room, Your Grace. Don't you want to change first, Your Grace?" Maude called after her as she rushed out.

Edwina was seated outside the Lavender Room, a book open on her lap. The look she gave Margaret at her approach was ironic. "This is as seemly as we could manage," she said apologetically. "Mr. Bartlett insists on staying with her. Alone."

"Good," Margaret said.

"Mummy's in shock."

Margaret didn't pause to inquire further into the disrupted state of her mother-in-law's sensibilities. She opened the door and went inside.

Frances was not asleep. She was propped up on a mountain of lace and velvet pillows. Her gaze was unswervingly on Adam Bartlett's radiantly happy face. Her hand was in his as he sat in a chair beside her. Neither one of them noticed her as she came forward.

A tight fist of anger coiled in Margaret's stomach as she took in the details of her sister's appearance. She was neat and clean and tucked into an embroidered linen nightgown, but she looked more to be swimming in the gown than wearing it. She was thin, so thin, so bruised and worn-looking. Margaret had no trouble making out the flecks of silver in her sister's fine golden hair. Silver. And Frances was only twenty-one. A year younger than she was.

"Oh, Frances," she said, voice tight with emotion.

Her sister looked at her, and held out her arms. As Bartlett moved to make room, Margaret ran forward, flinging herself into the waiting embrace. They held onto each other tightly for a long time, tearful and wordless. Margaret could feel her sister's ribs through the crisp material of the nightgown.

"I'm not going back," Frances said vehemently. "No matter what. I'm not going back to him."

"Of course you're not," Margaret said. She heard Adam's deep voice echo her words.

After a few moments of holding each other, it was Frances who broke away first. She wiped away Margaret's tears. "I truly am all right," she said. She gave an unconvincing laugh. "A few weeks in Bedlam made for quite a holiday, really. It was preferable to *his* company, at least."

Margaret wanted to give some bright and cheerful reply, such as *He's going to die horribly, with wolves gnawing at his vitals—even if I have to import the wolves from France*. But instead of mentioning French wolves, she said, "Everything's all right now. You'll be healthy in no time and—"

"You've changed dressmakers, haven't you?" Frances asked. "I knew there was something different about you. And perfumes."

She heard a low chuckle from Bartlett as she recalled her disreputable appearance. "Yes, well, I've been—"

"Adam told me all about it. He says you love this husband you went off to rescue."

Margaret considered this statement. "My husband," she said at last, "is the most difficult, dour, upright, stiff-necked, moralizing piece of work ever to hold up a coach on Hounslow Heath. Though he has his better moments. Not at present," she added.

"But do you love him?" Frances asked anxiously. "Is he good to you? Does he love you?"

Does he love me? Do I love him? Margaret sighed in exasperation. "Of course I love him. I just don't like him very much at present." She took her sister's thin hands in hers. "Don't fret, my dear. Jamie and I deal well enough together."

"I do worry," Frances said. "After *him*. I want you to be happy, Margaret. I want to know your Jamie takes good care of you."

"You have nothing to fear on that account." Margaret hugged Frances again, briefly. "I've missed you so much."

"And I you." Frances's gaze shifted to Bartlett. "And you, my love." Adam smiled and stroked Frances braided hair.

Margaret was shocked at the intimate possessiveness of the gesture. Of course she knew they loved each other, but she'd never before seen them as a grown man and woman who were lovers. Until loving Jamie, she'd never understood just how physically as well as emotionally connected two people could be. Dear, dear Jamie, she thought. Annoying creature.

She forced her attention back to Frances. "You must get well soon. We have so much to catch up on."

"And so little time," Frances said.

"You're safe." Margaret squeezed her hands. "I promise he won't take you away."

"No," Bartlett said. "He won't. I'm taking her away."

Margaret stared uncomprehendingly at her friend. "What?"

"We're going to—where is it, Adam?"

"Boston."

"It's in the American colonies, Maggie," Frances said.

"I've heard of the place."

"Apparently you own a shipping business of some sort in the colony."

"I do?"

"Yes," Adam told her. "I'm going to manage your properties in the colonies from Boston. In Boston no one will know who we are." He smiled down at his love. "We can start over."

"We can be ourselves at last," Frances added.

But . . . Margaret looked from one to the other. What could she say? What should she say? That Lady Frances and the groom's son had no right to be together? What God had ordained such an immutable separation of the classes? Should she remind them they were proposing an adulterous relationship? How? When Adam and Frances had been married in their hearts all their lives.

They watched her steadily, a little defiantly, while she absorbed and accepted their intentions. At last she sighed and said only, "I shall miss you both terribly."

Adam frowned. "I'm prepared for a logical argument, Your Grace. You're making this altogether too easy."

Margaret laughed. "Sweet Jesus, Adam. If I can marry a highwayman, you can live in sin with my sister in New England."

A knock on the door interrupted any answer from the happy couple. Edwina stuck her head in and announced, "Dominick says Lord Edgware has returned from the king. You'll want to see him, I expect. I know I certainly do," she added as Margaret immediately joined her in the hall.

"Fetch Jamie," Margaret told the girl. "Have him meet us in the morning room."

* * *

"His Majesty is perfectly willing to dismiss the whole incident as a prank," Edgware told the group gathered in the morning room.

"Including the escape?" Margaret asked hopefully.

Jamie shot his irrepressible wife a reproving look. She shot him one right back. She was still annoyed, he saw. Well, he'd deal with her later, in private.

"The whole arrest and imprisonment was nothing more than a vicious prank, I trust?" Fielding spoke from his chair in the center of the crowded room. "The duke is not really Jamie Scott?"

"Of course not!" Jamie, Margaret, Granny McKay, Samantha, Edwina, and Edgware all chorused.

Fielding steepled his fingers. "It's unanimous, I see."

Jamie noted that the magistrate seemed more amused than convinced. He chose to ignore the man's skepticism. It was the king's opinion that counted.

"However . . ." Edgware handed Jamie a folded document. "His Majesty would like Bonham's signature on this. A mere formality, really," he added.

"What?" Margaret asked worriedly as Jamie read. When he was finished he slapped the paper down on the writing desk and muttered, "God's death! Now I've got to go find Bonham. Ah, well," he added as a babble of questioning voices rose around him. "I want my earring back from the thieving cove, anyway."

Margaret picked up the document. As she read it, standing next to Jamie, she could feel anger building in him. Like heat rising off a newly caught fire. Jamie was recently bathed, finely groomed, and dressed in a fresh suit of clothes. He looked every inch the duke, but Margaret was well aware of the danger lurking beneath the surface.

"Well, girl, what does it say?"

Margaret looked at Granny McKay. "It's a formal

apology for both inconveniencing the duke and misusing the king's justice. It says it was all a boyish prank, no harm was intended to the duke's person or property and he wishes heartily to be forgiven. It also says he wishes to make up for his wretched behavior by taking up a commission to serve in the army. In India."

"Once Bonham signs that, all will be forgotten," Edgware said. He gave a cheerful laugh. "All we have to do is wrestle him to the ground and force him to put pen to paper."

"He'll be at Lake's," Jamie said.

Margaret heard the cold anticipation in her husband's voice. She looked at him in confused wonder. How could the man be so mild and penitent one moment, and hard and fierce the next? She didn't know. She wasn't sure if it was proper. She did know she liked it. The danger in Jamie's mood sent a hot rush of pleasure throbbing through her. She recognized her reaction as a shot of pure lust, which only served to confuse her emotions more. How could she want the man when she thought she was angry with him?

She looked away from Jamie and saw Granny McKay give a solemn nod. The old woman's eyes were as cold as ice. "A trip to Lake's seems to be in order," Granny said. "Go, Jamie."

Margaret knew exactly what Granny wanted. What Jamie intended. She couldn't bring herself to object. It was time Lake answered for everything.

Fielding obviously understood Jamie's intentions as well. "Might I accompany you, Your Grace?" he requested. "There are a few questions I'd like to ask General Lake. I've heard a number of interesting things about him in the last few days. Enough to make this a matter for the courts, I think," he added.

The magistrate's sharp gaze bored into him, and Jamie couldn't help but heed the man's warning. He'd been considering a duel, or even a flat-out murder if he could bring himself to do the deed. But perhaps justice could prevail in a more regular manner after all. If not . . .

"Very well," he agreed. "Follow in a coach. Edgware and I will ride ahead. Come on."

Jamie left quickly, without even saying so much as good-bye to his wife. Margaret stared after him, dumbfounded at first, then furious as Edgware and Fielding trooped out after him. It seemed that her husband had forgotten everything but his quest for revenge.

"Well," she said at last, after noticing the other women in the room staring at her. "Well!" She gave them an imperious look. "That's the last time I break him out of prison," she told them and marched out to the unsupressed laughter of Samantha and Edwina.

"Absentminded Scotsman," she muttered as she climbed the stairs to her rooms. By the time she reached her door, she didn't know if she was annoyed or amused at his single-minded quest after the villain of the piece.

Huseby was stationed at his usual spot, holding up the wall across from her door. She gave him a fond smile as he snapped to attention. He grinned and hurried to open the door for her. Once in her bedchamber she looked at Maude and said, "Just help me out of this rag, then leave me alone."

"A bath's been kept warm for you, Your Grace," the maid informed her as the dress came off.

Margaret ran her hands over her face. "Fine," she said. She pulled pins out of her hair. She was so tired. How long had it been since she'd had any real sleep? Since the night she'd shared the bed with Jamie at Lake's house. She couldn't even remember how long ago that had been. Too long. Would Jamie return home tonight? Would he remember his wife, alone in her big, soft bed? Would he care?

Lord, but she was melancholy all of a sudden. Another maid took the soiled dress from Maude. Margaret waved away the hairdresser who appeared from the dressing room. "Just leave me alone," she said. "Everyone just leave me alone."

"The bath?" Maude asked.

Margaret ran her hands through the loose strands of her hair. It smelled as if she'd washed it in sewer water. "Yes. I definitely need the bath. Just point me at it and leave me alone."

"But—"

Margaret gave Maude a repressive look.

Maude sniffed. "The last time I left you alone you got robbed," the maid reminded her.

"I'll be fine," Margaret insisted. She crossed the wide room and disappeared behind the painted screen that shielded the bath from public view. The steaming, scented water in the small porcelain tub drew her inexorably. She could only assume Maude and the others were gone by the silence which surrounded her as she lowered herself into the warm water. She washed the grime off quickly, as she looked forward to taking a good, long nap.

She found a nightgown and robe neatly laid out for her when she finished rubbing herself dry. When she came out from behind the screen there wasn't a person in sight. She smiled as she crossed the room. She luxuriated in the feel as her bare feet sank into the carpet with each step. It was a luxury she was used to, but after a journey to Newgate she appreciated her life anew. Before she reached the bed she stopped to stretch and yawn, closing her eyes as she rolled her shoulders to work out a stiff kink.

When she opened her eyes she saw the man watching

her just inside the balcony door. When Lake smiled at her she knew her worst nightmare had come to pass. He was there to kill her. She looked from his face to the pistol in his hand. There was another holstered in his belt. Maude had put her guns away, and she couldn't get to them without Lake putting a pistol ball through her first.

"You're looking at the bed, Maggie," Lake quietly sneered. "Have you realized what I want from you, at last?"

She blinked. "What?"

He moved closer, stalking like a lazy cat, dangerous but at ease. He had none of Jamie's coiled, supressed violence. But then, Jamie was only violent out of anger or necessity. Lake was violent out of his own evil nature.

"How did you get in here?" she demanded, hoping to disguise terror with a show of arrogance. "Just what are you doing here?" Please, God, don't let him know Frances is here.

"Someone was washing windows. I borrowed a ladder. Convenient for a dramatic entrance, isn't it?" he asked. "I've so looked forward to some time alone with you, my sweet."

"Get out."

He came close to her. While the pistol barrel rested, a cold weight against her stomach, he stroked her hair with his free hand. "Were you making yourself beautiful for me, Maggie?"

While she stood silent, rooted in shock, he undid the top ribbon of her gown. "It will be good between us," he promised, voice a soft, senual purr. "You've always been such a foolish girl. So full of games. The game's all mine now. You'll be a widow soon, if the deed isn't already done. Frances won't last too long where I've sent her. It's just us now, Maggie. The way it should always have been." He undid the second ribbon, revealing the deep cleft of her breasts. His smile grew wide as he took in the sight.

It occurred to her suddenly that perhaps he hadn't come to kill her. Not right away. A bolt of emotion shot through her; she wasn't sure if it was anger or a stronger jolt of terror. It gave her strength enough to back quickly away.

He raised the gun. "Not another step. Come here."

She couldn't help but smile, stiff with fear though the gesture was. "But you just said—"

"Shut up," he said. "Get over here, and don't make another sound."

She had never been able to do anything the man said. So she opened her mouth and screamed.

There was something Jamie had forgotten, something important. It had nagged at him while he paced around the stable waiting for his black mare to be saddled, and while he arranged a coach for the magistrate and the head groom filled him in on the adventures of the steward and Margaret's sister.

It was Margaret who filled his thoughts. Margaret, and the way he'd left her. It was something he'd learned early in life, a cardinal rule of the McKay family. It was a rule both his parents and grandparents had lived by, and it was a good one. Never, ever, he had been carefully taught, let the sun set on your anger. His family fought. His family was famous for fighting, squabbling, shouting like fishwives, and then making it all up as quickly as it began.

Margaret had finally learned how to fight; he should tell her he was proud of her standing up to him. He'd been acting like a fool, and he should apologize for it. Well, perhaps not a fool, but his timing had been less than perfect.

It would be long after sunset, if not the next day, before he could get back from Lake's estate fifteen miles away. The sun would have set on their argument, and perhaps tomorrow would be too late to make up for it.

Edgware came up to him. The young man looked tired, but his smile had an eager glint. "Shall we go?"

Jamie looked back toward the house. The emotion compelling him to go back was too strong to ignore. He ran a hand through his hair, loosening the ribbon holding it at the back of his neck. "You ride on," he told Edgware. "I'll catch you up. I have to say good-bye to my wife."

Jamie heard a distant noise as he loped two steps at a time up the impressive sweep of the grand staircase. He paused to listen carefully. He knew he must be mistaken, but it had sounded like a scream. He shrugged and hurried on. He was not mistaken about hearing the sharp report of a gunshot as he reached the landing.

"Lake!"

He knew it as sure as he breathed. It was Lake, and he had Margaret.

Jamie came barreling into her bedchamber with both sword and pistol drawn, almost tripping over a prone body just inside the doorway. Gunsmoke hung in the air, ghostly white and bitter. It took him a moment to realize it was Huseby lying in a pool of blood on the floor. He scanned the room quickly, but no one else was there. Cold fear curdled in his veins when Margaret was nowhere to be seen.

The footman groaned as Jamie knelt beside him. His eyes fluttered open as Jamie put down his weapons to examine him quickly. Clean through the shoulder. He propped Huseby up against the wall. "Stay still," he whispered. He tore off his neckcloth. "Hold this. Right there. Don't move. Where's Margaret?"

Huseby's eyes weren't quite focused. When he opened his mouth nothing but a weak groan came out. He did manage to point toward the balcony. The French door was open, and the heavy velvet curtains moved in the breeze. Jamie slammed the bedroom door as curious people gathered in the hall. The last thing he needed were bystanders getting in the way of more bullets!

If he'd harmed her . . .

Jamie stopped the thought, bridled the anger. He picked up his weapons and moved swiftly toward the balcony.

Before he reached the French door, Lake's angry voice exploded from outside. "Climb down that ladder, or I'll kill you!"

There were sounds of a scuffle, then Margaret raced in off the balcony. She was dressed in only a torn linen nightshift. Lake was right behind her. Jamie raised his pistol, but Lake had Margaret around the waist before he could aim and fire. Her body shielded her attacker even as she struggled to get away from him.

Lake rested the tip of the gun against her forehead and murmured lovingly, "Hush." Then he looked up and locked gazes with Jamie.

Mad, Jamie saw. Totally mad. And surprised to see him. Jamie raised his pistol. But what could he do? Margaret was in too much danger . . .

"You could shoot him," she suggested. Her voice shook despite the calmness of her words.

"I'm sure I shall, my dear." It was Lake who answered her. "The bastard's got more lives than a cat," he added. He pressed the edge of the pistol barrel suggestively against Margaret's temple. "You will drop your weapons, McKay."

Jamie let his gun and sword drop to the floor. The dull double thud of their landing was a doomsday sound. He carefully took a step back, wondering what other weapon might come to hand. Didn't Margaret have a brace of dueling pistols around here somewhere?

"Stand very still, my dear," Lake directed his captive. He pointed the gun at Jamie's chest.

Jamie noticed that Margaret was staring off into the distance, toward the pillows piled high on her bed.

"You're tougher than I thought, McKay," Lake said, voice as calm and even as if he were having a drawing room conversation. "I should never have sent anyone else to finish you off. I thought Newgate would be the end of you, one way or another. But here you are. It's for the best, really. I'll enjoy this more."

Jamie kept his attention on Lake's mad eyes, trying to discern what he would do next. Margaret kept perfectly still.

"Let her go," Jamie suggested quietly. "You don't want her dead."

"Of course I don't want her dead," Lake agreed. "I love her." His eyes narrowed angrily. "You've had her, haven't you? She'll pay for that. You'll pay for it." His face split in an evil grin. "You'll see, before you die. You'll see it's me she wants. I'll take your wife in front of you, McKay. Then I'll blow your brains out while you're still swearing at the sight." Lake looked around the room. "That'll do. Go to the head of the bed, McKay. Pull down the cord holding the bedcurtain."

"Why?"

"I'm going to tie you with it. Tie you so you can watch.

We'll do it in the light, in front of the window so you can see it all. Go on." He gestured with the gun. "Do as I say."

He began to push Margaret to the open French door, moving sideways, his attention never off Jamie for an instant. Margaret's gaze never wavered from the pile of pillows.

Jamie walked to the head of the bed. He tugged down the cord while his mind raced.

"Jamie," she said, both a plea and a suggestion in her voice.

Then Jamie knew. He smiled as he scattered pillows with his left hand and snatched up Margaret's pistol with his right.

"Down!" he shouted as he whirled. And pointed. And fired.

Head down, Margaret dove forward. Lake reeled back, a dark hole in the center of his forehead. The man stumbled and whirled across the balcony. He teetered briefly against the railing before momentum carried him over the edge down to the brick terrace below.

Margaret and Jamie rushed into each other's arms. They shared only a brief instant of closeness, punctuated by a healing, fiery kiss before they both said, "Huseby!" and turned to tend to the wounded footman.

Bartlett flung open the door as they reached Huseby's side. "What?" he demanded anxiously.

Margaret knelt beside Huseby. "Oh, my dear," she soothed as she pulled back Jamie's makeshift bandage. Huseby's eyes fluttered open, and he managed a weak smile for her.

Maude came in with a bundle of cloth strips and knelt beside her mistress. "We'll get the lad moved and attended to," she assured Margaret. "Best you put on some clothes,

Your Grace," she added with a glance at Margaret's night-gown.

Margaret stood. She retied the gown's ribbons while she watched Maude efficiently begin work on Huseby's shoulder. "We best send for the doctor," she said.

"Yes," Bartlett agreed anxiously. The man looked wildly between her and Jamie. "But what happened? Was it Lake?"

Margaret and Jamie exchanged a look, then led Bartlett onto the balcony without a word.

The steward looked down at the body lying on the terrace. A small group of servants were gathered around the man's awkwardly sprawled form. A curious buzz of questioning drifted up from below.

"It's Lake," Bartlett said.

Margaret heard the relief in the man's voice. "We have nothing to fear from him anymore." Having said the words it took her a moment to realize they were really true. She looked at her husband. "Oh, Jamie."

He nodded solemnly, his arm going comfortingly around her waist. "You're safe."

"I'm sorry you had to kill him, my love," she told him.

Jamie's brows lowered into a line. "Why?"

"I hate to think of him bothering your conscience." She ducked her head. "I should be praying for his soul, I suppose, but I hope he rots in hell."

"So do I," Jamie agreed fervently.

"And I," said Bartlett.

"He would have killed us, and worse," Jamie said. He turned Margaret so he could cup her face in his hands. "Never fear about my conscience when it comes to Lake. There was nothing else I could do." He would have had to kill Lake one way or another to stop him. Jamie was glad it had come down to a matter of self-defense.

"See to him, and everything, will you, Bartlett?" he said to the steward. "Come, love, let's get you away from here."

"I should tell Frances," she said.

"Not while you're shaking like a leaf," Jamie told her.

"Am I? Yes, I see I am. I'm cold too, Jamie."

"It's just your nerves finding time to react now that the crisis is over." He circled her with his arm and helped her to walk from her room, through the dressing room, and into the bedroom beyond. His bedroom. He led her to the bed, and they sat down in a close huddle of entwined arms. She put her head on his shoulder, and left it there a long time. Until the shaking stopped.

When she was finally under control, she looked him in the eye. Wonderful eyes, she thought. Beautiful, expressive, big brown eyes. She'd always thought so. "I borrowed your red scarf," she told him, surprised at the inanity of her words. "Granny McKay said you wouldn't mind."

"Babble on, love," he said, and kissed the tip of her nose. "I like the sound of your voice."

"Mmm. What about Bonham?" she asked as she recalled one of their other problems.

He waved it away. "Let Edgware see to it." He gave a low chuckle. "If he wants to be my brother-in-law as badly as I think he does, he'll take care of Bonham right smartly."

"Good. This is a nice bed," she commented as he laid her back on it. He leaned over her, hands resting on the mattress on either side of her. "We've never made love in a bed, have we?" she questioned. "Why is that, do you think?"

"I don't know." He kissed her, long and luxuriously,

leaving her panting and tingling from head to foot. "I think we should make love in a bed," he said.

"This one?"

"Yes."

"Right now?"

"Yes." He untied the ribbons of her gown. He smiled, hands poised over her bared breasts. "With thumbs or without?" he teased.

"With," she answered, drawing his big hands down to cover her. "Definitely with."

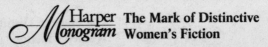

COMING NEXT MONTH

DREAM KEEPER by Parris Afton Bonds

The spellbinding Australian saga begun with *Dream Time* continues with the lives and loves of estranged twins and their children, who were destined to one day fulfill the Dream Time legacy. An unforgettable love story.

DIAMOND IN THE ROUGH by Millie Criswell

Brock Peters was a drifter—a man with no ties and no possessions other than his horse and gun. He didn't like entanglements, didn't like getting involved, until he met the meanest spinster in Colorado, Prudence Daniels. "Poignant, humorous, and heartwarming."—*Romantic Times*

LADY ADVENTURESS by Helen Archery

A delightful Regency by the author of *The Season of Loving*. In need of money, Stara Carltons resorted to pretending to be the notorious highwayman, One-Jewel Jack, and held up the coach containing Lady Gwendolen and Marcus Justus. Her ruse was successful for a time until Marcus learned who Stara really was and decided to turn the tables on her.

PRELUDE TO HEAVEN by Laura Lee Guhrke

A passionate and tender historical romance of true love between a fragile English beauty and a handsome, reclusive French painter. "Brilliant debut novel! Laura Lee Guhrke has written a classic love story that will touch your heart."—*Robin Lee Hatcher*

PRAIRIE LIGHT by Margaret Carroll

Growing up as the adopted daughter of a prominent Boston family, Kat Norton always knew she must eventually come face-to-face with her destiny. When she travels to the wilds of Montana, she discovers her Native American roots and the love of one man who has always denied his own roots.

A TIME TO LOVE by Kathleen Bryant

A heartwarming story of a man and woman driven apart by grief who reunite years later to learn that love can survive anything. Eighteen years before, a family tragedy ended a budding romance between Christian Foster and his best friend's younger sister, Willa. Now a grown woman, Willa returns to the family island resort in Minnesota to say good-bye to the past once and for all, only to discover that Christian doesn't intend to let her go.

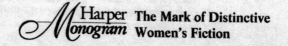 **Harper Monogram** **The Mark of Distinctive Women's Fiction**

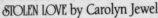

YESTERDAY'S SHADOWS
by Marianne Willman

Bettany Howard was a young orphan traveling west searching for the father who left her years ago. Wolf Star was a Cheyenne brave who longed to know who abandoned him—a white child with a jeweled talisman. Fate decreed they'd meet and try to seize the passion promised. 0-06-104044-4

MIDNIGHT ROSE by Patricia Hagan

From the rolling plantations of Richmond to the underground slave movement of Philadelphia, Erin Sterling and Ryan Youngblood would pursue their wild, breathless passion and finally surrender to the promise of a bold and unexpected love. 0-06-104023-1

WINTER TAPESTRY
by Kathy Lynn Emerson

Cordell vows to revenge the murder of her father. Roger Allington is honor bound to protect his friend's daughter but has no liking for her reckless ways. Yet his heart tells him he must pursue this beauty through a maze of plots to win her love and ignite their smoldering passion. 0-06-100220-8